TULIP Final Report

T U L I P

Final Report

Contributors

Marthyn Borghuis
Hans Brinckman
Albert Fischer
Karen Hunter
Eleonore van der Loo
Rob ter Mors
Paul Mostert
Jaco Zijlstra

4

TULIP Final report

Correspondence address

Elsevier Science
attn: Mrs. K. Hunter
655 Avenue of the Americas
New York, NY 10010
United States of America
phone   :   +1 212-633 3787
fax   :   +1 212-633 3764
e-mail   :   K.Hunter@Elsevier.com

ISBN 0-444-82540-1

Table of contents

Appendices

Executive summary

The *U*niversity *Li*censing *P*rogram (**TULIP**), which started in early 1991 and concluded at the end of 1995, has been very rewarding for all partners, who have learned many valuable lessons in the course of the project that will enable them to better face the long transition phase towards digital libraries. Participants in this collaborative project were Elsevier Science and nine leading universities in the USA: Carnegie Mellon University, Cornell University, Georgia Institute of Technology, Massachusetts Institute of Technology, University of California (all campuses), University of Michigan, University of Tennessee, University of Washington and Virginia Polytechnic Institute and State University.

The goal of the project was to jointly test systems for networked delivery to, and use of journals at the user's desktop. In the **TULIP** project, the scanned page images plus bibliographic data and unedited, OCR generated, 'raw' ASCII full text of 43 Elsevier and Pergamon materials science and engineering journals, were provided by Elsevier Science to the universities, which developed or adapted systems to deliver these journals in electronic form to the desktops of their end users. The focus of the research was on technical issues, on user behavior and on organizational and economic questions.

The major focus of at least the first half of the project, was at the technical side of **TULIP**. When this project started, there were very few institutions willing or able to bring up large scale implementations, aimed at bringing primary information to the desktop on their entire campuses. Many of the participants did just that. The lessons learned here, have already had an important impact on the implementation of the digital library (components) at the participating universities, as well as on the directions Elsevier Science is taking.

Technical conclusions:

- Most universities decided to 'shift to the Web', thereby abandoning X-Windows and MS-Windows applications, as the advantages plus the sheer user-pull outweigh any disadvantages such as fewer possibilities to provide 'real-time' functionality (e.g. image-zooming).
- Large-scale Internet FTP transfer is not feasible with the current transmission schemes and restricted bandwidth. Scalability of **TULIP**-like systems, will also be hindered by the limits of current massive storage technology. It is expected that a 'staged' approach to electronic collection building will emerge, which is composed of local servers for primary relevant material and remote (perhaps regional) servers for material of secondary importance to the particular institution.
- Speed is crucial for image viewing on the screen. The components of the system, influencing the (perceived) speed, are the server/storage speed, the network speed, the client machine speed and application software image caching 'smarts'.
- Printing page images is an important concern, but becomes viable with the advent of printers, that understand compressed Group IV fax images, and require careful attention to setup. Printing of images from other than directly IP-attached laser printers, should be avoided.

The objective of the user behavior research, was to obtain specific feedback about **TULIP** from endusers, to guide future developments of delivering journal information to the desktop, in order to get insights on the requirements for electronic services to be attractive and valuable, both from the content provider's and infrastructure provider's side.

Two types of research were done: quantitative and qualitative. The quantitative research consisted mainly of analysis of the logfiles, i.e. records of user actions. Penetration, defined here as a function of repeat usage, rather than just number of actions, varied widely among the universities. The qualitative research, which consisted mainly of focus groups and one-on-one interviews, using basically the same interview guides for each site, was aimed at answering the questions raised by the quantitative research. For instance, what makes (and keeps) users interested in electronic products; which requirements should electronic products meet to be attractive and valuable; how should we bring electronic (full text) information to the desktop?

Users seem to have the following requirements, regarding functionality, ease of use and critical mass of electronic information services:
- ease to use: as intuitive as possible, and preferably using a familiar interface;
- access to all information from one source;
- effective search capabilities;
- high processing speed (downloading and printing);
- high publishing speed (timeliness of the information);
- good image text quality;
- sufficient journal and time coverage;
- linking of information.

This is the enduser's definition of convenience.

Other conclusions to be drawn from the user studies, include the following:
- The general concept underlying the TULIP project is very well received by students and faculty. This concept consists of desktop access to full text/image articles; fast and easy to search, to read and to print.
- Hardware and software are serious obstacles for convenient use of the TULIP information at most sites.
- Most users consider the coverage (in number of titles and in time) of the journals in the TULIP project to be insufficient. This insufficient coverage (not all core journals - those not published by Elsevier - are available in the database) requires endusers to search additional information elsewhere, which is considered time-consuming and redundant; not contributing to an increased convenience.
- Graduate students use TULIP more frequently than faculty.
- There is enthusiasm about the concept of desktop access to electronic information, but the end of paper products seems to be far away still. Besides some practical benefits of paper products, 'emotional' ties with paper and the library also seem to exist.
- Although there clearly are a whole suite of conditions for a service such as TULIP to become a regularly used tool, such as overcoming the technical hurdles mentioned above, meeting user expectations, sufficient coverage, etc., promotion does play an important and continued role in the degree of success that can be achieved. Recognizing the fact that meeting user needs is primary; promotion and training are crucial for a service such as TULIP, to develop a base of regular users.

The organizational and economic issues summarized below, have been derived mainly from a series of interviews with key players at the universities.

There seem to be four major factors which can make or break a project like TULIP:
- The (project) organization, that is: dedicated project management, cooperation among the parties involved and having the right resources available at the right time. Politics, lack of priority and lack of responsibilities can cause long delays and have all but killed the project in a few of the TULIP universities.
- Understanding your user community's possibilities and needs, is also a key. A few universities stated, that they felt, in hindsight, that the first step of the project should have been to consult and involve their endusers.
- If there is no adequate infrastructure in place, a project like TULIP can not be implemented, even with committed team members, who know what their users want. Infrastructure includes systems and systems development (most universities stated they had underestimated this), networking and (non-local) printing infrastructure, the ability of the (inter-)campus networks to deal with bandwidth-consuming graphical data, and user desktop systems.
- Promotion, which was not viewed as a major issue at the beginning of the project at most universities, is clearly important for electronic information services. At sites, which did more extensive promotion, we see a significantly higher use of TULIP.

Although the universities and Elsevier Science have not resolved one critical issue, that of how to make the transition to digital libraries work economically, TULIP still helped us a great deal in the development of ideas about these issues, specifically about cost. All participants have been confronted with the harsh economic realities of building even a prototype of an electronic journals system: on Elsevier Science's side, the costs of conversion and distribution,; on the universities' side, the costs of implementation of their respective systems. These experiences guide us in determining what we want to and can do in a full scale production. Some universities referred to high costs, especially of storage, as an important factor inhibiting the development of their TULIP systems, and view these costs as a major roadblock for further development. However, at MIT the effort has been characterized as a '*relatively inexpensive effort with a highreturn on investment*'.

As part of the process of evaluating the TULIP project, university participants were also asked their views on what they have learned form the TULIP experience.
'*Too often, work on digital libraries , not to mention much theoretical discussion, proceeds without a thorough grounding in the realities of costs. There are certain assumptions, which precede this state of affairs, among them the notion that digital libraries somehow will be cheaper than print libraries, perhaps even free. One suspects that this arises from the misplaced hope that digital libraries will liberate us from the difficult cost dynamics of print libraries.*' TULIP proved to its participants beyond a doubt, that building digital libraries will be a costly and lengthy process. Also, we can say, that making additional funds available for electronic content, will not be a trivial issue for these universities.

The **TULIP** participants' view on the role of the libraries in the development of digital libraries reflects this focus on a lengthy transition period. Many information specialists said that the crucial role for libraries is the role of agents for the universities' information needs. '*What I see, is moving from content to context. Right now, we deliver page images, but in the future, libraries will be delivering an array of information in a lot of different digital media, that provide an information environment for the user*'.

All see the role of libraries increasing instead of decreasing, fulfilling the following roles: finding, selecting and providing the information needed by the community, and leading people to the right information, as well as protection of holdings.
'*If there are no libraries, users are going to be confronted by a lot of inconsistent interfaces, financial arrangements, delivery vehicles ... and the library can, at least potentially, add value, by making that coherent.*'
However, the endusers are seen as the driving force behind a lot of what libraries are going to do, and they will often be one step ahead. '*It all depends on how individuals value information.*'

Most see a continued role for publishers: '*Publishers enhance the credibility of information*'. More informal and preprint publishing is expected, but in the overflow of information, publishers can help in selecting the quality information. '*I don't see the publisher's contribution to the scholarly process changing drastically. I think the way they do it, is dramatically changing. But they remain the same in terms of managing a process and adding value to content.*' There does not seem to be a consensus among participants about the role of publishers in the archiving of the electronic content. While some universities are quite willing to let the publisher be the ultimate archive for electronical material, others are much more apprehensive to leave this role up to the publisher, either for reasons of continuous availability (publishers can go broke) or for reasons of continuous access.

A common view which all TULIP participants share is, that the transition to a digital library will go slower than they had expected before starting the project. No one can predict the actual transition speed, but TULIP generated some more important insights, concerning this question:
● At the moment, managing large digital collections locally, is harder and more expensive than managing a comparable print collection.
● Not everyone is ready for digital collections, nor will they be soon. Saying it is harder and more expensive, is to say that the leading edge market is still small. Whether one talks of large local stores of data, or regional networked collections, or single remote hosts, the number of academic libraries, really ready to support digital collections, is still small.
● Users will only move to electronic publications when they find the content they need in sufficient quantity. Having journals in electronic form and bringing them to the desktop, are necessary but not sufficient conditions for the scholarly user. You must deliver a certain 'critical mass' of needed information, to warrant learning a new system or accessing information in a different way.
● For the publisher, expanding electronic publishing (internationally) offers challenges very different from paper publishing. Elsevier Science has been delivering a uniform product which required little local training or support all over the world. With electronics, this is not the same; the process is more complicated and requires a different involvement from the publisher.

A personal note

Almost exactly five years ago, I started out on an adventure with a group of innovative and stimulating university librarians and university computing center directors. We decided to take a number of highly-visible risks in search of learning more about moving large scale journal delivery from paper to electronic and from the library shelves to the users' desktops. We started and stayed within the supportive ambiance of the Coalition for Networked Information and I want to thank Paul Evan Peters for his steady interest and support.

Some of my original colleagues in the participating universities are now in other institutions. Others have been with the **TULIP** project from the very first meeting. My own day-to-day role diminished after the first years, due to the very capable management provided by the Elsevier Science project manager, Jaco Zijlstra, and the equally dedicated supporting teams in the universities and within Elsevier.

> Karen Hunter
> Elsevier Science

Introduction

This is the concluding report on *The University Licensing Progam* (**TULIP**), a collaborative project of Elsevier Science and nine leading universities in the USA. This report reflects the experiences gained and research conducted in the project. All universities have contributed a report on their implementation and experiences. These reports, combined with input from a series of interviews conducted with key participants at the universities, as well as input from the Elsevier Science staff involved in the project, are the basis for this report. The university reports are attached as appendices I-IX.

The first four chapters of this report contain the report per se: describing the project and its findings. This part starts with a description of the participants (chapter I), followed by a description of the technical aspects of the project (chapter II). The third chapter deals with promotion. The fourth chapter contains a detailed account of the user behavior encountered in the project as well as of the research done to try to explain and learn from user behavior.

The second part of the report contains the conclusions drawn by participants at the end of the project and the recommendations that can be derived from the **TULIP** experience, which could be of value for others contemplating a 'digital library project'. These experiences have furthermore been summarized in appendix X (a checklist for institutions contemplating a **TULIP**-like implementation, and a summary of aspects to be considered). In the fifth chapter, organizational and economic issues are discussed. Finally, in chapter VI, the implications of this project for the future of digital libraries is addressed.

I   Description of the project and participants

I 1.   TULIP origins

TULIP started in early 1991. University systems and library leaders at a number of schools had been talking with Elsevier to find a way to accelerate the development of large scale systems for the distribution in electronic form of traditional journal information - information presently found only in print. Elsevier Science was looking at the same question from the publisher's side and was looking for experience on which to make strategic developmental and investment decisions, whether in search software, document delivery systems, PostScript or SGML database files or network development. During two Coalition for Networked Information (CNI) meetings in the spring of 1991, it was agreed that if ten or fifteen universities would commit to the same basic experiment, then a publisher could justify investing in the creation of a major test bed. University participants outlined a project and organized a group of universities on the spot and so **TULIP** was started. The universities were invited to submit project proposals, and Elsevier Science started to establish the technical and organizational framework necessary for such a large project.

Ultimately, the **TULIP** program became operational in January 1993, and nine universities had decided to participate: Carnegie Mellon University, Cornell University, Georgia Institute of Technology, Massachusetts Institute of Technology, University of California (all campuses), University of Michigan, University of Tennessee, University of Washington and Virginia Polytechnic Institute and State University.

The participating universities have in common strengths in the physical and engineering sciences. In looking within these disciplines for a target area, a field was preferred in which the researchers were comfortable with computer applications and had a higher than average installed base of workstations. An obvious choice might have been computer science itself, but these users were expected to be atypical in their computer facility, as to make it hard to generalize results to other disciplines. Material science provided a field in which there was both a sufficiently large corpus of frequently-cited material within one publishing company and interested faculties.

TULIP files consist of the scanned page images plus bibliographic data and unedited, OCR generated, 'raw' ASCII full text of 43 Elsevier and Pergamon materials science and engineering journals. The project started in January 1993 with the 1992 back file and continued for three additional years, totaling more than 500,000 pages.

I 2.   TULIP objectives

TULIP is a cooperative research project testing systems for networked delivery and use of journals to the user desktop. The participants set three objectives at the outset:

Technical:
    To determine the technical feasibility of networked distribution to and across institutions with varying levels of sophistication in their technical infrastructure. 'Networked distribution' means sending the information both across the national Internet and over campus networks to the desktops of students and faculty. Elsevier will deliver the journal information to participating universities in standard formats. The universities will incorporate in local prototype or operational systems. A wide variety of delivery alternatives, search and retrieval systems and print-on-demand options will be compared.

Organizational and economic:
    To understand through the implementation of prototypes, alternative costing, pricing, subscription and market models that may be 'viable' in electronic distribution scenarios; comparing such models with existing print-then-distribute models; and understanding the role of campus organizational units under such scenarios. The overall goal is to reduce the unit cost of information delivery and retrieval. 'Viable' means economically and functionally acceptable to all parties.

User behavior:

To study reader usage patterns under different distribution (technical, organizational and economic) situations. Improvement in the functionality of the information, whether as to article structure or retrieval tools, will also be considered. Certain data will be collected uniformly at all sites for analysis in the aggregate and for comparison among different systems.

The technical issues are discussed in chapter II. The organizational/economic issues are discussed in chapter V and user behavior is the subject of chapter IV.

I 3. TULIP chronology

The **TULIP** project, some highlights:

1991
- In March the **TULIP** project was initiated at the CNI Spring Task Force Meeting.
- In the remainder of the year Elsevier Science made a choice of suppliers who could process the required material, and of the tools they would be using to do this.

1992
- Meeting between Elsevier Science management and university administrators to agree on the project's goals and on the roles and contributions of the participants.
- Nine universities of the initial group of about 15 submitted a proposal to participate in the project.
- The open exchange format (=**TULIP** Technical Specifications) was specified and refined further, based on experiences and demands from universities.
- Purchase of equipment and development of production facilities at Elsevier Science took place to provide large-scale page scanning, OCR-ing and editing references.
- Purchase of equipment, setup of Internet facilities and development of Dataset loading, customization (=creating Dataset 'subsets' per university) and subsequent delivery procedures took place at Engineering Information (Ei). This included development of an E-mail-driven facility for single article delivery.

1993
- First of the 'regular' **TULIP** group meetings at the bi-annual CNI Task Force meetings, involving Elsevier Science staff, university participants and 'observers' from the universities which had decided not to participate.
- Processing of **TULIP** data. Dispatch of material was split in two parallel streams:
  • 1992 backlog material was directly dispatched on CD Rom to all universities;
  • 1993 current material was dispatched by Ei over the Internet.
  This delivery of **TULIP** data was based on a so called 'Push' mechanism in which Ei initiated the sending.
- At the universities development and/or adaptation of local library systems took place.
  The technological infrastructure at the universities determined to a large extent the technical solutions that were chosen: 'hi-tech' X-Windows/UNIX based systems with which it was possible to view page images on screen, vs 'low-end' Telnet based systems for less sophisticated workstations.
- The University of Michigan system went 'live' in June.
- In the fall, the first technical meeting, uniting technical implementers from all the universities was held, hosted by the University of Michigan. This meeting proved very valuable in the exchange of ideas, which continued to take place on the **TULIP**TECH-L listserv.

1994
- At Elsevier Science, a stabilized production and distribution environment was established after the backlog was eliminated.
- Based on experiences, the quality and validation of the material (notably page images) was enhanced and a checksum facility was introduced.
- At Ei the initial 'push' strategy of FTP deliveries was changed to a 'kicked-off push' in which university staff initiated a Dataset delivery after ensuring that enough resources were available for receipt of a Dataset.

- A number of **TULIP** systems at the universities went 'live'.
- In addition to numerous local promotional activities, Elsevier Science produced posters, banners, lapel pins, newsletters and a **TULIP** home page on the WWW to support the promotion of the project at the universities.
- Logfiles, the electronic records of user activity, started to be delivered to Elsevier Science.
- Universities started to investigate and/or implement MS-Windows and World Wide Web/Mosaic based systems, because the X-Windows platform was found to have too little 'critical mass' in many places.
- Elsevier Science cranked up its internal initiatives to redesign its internal production operations and to develop an 'electronic warehouse'.
- Elsevier Science started to scan all 1,100+ Elsevier journals based on the **TULIP** model for its Electronic Subscriptions project.
- The second technical meeting, hosted by Carnegie Mellon University, was held in the fall.

1995
- SGML bibliographic data files were added to **TULIP** Datasets, resulting in a moderate backlog at the scanning office.
- The number of **TULIP** journal titles increased from 43 to 83 journal titles, derived from the Electronic Subscriptions operation. Not all universities decided to take the additional titles.
- Because of problems with FTP deliveries resulting in large backlogs, it was decided to shift to CD Rom deliveries of Datasets.
- Focus groups and interviews, organized by Elsevier Science, took place at the University of Michigan, MIT and the University of California to research (changes in) user behavior and user needs as well as to have users evaluate the project. The University of Tennessee and Carnegie Mellon University also conducted focus group research.
- At the bi-annual **TULIP** group meeting, a separate discussion session on economic models was held.
- Most universities were busy investigating and developing World Wide Web functionality. A number of those developments were put into operation in 1995.
- At Elsevier Science, a new scanner was installed in the last quarter, resulting in significant improvements in the gray scale parts of the journals, such as photographs.
- Announcement of Elsevier Electronic Subscriptions, making all Elsevier Science journal information available in electronic form.
- The third and final technical meeting took place in the spring, hosted by Elsevier Science in Amsterdam. Besides the usual exchange of experiences and ideas, this meeting included an introduction to Elsevier Science publishing systems, and some brainstorming sessions on the next steps to be taken towards full scale implementations from a technical viewpoint.

1996
- Publication of the **TULIP** final report.
- **TULIP** is being succeeded by a full scale production commercial program, called Elsevier Electronic Subscriptions (EES). All of Elsevier's 1,100 plus titles are available in electronic format. Elsevier Science is offering EES to a number of selected ('high end') customers, among which obviously are the **TULIP** participants.
- Of the **TULIP** participants, some are going to a 'full blown' EES implementation, meaning that they will receive all their subscriptions in both paper and electronic form. Others have found that they are not ready or willing to implement an EES based digital library on a full scale, due to technical, organizational or budget constraints. Finally, there are two instances in which the universities feel that they have not learnt enough, and have asked Elsevier for an extension of the experimental period.

I 4. Profile of participants

I 4.1 Elsevier Science

With headquarters in Amsterdam, Elsevier Science has companies in Oxford, New York, Tokyo, Lausanne, Paris, Seoul, Rio de Janeiro and Shannon. Elsevier Science aims at linking scientists from all over the world through a comprehensive publishing program. Scientific progress is highly dependent on certified and refereed information and on the access to the information. Some of Elsevier's hallmarks are close cooperation with authors and editors, support of the refereeing system, speedy preparation of material for publication, commitment to innovative products and services, expertise in international marketing and distribution and quality control throughout the process. Elsevier Science aims to advance science, technology, and medical science by fulfilling the communication needs specific to the international community of scientists and engineers, and associated professions. Elsevier Science wishes to collaborate in this with libraries anywhere in the world where possible.

Elsevier Science is committed to converting all of its production processes at its different publishing houses (over 1,100 journals and 1.8 million pages published in ten locations in a previously non-standardized way) to produce media-neutral databases based upon SGML tagging as its primary output, generating the print as well as electronic products from that electronic source-material. This fundamental change in Elsevier Science's production, which involves changing almost all production procedures, hardware as well as software, and most importantly, hundreds of people's jobs, is currently under way, to be completed at the end of 1996. In the meanwhile, Elsevier Science is providing all its journals in electronic form by scanning the paper journals, as was done in the **TULIP** project.

I 4.2 Universities

I 4.2.1 Description of universities

The **TULIP** project unites nine of the leading universities in the USA. Although they have in common the drive to be at the forefront of the transition to digital libraries, they differ vastly in size, scope, resources, etc. On the one hand, very large institutions like the University of California system were participating in the **TULIP** project, on the other hand there were also much smaller institutions like the University of Tennessee participating. This diversity was reflected in the approaches of the projects, in their execution and in their results. Below is a short overview of the characteristics of each of the participants; more details can be found in the university reports (appendices I through IX).

- **Carnegie Mellon University**
  Carnegie Mellon University has seven teaching colleges or schools, most of which offer undergraduate as well as graduate programs, as well as over 50 interdisciplinary research centers. The annual budget of the university is approx. $360 million, including funded research. The University Librarian is responsible for library operations at Carnegie Mellon and reports to the provost. The staff includes 36 professionals and 50 staff, plus a significant workforce of students, around 45 FTE in all. The University libraries' collections include more than 852,000 volumes; over 900,000 microforms and graphics; and 3,850 periodical subscriptions housed in three locations. The Library Information Technology (LIT) department is responsible for day-to-day operations (eight FTE) as well as research and development (five FTE). The head of R&D is responsible to the head of LIT who reports to the University Librarian. In addition to **TULIP**, LIT is currently supporting several major technology R&D projects valued at around $2,000,000.

- **Cornell University**
  Cornell University is partially public (it is the land grant university for the State of New York), and partially private. The university consists of thirteen colleges; eleven of these are in Ithaca, and two (the Medical College and the Graduate School of Medical Studies), are located in New York City. The Cornell University Library system contains 5.8 million volumes, 6.8 million microform items, as well as large collections of maps, videos, sound recordings, and computer files. The library system consists of nineteen libraries, two of which - the Engineering Library and the Physical Sciences Library - were the

primary Cornell participants in the **TULIP** project. The Engineering and Physical Sciences librarians report to an associate university librarian, who reports to the University Librarian. The University Librarian reports to the provost. Cornell Information Technologies (CIT) consists of approximately 325 staff members, divided into three divisions: (a) Information Resources, (b) Support Services and Academic Computing, and (c) Network Resources.

● **Georgia Institute of Technology (Georgia Tech)**
Georgia Institute of Technology has five colleges, plus the Georgia Tech Research Institute. Research is an integral part of the education process at Georgia Tech and has grown to over $168 million annually, including research in the colleges and at the Georgia Tech Research Institute. Research activities are diversified and are centered on areas where the nation has a vital interest - defense, manufacturing, health and the environment, and electronics. Students and faculty have access to a catalog collection of over 2,929,507 bibliographic units in the Price Gilbert Memorial Library. Technical reports number approximately 2,375,000. There are over 5,130,000 patents; government documents include over 623,000 publications and nearly 173,680 maps. Approximately 75% of the total collection is in scientific or technical fields. Literature searches and other reference services are provided from more than 500 bibliographic and factual data bases. There are about 100 library staff, of which eight are systems staff.

● **Massachusetts Institute of Technology (MIT)**
MIT is an independent, coeducational, privately endowed university, broadly organized into five academic schools, housing 21 academic departments, complemented by many interdepartmental laboratories, centers, and divisions. MIT has a total budget of approximately $1.4 billion and research revenues of approximately $700 million. Reporting to the provost and with a total staff of about 200, the MIT libraries' resources comprise more than 21,000 current journals and periodicals and extensive back files totaling more than 2.3 million volumes. The library system is composed of five major (divisional) libraries as well as a number of smaller branch libraries.
Reporting to the senior vice president and with a total staff of about 240, Information Systems (IS) provides comprehensive computing, networking, and telecommunications services for all of MIT. IS services and facilities support the academic, research, and administrative use of a broad scope of information and computing technology, and include responsibility for the Athena Computing Environment and MITnet, the campus-wide computer network. The Athena Computing Environment offers computing resources designed for educational use by students and faculty. MITnet connects thousands of computers across the campus and to the Internet.

● **The University of California**
The University of California is one of the largest institutions of higher education in the world. It has academic programs in over 150 disciplines, and ten percent of all Ph.D.'s awarded in the United States come from the University of California. Its library system contains over 100 libraries on the nine campuses, with collections totaling over 27 million volumes. The Division of Library Automation (DLA) is responsible for the University of California system-wide MELVYL system, a computer based library system providing access to a variety of bibliographic databases. DLA is also responsible for operating the inter-campus TCP/IP data communications network. In 1995 this network was upgraded from a network running at fractional T1 speeds to an SMDS network. One of the major justifications for this large increase in bandwidth was the need to adequately support applications like **TULIP**.

● **The University of Michigan**
The University of Michigan, located in Ann Arbor, contains 18 schools and colleges. During fiscal year 93-94, the University had grant research income of $386 million, the largest of any U.S. university. Although the university's schools and colleges are managed through a decentralized organizational structure, there is a central agency for information technology, ITD (Information Technology Division), managed by the Vice-Provost for Information Technology. This unit provides basic IT infrastructure and support, maintains public computing sites, advises on hardware and software, and cooperates with others to meet University needs. Some of the schools and colleges have their own information technology support groups. This is the case for both the University Library which manages MIRLYN, the campus library management system, and the College of Engineering which oversees the Computer-Aided Engineering Network (CAEN). The School of Information and Library Studies (SILS) is also a contributor to the University's development of electronic services. Consistent with Michigan's tradition of

interdisciplinary activities, ITD, the University Library, CAEN, and SILS are collaborating under the umbrella of the Digital Library program. **TULIP**, NSF-UMDL, a project funded by the National Science Foundation and others, and JSTOR are part of this University of Michigan Digital Library (UMDL) umbrella. The units are working together in development and production activities.

- **The University of Tennessee**
  The University of Tennessee is the official land grant institution for the State of Tennessee, with its main campus in Knoxville. The University offers more than 300 degree programs. Developments in graduate education have been accompanied by expanded cooperation with Oak Ridge National Laboratory (ORNL) and the Tennessee Valley Authority, and by growth of major research programs including those in the fields of energy, biotechnology, and robotics. The University of Tennessee, Knoxville libraries own approximately 2 million volumes, more than 3.5 million manuscripts, 2 million microforms, 32,000 audio and video recordings, plus United States and United Nations documents. The University of Tennessee libraries employ 185 full-time staff, and subscribe to more than 11,000 periodicals and other serial titles. **TULIP** was implemented at The University of Tennessee by a team of library staff that included an information sciences professor, independent of the computing and telecommunications services.

- **The University of Washington**
  The University of Washington, a public research university with a main campus in Seattle and branch campuses in Tacoma and Bothell, has 16 major schools and colleges. The University of Washington libraries system is one of the largest research libraries in North America. Its collections exceed five million catalogued volumes, an equal number in microform, several million items in other formats, and more than 50,000 serial titles. The libraries system is composed of the Suzzallo and Allen Libraries with collections primarily in the humanities, natural sciences and social sciences, three other major libraries, 18 specialized branch libraries and two branch campus libraries. Computing at the University of Washington is the responsibility of Computing & Communications (C&C), which has experienced a more than 25 percent annual growth rate in active accounts in the last five years. There are now over 40,000 individuals using the the University of Washington Uniform Access computers. The services offered by C&C encompass a wide array of computing and networking environments.

- **Virginia Polytechnic Institute and State University (Virginia Tech)**
  Virginia Tech, the largest state supported institution of higher education in the Commonwealth of Virginia and a land grant institution, has nine different colleges, the largest being the College of Engineering. The Virginia Tech libraries consist of a main library, three branch libraries at the main campus in Blacksburg, and another branch library in Fairfax, Va. There are six administrative units that comprise the University libraries - Administrative Services, Collection Development, Library Automation, Special Collections, Technical Services, and User Services. Library personnel consists of 40 professional librarians, 110 support staff, and approximately 63 FTE of student assistants, reporting to the Dean of University Libraries, who in turn reports to the Vice President for Information Systems. Within the University libraries all IT services, equipment installation and repairs, software and network maintenance, etc., are provided by the Library Automation Department. Campus-wide IT services are provided mainly by other information systems groups, such as the Computing Center, Communications Network Services, and Media Services, but library personnel does participate in various IT outreach projects that affect a broad spectrum of the university community.

I 4.2.2   Project organization

The project was implemented under different organizational structures at different universities. At all sites the libraries were involved, at some sites the computer centers; other technical organizations and library schools were involved in the project as well.

- At Carnegie Mellon University, the project started out as a joint activity between the Computing Services and the University libraries. This turned out to be an unworkable solution, because nobody was focussed on the effort and as a result the work did not get done. After about a year, **TULIP** became the full responsibility of the libraries, which allowed them to supply the necessary effort to the implementation of **TULIP** much more quickly than had been the case before.

- Cornell University had two separate groups involved in the project: the Cornell Information Technologies and the library. While the library provided administrative and public service support for **TULIP**, the main technical work on the project was done by a combination of special support from CIT and grant funding received to further the creation of the Cornell digital library. CIT also assumed responsibility for archiving the **TULIP** materials. Part way through the **TULIP** project, the library made the decision to divide organizationally those projects considered to be experimental, such as **TULIP**, from regular and routine online services (e.g. online catalog maintenance) already in production. This was done mainly in order to protect the support for basic online services. This decision had the advantage of clarifying reporting relationships, which resulted in significant improvements in productivity allowing Cornell to better guide the development of the **TULIP** effort.

- Georgia Institute of Technology managed the project with library staff exclusively, no computer center staff was involved. Georgia Tech has a fairly large systems staff incorporated within the library, dedicated to library projects, who really understand library issues. The implementation could be done 'in-house', so there were no organizational problems; as Georgia Tech already had staff support for the database on which the **TULIP** implementation was based, it was relatively easy to implement **TULIP** on this site.

- At the Massachusetts Institute of Technology, organization of the **TULIP** experiment took place within the context of the MIT Distributed Library Initiative (DLI), a collaborative effort led by the MIT Libraries and Information Systems. The **TULIP** implementation team was called BULB and was comprised of public services staff from the libraries, programmer analyst expertise from information systems, a research associate from the Dept. of Materials Science, and a counselor from the MIT Intellectual Property Office.

- At the University of California, the university libraries of all nine campuses were involved by means of an advisory/liaison group of librarians. The project was managed by the Division of Library Automation (DLA) at the office of the president, where all the technical implementation took place.

- As mentioned above, at the University of Michigan the project was carried out under the umbrella of a joint undertaking of the Information Technology Division, the College of Engineering, the School of Information and Library Studies and the University library. A joint team with representatives from each group guided developments through each step of the **TULIP** project.

- The University of Tennessee had involvement from the library only; a team of library staff with responsibility in public service, networking, and systems implemented the **TULIP** application. A professor from the School of Information Sciences was involved throughout the project and participated in promotion, training and research activities.

- The project at the University of Washington was rooted in the systems side of the libraries and the university information systems. The branch librarians dealing with the potential users were only marginally involved in the development of the application. The University of Washington abandoned their **TULIP** implementation two years into the project, because they wanted to move all development to the Web environment and because they felt the project did not have enough of a potential user base on their campus to make it a success.

- At Virginia Tech, the project was managed by the University libraries, while resources were provided by both the libraries and the Computer Center. User contact was maintained through an interested professor in the Department of Material Science and Engineering in the College of Engineering.

I 4.2.3 **User demographics**

The total numbers of faculty and students per university are listed below and where available the primary target departments and their user groups for the **TULIP** project are also listed.

- Carnegie Mellon is a highly selective small, private, coeducational university with approximately 4,300 undergraduate students, 2,400 graduate students, and over 550 regular faculty. Some 30 faculty, 55 graduate students and 50 undergraduate students could be considered the primary target group for the **TULIP** material, while there is a group of about three times as many people who could have an interest in parts of the **TULIP** journals list.

● Cornell University has a current enrollment of 19,000 students (13,000 undergraduates and 6,000 graduate students), and a faculty of 1,600. The College of Engineering (218 faculty, 1,055 graduate students) as well as the science faculty and students in the College of Arts and Sciences, especially in the fields of physics (45 faculty, 190 graduate students, two research associates), and chemistry (31 faculty, 145 graduate students, 15 research associates) are the primary target groups for the **TULIP** content.

● Georgia Institute of Technology has about 5,000 faculty and staff, 4,000 graduate students and about 8,000 undergraduates. Of these, about 220 can be considered potential users of the **TULIP** material.

● Massachusetts Institute of Technology's total enrollment is approximately 9,800 students, with somewhat fewer undergraduates than graduate students. The MIT faculty numbers approximately 1,100, with a total teaching staff of over 2,000. The potential user group of the **TULIP** files is estimated at about 450, the primary group being the Materials Research Department, but some of the material may be of interest for users in at least nine other departments.

● The University of California's nine campuses comprise 167,000 students and 130,000 faculty and staff. They are composed of approximately 122,000 undergraduate and 45,000 graduate students, and 7,000 faculty and 32,000 other academic personnel. Of the nine campuses, eight have more or less substantial departments involved with material science/engineering. The total potential user group for the **TULIP** files at the University of California is almost 3,400, but many of these can not be considered potential 'core users' of the **TULIP** files, as their primary research interests are not represented in the **TULIP** journal list.

● The University of Michigan has an enrollment of 37,000 students, of which 30% are graduate students. The College of Engineering contains the largest number of materials scientists as well as computer scientists and others interested in the **TULIP** titles. However, users can also be found in the physics and chemistry departments, and to a lesser extent in the Dental, Medical and Pharmacy schools. Altogether, a potential user community of 360 faculty and graduate students is estimated.

● The University of Tennessee has an enrollment of 26,000 students and employs 1,600 faculty. The **TULIP** audience included faculty and graduate students in the University of Tennessee, College of Engineering Department of Materials Science and Engineering, as well as ORNL researchers whose work involved materials science. There are 15 Materials Science faculty and approximately 100 graduate students. The Materials Science Department also has a small undergraduate program with 75-80 students enrolled.

● The University of Washington is populated by about 3,500 teaching and research faculty, about 13,000 staff and about 35,000 students, of which 8,000 are graduate students. The primary target group for the **TULIP** material would be in the College of Engineering, which offers education in traditional fields dealing with transportation systems, manufacturing and process industries in the Departments of Aeronautics and Astronautics, Civil Engineering, Chemical Engineering, Electrical Engineering and Mechanical Engineering, and also rapidly-growing new fields in bioengineering, computer science and engineering, materials science and engineering and technical communication.

● Virginia Tech has over 23,000 students enrolled in graduate and undergraduate education, while the College of Engineering alone has over 5,000 students enrolled. The primary target group for this project was to consist mainly of the faculty, graduate and undergraduate students in the area of materials science, consisting of the Materials Science and Engineering Department, with 20 faculty, approximately 50 graduate students and 50 undergraduate students, complemented by approximately 50 additional faculty and 50 graduate students from related fields such as Chemical Engineering, Chemistry, Engineering Science and Mechanics, Electrical Engineering, Mechanical Engineering, and Physics. The initial user group will be the MSE department.

II   Technical aspects

This chapter describes the technical side of the **TULIP** project, which has been the major focus of at least the first half of the project. The lessons learned here have already had an important impact on the directions Elsevier Science is taking, as well as on the implementation of the digital library (components) at the participating universities. Because we think that some of these lessons could be equally valuable for other institutions looking to get started in this field, we have summarized them below, and prepared some general guidelines and checklist (appendix X).

To give a better feel for the size of the **TULIP** project, we have listed some key numbers in the box below (next page).

II 1.   Production at Elsevier Science

This chapter describes the phases of production at Elsevier Science and its partners to generate and deliver electronic journal issues for the **TULIP** project. This can be broken down in three main phases:
- the (traditional) production from manuscript to journal issue;
- the scanning and capturing of journal issues in full **TULIP** Datasets;
- the customization and delivery of Datasets to the libraries involved in **TULIP**.

II 1.1   Description of paper journal production

'Traditional' paper journal production is done in several phases. We briefly describe the steps from manuscript written by the author to the journal issue received by the librarian. Variations exist for particular types of publications, but the majority of articles is handled in the following order:

a. The author creates the manuscript and submits this manuscript to the editor of a journal.
b. The editor distributes the manuscript to a small number of reviewers to assess its scientific value. Based on their reports and possibly subsequent modifications by the author, the editor decides to accept or reject the manuscript for publication in the journal. Accepted manuscripts are submitted to the publisher.
c. The accepted manuscript is received by the publisher, where the details are entered in the tracking system which monitors production flow. Electronically delivered manuscripts (nicknamed 'compuscripts') are converted to a generic word processing format (SGML).
d. The text is marked up according to the style of the journal and spelling- and other checks are done. 'Anchors' are inserted for the artwork.
e. Artwork (figures, charts, photographs, etc.) is prepared and converted to electronic files by conversion, redrawing or high quality scanning.
f. The resulting manuscript including artwork is proofed by the typesetter to obtain a draft version of the article, which is mailed to the author for approval.
g. The corrections returned by the author are inserted in the article text or artwork files. The article is ready for issue assembly.
h. Based on the publication scheme (weekly, biweekly, monthly, etc.) of the journal, finished articles are assembled in a journal issue. Page numbers are assigned, a table of contents, author and subject index, and other editorial material is added and the full issue is sent to the typesetter.
i. The typesetter produces high quality Camera Ready Output (CRC) on film or print plate for further processing.
j. The CRC material is printed in 'quires' (sixteen pages on one piece of paper, to be folded and cut) and these are collected and bound into journal issues. Packages of printed issues are dispatched to the publishers' distribution center.
k. The distribution center packages the issues into envelopes with address labels. The issues are bundled by geographical area and dispatched to customers by mail, airmail or courier service (based on subscription arrangements).

The Tulip project in key numbers

Number of journal titles	43
Additional number of journal titles in 1995	40
Number of Datasets - in original titles - in additional journal titles	99 86 13
Number of issues - in original titles - in additional journal titles	2,784 2,427 357
Number of articles - in original titles - in additional journal titles	74,096 66,569 7,527
Number of pages - in original titles - in additional journal titles	536,946 470,040 66,906
Storage space per Dataset - Average Dataset - Biggest Dataset	 380 Megabytes 530 Megabytes
Storage space per issue - Average page image - Average issue - Largest issue	 72 Kilobytes 14 Megabytes ($\pm$ 193 pages) 86 Megabytes (1,200 pages)
Total storage space (approximate)	39 Gigabytes
Average transmission time per Dataset *) - Quickest school average - Slowest school average *) raw throughput time; failures and overhead excluded	6h 42m 4h 21m 11h 2m
Number of **TULIP** universities	9
Number of different solutions (including abandoned and prototype versions) - Number of MS Windows implementations - Number of X-Windows implementations - Number of Telnet implementations - Number of Gopher implementations - Number of WWW implementations	 2 6 3 1 4

II **1.2**   **Description of production of electronic version**

II **1.2.1**   **Introduction**

As a result of historical technological differences and more recent acquisitions, there was no single production flow mechanism covering all journal titles within the Elsevier Science organization in 1992. Elsevier Science consists of several larger or smaller publishing offices, each with its own publishing portfolio, working procedures and technologies as well as its own third-party suppliers such as typesetting, artwork preparation and printing companies. For instance, the 43 initial journals in **TULIP** were published by four different offices in Amsterdam (The Netherlands), Oxford (UK), Lausanne (Switzerland) and New York (USA). These 43 titles are typeset by some 18 different typesetting companies. In 1992, PostScript had not gained the popularity it currently has for scientific typesetting, hence both PostScript and non-PostScript routines were used.

At present, Elsevier Science is consolidating all these different production methods to streamline the output into standard electronic formats, such as SGML, PostScript, PDF, JPEG and TIFF, which then become the basic material to not only produce paper versions of the journals in their most appropriate typeset form, but also to provide 'real' electronic versions of the journals based on SGML. In the future we should experience a state where paper is the derivative of the electronic journal, the reverse of the situation in **TULIP**.

As an intermediate step, however, for the **TULIP** project we used the paper version of the journals to produce scanned images as the electronic form of the journals. It was decided that it would be preferable to use and digitize the finished paper product (end of phase j, see above) rather than trying to obtain production files in a diversity of (sometimes proprietary) electronic formats from these different sources. This was based on the following observations:

- The material from the production files is not a 'clean cut' version, i.e. the pages have an extra margin, that contains crop marks and production remarks, which is cut away later.
- The cover is not the final one. In a number of cases the 'blank' color cover is held at the printer in a large stock on which only the volume, issue and cover date information is added per issue.
- Some of the material is in the form of plastic film with transparent text on a black background, impossible to process with currently used plain paper page scanners.
- The typesetter and printer are changing to electronic delivery of CRC. This exchange is based on PostScript, but the resulting files are totally unusable for **TULIP**, since these are imposition prints with e.g. a complete one sided quire with half of the pages upside down in one large print file.
- Typesetters and printers work with tight production schedules. There was a hazard that the introduction of new requirements would disturb their production flow.

II **1.2.2**   **The Dataset**

TULIP is based on electronic subscription-based regular delivery of large volumes of journal information. No standard existed for this kind of delivery. Available standards for document delivery dealt with the concept of demand-driven single document requests, which appeared to be inapplicable for supply-driven electronic delivery of entire journal issues. Therefore, in **TULIP**'s first year the concept of the **TULIP** Dataset was created in close cooperation with the different internal production and delivery partners, and with the technical coordinators at the universities.

A Dataset holds a number of page image and text files from several journal issues, collected biweekly in this particular case. The structure and format of a Dataset follows the ISO 9660 Mode 1 standard for CD-Rom mastering, which is more or less similar to regular MS-DOS conventions for file names and directory structures. This convention can easily be used in other computer platforms, such as Apple Macintosh and UNIX operating systems.

The directory-structure of the Dataset directly reflects the division into journals (identified by their International Standard Serial Number — ISSN), journal issues and pages/articles. The files in the Dataset are page images, 'raw' ASCII files, SGML-coded citation files and a master index containing bibliographic information and pointers connecting the files.

- Every page from a journal issue (cover-to-cover) corresponds with a page image file. These are standard black/white single-page Tagged Image File Format (TIFF) files with a resolution of 300 dots per inch. The page-sizes differ from journal to journal. The maximum size is European A4, i.e. 21 x 29.7 cm or 8.27 x 11.69 inch. The compression method used is the International Telecommunications Union (ITU; formerly known as CCITT) Fax Group IV encoding scheme, with which it is possible to reduce the average 1 megabyte image to a TIFF file of 80 kilobytes (Kb).
- Every page has a corresponding text file with the full text. This ASCII file is the result of Optical Character Recognition (OCR). These files are provided in unedited ('raw') format, since no further keyboarding/editing/spell checking is performed on them.
- Every editorial item (e.g. full length scientific article, product review, correspondence letter, editorial note, etc.) has a corresponding Standard Generalized Markup Language (SGML) file, holding the full bibliographic information (e.g. title, authors, abstract, keyword, page range, etc.). The Document Type Definition (DTD) for these SGML files is Elsevier's Full Length Article DTD. These SGML files were initially not part of the **TULIP** Datasets, but were added in 1995 when **TULIP** production became part of the Elsevier Electronic Subscriptions production.
- Each Dataset has one master index file, the so-called DATASET.TOC file, which holds complete bibliographic information as well as all relevant cross reference data, i.e. which page images are related to which articles and which articles are in a particular journal issue.

An important characteristic of the **TULIP** project is the large storage requirement. Traditional text oriented database systems normally deal with small, plain-text bibliographic records, averaging 2 to 3 Kb (with abstract). The information delivered in **TULIP** averages 840 Kb per article, roughly 400 times this size.

The storage requirements for a typical journal issue, holding 20 articles plus cover pages, editorial notes, table of contents, etc. on 200 pages, are approximately 17 megabytes (Mb):
- A single page TIFF image file takes about 80 Kb, 200 pages are approx. 16 Mb.
- The corresponding unedited ('raw') OCR-quality ASCII file takes up 4 Kb, that is 800 Kb for all 200 pages.
- The SGML file, which holds the bibliographic data of a given article, is on average 4 Kb. For 20 articles this amounts to 80 Kb.
- The index data comprises some 4 Kb per article, adding up to 80 Kb for an average issue.

For the **TULIP** titles the average subscription frequency is 14 issues per year, that is 238 Mb per journal per year. However there is a wide variation in volume and frequency between the journal titles.

II **1.2.3   Overview of production steps**

TULIP operational units transform printed journal issues into their electronic equivalents as follows:

a. Dispatch of journal issues to the scanning offices:
    Journal issues for **TULIP** follow the usual internal production routines for typesetting, printing and binding. The Elsevier distribution centers ship the journal issues via air mail delivery to the **TULIP** scanning offices.

b. Receipt and verification of journal issues:
    As soon as the journal issue arrives at the scanning office, it is checked for completeness and registered in the tracking system at the scanning office.

c. Page image scanning:
    The spine of the issue is cut and the pages are fed into a high-volume (40 pages per minute) double-sided scanner. Care is taken that the order of the pages is correct, the pages are not fed skewed and that the printed page numbers correspond with the actual pages, including certification of pages without page numbers (such as advertisements) and oddly numbered pages (such as roman numbered pages with *iii, iv, xi*).
    The pages are scanned at 300 dots per inch (dpi) and directly compressed by means of hardware based compression boards in order to keep storage space manageable.

At the start of the project in 1992 the decision was made to base page images on 300 dots per inch, black/white TIFF according to the ITU/CCITT Fax Group IV compression scheme. This decision was based on a good ratio of image quality versus storage consumption and production costs. No affordable high-volume 600 dpi scanners were available at that time and the quality of text and line art was regarded as good, somewhere between office laser printer and photocopier quality. The implication of this choice is that color is not possible with this format and that the quality of photographs can be unsatisfactory, especially for photographs with little contrast such as electromicrographs.

d. Optical character recognition (OCR):
   After the page images are scanned and cropped they are processed in a background process on a sepa-rate machine in the same network. This machine automatically picks up a page image and performs optical character recognition to generate the corresponding ASCII file. The OCR process takes longer to process a page image than the actual scanning. At **TULIP**'s start, hardware OCR equipment was used, but with the advent of faster machines and better algorithms OCR is performed entirely in software and takes thirty seconds to a whole minute per page. The quality of the resulting files has improved greatly in the past years, but mathematical symbols and other typographic codes remain a problem. Even now, there is no software available to handle complicated scientific texts successfully.

e. Editing of OCR texts to obtain SGML files and bibliographic records:
   Page images and OCR texts are used in a production editor environment to generate the bibliographic records and the SGML files for each article. Because each journal title has a different presentation and layout for article elements such as titles, abstracts, article texts, etc., it is not possible to fully automate this process. Despite efforts in artificial intelligence, only a human being can comprehend the whole scope of a scientific article. Associating page images with articles, i.e. identifying the pages which 'belong' to an article, is an integral part of the production editor process.

f. Collecting material in Datasets:
   The **TULIP** production schedule results in biweekly delivery of Datasets. All material that has passed the final quality control step is collected into the directory structure of a Dataset. All edited bibliographic information and relevant cross reference data are compiled into the DATASET.TOC file which is the primary index for each Dataset. A final quality control step is performed on the entire Dataset and checksum files are generated (for a description of this facility, see below). The resulting Dataset is finally copied onto CD-Recordable disk. This disk was shipped by courier to the customizing and delivery office, located in the USA. Due to the problems in Internet file transfer procedures (see below), it was decided in 1994 to discontinue network delivery and to send CD-Rom's directly to the universities.

II **1.3**   **Description of customizing and Internet distribution**

Elsevier Science worked together with Article Express* to customize Datasets to reflect universities' sub-scriptions and to deliver those customized Datasets via the Internet. The original implementation that was agreed on by Elsevier and the collaborating universities in early 1993 was a so called 'push' model. After the Dataset has been received and customized, it is ready for delivery. It was 'pushed' from Article Express to all universities by means of a series of FTP scripts. Tracking and validation was based on the assumption that FTP could be used for the 'push' model of delivering large Datasets with very many pieces.

II **1.3.1**   **Customizing Datasets**

Upon receipt of a new Dataset on CD-Rom from the scanning office, the entire content of the CD-Rom is copied to large capacity magnetic disk. Article Express holds a database including among other things, which universities subscribe to which journal titles, since not every university subscribes to all journal titles. Universities only receive electronic equivalents of journals of which they hold a subscription. A num-

---

* Originally a combined operation of Engineering Information, Inc. and Dialog Inc., Article Express was later run by Dialog, after Engineering Information was bought out.

ber of different 'logical' Datasets (based on pointers to relevant files, not by duplicating entire Datasets) is derived, one for each university. Also, different DATASET.TOC files are generated for each university. Subsequently a number of FTP scripts is generated, also one for each university. As soon as this preparatory work is done, the different logical Datasets are ready for dispatch.

II 1.3.2   Internet Delivery

The original delivery process worked as follows:
- In a series of FTP sessions (one per directory holding a journal issue) the entire content of the customized Datasets was transferred.
- The following step was an FTP session in which all transferred directories were checked against the original data.
- For any mismatch (missing files or ones which had a different file size than intended) the files were retransmitted and revalidated. If the validation still failed, an automatic message was generated for the service provider.
- As a final step, after all validation had been accomplished, the customized DATASET.TOC file with all bibliographic data and the relevant cross reference data was transferred to indicate the successful completion of Dataset delivery.

On average Datasets are between 200 and 300 Mb in size. FTP deliveries tended to fluctuate between two to 14 hours with an average of 6.5 hours, dependent on a number of visible or less visible factors such as time of day, Internet rerouting, type of connection (T1 = 1.5 Mbit/second or T3 = 45 Mbit/second), high user load, etc.

The initial 'push' strategy was based on the assumption that all universities would be able to start receiving **TULIP** Datasets within the same time frame and that there would be 'enough' storage space available at the universities' end to receive the information. The idea was that after receipt of a Dataset from the scanning office it would be transmitted without delay from Article Express to all universities. However, because not all universities were ready to receive at the same time due to differences in their implementation schedules, this did not work very well.

Therefore during the course of the project the 'push' strategy was changed to a 'push on demand' strategy. From time to time (at least weekly), the local **TULIP** coordinator at a university connects via Telnet to the dedicated dispatch machine at Article Express to see if there are any new Datasets available and what the estimated size of the Dataset is in Mb. If there is a new Dataset, he/she indicates which one(s) to deliver (in **TULIP** terms: 'kicking it off') and then exits the Telnet session.

Implementation of this 'kick-off' facility allowed for the university staff to initiate the transfer of a Dataset when they were ready to accommodate the data. This helped considerably because it enabled the universities to process Datasets at their convenience when they had sufficient disk resources. It proved very successful in the case where one late starter began receiving Datasets about one year after other sites and had a pretty large backlog. A complete year of Datasets was transmitted within a few weeks.

Nevertheless, the amount of errors (detailed below) remained high. Therefore, it was decided to cease the delivery of Datasets via the Internet and to revert to CD-Rom distribution.

II 1.3.3   Single article delivery

At **TULIP**'s start, a facility was designed at Engineering Information for single article delivery over the Internet. Universities were entitled to receive all bibliographic records of the **TULIP** titles, even if no subscription was kept on certain titles. If a researcher found an article of interest in one of the non-subscribed titles, it was possible to request this article by means of a formatted electronic mail message. To accomplish this facility a separate WORM-based optical storage system was developed by Engineering Information staff. It was the intention that this multi-gigabyte storage system would hold all Datasets after these were dispatched to the universities.

The development of this system suffered from several technical problems, most of them due to the incompatibility to connect optical devices to the UNIX systems at Engineering Information. Therefore this system never became fully operational. The solution was to use a manual procedure, but this resulted in long delivery delays, and those universities that tried this system, found it did not work satisfactorily. The demand for this system turned out to be very low. Most of the universities subscribed to nearly all journals and so did not need to request single documents. The only exception was the University of Tennessee, which did not receive and store page images and relied on this facility to order page images. However, besides some troublesome experimenting, there was no demand for single articles and so the facility was practically abandoned in 1994.

II **1.4**   **Lessons learned concerning production**

Below is an overview of some of the standards that have been adopted in the course of the **TULIP** project, of some of the problems that were faced during the four years of producing **TULIP**, and of the solutions found and implemented to solve these problems.

II **1.4.1**   **Dataset structure**

The Dataset structure with directories and a single 'DATASET.TOC' master index file has proven to be a stable and robust 'envelope' format to collect and transmit large quantities of electronic material, independent of medium. It is simple to generate, load and convert in different systems and it is open to add formats like full text SGML files and MPEG videos, without violating the original structure. This Dataset structure format, nicknamed EFFECT, Exchange Format For Electronic Components and Texts, has been offered to the Internet Engineering Task Force (IETF) as a possible Internet standard. The format has been applied in other projects, such as the EASE project in which Elsevier Science is cooperating with Tilburg University in the Netherlands, and in the JSTOR project at the University of Michigan.

II **1.4.2**   **Page image cropping**

There is a large variation in journal heights and widths. Scanning is performed at maximum page size regardless of journal size. The resulting page images therefore initially had black borders, meaning wasted disk storage space and high laser printer toner consumption.
- The first cut at this problem was to manually measure each journal issue before it was fed into the scanner and to have the scanner operator enter height and width. This proved to be too laborious and error prone to work satisfactorily.
- Image enhancement programs, which automatically crop pages based on visual aids on the page image, have also been investigated, but proved too inaccurate. Sometimes fine horizontal or vertical lines in a table or page footer were taken as the page margin, resulting in too much cropping. Automatic cropping also results in different dimensions for each page. This proved unsatisfactory for screen display purposes as the (left and right) page images 'jump' on the screen when browsing through an article.
- The following procedure, which is based on a separate cropping operation step, was finally adopted. Every journal title typically has its own fixed dimensions. In the cropping step a different 'mask' is applied per journal title which removes a fixed number of pixels from the right and bottom sides from odd pages and the same amount of pixels from the left and bottom sides from even pages (due to the dual page scanning method both sides of the page are scanned at the same time). The result is equal size page images per journal issue, with minimal black borders.
- No good solution has been found yet for fold-out pages, which don't appear in **TULIP** journals very often, but are frequently present in medical and geological journals for large maps, charts or tables. Fold-out pages are simply cut into several page images, losing the intended overview of the fold-out. It could be considered to add the entire fold-out at 70% size, enabling users to get an overview of the entire chart, scheme or table.

II 1.4.3 Halftone quality

Page image scanning quality has enhanced considerably in the past years. Image enhancement technology improved and scanning staff became more experienced, resulting in crisp text and good artwork. The only exception is the quality of scanned photographs, which is less than satisfactory. This holds especially for those photographs with little contrast such as electron microscope or other micrograph-optical reproductions. This is inherent of the image format chosen, which is bi-level bitmaps. Each pixel in a bi-level file denotes either black or white as opposed to halftone or color bitmaps. Each pixel in a bi-level bitmap is only one bit, while pixels in halftone or color files can be many bits to represent different colors or gray values. Bi-level bitmaps are therefore relatively small and can furthermore be compressed excellently with the Fax Group IV compression scheme, the TIFF format is well established and software/hardware tools are readily available.

However, when scanning a halftone photograph into a bi-level bitmap, an image scanner has to decide for each pixel area (typically 1/300 square inch), whether the gray value is above or below a certain threshold and should be represented as a black or white dot only. In some cases, photographs with large gray areas result in smudgy black rectangles on the page images. This problem is further complicated by the symptom of 'moiré patterns', because of interference of the print screening (the angled tiny raster which is visible when observing printed photographs with a magnifying glass), and the scanner.

New scanning technology came on to the market recently to tackle this particular problem, however this came 'too late' for the **TULIP** project. A new line of high volume image scanners recognizes halftone areas on the page and performs a sophisticated dithering technique on these areas, leaving the text areas untouched. The result is a considerably better scanned photograph quality, although still not equivalent to the original photograph. Scanners of this type will be used for future electronic projects.

II 1.4.4 CD Rom mastering

In 1992, CD Rom mastering equipment based on CD Recordable write-once (golden) disks was not readily available and had its teething problems. Some of these first generation problems were encountered in 1993, when it was necessary to produce a large quantity of CD Rom's due to the 1992 backlog. The situation has now become more stable, but needs continued attention because the technology is still not 100% error proof.

II 1.4.5 Checksums

TIFF page images are very sensitive to 'corruption'. One single incorrect bit in a page image makes the file useless. Errors occasionally occur in CD-Rom mastering as well as in Internet file transfers, although at the outset these two technologies were expected to have sufficient error recovery facilities. On average we have encountered one incorrect bit, resulting in a fully incorrect image per maybe 20,000 correct images, equaling one wrong bit per 1.6 gigabyte.

It is impossible to determine a pattern in the occurrence of erroneous files. To detect possible problems a checksum file is generated for each subdirectory as a final step in the quality control phase. These checksum files are checked after the CD Rom is written. Only validated CD Rom's are shipped to the universities. As a precautionary measure the receiving universities also validate all incoming Datasets against the checksum files. They have indicated that this is of high relevance to safeguard the integrity of their electronic holdings.

Checksums were introduced in the beginning of 1994. The first checksums were based on the 'sum' routine, available as a UNIX command. However, this routine was dependent on the byte order of the central processing unit and on the UNIX 'dialect' (Berkeley BSD or AT&T System V), and therefore not universally useable. Since mid 1995, the checksums are based on the publicly available MD5 signature algorithm, developed by RSA Data Security, Inc., which is independent of byte order and CPU and is more robust.

II **1.4.6   Unique identifiers**

One of the things we have learned in **TULIP** is, that in a large scale database environment it is necessary to have a unique and unambiguous way of identifying journals, issues and articles.

a. *Journal identifiers*
   As a unique journal identifier, the International Standard Serials Number (ISSN) has been chosen. This however, posed problems with journal titles which are renamed, are split up, or are joined.
   Nevertheless, the ISSN proved standard 'enough' for the majority of journals, thereby avoiding the need for a 'new' standard.

b. *Issue identifiers*
   No short and simple unambiguous scheme existed for identifying journal issues. Normally a journal issue is identified by a volume and issue number (e.g. *Volume 193, Issue 4*). However, it appeared that there exist many troubling exceptions to this rule, such as combined issues (e.g. *Issues 1-4*), combined volumes (e.g. *Volumes 192-194*) and special issues (such as indexes, supplements and proceedings issues). To avoid any inconsistencies, a simple generic sequence number, unrelated to the printed volume and issue numbers, has been adopted for **TULIP**.

c. *Item identifiers*
   The standard adapted in this project is the Standard Serial Document Identifier (SSDI) (previously known as the ADONIS numbering scheme).
   The proposed NISO Z39.56 standard, also known as SICI (Serial Item and Contribution Identifier), has also been considered. While Z39.56 is an excellent format for retrospectively assigning a unique and unambiguous identifier to paper-based information, and it is very easy for a librarian to assign a Z39.56 code to an article in his collection (even if this article was published centuries ago), it has two major disadvantages in the electronic era:
   - It is restricted to paper-based material. Volume, issue and page numbers, relevant for paper forms, are being used, which could be irrelevant in electronic environments where a page paradigm is not applicable like for instance, a hierarchy of HTML-files published as part of a World Wide Web service.
   - It is restricted to material that is ready for publication. This means that it is not possible to denote an article with a Z39.56 code before it is certain what the volume, issue, page number and publication date exactly are. For instance, publishers often provide information in 'current awareness' or 'pipeline' services about articles in forthcoming publications, when all the above specifications are not yet finally available.

   The SSDI scheme chosen in **TULIP** could be regarded as a 'social security number' for documents. The SSDI is assigned at the moment that the article is accepted for publication; it is used as a reference number for the authors during production phases and it is printed on each page of the article in the issue. As it is relatively short (a fixed 16 digit number), the SSDI is very usable as a primary key in computer environments. Since this number is based on the ISSN, it is not restricted to Elsevier, but allows every publisher in the world the ability to assign SSDI's.

   In 1995, the (slightly adapted) SSDI was incorporated in the Publisher Item Identifier (PII) initiative, encouraged by a cooperation of major publishers and societies. This cooperation includes the American Chemical Society (ACS), the American Institute of Physics (AIP), the American Physical Society (APS), the Institute of Electrical and Electronics Engineers (IEEE) and Elsevier Science.

   The Z39.56 Standard Committee has apparently taken the concerns mentioned above into consideration and will incorporate publisher-assigned identifiers in a forthcoming release of Z39.56.

d. *Section identifiers*
   One point not attempted to be solved in **TULIP** is the need to divide articles into groups or sections within a journal issue. A few journal titles (especially the larger ones), have an editorial setup to divide journal issues into several subject areas or sections. Articles about a given topic within the scope of the journal are collected together and identified by means of special separation pages and/or with a categorization in the table of contents. Future projects could consider adopting a sectioning strategy.

II 1.4.7 Production backlogs

When the **TULIP** project started in 1992, it was based on rather new, uncommon technologies such as high-volume scanning, optical character recognition, CD-Rom mastering, Internet file transfer, etc. It took almost a year to develop and test the procedures. Therefore reliable, stable production was only possible beginning in January, 1993. Since the decision had been made to begin the **TULIP** journal data with the 1992 subscription year, it was necessary to produce two years of data in 1993, beginning with the 1992 backlog. The 1992 material was done retrospectively as much as possible (more recent journal issues were done first, going backward in time). Due to several teething problems, it took the full year 1993 to work away the 1992 backlog. In February 1994, the production systems became stable with a regular biweekly frequency.

In the beginning of 1995, a smaller backlog arose when SGML files were added to **TULIP** Datasets. It took until the end of the summer to catch up and return to the regular schedule.
The lesson here is to be extremely careful with introducing new pioneering technologies in smoothly operating environments. Procedures which perform nicely in a small-scale situation without deadlines are not easily transferable to large-scale, tightly scheduled operations. New technologies require extra administration, operator training, good feedback of teething errors to developers, motivation of staff, etc. All those aspects are easily overlooked in the laboratory stages in which only 'proof of principle' has to be defined.

II 1.4.8 Logistics in the scanning offices

During the **TULIP** project electronic material was lagging behind the paper journal issues, due to the decision to not intercept intermediate (possibly incomplete) articles, but instead to scan final journal issues after these were printed and bound. There were efforts during the **TULIP** project to accelerate the electronic delivery of material to correspond as much as possible with the printed journal. However, two to three weeks has been the practical minimum lag time.

II 1.5 Lessons learned about customizing and Internet distribution

II 1.5.1 Lessons learned on customizing

From a technical viewpoint, customizing a Dataset to only include those journals a university subscribes to is not difficult, a simple database table compares which journal titles which university is supposed to get. A few UNIX command scripts performed the task of constructing logical directory sub-trees and removing un-subscribed material from the DATASET.TOC master index file.

One difficulty is that there is no recognizable link between the cover date printed on the journal issues and the subscription year based on volume numbers. At the end of a year, subscription cancellations can pose problems when 'late' issues (part of last year's subscription) are published with cover dates of the following year. These should be sent to the universities, even though there is no current subscription. In **TULIP**, there were no cancellations during the project period. However, in the reverse situation where a university requested 'older' material to complete their holdings retrospectively, a few minor complications arose.

II 1.5.2 Lessons learned on Internet delivery

Lack of experience with delivering large Datasets with many pieces led to the original design of an FTP 'push' model which proved unreliable. Near the end of the project several of the technical collaborators discussed a design for an FTP 'pull' system that would still allow subscription control, but would be a better match for FTP's design strengths.

Different types of problems occurred with Internet delivery, ranging from operational problems at the sending or receiving side to more generic problems with the Internet and the FTP protocol (see appendix

XI for more detail). The large amount of FTP problems made the delivery process unmanageable. It was decided to temporarily discard FTP deliveries and to revert to CD Rom delivery of Datasets. Most universities have adapted to this change in procedures without problems, although they have expressed their long-term preference to use Internet as a delivery method.

Studies are currently under way to develop a 'full pull' strategy based on FTP mirroring technology with automatic E-mail functionality, FTP and Perl scripts. This would work as follows: As soon as a Dataset is available for dispatch, a structured E-mail message is sent to a dedicated E-mail address. An automated process at each university picks up these messages and starts a standard series of pull-and-validate scripts. All transfer errors would be recorded and checked by the **TULIP** operator at the university.

II 2.   Technical implementation at the universities

In this part, a brief overview will be given of the major similarities and differences between the **TULIP** implementations, as well as of the major experiences and lessons learned by the universities as described in their final reports. All detailed information on these implementations can be found in these final reports (appendices I-IX).

II 2.1   Organization of IT/Information services

The **TULIP** universities are medium to large, or very large organizations with relatively high-tech environments, with good campus networks and highly skilled personnel. The library and the computer center normally are separate organizational units. Some libraries have their own development staff who operate independently from the computer center. In one case (Michigan) staff from the College of Engineering collaborated on the project.

II 2.2   TULIP systems development

The approaches to **TULIP** are all different, no system is the same. Some of the components used to build the **TULIP** implementation can be the same, but the actual implementations differ greatly. BRS Search, Kerberos, Adabas, Notis and Newton are mentioned more than once as a component, but the way these components are used in the implementations differs remarkably. Also, development phases are quite incomparable. It is noteworthy that nearly every university has tried more than one different alternative/prototype, except the University of California and Virginia Tech, but even these are considering a Web implementation as an alternative to their current solutions.

Also, **TULIP**-like systems are very different from traditional library systems. At several universities, where there has been a change of personnel during the project period, this has meant a very steep learning curve for those getting involved in the project, due to the fact that the (development of the) **TULIP** system was completely uncharted territory.

II 2.2.1   Development process

Development was a lot harder and different than expected. It was not necessarily the technology that was the major problem, but more the scale and infrastructure of the project.
'Perhaps, the major general lesson that has come out of doing TULIP is that systems like TULIP are a lot harder to develop and deploy than might be apparent. And the reason for these difficulties has less to do with the technologies used to build such systems than with the infrastructures needed to support them.'

Some of the characteristics of the development process are:
● Most of the systems were assembled from different components resulting in rather proprietary solutions, not easily transferable to other organizations.

- Cheap or free-of-charge public domain, or shareware software components, were used wherever possible, and there also seemed to be a preference to make something bespoke themselves rather than purchasing off-the-shelf software.
- In most cases the **TULIP** development was done by one person or the combined effort of a small group.

II **2.2.2 Migration to production**

None of the **TULIP** systems became 'mature' in the sense that prototypes were handed over to production departments. All systems remained prototypes, with all typical evidence of prototype systems, such as lack of proper documentation, backup-restore procedures, management tools, etc.

At a few universities plans are being made to move towards more production-type operations.

II **2.3 TULIP functionality**

II **2.3.1 Searching vs browsing**

- Most of the universities, with the exception of the University of California, implemented a browsing facility, that is the possibility to choose a journal, then an issue, then an article from the table of contents.
- All of the universities developed a searching facility, mostly restricted to boolean logic and proximity searching.

II **2.3.2 Separate system vs based on/integrated with OPAC or A&I services**

Three basic types of implementations were built:
a. a separate database and user interface;
b. a separate database but using a common/known interface;
c. integration with an existing information service, i.e. access to the image files through comprehensive secondary databases.

Re a. A number of solutions were stand alone implementations, where **TULIP** was not only offered as a new database, but also had a 'new' (proprietary) interface, mostly based on X-windows. However, a number of Web implementations have also been developed, for which obviously the client (interface) is very well known, even though the **TULIP** files are in stand alone databases.
In all these cases, systems based on RS6000/AIX, Decstation/Ultrix and SunSparcstations/Solaris, were most popular.

Re b. All universities had an existing OPAC (library catalogue), most of which were IBM mainframe or UNIX based. In two cases, **TULIP** was implemented as an adaptation of the existing OPAC (GTEL at GT, MIRLYN at the University of Michigan). In the OPAC-based environments, the OPAC was used for searching and browsing bibliographic records only. The page images were stored separately from the OPAC on one of the UNIX systems mentioned above.

Re c. At the University of California, the initial access to the **TULIP** files was through the existing Inspec or current contents databases on the MELVYL system, after which page images could be displayed and printed through a proprietary X-windows based viewer.

II 2.4   Client systems

II 2.4.1   Clients

In **TULIP**, efforts have been made to build several client systems, usable in a multitude of client systems, such as MS-Windows PCs, Apple Macintoshes, a diversity of UNIX systems (IBM AIX, Dec Ultrix, Sun Solaris, Motif, SCO Unix, Linux, Indigo IRIX, etc.) and for several terminal oriented mainframe systems, notably VT100 and IBM3270-based. Upscaling and broadening would create huge maintenance problems because all client systems should be kept in line with upcoming new facilities and emerging new processors (e.g. PowerPC) and operating systems (e.g. OS/2, Windows95, Windows NT).

In the early days of the project many different approaches reflecting this variety, were tried, with more or less satisfactory results:
- Telnet
- X-Windows-based proprietary developments
- MS-Windows/Visual Basic-based developments
- MS-Windows/Proprietary developments such as OCLC's Guidon
- Gopher

It became clear however, that there are basically two ways to support an application on many different client platforms:
- One is to develop, test, install and upgrade a client system on these different platforms in synchronization with each other.
- The other is to develop an application which works on the lowest common denominator platform, i.e., a terminal emulation which could be done on all client platforms.

Both solutions were not satisfactory, as in the first case extraneous amounts of development time are required, and in the second case the functionality that can be offered is very low, whereas one wants to offer a system that is an improvement over existing systems, with high sophistication and functionality.

The advent of the World Wide Web provided a solution for this dilemma. One of the crucial advantages is the availability of ready-to-use, publicly available, user friendly, graphical Web browsers on all prevalent platforms. The Web environment allows developers to concentrate fully on the server part and not to bother any further with the client part.

The standard which has been set with HTML and HTTP and portable WWW-clients such as NCSA Mosaic and Netscape Navigator solves the maintenance problem, freeing time to concentrate on server developments. The current WWW tools are somewhat unstable and rather restricted in functionality, but it is expected that limitations will quickly decrease over time and new functions (such as Hot Java and embedded viewers), will be added. Another major advantage is that, since these clients are so generally available and are easy to use, the need for support and training is minimal. However, a disadvantage is that WWW clients are restricted in programmability if you want to add functions the client itself does not fulfill. For instance, there is no satisfactory solution as yet within the Web environment for printing high quality images. At the University of Michigan, a so-called helper application takes care of the printing. It is expected that future possibilities such as Java will alleviate current constraints.
Also, the possible future pricing and licensing strategy for these products is a major concern for academic institutions.

There was a general consensus among **TULIP** developers, that writing good, stable client software has proved to be a major, often underestimated task. And maintaining this software in different computer environments is not very rewarding.

So while the Web browsers have some limitations with regard to the required **TULIP** functionality, both the benefits for development and the popularity of the Web are so pervasive, that most developers feel that the Web is the only way to go at the moment.

II 2.4.2 Viewing

The majority of the universities have implemented page image viewing for their **TULIP** systems. A few observations of those who implemented this facility follow:

- The utilized Group IV compression algorithm is a straightforward method, but it demands high resources for scanning, viewing and printing. At the start of **TULIP**, common technology to deal sufficiently fast with page images was not readily available. For scanning and printing, special acceleration boards were used, and only high-end UNIX workstations were able to perform page viewing. In the past four years, computer and printer technology has evolved to the extent that no special purpose equipment is needed to achieve near-instantaneous image viewing and printing.

- The first page image viewing applications were based on X-Windows, which lacked image compression. In those cases where networks links between imaging application and user screens were slow, this resulted in relatively long response times because entire uncompressed page images were transmitted over the networks. This was true in particular for the University of California system. However, in other cases the response times were well under two seconds, which is what users have said they want.
  In practice, X-Windows was restricted to UNIX machines. PCs and Macs are considered as too slow or too cumbersome for X-Windows emulation. Also, X-Windows requires a rather difficult installation procedure compared to what is 'usual' for PC applications, for which any user can typically run a fool-proof Install or Setup program, without user-hostile parameter settings.

- In most page image viewing applications, a technique known as 'gray scaling' or 'anti-aliasing' is applied to enhance page images (see appendix XII for an elaboration on these techniques).

- Page viewing, also known as page flipping, needs to be very fast in order to avoid user annoyance. Typical flip times must be below two seconds. To speed this up, the faster implementations apply technologies such as pre-fetching (i.e. requesting - in the background - the most probable 'next' page in advance so that it is readily available when the user asks for it), and caching (i.e. keeping a few page images temporarily stored 'at hand' in case the user wants to see them again).

- Experience shows that, even with anti-aliasing technology, page images displayed on the computer screen are not really used for reading. As ascertained by the log files, the average duration a page image is shown is far below one minute. This allows for a brief scan of the page to discern the relevance of the article, but not for exhaustive reading. None of the implementations allows for online highlighting and/or annotations, which is 'less' than the functional equivalent of the paper.

- Most implementations did not allow viewing of pages outside the scope of 'full articles'. Page viewing starts as the result of either browsing or searching. After selection of an article, the first page of the article is displayed. Buttons enable navigation to the previous, next, first or last page (within the same article), or to another article. However, none of the implementations, except for the University of California's, allowed for easy browsing through an entire journal issue, including the pages with advertisements, announcements, obituaries, etc., which were not represented in the table of contents.

II 2.4.3 Printing

Printing of page images has proven to be a major concern for all universities. The large size of the 300 dpi page images in combination with the utilized compression scheme, is a highly demanding exercise for older laser printers and even the newer high capacity laser printers could show an exceptionally slow throughput compared to more regular print jobs if not properly set up. And even if properly set up, page images are large compared to other regular office print jobs and could easily drain network resources and congest print queues. Printing of images from other than directly IP-attached laser printers should be avoided. However, keeping track of local laser printers, attached to the network, is troublesome. In large organizations there is too much change (moving printers, modification of local sub-nets) to allow for proper and easy central print management.

Early in the project, printing of non-compressed page images could easily take between 15 and 30 minutes per page. The advent of affordable PostScript Level 2 printers, supporting compressed image printing, instigated the shared development by the **TULIP** participants of a **TULIP**-endorsed subroutine to print page images (available at *ftp.elsevier.nl/TULIP*) within 30 seconds on HP LaserJet 4MX laser printers or compatibles. This printing code was the product of a concerted collaborative effort. Distributed printing is a key infrastrucuture issue for all campuses. This collaboration underscores the shared nature of this problem.

To prevent network congestion, most universities have central printing facilities in which a high capacity laser printer is directly connected to the image server. However, these implementations did not seem very popular in the **TULIP** context. Users seemed to prefer a quickly available local print in lower quality over high-quality central prints which took time to arrive at their desk.

II 2.4.4   Exporting/faxing

Export of material other than for viewing or printing, for instance for supplying texts in wordprocessor formats, has not been implemented by any of the universities. In Web implementations limited cutting and pasting of text is possible, by using the source 'code'.

Georgia Tech has developed a fax service supplementing the print service, with which it is possible to provide page images directly to fax machines.

II 2.5   Server systems

II 2.5.1   Search engine

Each university uses a different system or approach for searching. Universities using OPAC-based **TULIP** systems use the native OPAC search engine. Non-OPAC based systems use a full text search system. Choices range from proprietary 'home-grown' systems (e.g. FTL), to public domain or experimental software (e.g. WAIS, Clarit), to commercially available systems (e.g. BRS, Newton, SiteSearch). All those systems provided basic search possibilities such as Boolean logic and word proximity. A few sites have tentatively investigated natural language systems, but were unable to implement this functionality within the life span of this project.

Most universities choose to implement fielded search on the bibliographic data provided in the DATASET.TOC file only. This information is divided into well-defined structured fields such as article title, authors, keywords, journal name, publication date, and abstract. Searching can be done on all of these fields, including on words in, for instance, title and abstract.

'Raw' ASCII files were available for additional searching. The quality of these OCR-ed files has improved considerably in the course of the project. Two of the universities (University of Michigan and Virginia Tech), have implemented full text searching on the basis of the raw ASCII files. The main reasons for not implementing searching of the full text ASCII for the other sites were:
- the relatively low quality of these ASCII files;
- keyword-Boolean retrieval does not perform very well on these files, Carnegie Mellon University plans to start using the full text when Claritech natural language retrieval is being put into production, which performs better on the raw ASCII files;
- the added complexity/system load of loading these large files into their full text database systems.

The implementation at the University of California was different from the others:
All universities except the University of California implemented **TULIP** as a closed collection, that is the **TULIP** system only gave access to the limited set of journals in the **TULIP** project. For other information (e.g. other journals from other publishers), users had to rely on their traditional ways of accessing those collections. The University of California used a different approach for **TULIP** to overcome the lack of comprehensiveness. A procedure of semi-automatic matching between their Inspec and Current Contents (CC) databases and **TULIP** was developed, in which every incoming **TULIP** Dataset was checked against Inspec

and CC, and matching records were marked. When searching in Inspec or CC, users find **TULIP** records with an indication that the full article is available. Subsequently, issuing the 'display' command starts the page image viewer. The users' regular searching/browsing in Inspec or CC leads them to the **TULIP** pointer, and they can access the page images directly.

Another feature worth mentioning here is the 'profiling' feature implemented at the University of Michigan, which means the ability to store queries that are automatically run against new **TULIP** Datasets when they arrive. For this facility, end users specified a profile with a predefined set of keywords based on their interests. Each incoming Dataset was scanned using this profile and users were notified about articles of potential interest to them by means of electronic mail messages containing the abstracts of matching articles.

II 2.5.2   Data loading

As described earlier, the File Transfer Protocol (FTP) as a mechanism for large-scale bulk delivery was an aggravating experience. Even if a better and stable mechanism were developed (e.g. 'pull' as opposed to the employed 'push' method), FTP is considered not to be scalable to larger collections and to more customers with the current technologies and network bandwidth. However, **TULIP** participants think that in a more remote future, these restrictions will disappear and that will make network delivery the preferred method again. Therefore development should continue.

One reason most universities prefer network delivery over CD Rom deliveries is that completely automated delivery is possible, as opposed to CD Rom, where manual loading procedures remain necessary.

Because all **TULIP** systems are different, loading new data is also different for all universities. New Datasets mostly are verified, separated into several image and full text databases, the text is indexed and images prepared. Sometimes loading errors are encountered which necessitate human intervention. Especially in the beginning of the project, this process needed constant oversight.

II 2.5.3   Storage

In the first years of **TULIP**, magnetic media prices were very high. Most universities have investigated optical storage technologies, in view of the lower price. However, a number of disadvantages became evident:
- Optical media are slow compared to magnetic ones, especially when applied with jukeboxes. This is an important disadvantage in an operation geared for quick response such as near-instantaneous page viewing. Magnetic disk caches relieve this somewhat but result in variable delays, which could annoy users (less frequently requested or older material takes longer to fetch, but the user doesn't know why some material takes longer to display than other material).
- The optical media used are basically read-only. This was counter-productive in an experimental environment in which sometimes rearrangements or modifications of files were needed.
- Optical media are relatively new and unknown in combination with server systems, resulting in a considerable amount of incompatibility problems.

In the past four years magnetic disks have decreased dramatically (a factor of 1.5 to 2 per year). Especially the new RAID (Redundant Array of Inexpensive Disks) technology is favored as a good option for applications with massive storage requirements, combining a good price/performance ratio with reliability and compatibility with any server system.

The very large volume of **TULIP** data also presented some problems with backing up, which apparently have not been solved at all universities. A few times requests were made to Elsevier to borrow its spare CD's to reload data lost due to disk crashes or other calamities. New ways will have to be found to routinely back up the page images and other data files. Delivery on CD Rom obviously alleviates this problem somewhat, as these contain all the data, but not the indexes etc. generated by the university's application.

New data formats such as SGML, HTML and Acrobat PDF do not appear to reduce the need for large storage space. There are strong indications that data in these formats is equally large in file size, but has better information search, retrieval and presentation possibilities.

II 2.5.4   Security and authentication

The **TULIP** license allowed for unlimited on-site electronic distribution and use of the data, but restricted off-site delivery. Also, use should be registered and reports on use generated.

User name/password schemes restricting usage to legitimate users were the obvious way to do this. For some institutions unaccustomed to authorized usage this proved problematic. Management of user names and passwords in large, non-constant environments such as a university with many students, departments, locations, etc., and with continuous changes, is troublesome at best.

There was initial concern regarding logfile delivery to Elsevier because of privacy breach. This was overcome by implementing anonymous code schemes, which make it impossible to track certain use to a particular user.

The advent of the World Wide Web complicated this even further because of its inherent limitations. Restrictions can be set on machines and IP addresses, but not easily on authorized persons without user-hostile password procedures. Nevertheless, Web server logging facilities provided possibilities to generate usage information, if care was taken to include this in the design of the particular Web system. New generic WWW authentication, security and encryption technologies to master this problem, are emerging.

II 2.6   Network delivery to end users

TULIP page images, which are much more voluminous than plain bibliographic records, take longer to transmit from a central storage and retrieval system to the end user's desktop. A large scale implementation involving massive transfer of page images in a typical network infrastructure can easily drain available resources.

Users expect that a system which allows them to view page images on their screens and to print them locally, has fast response times. Especially image viewing should be almost instantaneous to prevent user rejection, which puts a considerable strain on available network bandwidth and on the capacity to retrieve from the storage media described above.

It became clear during the **TULIP** project, that for 'usable' page image viewing and printing, a local area network should minimally support 'normal' Ethernet speeds of 10 megabit/second. Modem or ISDN based SLIP or PPP connections are too slow to provide fast response times.

In the early days of the **TULIP** project, printing contributed significantly to network congestion, as the image files had to be sent uncompressed to local printers (see also paragraph II 2.4.3. on printing). This improved with the arrival of PostScript Level 2 printers supporting the Fax Group IV compression scheme.

Contrary to other **TULIP** universities, the campuses of the University of California are spread across the entire state, interconnected with (fractional) T1 lines of 1.5 Megabit per second. The computer center at the office of the president in Oakland held the **TULIP** data, there was no local storage at campus. The network capacity proved to be detrimental to system response, leaving users waiting a long time for images to appear on their screens. This experience provided support for an initiative to increase the bandwidth of the University of California's network, since it is expected that more image and multimedia projects will be launched in the foreseeable future, which will require bandwidth similar to the **TULIP** project.

II 3.   Conclusions and recommendations

Some of the main problem areas identified are:
a. maintaining suites of client software;
b. FTP and the Internet as a means of large scale delivery;
c. storage;
d. (infrastructure for) viewing and printing.

Re a. Most universities decided to 'shift to the Web' on a shorter or longer term, thereby abandoning X-Windows and MS Windows applications. This has the advantage for developers of easier cross plat-form portability, because developing, maintaining and upgrading several software clients in a distrib-uted environment (Mac, PC, UNIX) is a cumbersome task. In the Web environment, development work is concentrated on the server side. Furthermore, support and training efforts decrease, and user documentation needs minimal emphasis. However, Web applications have fewer possibilities to pro-vide 'real-time' functionality such as image zooming.
Basically, the Web can not be ignored. The advantages plus the sheer user-pull outweigh any disad-vantages.

Re b. Large-scale Internet FTP transfer is not scalable with the current transmission schemes and restrict-ed bandwidth. Suggestions for a robust 'full pull' strategy have been discussed, but no conclusion has been reached.

Re c. Scalability of **TULIP**-like systems will also be problematic. Current massive storage technology and network bandwidth capacities practically limit electronic collections to a small percentage of the total library collections. It is expected that a 'staged' approach to electronic collection-building will emerge, which is composed of local servers for primary relevant material, and remote (for instance regional) servers for material of secondary importance to the particular institution.

Re d. Image viewing on the screen requires a high-speed infrastructure, as (perceived) speed to the user's desktop is crucial. The components of the system influencing this are:
● server/storage speed (optical storage on jukeboxes will be slower than magnetic storage);
● network speed ('real' LAN is a minimum);
● client machine speed;
● application software image caching 'smarts'.

Printing page images is an important concern. With the advent of printers that understand com-pressed Group IV fax images, and careful attention to setup, this aspect becomes viable. The older laser printers are not equipped to deal with the large size of the 300 dpi page images in combination with the utilized compression scheme. Printing of images from other than directly IP-attached laser printer should be avoided.
When sent as compressed Group IV fax, the images are actually smaller than the PostScript files that you would normally see as output from a word processor. Even so, network congestion can be an issue and in some cases a central printing facility was used in which a high capacity laser printer is directly connected to the image server.

Other:
● Bi-tonal (black/white) scanned page images are good for text and line art, but the quality is unsatisfac-tory for gray scale images and color artwork.

● A well documented data structure is important for large scale delivery of electronic files. This structure must be medium independent in order to allow for different transfer methods and/or media.

● Data shipments as large as in the **TULIP** project need to be checked for corruption by some checksum facility. Ultimately a platform-independent, portable and robust checksum facility was adapted for **TULIP**, the 'MD5' algorithm of RSA Data Security, Inc.

III Promotion

III 1. Overview of promotional activities undertaken

III 1.1 By Elsevier Science

The launch of **TULIP** and the related promotional activities were the primary responsibility of the universities. To support the universities a toolkit was developed, consisting of:
- posters;
- banners;
- **TULIP** lapel pins;
- newsletters;
- **TULIP** home page on the Elsevier WWW;
- server with links to the journal entries in the Elsevier Internet Catalogue;
- sample copies of **TULIP** journals.

All of these were offered to the universities during the course of the project, with the largest interest being in the posters, which were customized per university to give relevant information on the specifics of that university's implementation. In addition, some initiatives were taken to develop promotional material together with individual universities, with varied success.

III 1.2 By the TULIP universities

In addition to the promotional material made available by Elsevier Science, the universities utilized a wide range of promotional items and activities, such as:
- Web promotion: e.g. pointing to new services on home pages;
- announcements on electronic bulletin boards;
- E-mail messages;
- letters sent out to faculty with printouts of one of their articles from **TULIP** database;
- other targeted direct mail;
- announcements on departmental (physical) bulletin boards;
- attract attention in the library (e.g. balloons), if a new database like **TULIP** is installed;
- articles in campus newspapers, faculty newsletters, etc.;
- (display of) handouts with information and instructions;
- organizing introduction meetings;
- training sessions for groups as part of regular library services trainings or separate ('introduction of');
- one-on-one training of key potential users;
- trainings for faculty who in turn will train classes.

Most universities felt that training should be minimal, either because the users were already accustomed to the interface (library systems interface or Web interface), or because they felt a system such as this should be fairly self-explanatory. Minimal attendance at training sessions and the results from the focus groups seem to corroborate this view.

For more detailed descriptions of the universities' actions, please see the university reports (appendices I-IX).

III 2. Conclusions and recommendations

Although there clearly are a whole suite of conditions for a service such as **TULIP** to become a regularly used tool, such as technical, user expectations, contents, etc., promotion does have an important and continued role in the degree of success that can be achieved. Recognizing that meeting user needs is primary, promotion and training are crucial for a service such as **TULIP** to develop a base of regular users. Most of the **TULIP** universities do not actively promote the paper product since it is deeply ingrained in people's research method and people know where and how to find journals. However, there is a definite difference between the need for promotion of paper and electronic products.

Some quotes from university reports:

'It is clear, though, that any new service that challenges a user's pattern of work requires a steady diet of promotion and training. Because faculty members (perhaps our most significant, and certainly our most stable, user group) have typically found a pattern of journal use that satisfies them, changes to this pattern have to be sold to them before they will use a new service such as TULIP. Promotion clearly fulfills this role. Training is also essential, but in a different way. If an information product requires a steep learning curve, users who have either already found a simple method for getting similar information or have invested time in learning an alternative way of getting similar information, will hesitate to switch. The new system will be most readily accepted if it requires minimal training. So, it is essential to promote a new delivery mechanism as not only as good as the one it replaces (or, in the short term, supplements) but better. In terms of training, users will require, and often request a brief introduction. After this, though, the delivery mechanism will have to prove itself as not merely as easy to use as their previous methods, but easier.'

and:

'TULIP clearly demonstrated that student and faculty use of electronic journals for actual study and research requires a behavioral change. There is some evidence that this is beginning to happen, but it will not happen until such time as electronic texts are delivered in a way that fits the use that the individual has for the information. Promotion should be continued, but will only be useful if the product is one that meets users' needs and the quality is such that they will continue to use the product. Training should be incorporated into the regular ongoing library instruction teaching that is already occurring.'

Although many people like electronic information services, these electronic services need more promotion. There are many new products and services; people do get confused. They must be shown that there are new means available that might answer their research questions. It is important for any new service to get a position in the 'research toolkit' a scientist is using to stay up to date and to find information to solve his specific problem-oriented information needs. The key question is how to create awareness, get users to try the system and then generate repeat usage. To achieve this, (repeated) promotion is important, to keep the service 'fresh in the mind' of the end user.

Even in cases where repeated promotional activities took place, several universities reported that a segment of the user population could apparently not be reached:

'Despite all of this promotion, however, one of the most frequent comments by users on the paper survey forms was that they were unaware of the availability of the online versions. This is perhaps indicative of the endemic communication difficulties within the academy'.

Furthermore, as was also the case with, for instance, the technical implementation, the amount of effort needed for the promotion and training has been systematically underestimated in many places:

'Promotion and training is a time consuming effort, but is a very important component in the attempt to modify users' behavior in regard to journal use. However, the amount of promotion and training that can realistically be done needs to be balanced with the degree of stability and long term availability of the program being promoted'.

and:

'As with so many other aspects of the TULIP project, our promotion and training effort seemed to require of us much more work than the final results appeared to justify. Despite frequent references to TULIP, we were unable to shift much use from the paper to the electronic versions, and we did not bring in nearly as many users (especially faculty) to our training sessions as we had hoped'.

IV User behavior

IV 1. Goal of the research

The continued objective of the research was to obtain specific feedback about **TULIP** from end-users to guide future developments of delivering journal information to the desktop, to get insights on the requirements for electronic services to be attractive and valuable, both from the content provider and infrastructure provider's side. Several areas of user behavior and perceptions were investigated:

1. Generic and basic understanding of information behavior of scientists and librarians.
2. What gets (and keeps) users interested in electronic products in general? What are the 'pull' and what are the 'push' factors?
   - pull: what is perceived added value? Why do they want desktop access?
   - push: what is unattractive in the current situation and can be improved on in a 'full text' electronic environment?
3. Which requirements should electronic products meet to be attractive and valuable?
4. How should we bring electronic (full text) information to the desktop?
5. How should we promote?

These general research areas were translated to a number of specific topics:
- Current information needs, including various professional roles which require respondents to seek information, primary information needs and sources used.
- Background information including problems encountered in the daily search for information or data, changes in respondents' method of reading or searching for information over the past year, expected changes in the future and typical pattern used to review journals.
- Specific questions about electronic information sources, including the amount of time spent in front of a computer each day and how that time is allocated, the amount of time spent using WWW browsers and usage of specific databases, perceived benefits and drawbacks of electronic information, desired improvement with regard to desktop access, perceived role of the library as electronic information services become more widespread, and payment for use of electronic information sources.
- Usage and adoption of the **TULIP** files, penetration of the potential user group.
- Evaluation of **TULIP** including sources of awareness and information about the program, initial expectations and whether or not these expectations were met, frequency of use, reasons for use, effect of **TULIP** on readership of paper journals, missing items, evaluation of specific features of the program (i.e. journal coverage, search features, printing facilities etc.) and suggestions for improvement.
- Reasons for not using **TULIP** among respondents who have either used it in the past and stopped using it or do so only occasionally or who have never tried it.

The actual research done as part of the **TULIP** project can be divided in two categories, quantitative and qualitative.

IV 2. Quantitative Research

IV 2.1 Research methods used

The major part of the quantitative research is based on the analysis of computer generated files in which the actions of end users are recorded (logfiles). The main elements of these logfiles are:
- type (faculty, student), department and location of user;
- actions like reading the abstract, viewing full text, printing etc.;
- journal article, page(s);
- date and time of (beginning and end of) usage, per action.

The logfile analysis is based on the *actions* users carry out, the most important ones being browsing of abstracts, browsing of page images (per page) and printing (one action per abstract or article printed). The relation between these three major types of actions differs from **TULIP** site to site because of the differences in infrastructure. As an example: at the University of California, access to the **TULIP** page images is through a search action in the secondary databases Inspec and Current Contents on the central MELVYL library system; the actions in MELVYL, including viewing the abstract in Inspec, are not captured in the **TULIP** logfile for this university. On the other hand, at the University of Michigan, the **TULIP** implementation itself incorporates all searches, therefore each abstract or page viewed as well as each abstract or article printed is registered as an action.

Repeat users and penetration:
The primary question to be answered was how the acceptance of **TULIP** at the various sites has developed, which was translated as:
How many users in the primary user groups (faculty and graduate students) use **TULIP** repeatedly?

Information from the focus groups and interviews shows that graduate students and faculty visit the library on average every two to three months. Analysis of the logfiles showed a similar frequency emerging, therefore we have defined a repeat user as follows:
A *repeat user* is a user (faculty or graduate) who used **TULIP** in at least two (not necessarily consecutive) months within a six months period.
The *degree of penetration*, which tells us the relative importance of the number of repeat users, is defined as follows: the number of repeat users (faculty or graduate students), divided by the potential user group of **TULIP** at a site.

So the degree of penetration is dependent both on the actual number of repeat users and on the size of the potential user group. As the number of repeat users grows or declines, the penetration curve indicates the acceptance of **TULIP** by the potential user group.

As Materials Science is a rather interdisciplinary subject area, the potential user group not only consists of 'core user groups' in the Materials Science departments. Faculty and graduate students from, for instance, the general physics and chemistry departments, can also be part of the potential user group. For calculation of the size of the potential user groups we relied on information provided by the **TULIP** contact persons at the various sites.

This analysis was carried out for all sites which provided usable logfiles and allowed for comparing the degree of acceptance of **TULIP**. This comparison led to further questions about the reasons behind a certain degree of penetration. These questions were then asked during the focus group sessions and interviews in order to generate insights into why the acceptance of **TULIP** differed strongly from site to site.

Further questions that were answered by logfile analysis are:
● What is the share of usage of the various user groups (faculty, graduate students, staff, undergraduates, others)?
● What is the relation between different types of usage, mainly browsing abstracts/page images and printing?

Eventually, four types of analysis were carried out for all sites:
● an overview of the *usage by type* (browsing abstracts or page images/printing/other) per site per month for all users (graph & table 1); for the University of California this analysis was done separately for the large, medium and small sites;.
● an overview of *usage by all user types* per month (faculty, graduate students, undergraduates, library staff, staff, others, and unknown) (graph & table 2);
● the same analysis, but only of the *usage of the core user groups*: faculty and graduate students (graph & table 3);
● a month by month report on the development of the *number of users and repeat users* for the faculty & graduate students (graph & table 4).

Analysis of the following logfiles has been carried out:
● Carnegie Mellon University (September 1994 to October 1995);
● Cornell University (October 1994 to October 1995);
● Georgia Tech (September 1994 to October 1995);
● MIT (July 1994 to October 1995);

- University of California (January 1994 to October 1995) for all nine campuses;
- University of Michigan (January 1994 to October 1995);
- Integrated logfile-analysis of the three environments (MASC, TULIPView and WWW);
- University of Tennessee.

At the moment the logfile analysis started, the October 1995 logfiles were the latest available for all universities, therefore no later logfiles were included in the analysis.

We have to repeat here that there are several different types of TULIP implementations, which has consequences for the interpretation of the graphs:

- The implementations at the University of Michigan (TULIPView and WWW) are stand alone TULIP implications in which the use of the abstracts is registered, as well as the use of the page images for viewing or printing.
- In the implementations at the University of California and MIT, only the viewing and printing of the page images is registered as an action. The actions of the users on the abstracts are not logged.
- At Georgia Tech, only usage of the abstracts and printing are logged, as there is no viewing of page images available in this service.
- For Carnegie Mellon's system we can not differentiate between any kind of actions.

Additional quantitative research by two universities consists of 'reshelving studies', a method to calculate the usage of the paper-versions of the journals in the library by counting the number of times (unbound) journal issues are used. The question behind these studies is whether the TULIP project increased or decreased the usage of the paper versions of the journals in the project in the library. Studies of this kind were carried out by the library staff at the University of Michigan and Tennessee, results are discussed below in IV 2.2.3.

IV 2.2 Results of the logfile-analysis per TULIP-site

IV 2.2.1 Carnegie Mellon University

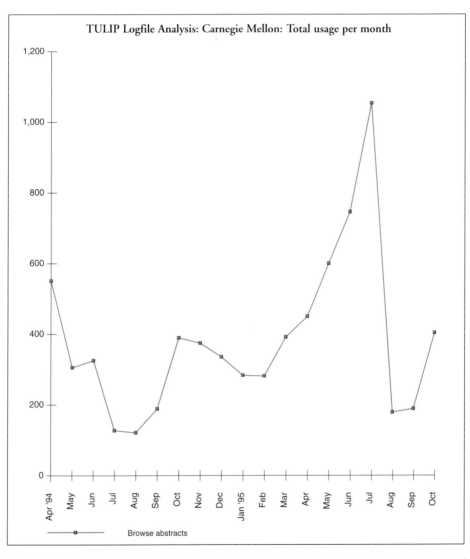

TULIP Logfile Analysis: Carnegie Mellon: Total usage per month

Browse abstracts

Usage Type	Apr '94	May	Jun	Jul	Aug	Sep	Oct	Nov	Dec	Jan '95	Feb	Mar	Apr	May	Jun	Jul	Aug	Sep	Oct
Browse	551	306	326	128	122	189	390	375	336	284	282	392	450	600	746	1054	179	189	404
		Graph & Table 1																	

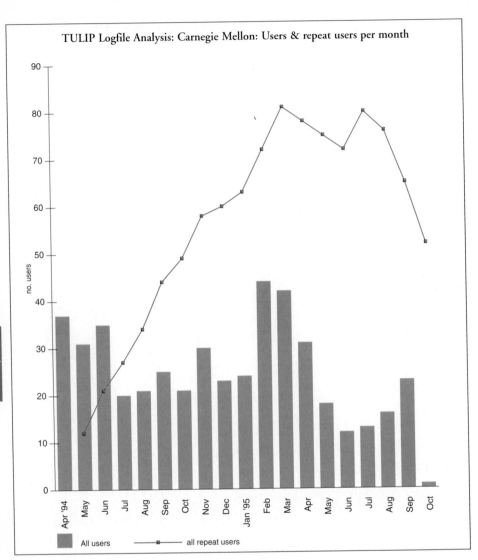

TULIP Logfile Analysis: Carnegie Mellon: Users & repeat users per month

Legend: █ All users ■ all repeat users

Type	Apr '94	May	Jun	Jul	Aug	Sep	Oct	Nov	Dec	Jan '95	Feb	Mar	Apr	May	Jun	Jul	Aug	Sep	Oct
all	37	31	35	20	21	25	21	30	23	24	44	42	31	18	12	13	16	23	1
repeatedly used by:																			
all		12	21	27	34	44	49	58	60	63	72	81	78	75	72	80	76	65	52
Penetration								9%	9%	10%	11%	12%	12%	11%	11%	12%	12%	10%	8%
Potential User Group:														fc	90				
														gr	165				
														Others	400				
														total	665				
Note: included are all users groups (CMU has no type of user identification)																			
	Graph & Table 4																		

a. Usage

Usage only exceeded 1,000 actions per month in July 1995 (which peak was mainly caused by usage of a few library staff for testing reasons), which in comparison to other sites is rather low. Important factors were:

- only 1992 data was available up until early 1995;
- **TULIP** was not actively introduced until Spring 1995;
- when there was access to the images, it was with an interface previously rejected in user tests.

b. Printing

No data available, as printing was impossible throughout the project.

c. Users and repeat users

Despite the rather low usage figures more than 100 users used the system at least once, of which a high percentage returned. The number of repeat users peaked in March/April and July/August 1995. The log-files did not differentiate usage between the various user types. The potential user group is about 650, there are between 80 and 50 repeat users, which means a penetration of between 12% in the middle of 1995 and 8% in October 1995. However, it is not clear how usage by development and library staff distorts this picture.

IV **2.2.2 Cornell University**

a. Usage

There is no data available on the usage of the X-Windows based system which has been available to end users with limited files for about a year and a half at Cornell. This system was based on a book paradigm, developed for a book preservation project. Usage of this implementation was very low. The connection to the Web implementation at the University of Michigan is 'live' since March 1995. Usage, however, does not exceed a few hundred hits, of which 80% are from one user.

b. Printing

No printing is registered.

c. Users and repeat users

In total one graduate student and 23 'unknown' users have used the system. Only two users can be classified as repeat users. A concluding remark is, therefore, that **TULIP** has no substantial user base at Cornell.

2.2.3 Georgia Institute of Technology

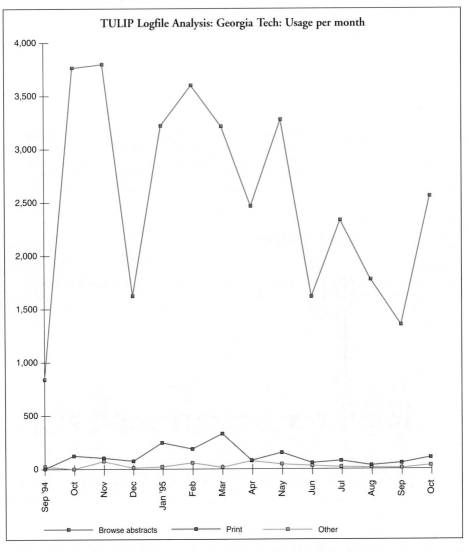

TULIP Logfile Analysis: Georgia Tech: Usage per month

Usage Type	Sep '94	Oct	Nov	Dec	Jan '95	Feb	Mar	Apr	May	Jun	Jul	Aug	Sep	Oct
Browse abstracts	840	3,765	3,799	1,623	3,222	3,599	3,215	2,466	3,278	1,616	2,333	1,776	1,353	2,560
Print	3	124	104	75	246	188	330	80	153	56	77	34	57	108
Other	24	1	74	12	22	59	17	77	46	31	19	15	11	36
Graph & Table 1														

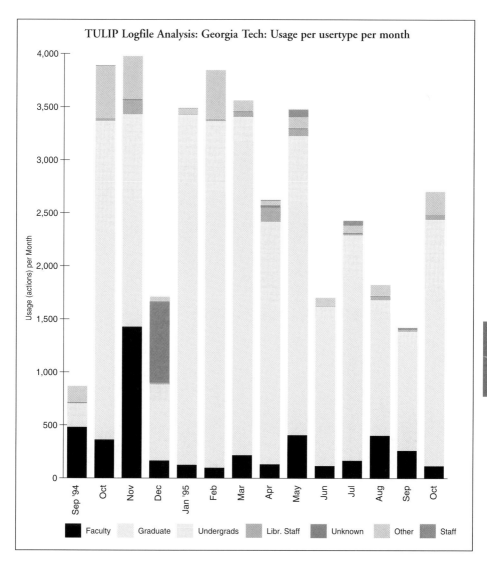

TULIP Logfile Analysis: Georgia Tech: Usage per usertype per month

User Type	Total	Sep '94	Oct	Nov	Dec	Jan '95	Feb	Mar	Apr	May	Jun	Jul	Aug	Sep	Oct
Unknown	847	7		13	767		3	8	22	8		10	7	1	
Faculty	4,872	482	364	1,427	166	126	99	219	132	408	117	167	404	263	117
Graduate	25,224	103	1,961	1,198	559	2,660	2,593	2,959	1,471	2,168	1,381	1,711	1,154	982	1,671
Libr. Staff	644	8	26	134	20	6	15	49	137	69	5	16	35	14	48
Other	2,543	150	494	403	42	58	464	101	39	103	84	66	103	1	217
Staff	183	1	6			4			9	73		46		22	
Undergrads	7,335	116	1.039	802	156	636	672	226	813	648	116	413	122	137	650
		Graph & Table 2													

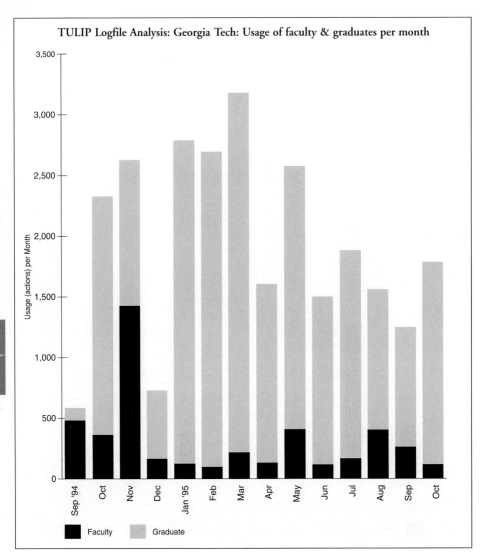

TULIP Logfile Analysis: Georgia Tech: Usage of faculty & graduates per month

User Type	Total	Sep '94	Oct	Nov	Dec	Jan '95	Feb	Mar	Apr	May	Jun	Jul	Aug	Sep	Oct
Faculty	4872	482	364	1427	166	126	99	219	132	408	117	167	404	263	117
Graduate	25224	103	1961	1198	559	2660	2593	2959	1471	2168	1381	1711	1154	982	1671
	Graph & Table 3														

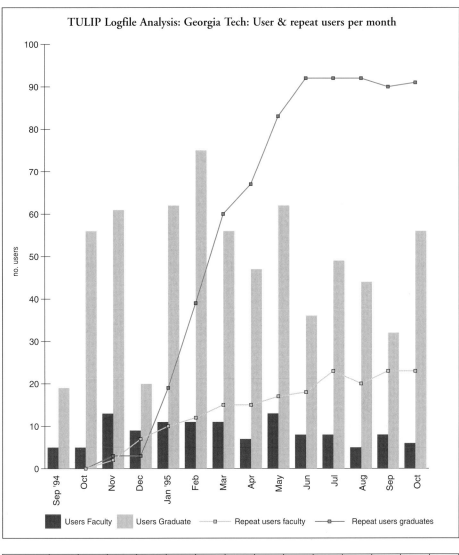

TULIP Logfile Analysis: Georgia Tech: User & repeat users per month

Usage Type	Sep '94	Oct	Nov	Dec	Jan '95	Feb	Mar	Apr	May	Jun	Jul	Aug	Sep	Oct
fc	5	5	13	9	11	11	11	7	13	8	8	5	8	6
gr	19	56	61	20	62	75	56	47	62	36	49	44	32	56
repeated used by:														
fc		0	2	7	10	12	15	15	17	18	23	20	23	23
gr		0	3	3	19	39	60	67	83	92	92	92	90	91
Penetration			2%	5%	13%	23%	34%	37%	45%	50%	52%	51%	51%	52%
Potential User Group:									fc		50			
									gr		170			
									total		220			
Graph & Table 4														

a. Usage

At this site, users can either search the **TULIP** citations and abstracts file connected to the library's OPAC, or select journal titles and browse their table of contents. Desktop viewing of articles is not possible.

Both usage-peaks and lows are more frequent here than at other **TULIP** sites. Remarkable is also that these fluctuations remained within certain boundaries, with peaks of around 4,000 actions per month, and lows of about 1,500 user actions per month. This pattern seemed to continue in the remaining months of 1995.

b. Printing

At Georgia Tech, printing was done on a central campus facility, then the printed articles were delivered to the requester using an existing campus-courier service, a nice combination of new and old technology. Compared with other sites, printing remained at a rather low level of about 100 prints per month.

c. Users and repeat users

In total, some 440 people used the system at least once. The number of users per month is now stable around 50 to 55 graduate students per month, and five to eight faculty. These numbers were already reached a few months after the launch of **TULIP** at Georgia Tech. A plausible explanation is, that Georgia Tech already had an on-line library service in place which gave access to bibliographic data. **TULIP** added the availability of abstracts and direct ordering of the articles, although before that, the service to deliver articles identified otherwise was already in place. **TULIP** was, therefore, a logical extension of this service, with better access to the bibliographic data, including abstracts, and faster delivery of the actual articles. Adapting this new service did not require much training or explanation, while offering direct benefits.

Repeat users developed rapidly among graduate students, reaching a peak in May 1995 and stabilizing since then. With 220 estimated potential users among the faculty and graduate students, Georgia Tech reached a penetration of over 50%.

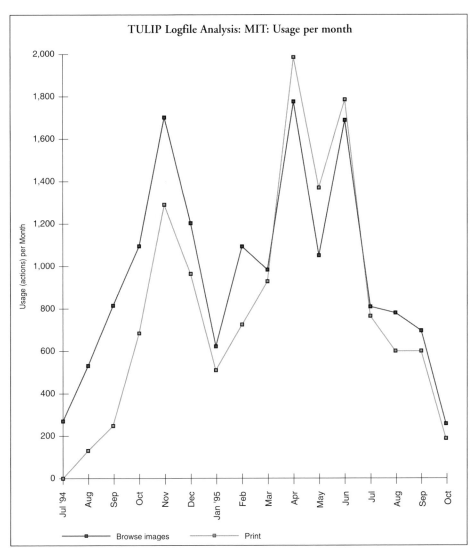

TULIP Logfile Analysis: MIT: Usage per month

Usage Type	Jul '94	Aug	Sep	Oct	Nov	Dec	Jan '95	Feb	Mar	Apr	May	Jun	Jul	Aug	Sep	Oct
Browse images	270	531	815	1095	1702	1203	622	1093	983	1776	1051	1689	809	780	696	257
Print	0	131	248	684	1290	964	510	725	928	1985	1370	1785	765	600	600	188
	Graph & Table 1															

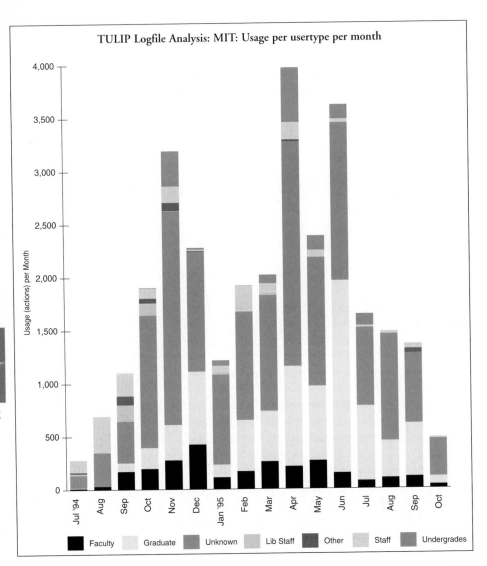

TULIP Logfile Analysis: MIT: Usage per usertype per month

User Type	Jul '94	Aug	Sep	Oct	Nov	Dec	Jan '95	Feb	Mar	Apr	May	Jun	Jul	Aug	Sep	Oct
Unknown	118	318	393	1,250	2,015	1,131	850	1,022	1,094	2,120	1,212	1,488	739	1,007	660	357
Faculty	12	32	171	197	277	424	112	168	260	212	267	149	74	101	112	36
Graduate	6	0	81	197	332	686	120	482	473	943	701	1812	704	348	501	75
Lib Staff	14	9	153	114	3	0	31	13	27	0	0	10	6	0	0	0
Other	14	0	86	45	78	8	0	0	0	17	0	0	0	0	43	0
Staff	117	335	218	95	157	14	52	231	84	164	70	27	13	25	46	13
Undergrades	1	0	0	6	332	17	52	4	82	517	137	137	112	0	0	0
Graph & Table 2																

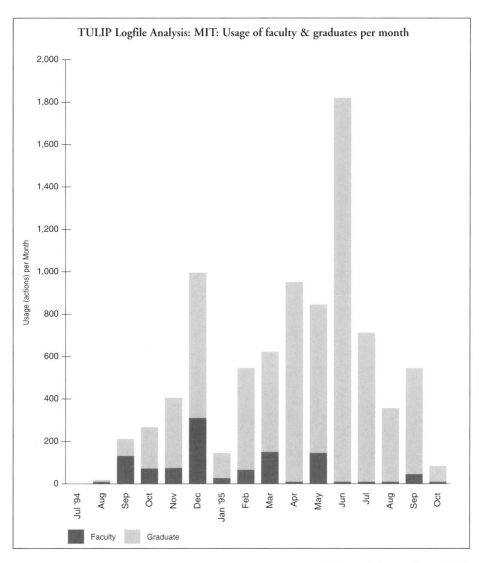

TULIP Logfile Analysis: MIT: Usage of faculty & graduates per month

Usage (actions) per Month

■ Faculty   ▨ Graduate

User Type	Jul '94	Aug	Sep	Oct	Nov	Dec	Jan '95	Feb	Mar	Apr	May	Jun	Jul	Aug	Sep	Oct
Faculty		10	132	72	75	311	27	66	151	10	146	10	10	10	46	10
Graduate	6	10	81	197	332	686	120	482	473	943	701	1812	704	348	501	75
Graph & Table 3																

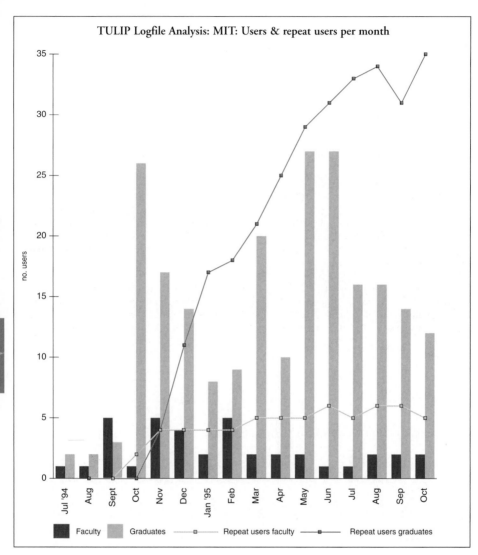

TULIP Logfile Analysis: MIT: Users & repeat users per month

Type	Jul '94	Aug	Sep	Oct	Nov	Dec	Jan '95	Feb	Mar	Apr	May	Jun	Jul	Aug	Sep	Oct
fc	1	1	5	1	5	4	2	5	2	2	2	1	1	2	2	2
gr	2	2	3	26	17	14	8	9	20	10	27	27	16	16	14	12
repeated used by:																
fc		0	0	2	4	4	4	4	5	5	5	6	5	6	6	5
gr		0	0	0	4	11	17	18	21	25	29	31	33	34	31	35
Degree of Penetration:			0%	2%	3%	5%	5%	6%	7%	8%	8%	8%	9%	8%	9%
Potential Number of Users									fc		150					
									gr		300					
									total		450					
	Graph & Table 4															

a. Usage
Usage at MIT, which was rather low in the beginning, increased gradually to a peak in April 1995, with a sharp spike in June (probably due to the fact that graduate students were being asked to participate in focus groups), and then flattened out on a lower level.

b. Printing
Unlike, for instance, the University of Michigan, where both browsing in the citation file and viewing/printing the page images are logged, MIT logfiles only registered actions on the image files. Selecting articles for printing, which was carried out in either a Willow or a Web table of contents browser, were not registered as actions in the logfiles. Therefore, the number of printing actions are close to the browsing actions, as all other actions concerning the citation file remain outside the logfiles.

c. Users and repeat users
At MIT, some 314 people viewed and/or printed **TULIP** images at least once.
Users at MIT had the option to log in either with their user type code (faculty, graduate student, etc.) or as 'unknown'; this makes it rather difficult to identify the various user groups and thus to calculate their size and growth. To obtain a good estimate of the real number of faculty and graduate students using **TULIP**, a proportional share of the unknown category is assumed to be faculty and graduate students, and is added on a monthly basis.

The number of users per month at MIT developed from an initial two to a peak of 27 graduate students; by October 1995, this had gone down to 12. Faculty remained stable around two users. Penetration, with a potential user group of Materials Researchers of 450, developed from 2% in November 1994, to 8-9% in September/October 1995. **TULIP** was also used by faculty and graduate students from nine other departments.

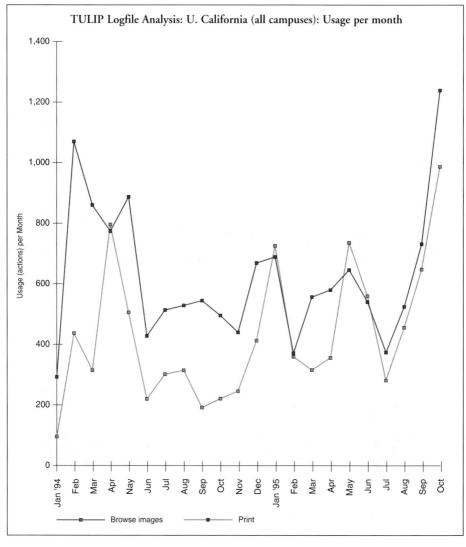

TULIP Logfile Analysis: U. California (all campuses): Usage per month

Usage Type	Jan '94	Feb	Mar	Apr	May	Jun	Jul	Aug	Sep	Oct	Nov	Dec	Jan '95	Feb	Mar	Apr	May	Jun	Jul	Aug	Sep	Oct
Browse images	293	1070	860	774	887	428	514	529	545	496	440	669	689	371	557	580	646	541	374	525	732	1239
Print	96	437	315	796	506	220	302	315	192	221	246	413	726	360	316	356	736	560	282	456	648	987

Graph & Table 1

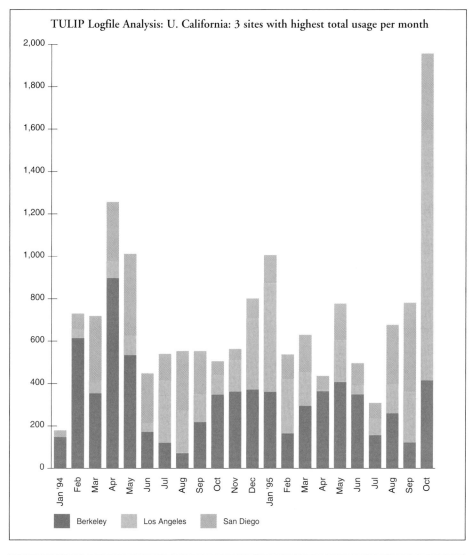

TULIP Logfile Analysis: U. California: 3 sites with highest total usage per month

UC Campus	Jan '94	Feb	Mar	Apr	May	Jun	Jul	Aug	Sep	Oct	Nov	Dec	Jan '95	Feb	Mar	Apr	May	Jun	Jul	Aug	Sep	Oct
Berkeley	148	615	355	898	535	173	122	73	219	349	363	373	362	166	295	365	408	350	157	260	123	416
Los Angeles	0	40	61	78	92	43	293	201	130	91	148	335	511	256	159	8	196	41	78	135	239	1180
San Diego	32	76	304	281	386	233	126	280	205	66	53	94	134	116	176	64	174	106	74	283	420	361
Graph & Table 1a																						

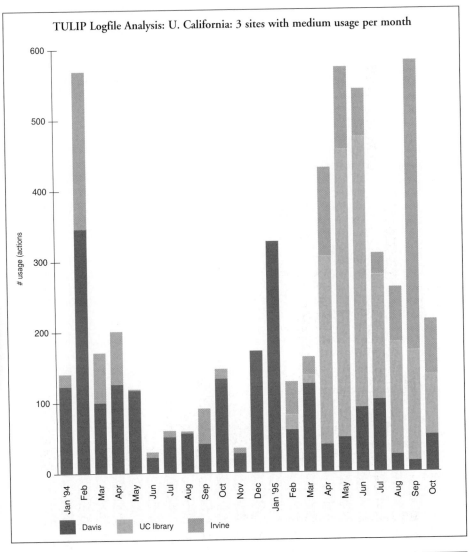

TULIP Logfile Analysis: U. California: 3 sites with medium usage per month

UC Campus	Jan '94	Feb	Mar	Apr	May	Jun	Jul	Aug	Sep	Oct	Nov	Dec	Jan '95	Feb	Mar	Apr	May	Jun	Jul	Aug	Sep	Oct
Davis	123	346	100	126	117	22	51	56	41	133	27	172	327	60	125	39	49	91	102	24	15	52
UC library	0	0	0	0	0	0	0	0	0	0	0	0	0	21	12	266	407	383	177	159	156	85
Irvine	18	223	71	75	2	8	9	3	50	14	8	0	0	47	26	126	117	68	30	78	411	78
	Graph & Table 1b																					

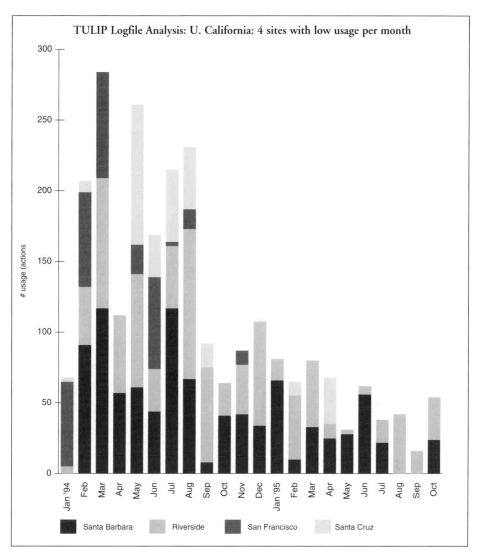

TULIP Logfile Analysis: U. California: 4 sites with low usage per month

UC Campus	Jan '94	Feb	Mar	Apr	May	Jun	Jul	Aug	Sep	Oct	Nov	Dec	Jan '95	Feb	Mar	Apr	May	Jun	Jul	Aug	Sep	Oct
Santa Barbara	0	91	117	57	61	44	117	67	8	41	42	34	66	10	33	25	28	56	22	0	0	24
Riverside	5	41	92	55	80	30	44	106	67	23	35	73	15	45	47	10	3	6	16	42	16	30
San Francisco	60	67	75	0	21	65	3	14	0	0	10	0	0	0	0	0	0	0	0	0	0	0
Santa Cruz	3	8	0	0	99	30	51	44	17	0	0	1	0	10	0-	33	0	0	0	0	0	0
	Graph & Table 1c																					

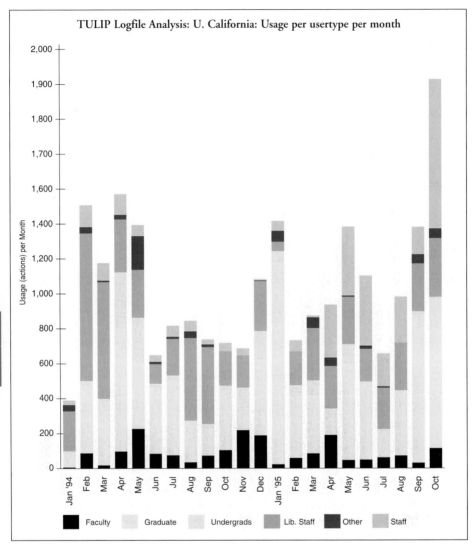

TULIP Logfile Analysis: U. California: Usage per usertype per month

Usage (actions) per Month

Legend: Faculty · Graduate · Undergrads · Lib. Staff · Other · Staff

Usage Type	Total	Jan '94	Feb	Mar	Apr	May	Jun	Jul	Aug	Sep	Oct	Nov	Dec	Jan '95	Feb	Mar	Apr	May	Jun	Jul	Aug	Sep	Oct
Faculty	1950	6	87	18	98	227	84	75	35	73	105	219	189	23	59	85	191	47	49	62	72	31	115
Graduate	9195	83	387	353	706	379	380	434	234	160	345	130	436	1157	351	336	98	556	445	150	368	850	857
Lib. Staff	6635	231	847	671	306	277	115	211	475	442	198	186	289	57	195	301	246	274	189	238	273	276	338
Other	708	36	37	9	27	194	14	13	39	16			4	63		62	49	8	19	9		53	56
Staff	3391	25	124	99	117	62	37	62	59	27	48	41	6	55	64	9	302	393	399	187	265	156	854
Undergrads	1366	8	25	25	316	254	18	21	2	19	21	110	158	60	62	80	50	104		10	3	14	6

Graph & Table 2

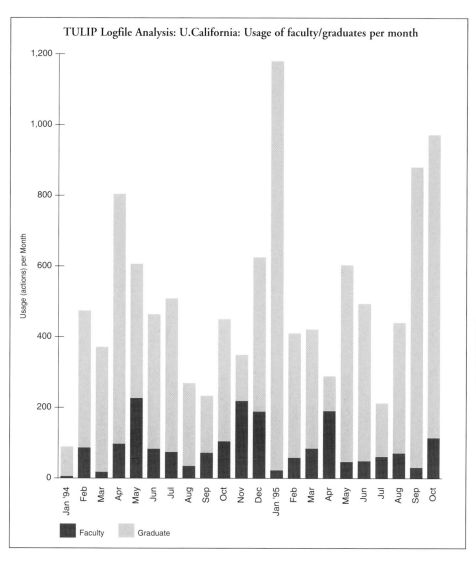

TULIP Logfile Analysis: U.California: Usage of faculty/graduates per month

User Type	Total	Jan '94	Feb	Mar	Apr	May	Jun	Jul	Aug	Sep	Oct	Nov	Dec	Jan '95	Feb	Mar	Apr	May	Jun	Jul	Aug	Sep	Oct
Faculty	1950	6	87	18	98	227	84	75	35	73	105	219	189	23	59	85	191	47	49	62	72	31	115
Graduate	9195	83	387	353	706	379	380	434	234	160	345	130	436	1157	351	336	98	556	445	150	368	850	857
	Graph & Table 3																						

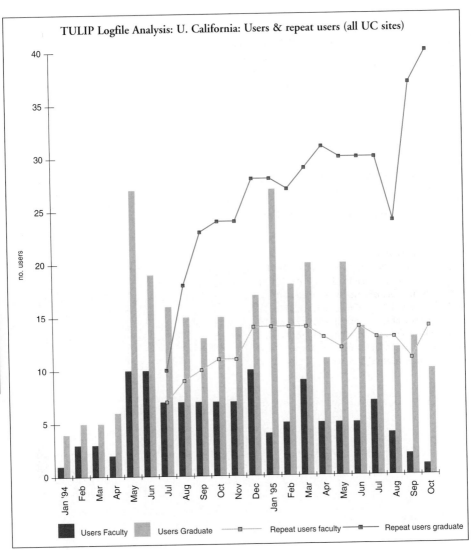

TULIP Logfile Analysis: U. California: Users & repeat users (all UC sites)

Type	Jan '94	Feb	Mar	Apr	May	Jun	Jul	Aug	Sep	Oct	Nov	Dec	Jan '95	Feb	Mar	Apr	May	Jun	Jul	Aug	Sep	Oct
fc	1	3	3	2	10	10	7	7	7	7	7	10	4	5	9	5	5	5	7	4	2	1
gr	4	5	5	6	27	19	16	15	13	15	14	17	27	18	20	11	20	14	13	12	13	10
repeatedly used by:																						
fc							7	9	10	11	11	14	14	14	14	13	12	14	13	13	11	14
gr							10	18	23	24	24	28	28	27	29	31	30	30	30	24	37	40
Penetration							1%	1%	1%	1%	1%	1%	1%	1%	1%	1%	1%	1%	1%	1%	1%	2%
Number of potential users at UC:										fc	646											
										gr	2711											
										total	3357											
	Graph & Table 4																					

a. Usage

If one compares the months with the highest and lowest usage in 1994 and 1995, it is clear that at the University of California the usage of **TULIP** only recently increased, but remains at a rather low level overall. October 1995, has the highest usage of the whole project period. This recent increase however is almost completely due to the activity of a few users at UCLA.

Three campuses (Berkeley, Los Angeles and San Diego), account for about two-thirds of the total usage at the University of California. Usage is almost zero at four other campuses (Santa Barbara, Riverside, San Francisco and Santa Cruz). These campuses are not very strong in Materials Research, which is not only reflected in the low number of potential users, but also in the fact that there are few subscriptions to the paper journals at these campuses.

b. Printing

Because the **TULIP** application at the University of California is linked with the MELVYL library system, providing direct access to Inspec and Current Contents, searching and selecting relevant items is not recorded in the **TULIP** logfiles. Only once people decide to look at the page images, are subsequent actions logged. This situation, similar to the MIT logfiles, leads to an almost equal number of printing and browsing actions.

c. Users and repeat users

There have been 253 people who have used the University of California **TULIP** images at least once. The number of users has been declining since May 1995, and since then is lower than in the same period of 1994. The number of repeat users increased somewhat in October 1995, after remaining stable for a while, at 13 faculty and 30 graduate students, probably because of the announcement of focus group research at the University of California campuses in that month. With a total potential user group at the University of California of almost 3,400, penetration does not grow above 1-2%. However, this potential user group seems to include many 'non-core' potential users. Certainly, at those sites where the usage is heaviest, penetration will be relatively higher.

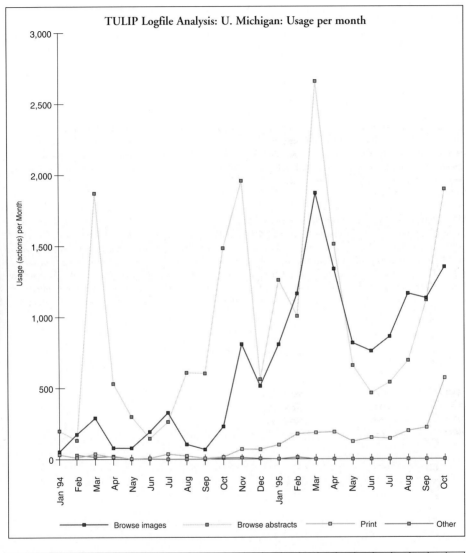

TULIP Logfile Analysis: U. Michigan: Usage per month

Type	Jan '94	Feb	Mar	Apr	May	Jun	Jul	Aug	Sep	Oct	Nov	Dec	Jan '95	Feb	Mar	Apr	May	Jun	Jul	Aug	Sep	Oct
Browse images	52	174	289	79	78	192	326	104	68	229	808	514	806	1,163	1,872	1,338	816	759	862	1,164	1,131	1,351
Browse abstracts	198	132	1,871	531	298	145	262	608	603	1,484	1,958	561	1,259	1,006	2,658	1,512	658	465	540	693	1,118	1,898
Print	32	10	37	14	3	7	36	23	6	15	70	68	100	177	185	190	123	150	144	198	221	570
Other		29	16	20	1	2	0	0	0	8	10	4	1	13	0	0	0	0	0	0	0	0

Graph & Table 1

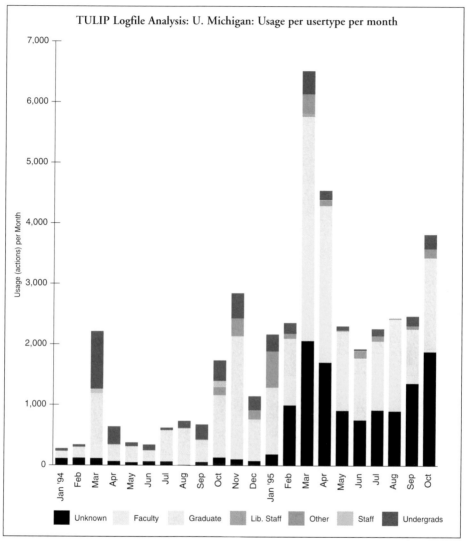

TULIP Logfile Analysis: U. Michigan: Usage per usertype per month

Legend: Unknown · Faculty · Graduate · Lib. Staff · Other · Staff · Undergrads

User Type	Jan '94	Feb	Mar	Apr	May	Jun	Jul	Aug	Sep	Oct	Nov	Dec	Jan '95	Feb	Mar	Apr	May	Jun	Jul	Aug	Sep	Oct
Unknown	118	126	119	72	53	69	68	9	58	133	105	77	188	995	2,059	1,703	909	753	916	901	1,360	1,881
Faculty	22	35	211	68	68	37	108	279	246	212	545	541	296	490	2,065	1,722	929	770	947	923	135	47
Graduate	98	143	851	191	188	143	401	309	106	815	1,483	143	804	609	1,631	863	377	246	189	589	756	1,501
Lib. Staff														60			7	7			8	8	5
Other						1	1			139	296	144	596	83	319	94	10	118	90	15	48	149
Staff			82	17	8		5	19	16	98		5			6	2	4		7	2		
Undergrads	44	41	950	296	63	96	41	119	251	339	417	237	282	182	381	155	72	29	120		161	236

Graph & Table 2

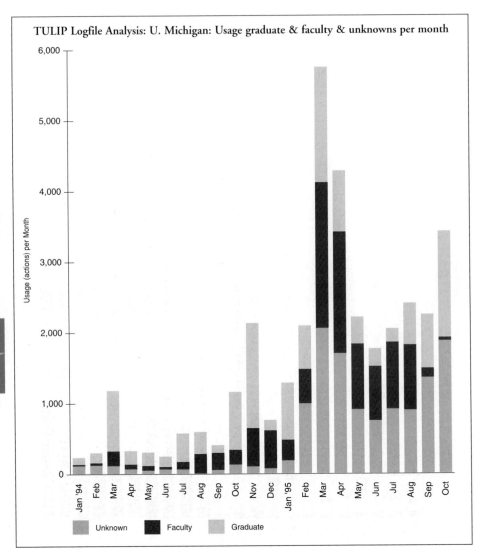

TULIP Logfile Analysis: U. Michigan: Usage graduate & faculty & unknowns per month

Type	Jan '94	Feb	Mar	Apr	May	Jun	Jul	Aug	Sep	Oct	Nov	Dec	Jan '95	Feb	Mar	Apr	May	Jun	Jul	Aug	Sep	Oct
Unknown	118	126	119	72	53	69	68	9	58	133	105	77	188	995	2,059	1,703	909	753	916	901	1,360	1,881
Faculty	22	35	211	68	68	37	108	279	246	212	545	541	296	490	2,065	1,722	929	770	947	923	135	47
Graduate	98	143	851	191	188	143	401	309	106	815	1,483	143	804	609	1,631	863	377	246	189	589	756	1,501

Graph & Table 3

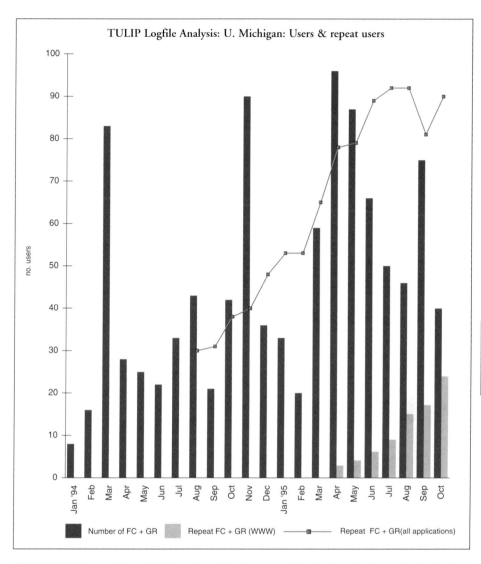

TULIP Logfile Analysis: U. Michigan: Users & repeat users

Legend: ■ Number of FC + GR ▨ Repeat FC + GR (WWW) ─■─ Repeat FC + GR(all applications)

Type	Jan '94	Feb	Mar	Apr	May	Jun	Jul	Aug	Sep	Oct	Nov	Dec	Jan '95	Feb	Mar	Apr	May	Jun	Jul	Aug	Sep	Oct
fc + gr	8	16	83	28	25	22	33	43	21	42	90	36	33	20	59	96	87	66	50	46	75	40
WWW															4	4	9	7	11	13	11	12
repeatedly used by:																						
Repeat (all applications)								30	31	38	40	48	53	53	65	78	79	89	92	92	81	90
Repeat FC + GR (WWW)																3	4	6	9	15	17	23
Degree of Penetration:								8%	9%	11%	11%	13%	15%	15%	18%	22%	22%	25%	26%	26%	23%	25%
Potential User Group											360											

Graph & Table 4

a. Usage

The University of Michigan's usage statistics show that **TULIP** usage in 1995 is higher overall than in 1994. If one compares the month of June, which shows lowest usage for both years, usage in June 1995 is almost four times as high as in June 1994. The same holds true if one compares the months with peak usage, which in both years occurred in March. March 1995 usage is almost twice as high as in the same month of the previous year. The trend, therefore, indicates a steady increase in usage in the second year of the **TULIP** project at the University of Michigan. This trend is especially clear in the development of page image viewing and printing (see graph 1).

This trend is probably partly influenced by the expansion of the number of **TULIP** journals included in the project from 43 to 82 per January 1, 1995.

b. Printing

Printing articles stays at a low level, but since the introduction of Web access to **TULIP** (in March 1995), printing has increased from 185 to 570 articles per month. As the Web version will probably be more frequently used, it can be expected that this trend will continue.

c. Users and repeat users

At the University of Michigan, 437 people have used the **TULIP**View, MASC or Web implementation at least once.

Due to changes in the logfile procedures (since March 1995), the number of faculty and graduate students are no longer registered by user type. Distinguishing between faculty and graduate students was no longer possible, and for continuity reasons we have had to combine the user types in the analysis.

The number of users per month fluctuates between 50 and 80 to 90. The share of Web users is steadily increasing. The number of repeat users developed significantly, from 30 in August 1994 to 90 in October 1995. Since June 1995, we have seen a stabilization occurring. Penetration, with an estimated potential user group of 360, is 25% as of October 1995.

IV 2.2.7 University of Tennessee

a. Usage

The logfiles of the University of Tennessee did not meet the agreed standards and can, therefore, not be analyzed here. The number of actions however, could be counted and did not exceed an average of 100 per month by all user types. This is also confirmed by analysis carried out at the University of Tennessee, which mentions the lowest usage in December 1994 (four actions), to a maximum of 812 actions in January 1995.

b. Printing

The number of requests for full text articles was no more than ten throughout 1994 and 1995.

c. Users and repeat users

As repeat usage could not be traced, there is no information about number of repeat users or penetration. The core user group consists of 15 faculty and about 100 graduate students, of whom 38 registered for a **TULIP** password. Conclusion: there was only moderate usage of **TULIP** at the University of Tennessee.

IV 2.3 Overall results and comparison of sites

Notwithstanding the diversity of the **TULIP** implementations and its consequences for the logfiles, we feel that we can compare the results of the University of Michigan, the University of California and MIT, because all three logged the usage of page images for viewing on screen and printing. Although the University of Michigan logfiles have the added registration of the use of the abstracts, this has proven not to be of influence on the number of repeat users. Analysis of the logfiles showed that the same users are browsing and printing both abstracts and image files on a regular basis, and thus the number of repeat users is not influenced. This means that the results of the University of Michigan, the University of California and MIT can be compared.

- The University of Michigan, which had a 25% penetration, invested a lot of time and effort in providing good and useful interfaces to the material, as well as in communicating the benefits of **TULIP** to the end users, training, and in the technical improvement of especially the printing facilities.
- At MIT, a penetration of about 10% overall was reached, however the number of faculty using the system remained rather low. There was high usage intensity, that is, the usage of the system, as measured by the number of pages viewed and printed, clearly demonstrates a strong interest in using the service. There are questions about the percentage of repeat usage the system received, however. We attribute the lack of repeat usage to a mismatch between the content and the needs of the users rather than in dissatisfaction with how the service was implemented.
- At the University of California (1-2% penetration), the technical infrastructure seems to be the major roadblock. Especially extreme difficulties with printing, sometimes excruciatingly slow response from the system, and the lack of computers running X-windows had a negative effect on repeat usage.

At Georgia Tech, more than 50% of the potential users regularly made use of the system. This service, which provided browsing of abstracts only and printing of the articles, can be considered highly succesful when compared to the other sites which had comparable systems (the University of Tennessee and Carnegie Mellon for much of the project lifetime).

The reason for this high user acceptance is most probably that their **TULIP** implementation was a logical extension of an existing service with better access to bibliographical data (including abstracts) and fast delivery of actual articles.

IV 2.4   Results of the Reshelving Studies

IV 2.4.1 University of Michigan

The results of the reshelving statistics at the University of Michigan indicate that *'TULIP publicity efforts increased awareness (...) of the TULIP journals in the first year of the experiment and thus the journals were used more in 1993 than in 1992'*. The continued promotion and the publicity around focus group research in early 1995 may have caused an increase in use in 1995 over 1994. However, the library staff at the University of Michigan, knowing the pitfalls of this type of usage studies, are rather cautious to draw too strong conclusions.

IV 2.4.2 University of Tennessee

The statistics kept in the Current Periodicals room of the library indicated that usage of (unbound) **TULIP** journal-issues was low and did not change very much during the project. This was also confirmed by lending statistics of bound volumes and the proportion of **TULIP** titles in interlibrary loan requests.

IV 2.4.3 Conclusion

Promotion of electronic access to the journals makes people aware of the availability of these journals on campus, which could lead to increased usage in the library.

IV 3.   Qualitative Research

IV 3.1   Research methods used

Two types of qualitative research have been used, structured individual interviews (with faculty) and focus groups (with graduate students). Although focus groups would have been preferable for both groups, structured interviews were used for faculty members, because focus groups proved not feasible for this group of respondents.

Focus groups were considered the preferred method of research, because they are an even better tool for getting an in-depth insight into the considerations, the motivations, the needs and other driving forces behind actual behavior than one-on-one interviews, because of the interaction between the participants.

The focus groups as well as the interviews were moderated by an external professional researcher and were based on an identical interview guide. The interview guide has been adapted for each site and included questions and discussion points regarding expectations, satisfaction and unfulfilled needs. In addition, preliminary conclusions from the other (quantitative) research activities have also been an important input for the formulation of the interview guides.

The following qualitative research activities have been carried out:
● University of Michigan (January, February 1995)
  • three personal pilot interviews among faculty members
  • one focus group with nine graduate students
  • ten interviews with faculty and graduate students
  • 15 telephone interviews with faculty and students who had either only tried to use **TULIP** once or who heard of **TULIP** but never tried to use it.

● MIT (July 1995)
  • one focus group session with nine graduate students.

● University of California (October 1995)
  at Santa Barbara:
  • one focus group session with ten graduate students
  • five interviews with faculty.
  at Berkeley:
  • one focus group with nine graduate students
  • five interviews with faculty.
  at Davis:
  • six interviews with faculty.

All focus groups lasted approximately two hours and the personal interviews approximately one hour each. The respondents of the focus groups and personal interviews were all **TULIP** users. The telephone interviews at the University of Michigan (of approximately 20 minutes each), were focused on getting information about the reasons of non-use.
Respondents who participated in the focus groups and personal interviews were paid an honorarium for their participation in the research.

Carnegie Mellon University and the University of Tennessee have conducted other qualitative research, the results of which can be found in their reports (appendices I and VII, respectively). To the extent that their research objectives were comparable to those of the research described above, their results are included in the analysis below.

IV 3.2   Major findings

The interview guides used for the focus groups and the one-on-one interviews have been adapted for each site in order to fit the particular implementations of **TULIP** and/or the specific situations on each campus (see appendix XIII for the interview guide used at MIT). Nevertheless, all interview guides covered the same issues so we were able to compare the results.

A summary of the findings is presented below. The detailed results of the qualitative research, following the sequence of the interview guides, are given in appendix XIV.

IV 3.2.1   Summary of the results

The results of the study are evaluated in the light of the five research objectives described in chapter IV 1.

Re 1. Generic and basic understanding of information behavior of scientists.

The major elements that have been learned or confirmed are:
- When searching for information a rather severe selection takes place based on the title, name of the author, abstract, pictures and tables. Therefore, in-depth reading of articles is relatively rare.
- Graduate students have a more active information seeking behavior than faculty members. Their focus is also broader.
- Graduate students use a larger number of journals with a lower frequency and in a more ad hoc manner.
- On the one hand, searching behavior of faculty is more focused, because their network of personal contacts, etc. indicates the relevant sources. On the other hand, they appreciate (more than graduate students do) the possibilities of browsing and the serendipity of paper.
- Faculty seem to be more limited by time constraints, they therefore rely heavily on reference librarians and graduate students to search for information.
- Faculty members in particular, also read journals at home.
- Library visits are often perceived as cumbersome: distance, parking problems, issues not available, etc. On the other hand, the library has some very appreciated elements such as social contacts and 'pleasure reading'. Many users have a kind of 'emotional' relationship with the library.

Re 2. 'Pull' and 'push' factors regarding electronic products

The reasons for accepting or rejecting innovative products like electronic information can be divided in 'pull' factors, the attractive elements of the new product, and 'push' factors, those elements that are unattractive in the current situation and will therefore motivate to look for other solutions.

There is no doubt that one of the major 'pull' factors for electronic products in general, and for desk top access to full text/image articles in particular, is convenience. Respondents like the idea of being able to search and select information and to print it out without leaving their desk. Therefore, the concept of **TULIP** as it is perceived by the end users (which is desktop access to full text/image information), is very well received. Another 'pull' factor of electronic products is the better search capabilities, mentioned in particular by those who were able to use INSPEC and Current Contents.

The major 'push' factors are the inconveniences of the current situation with a reliance on paper copies which are kept at the library. This method is cumbersome, time consuming, the relevant issues are not available, etc.

TULIP has made clear that the basic 'pull' factor for full text/image products is convenience. The usage statistics make clear that this is fairly difficult to achieve.

Re 3. Requirements for electronic products

Users seem to have the following requirements regarding functionality, ease of use and critical mass:
- ease of use: as intuitive as possible, and preferably using a familiar interface;
- access to all information from one source;
- effective search capabilities;
- high processing speed (downloading and printing);
- high publishing speed (timeliness of the information);
- good image text quality;
- sufficient journal and time coverage;
- linking of information.

This is the end user's definition of convenience.

Re 4. Distribution of electronic (full text) information to the desktop

There is no doubt that electronic distribution of full text/image information is very much appreciated, under the condition that convenience (as defined above) is really improved. Georgia Tech seems to be successful in implementing a non-electronic element in the distribution (delivery of the documents by special campus courier), assuring a fast distribution of good quality print. This illustrates clearly that not the medium is important, but the final results. The experience on several other sites demonstrates that the missing of only one link in the total distribution of the information, in particular smooth printing capabilities, can seriously limit the usage of electronic information. The electronic distribution seems to be more convenient for searching, while the easy-to-browse aspect of paper makes it more convenient for serendipity. That is also the reason why reading a paper version of a journal takes more time than using the electronic version: browsing gives greater likelihood of being 'sidetracked' by other information. Finally, most users prefer reading a hard copy to viewing information on the computer screen. Printing is therefore an important feature. It should be easy, fast and good quality.

Re 5. Promotion

Expectations regarding desk top access to full articles are in general very positive: once aware of the launch of a new product, many people (in particular graduate students), will give it a try. We see this relative ease of gaining interest in **TULIP** in the usage statistics: many new users are trying **TULIP** at each promotional activity.

However, it appears to be extremely difficult to influence decisions about repeat use with communication and/or promotional activities when the first experiences are not meeting the initial expectations, which is the case in many **TULIP** sites. In such a situation, there needs to be an on-going promotional effort to attract previous users and alert potential new users about improvements and updates made to the system.

IV 4.   Conclusions

The conclusions we can draw from the user studies are the following:

● The general concept underlying the **TULIP** project is very well received by students and faculty. This concept consists of desktop access to full text/image articles: fast and easy to search, to read, and to print.

● Hardware and software are serious obstacles for convenient use of the **TULIP** information at most of the sites. That is certainly a reason why it appears to be difficult at most **TULIP** sites to increase the user base.

● Most users consider the coverage (in number of titles and in time) of the journals in the **TULIP** project to be insufficient. This insufficient coverage (not all core journals - those not published by Elsevier - are available in the database) requires end users to search additional information elsewhere, which is considered time-consuming and redundant, not contributing to an increased convenience. However, we have no definite answer concerning the relative importance of coverage versus convenience. If a system is able to offer satisfactory convenience (more than **TULIP** did), is limited coverage still a major handicap for frequent use?

● For the users of **TULIP** there has been an accumulation of discouraging factors in many cases; limited coverage, slow response times, difficulties in accessing the system, printing problems, limited computer literacy, delays in adding new journal issues, etc. Some of these elements, the 'objective' ones, can be measured, such as response time and the number of issues that are delayed. However, there are also much more subjective elements determining (repeat) usage of the **TULIP** implementation on a campus, for instance the initial expectations users had of the convenience and performance of **TULIP**. These expectations influence greatly whether a user is satisfied with the service offered or not. Because of these subjective factors, it is impossible to isolate the impact of improvements of the objective factors. In other words, we are unable to indicate to what extent the acceptance and usage of **TULIP** will be influenced by improving each of the above mentioned factors. Their weight in the users' trade off of the value of **TULIP** compared with their existing 'research tool kit', remains unknown.

● Graduate students are using **TULIP** more frequently than faculty. This is probably due to a more active information seeking behavior of graduate students and their broader orientation. Also, faculty need a compelling reason to change - either it is so much more convenient or so much more complete. They are both more sceptical and less willing to invest in learning to use an electronic information tool due to severe time constraints and to a lack of computer literacy.

● Although the number of users might seem to be relatively low at some sites, it is difficult to evaluate these figures, because we lack reference points. For innovative products in consumer markets, a market penetration of 10 to 25% after one year is considered extremely high. However, for the type of market we are looking at here, where end users get the products and services free of charge, there are no comparable figures.

● The steadily declining number of users in many cases is cause for concern, because it is a clear indication of dissatisfaction.

● There is enthusiasm about the concept of desktop access to electronic information, but the end of paper products still seems to be far away. Besides some practical benefits of paper products, there also seem to be 'emotional' ties with paper and the library.

V   Organizational and economic issues

This chapter deals with the organizational and economic questions raised as the second objective of the **TULIP** project (chapter I 2). As many organizational, and to some extent economic (cost), issues have been discussed as part of the previous chapters, specifically chapter II, this chapter reflects the suggestions/conclusions/'lessons learned' contributed by participants in interviews and reports. Some 35 interviews were held in October/November 1995 with project managers, project liaisons, administrators, head librarians, (reference) librarians, and technical management and staff at the nine participating universities.

V 1.   Critical success factors for the implementation of TULIP

From the interviews conducted with key players at the **TULIP** universities, we have distilled four major factors which can make or break a project like **TULIP**: the (project) organization, understanding your user community's possibilities and needs, infrastructure and promotion-related factors.

V 1.1   Organization and project management

First of all, dedicated project management, cooperation among the parties involved and having the right resources available at the right time seem to be crucial to getting a large scale project off the ground. For instance, at the University of Michigan there were several groups that had interest in the information infrastructure, and a common goal to move ahead. Certain areas had expertise that would contribute to the whole, but no one area had all expertise. So they had to work together, and by working together they moved the agenda forward quickly. For an implementation like **TULIP** both technical and user expertise are necessary. Working together with both technical and 'contents' specialists is easier if common goals are set. In some cases, the systems staff and the librarians report to one person, facilitating setting priorities.

Almost all participants implemented **TULIP** in addition to their ongoing other tasks. To make this work, especially when priority projects come along, what is needed are very capable people who creatively manage their time. Like at MIT for example: *'We couldn't afford a large staff so we had to focus on getting the right people at the right time'*. A member of the BULB group, the persons who worked on **TULIP** at MIT, said: *'None of us have a lot of margin or excess staff or money lying around. So we had to think carefully about, in building the system, what were things that already existed, so that we didn't reinvent the wheel'*. During the first stage of the project they met weekly during lunch, then biweekly and during the last period once a month.

Another participant described it as follows: *'Spelling out a common set of values, common visions of the future and the divisions of responsibility and the role of each organization'*. Politics, lack of priority and lack of responsibilities can cause long delays. Problems of this kind have occurred at many of the **TULIP** universities, and all but killed the project in a few of them. Internal organizational/political problems can turn out to be very real stumbling blocks.

V 1.2   Comprehend end users' possibilities and needs

Knowing your users is the next key element for a successful implementation. What happens if there is an interface, up and running in the library, accessible on the desktop of users, and it appears not to be what users really want? One of the main lessons learned at the University of Washington was that you have to make sure that the product you implement is appropriate for your user community. The task force for library services is now working to acquire more information and to work more closely with major users to find out what their needs are.

A few universities actually stated, that they felt in hindsight that the first step of the project should have been to consult and involve their end users. This was especially true for those who attended the focus groups, which they found very useful for their assessments of user needs.

'Users said it (TULIP) was useful, but that it was only a piece of what they need. They want it (electronic information) on their desktop; they want electronic access to the full text (not just to citations); local, fast printing; and they want it now.'

Not all users like electronic information, though. A remark heard many times was, that in general, the graduate and undergraduate students are computer literate and were the heavy **TULIP** users. Faculty are coming along, but it varies per discipline and per person: *'the students are way ahead of them'*. But, if users are to be provided with the advantages of electronic access, one must understand what is important to them.

V 1.3   Resources and infrastructure
(see also chapter II)

If there is no adequate infrastructure in place, a project like **TULIP** can not be implemented, even with commited team members who know what their users want. There are three aspects to infrastructure here:
a. systems on which **TULIP** runs;
b. networking and (non-local) printing infrastructure;
c. user desktop systems.

Re a. Universities where **TULIP** was linked to their existing systems had less of a daunting challenge than those where the system was developed from scratch, but most universities have stated they had underestimated the amount of time, effort, and to a lesser extent money, it would take them to get their **TULIP** system up and running. These experiences are well documented in chapter II. Some additional comments: *'Libraries with less resources are advised to think twice before starting to make their own implementation: It won't do, in particular for small libraries, to be responsible in a way the TULIP participants were. They don't have the human resources and technology to do it. So they will have to turn to a vendor who can supply them with the right kind of clients to get at this information. They also won't have the capability of storing the data locally'.*

Re b. The ability of the (inter-)campus networks to deal with bandwidth-consuming graphical data is crucial. If you want to provide users with a system which enables them to access graphical information from their desktops, you need a high speed network able to transmit graphic information with acceptable response times. Although 'acceptable' is a highly relative term here, dependent on the users' expectations, there is a certain delay at which users will get frustrated and stop using the system. The printing infrastructure should also be ubiquitous, fast and easy.

In some cases network speeds and slow or difficult printing have been limiting factors. At Georgia Tech, this has been circumvented by implementing a service that did not offer desktop display but rather off-line printing. At the University of California however, where viewing was very slow and printing almost impossible for most campuses, this has been a major factor hindering success. Additionally, it led to an unwillingness on the part of some of the campus liaisons to promote a system which they knew did not work satisfactorily. The University of California will, on the basis of their experiences with **TULIP**, upgrade its inter-campus network to be able to deal with the increased requirements of image based information.

Re c. *'For a successful implementation, make sure the product is appropriate to your user community.'* Regarding the equipment on the desk of your users, there are two possibilities: either to provide high-end workstations (required for image viewing) to the users, like the Athena Project at MIT, or adapt your interface to a standard that can be used at the workstations your users have. However, hardware purchases are highly decentralized in many places, resulting in an amalgam of hardware configurations on users' desks. Several universities now require students to have high-end PCs. However, this is still rare and it may take a while before, as someone said: *'We'll end up with computers being in the same class as text books and calculators, something you can build into a financial aid package, averaging out over four years with a mid-point upgrade in two years'.* And even then the required hardware may vary from department to department. Furthermore, faculty and graduate students still have widely varying equipment.

The lowest common denominator then is a terminal emulation, which severely limits the possibilities of the application (no graphics at all), and therefore result in non-user friendly and uninteresting applications. With the advent of the Web, with clients for every platform, this situation has changed dramatically for the better, as you can now build a Web-based system which can be used by almost everyone, without having to write clients for all the platforms they use.

V 1.4   Introduction, promotion and training
(see also chapter III)

At most universities, promotion was not viewed as a major issue at the beginning of the project. However, over the course of time this attitude changed.

Some quotes:
- *'Products are not used unless you promote them. Promotion is a key issue and easily overlooked';*
- *'Promotion is absolutely necessary for electronic products. When a new database was installed, I put balloons above it to attract attention...'*

and
- *'There is so much out there, people get confused. You have to show them that there are many more things besides books to help them get answers to their questions.'*

Nevertheless, some librarians feel *'a perfect product will sell itself. But if no one knows a service exists, no one will use it. Initial promotion is a minimal requirement'.* At sites which did more extensive promotion we see a significantly higher use of **TULIP**. So, promotion does seem to be a condition to get your users interested and started. Continued promotion is obviously a necessity to attract new user groups. Additionally, the **TULIP** implementations were often far from perfect in the beginning. Therefore, continued promotional activities are needed to make users aware of improvements.

While general computer training, that is teaching the use of the basic tools needed for research, is seen as a requirement, many feel that separate training for a specific implementation should not be necessary. Users should be able to start using the implementation without specific knowledge, and discover the more advanced features as they start to need them.
'We begin to observe that people will use systems to a point of satisfaction. No matter how whiz-bang a system is, they are probably not going beyond the point where it satisfies their needs. Only when they become dissatisfied with their current capabilities, are they going to move forward and learn more about the system's possibilities and that is where the functionality begins to pay off.'
The kind of people who use scientific journals are said to generally prefer to experiment themselves instead of attending training. They want to be able to do what they intuitively think is right and prefer not to read the documentation.

V 2.   Economic issues

Of the objectives of the **TULIP** project (technical, organizational/economic, user behavior studies), the 'economic issues' part of the second objective is the least conclusive. This is in part due to the fact that it simply proved impossible to test some of the economic models as we had set out to do, and partly due to the fact that the project was still so much in an experimental phase, struggling with technical and user behavior issues, that the discussions about economic issues did not really start until close to the end of the project.

However, although we have not been able to directly test many economic models, **TULIP** still helped us a great deal in the development of ideas about theses issues, specifically about cost. Below is a summary of the views of the participants on economic issues, both from interviews conducted with them and the university reports (appendices I-IX), and of initiatives which were taken to test economic models.

V 2.1 Cost

V 2.1.1 Costs of implementing TULIP

All participants have been confronted with the harsh economic realities of building even a prototype of an electronic journals system, from Elsevier Science's side the costs of conversion and distribution, on the universities' side the costs of implementation of their respective systems. These experiences guide us in determining what we want to and can do in a full scale production.

Some universities referred to high costs, especially of storage, as an important factor inhibiting the development of their **TULIP** systems, and view these costs as a major roadblock for further development. However, MIT reports:

'The cost of building the Page Image Delivery System (PIDS) involved staff costs and technical costs. We estimate that the aggregate effort to build the delivery architecture has been three FTE for two years. Because MIT's infrastructure is already in place, hardware costs for TULIP consisted primarily of the server and storage, in total, approximately $100,000. This seems like a relatively inexpensive effort with high return on investment'.

V 2.1.2 Costs of storage

Storage costs have been a major factor in the **TULIP** project, as storage media had to be dedicated to the project, whereas use of people's time, use of the server etc. could be shared with (many) other projects. When **TULIP** started, most university technologists minimized the storage costs. But, it seems that storage costs remain a very important cost element, even though the costs of the media keep dropping:

'...the current cost for magnetic storage is 5.3 times greater than print, and jukebox storage on CDS is 1.2 times greater. It is also worth considering that the typical book stack will last well over 30 years, but not the information technology. The $16,891 server and magnetic storage will have to be replaced at least every eight to ten years, and this is stretching the point. Based on a ten-year replacement cycle, digital storage and access will cost academic libraries 16 times as much as print to store locally. It seems unlikely that a persuasive case can be made for the added value of electronic access and retrieval without a dramatic change in the ownership concept. ... one final note on comparative capital expense - the cost of building will continue to increase at something like the CPI, and (if recent past is a guide) the cost of servers and storage will continue to fall at a more rapid rate. The problem is guessing correctly when these trend lines will cross and make digital storage cheaper than print'.

Additionally, the costs of 'managing' large collections of electronic data must also not be underestimated. Consequently, Carnegie Mellon University argues:

'The traditional model of local ownership, which has dominated the vision of library organization and collection development for a century must change. The access model which is emerging will mean the libraries may subscribe or license access to information formerly packaged as a book or a journal, but it is not likely that they will store much of it on the local campus network. It only makes sense to share information technology resources among libraries and the cost of shared access to databases... It also seems likely that the library vendor and publishing community will provide some forms of access... However, these are all new relationships. They mean that the nature of ownership must be carefully redefined and this will take time and it may not be very easy to accomplish. Publishers will want to know that their materials are being used appropriately. They will expect that access is for the campus community, that ILL and reserve reading conform to 'fair use' and that authentication and authorization prevent the significant access to information for those who have not paid for it. Libraries will want to know that a subscription to a title gives them permanent access to the contents over time, that the server on which it is found will be consistently available, that the technology will be robust and stable, and that if the supplier (e.g., consortium, publisher, network) ever withdraws the service, then there is a plan for giving them the data they paid for. If such relationships are properly worked out, new types of subscribed access may be expected'.

V 2.1.3 Costs of content

While in the **TULIP** project access to the electronic journals was free on the basis of paper subscriptions, many universities expressed concern about the costs of the electronic journals after the experimental phase, for instance:

'Because the online versions of the TULIP journals received only light use, it is doubtful that we would have been ready to pay additional charges for the online versions at this time. The pressures on our science materials budgets are too great to justify such expenditures. We can no longer provide access to paper journals now needed. We would therefore need to consider very carefully purchasing 'added copies' online of items also held in paper at the expense of materials needed in paper form. If the costs of the online versions were less than the paper versions, then there would be some incentive to purchase online versions as an alternative to the paper - but the current Elsevier pricing policy (i.e., online versions on their own being more expensive than the paper versions) does not make that possible'.

And:

'With regards to continuing to purchase Elsevier electronic content, we have elected to discontinue loading content in the present mode primarily because the cost is too high and comes at a time of shrinking library budgets. We are excited about electronic content, and look forward to exploring other economic models that are a better fit with our economic realities. MIT is willing to pay for high value information but is under tremendous pressure to spend fewer dollars as time goes on. For example, electronic-only distributions are particularly attractive since they eliminate postal, paper, and packaging costs'.

V 2.1.4   Costs of full scale digital libraries

'Too often, work on digital libraries, not to mention much theoretical discussion, proceeds without a thorough grounding in the realities of cost. There are certain assumptions which precede this state of affairs, among them the notion that digital libraries somehow will be cheaper than print libraries, perhaps even free. One suspects that this arises from the misplaced hope that digital libraries will liberate us from the difficult cost dynamics of print libraries. There is also a presumption that electronic access will mean added value to library patrons, but it begs the question if the access is at a cost patrons are unwilling to pay.'

TULIP proved to its participants beyond a doubt that building digital libraries will be a costly and lengthy process. The future is highly uncertain: is it a remote access, single computer serving the world or the continuation of the building of local libraries, with local patrons, spending local budgets? The easy and undoubtedly correct answer is to say that it is both. But for both libraries and publishers, this may be the most difficult to deal with, as we have feet in both worlds and cannot easily balance the economics of parallel systems.

'The current publishing environment and the cost analysis of the work at Carnegie Mellon does not support the notion that digital libraries are about to happen. The world of publishing is anything but monolithic... In addition, the necessity to repeat capital expenditures on servers and storage will not encourage the development of digital libraries, even though hardware is becoming more of a commodity and storage costs may be trivial in the not-too-distant future.'

V 2.2   Economic models examined

The **TULIP** project did not provide definitive answers to the questions about economic issues surrounding the transition from a paper based situation to the electronic dissemination of (scientific) information. Testing of economic models has been limited, as described in some detail below.

V 2.2.1   Internal charging at universities

Some universities had plans to test some economic models on their campuses by charging for article printing. This proved to be impractical or unfeasible within the context of this project. For instance at the University of Michigan:

'From the project's inception, the team anticipated gaining a base of knowledge about system building for electronic resources, user behavior with digital journals, and economic models applicable to the evolving hybrid print and digital environment. They were successful in meeting the first two objectives but were unable to test economic models. The rapid evolution of the World Wide Web as an information environment presented the developers with a better approach to TULIP than possible during its initial implementation. However, the Web does not yet

support the kind of data collection that is necessary for testing economic models nor the level of security for financial transactions that we felt was necessary'.

V 2.2.2   Consortium model

Discussions had started between Elsevier Science and the University of Washington to refine a consortium model by working with NorthWestNet, but unfortunately that was not possible because of problems which Washington experienced with their implementation.

V 2.2.3   Subscriptions to electronic-only material

Elsevier Science wanted to explore a few possibilities to test specific economic models based on the subscription model, as both sides know that model and are comfortable with it. As the electronic versions of the subscribed-to **TULIP** journals were free, Elsevier Science offered the participating universities some additional options:
- Elsevier Science offered electronic copies of titles to which the participants did not have a paper subscription at a reduced rate from the beginning. There were few takers of this offer, partly because participants did not want to negate/counter collection development decisions, partly due to budget constraints, not only concerning the journal subscriptions, but also (and possibly even more so), because of additional storage/infrastructure costs.
- Elsevier Science also offered lower prices for a second group of titles for which again response was very limited, the major reason being budget constraints (cost of content as well as of storage). Other reasons included, that some universities perceived their systems to be incomplete (for instance the user interface), and did not want to invest in more content at that point. Also, as some universities were planning to discontinue providing access to the **TULIP** files after the experimental period, they did not want to extend the journal list.

In conclusion we can say that making additional funds available for electronic content will not be a trivial issue for these universities. As Carnegie Mellon University described it:
'In the first place, it seems clear that libraries will not have large amounts of new funding with which to purchase electronic materials, although it is not a zero-sum game. It follows that publishers may not expect to have large sources of new profits from the sales of electronic products that represent the scholarly information published today in books and journals'.

V 2.2.4   Pay per use - article delivery

Elsevier Science offered two article delivery related options:
- All participants were offered the opportunity from the beginning to use the files for article delivery to other non-participants if a royalty was collected; none of the participants actually implemented this. The reasons for this option not being taken up are somewhat unclear, however it seems that one important reason is that most universities' document delivery demand stems mostly from ILL requests, which they are bound to fulfill at little or no cost to the receiving university on the basis of reciprocity. Although the costs of fulfilling these requests by hand are much higher than the royalties to be paid in the **TULIP** option, these royalties are 'out of pocket' as opposed to the personnel cost involved with copying the original articles. Elsevier Science does not permit the electronic files to be used for ILL.
- Similarly, Elsevier Science encouraged universities to consider providing article delivery to their own constituents for titles not subscribed to (but included in the bibliographic information) by using Ei, in which case Elsevier would subsidize Ei's handling fee and only royalties would be collected; again, none of the participants did. It seems that the reasons here are the technical difficulty to implement this, or in some cases rather the lack of priority to implement it, as well as the inability to charge through to end users in combination with budget constraints.

In conclusion: it seems to be quite difficult to move away from the status quo as far as article delivery is concerned, either because of 'political differences' between publisher and universities, or because of the inadequate infrastructure provided by current technical and economic solutions.

V 2.2.5   Conclusions

There are no blueprints available of economic models in an electronic environment. In the **TULIP** project we took the first steps, addressing many of the issues - technical, organizational, user needs and preferences, and to some extent economic. Some of the practical problems with establishing and testing new economic models are mentioned above. However, towards the end of the project it also became clear that the expectations of (a number of) the universities and Elsevier Science on what kind of economic models would be tested were somewhat different. Discussions continue between individual universities and Elsevier Science, in the context of the Elsevier Electronic subscription (EES) program.

A final comment from the University of Michigan report (appendix VI):
'A review of faculty and student comments and patterns of use suggests how important a better understanding of economic models is if the TULIP concept is to be expanded. Clearly, we continue in a transitional phase with some users reporting their inability to sustain additional subscription costs for personal copies of favored journals and with the library, too, forced to make choices because of budget constraints. However, the scientists and students report a desire to retain a paper version as well as the electronic files as long as possible. Certainly, we need to know what are feasible pricing options that will enable us to continue to support our researchers' and students' information needs'.

V 3.   Conclusions and recommendations

The **TULIP** partners - universities and Elsevier Science - have learned many valuable lessons in the course of the project that will enable them to better face the long transition phase towards digital libraries. These lessons are shared in this report and the university reports with anyone facing similar challenges now or in the future. The **TULIP** project has been rewarding for all partners, even though not all objectives may have been met completely:

'Sustained communication among libraries and Elsevier Science as we probe electronic frontiers together has surely resulted in higher levels of understanding about the differing concerns that we bring to the arena of electronic journals. TULIP libraries have gained first-hand experience with a publisher's perspective on the costs of changing from a traditionally accepted format to an experimental, rapidly changing electronic medium. Perhaps Elsevier Science has benefitted from working closely with libraries in the developmental process to discover values and constraints that inform library acquisitions decision-making'.

'Elsevier Science sponsored TULIP at a timely juncture for the future of scholarly research and publishing. TULIP represented a unique collaboration among publishers, librarians, academic faculty and researchers for exploring delivery of full text to the desktop... At the time TULIP started, librarians and their clientele had had little exposure to scholarly electronic journals, and Gopher was an innovative development. With the advent of Web capabilities, we discovered a much more viable medium for image delivery. The fact that Elsevier Science journal tables of contents are now available via the Web suggests that this direction holds promise for the future'.

VI Implications of the TULIP project for the future of the development of digital libraries

The **TULIP** participants not only gained a lot of practical experience during the project, but also valuable insights on digital libraries and their development. The first part of this chapter (paragraphs 1 - 4) gives an overview of the implications of **TULIP** for the future as expressed by university participants during interviews and in their final reports. In paragraphs VI 1 and VI 2, the changing environment, the role of the library, librarians and publisher are discussed. The views of university participants on the transition period and possibilities for the distant future can be found in paragraphs VI 3 and VI 4. Paragraph VI 5 expresses the opinion of Elsevier Science on the implications of the **TULIP** project for a scientific publisher.

VI 1. Changing environment as viewed by participating universities

The technological possibilities keep growing, the information flow keeps increasing, the budgets remain tight and users demand more. In a nutshell, this determines the environments of the universities today.

Electronic information raises opportunities. Quick searches come within easy reach, the wish of many users to access information at their desktop becomes possible:
'The electronic environment brings people together faster so there is much quicker sharing of info. On their desktops, wherever they are, they can have access to this (electronic information) without having to come to the library to do it. What that does is make their time in the library more efficient and more productive'.

The Web was mentioned many times as the major external influence these days:
'At the time TULIP started, Gopher was an innovative development. With the advent of Web capabilities, we discovered a much more viable medium for image delivery'.
Someone else formulated it this way:
'The rapid evolution of the World Wide Web as an information environment presented the developers with a better approach to TULIP than possible during its initial implementation'.
Although experts notice many shortcomings of the Web, the number of users familiar with it and using it keeps increasing, influencing strategies of all parties involved.

At the same time, preprint publications and more informal publications appear. According to some information specialists this will even increase:
'I don't believe the money is around to support first rate, fully refereed, fully edited publications, everything people want to publish. Since it is becoming easier to become your own publisher, we will see more informal stuff. If this happens, we will have to ignore or sort through a great wave of junk before we get at the quality information'.

Within the groups of users of the library, we see changing demands. The librarians' perception of the changes in demands of graduate students and faculty mirror the findings in chapter IV 4.
In general, the graduate students are the early adopters of the new possibilities. They are most computer literate, are the heavy users of **TULIP** and ask in surveys and focus groups for full texts of everything, with all possibilities available on their desktop at home. According to the participants, the group of faculty is mixed. Some prefer browsing in paper journals and wish for information to remain in paper format as long as possible, while some others see and use the advantages of electronic media for scientific information and are early adopters as well. Undergraduate students differ per discipline and per institute. They need peer reviewed scientific publications less than graduate students and faculty, in general have access to less hi-tech equipment but in some places are trained right from the start to use computers to access information. In the coming years, when undergraduates become graduate students and some graduate students become faculty, more demand for electronic information is expected.

How do participants in the **TULIP** project look at these changes? How do they see the future roles of the traditional participants in the process of scholarly information?

VI 2. Future roles of the players in the field as viewed by participating universities

VI 2.1 The library - as viewed by TULIP universities

With the exception of only a few, all see the need for libraries increasing instead of decreasing in this environment.
'If there are no libraries, users are going to be confronted by a lot of inconsistent interfaces, financial arrangements, delivery vehicles...and the library can at least potentially add value by making that coherent.'

One of the specialists formulated it this way:
'I don't think faculty can be responsible for the information needs of their whole community. They can be responsible for their personal information needs. It is just a matter of centralization and cost efficiency'.

Many information specialists said that the crucial role for libraries is as agents for the universities' information needs. Traditionally, someone said, libraries were seen as storehouses:
'What I see is moving from content to context. Right now we deliver page images, but, in the future, libraries will be delivering an array of information in a lot of different digital media, that provide an information environment for the user'.

In their role of agents of the universities' information needs, five aspects were named as being crucial: *finding*, *selecting* and *providing* the information needed by the community and *leading* people to the right information. Finally, *protection of holdings* is seen as an increasingly important responsibility of the (future) library. Someone said that electronic material is absolutely necessary for a library to lead people to information in the increasing information flow, making the task of providing information more difficult in an intermediary period, but also more efficient for the end users.

VI 2.2 The 'physical' library - as viewed by TULIP universities

Where will users access the information? If the infrastructure is available, the desktop access is expected by most information specialists to increase enormously. But while almost all are certain that the remote visits to the library will increase, the views on the physical visits differ per university. In contrast to what might be expected, a few universities noticed that the physical visitors to the library increase when online databases are available:
'The more you put online, the higher traffic volume you see physically of people coming into the libraries'.
Users are more aware what information is available and will use more. In some of those cases librarians visit the users instead of users visiting the libraries. Librarians even have offices within departments and work together with 'their clients'. The number of physical visitors depends, of course, on the services offered by the library. There were views of participants that go beyond the roles mentioned above and which will influence the number of visitors to the physical library. Several information specialists see a learning space as one of the roles of future library: either for all study purposes or for collaborative learning. In the first scenario, the library could be opened 24 hours a day and provide all facilities necessary for quiet studying. In the other scenario, the notion of the library as being a quiet place for independent study will disappear. Instead, libraries will be a place for collaborative, joint learning, where people can come together and find the tools they need. An individual should be able to learn wherever they are, using their laptop as their gateway. The library may then become a high-tech seminar room where students gather and work together as teams, which in many ways emulates society these days. As one of the few neutral grounds on campuses, libraries can become community centers, meeting places.

VI 2.3 The librarians - as viewed by participating universities

Instead of less staff, most universities think they will need more librarians in the future. They will be the ones leading users to all kinds of information on all kinds of media. To quote one of the university's reports:

'Many people will have to move to more service-oriented positions, and less 'behind the scenes' activities will have to be done'.

Whether the resources for this will be available is another question. The librarians who have to deal with this overflow of information, the technology that will keep changing and with that the demand from users, while the budgets are not expected to grow apace with these two, need to have a lot of qualities. In this changing environment flexibility is crucial. Technological knowledge and good computer literacy help a lot. In their job, they mainly expect more emphasis on decision making and more training. But giving training on electronic products also requires more technological knowledge. As someone said:

'Librarians will become more technicians, and technicians will become more of librarians. For sure, good cooperation and understanding is essential in this'.

VI 2.4 The publisher - as viewed by participating universities

Most participants in the **TULIP** project see a continued role for publishers: *'Publishers enhance the credibility of information'.* More informal and preprint publishing is expected, but in the overflow of information, publishers can help in selecting the quality information. *'I don't see the publisher's contribution to the scholarly process changing drastically. I think the way they do it is dramatically changing. But they remain the same in terms of managing a process and adding value to content.'*

There does not seem to be a consensus among participants about the role of publishers in the archiving of the electronic content. While some universities are quite willing to let the publisher be the ultimate archive for electronic material, others are much more apprehensive about leaving this role up to the publisher, either for reasons of continuous availability (publishers can go broke), or for reasons of continuous access:

'If online access to standard science journals is to become a reality, that material will probably need to be archived at one or more institutions of higher learning--rather than maintained by the publisher. There is too much distrust on the part of many institutions that--because the primary objective of the publisher is revenue-- access could be denied or impaired as soon as it no longer generates revenue'.

VI 3. The transition to digital libraries - as viewed by participating universities

More of the technical information specialists who worked on **TULIP** foresee a faster change than others, but one of the common views which all **TULIP** participants share is that the transition to a digital library will be slower than they had expected before starting the project. The majority of the universities don't think that everything will be electronically available: not all information is suitable for it. And older information isn't expected to be completely available in electronic format. One university says that it seems certain that within two decades electronic networked access to scholarly information will be the norm. Estimates of what share of the journals would be provided by their institution electronically ten years from now ranged from 10% to almost 100%. Estimating is hard since many issues are still unsolved at this moment. The issue most often mentioned is the question what users want and would use: *'It all depends on how individuals value information'.* Users are seen as the driving force behind much of what libraries are going to do and they will often be one step ahead. The speed of contents which are made available electronically, the development of infrastructure, how access will be organized in the future with changing technologies, user authentication and identification on a university wide scope, copyrights and of course resources, are some of the other questions which need to be answered. Technologically, everyone wishes for one standard interface, on which all electronic information can be accessed. Unfortunately, no one expects this to happen in the near future. So we will have to deal with different software, different interfaces and different media. Most see this as something they just have to cope with in a transition period. Storage (see paragraph V 2.1.2) and archiving (VI 2.4) are also open issues.

VI 4.   Views on the library of the remote future

While solving the open issues will take more time than expected, there might come a day when most issues are solved and digital libraries are a standard. At that point, the way (scientific) literature is written might change, and the way people access/read/use information might be different as well. While reading an article from the screen is not practical at this moment, improvements in technology will change this.
Certainly, more people will be comfortable with electronic information. The infrastructure is expected to become much 'deeper and thicker' in the future: greater bandwidth, better delivery mechanisms, more efficient protocols. Then we can see information really beginning to flow. Eventually, everyone will be able to access the information from outside the physical library.
At the library itself, some expect a 'multimedia explosion', with the possibility of hearing and seeing an author giving a presentation from a computer, enhanced with interactive features.

VI 5.   Implications of the TULIP project for Elsevier Science

The **TULIP** project has allowed Elsevier Science to make better decisions on how to proceed with the conversion of its physical production process to produce digital output, on how to store and distribute electronic material, how to support its customers, how to work with end users, etc. Many of the lessons learned have already been translated into actions.

Looking towards the future, one of the most challenging aspects of publishing today comes in trying to judge the speed of change from the libraries' perspective as a purchaser, and the scholar as information consumer. Publishers must try to estimate how quickly a transition from paper to electronic (only) will occur.

TULIP has generated some important insights concerning this question:

● At the moment, managing large digital collections locally is harder and more expensive than managing a comparable print collection.

● Not everyone is ready for digital collections, nor will they be soon. Saying it is harder and more expensive, is to say that the leading edge market is still small. Whether one talks of large local stores of data or regional networked collections, or single remote hosts, the number of academic libraries really ready to support digital collections is still small.

● Users will only move to electronic publications when they find the content they need in sufficient quantity. Having journals in electronic form and bringing them to the desktop are necessary, but not sufficient, conditions for the scholarly user. You must deliver a certain 'critical mass' of needed information to warrant learning a new system or accessing information in a different way. Publishers have speculated about critical mass questions for years, but now are learning from doing. In **TULIP** some users loved the local system but did not find enough of 'their' journals to warrant regular use. Users don't have the time or inclination to be inefficient on a long-term basis. Novelty will only go so far. Then, organized collections (libraries) will be required to bring critical mass and retrieval across more databases.

● Expanding electronic publishing (internationally) offers very different challenges from paper. Elsevier Science has been delivering a uniform product which required little local training or support all over the world. With electronics, this is not the same. As we found out in **TULIP**, the process is more complicated and requires a different involvement from the publisher's side. The delivery of, and use of, the system – even if Web based – means still more publisher involvement with the library and user.

The universities and Elsevier Science have not resolved one critical issue, that of how to make the transition work economically. For Elsevier Science as a publisher the question is how to price your paper and electronic publications so that you have no vested interest in the media chosen. The goal - ideal - would be for the price to be media-neutral, to let purchasing decisions be value-based from the buyers' perspective. This, however, is *much* easier said than done.

TULIP

Appendix I

Carnegie Mellon University

Carnegie Mellon University Libraries
TULIP Final Report

Denise A. Troll
Head of Research and Development, Library Information Technology

Charles B. Lowry
University Librarian

Barbara G. Richards
Associate University Librarian

Brent R. Frye
Systems Manager, Library Information Technology

Carnegie Mellon University
© 1995

Table of Contents

PART I: USE AND CONCLUSIONS

PART II: TECHNICAL IMPLEMENTATION

List of Figures

List of Tables

PART I: USE AND CONCLUSIONS

PART II: TECHNICAL IMPLEMENTATION

PART I

USE & CONCLUSIONS

- UNIVERSITY PROFILE

- TULIP PROMOTION AND TRAINING

- TULIP USER BEHAVIOR

- TULIP ORGANIZATION AND ECONOMICS

- TULIP IMPLICATIONS FOR THE FUTURE

1. University Profile

1.1. Organization of Carnegie Mellon University

Carnegie Mellon was founded at the turn of the century, by industrialist and philanthropist Andrew Carnegie, to train young people for skilled positions in Pittsburgh's industries. The Carnegie Technical Schools, as the university was originally known, quickly evolved into an engineering college.

During the 1930s and early 1940s, the Carnegie Plan was developed -- a program that had an important influence on higher education in the United States. It emphasized curricula designed to prepare graduates to meet the technical, economic and social responsibilities they would encounter in their professional careers, to develop an appreciation of the cultural aspects of life, and to bring about a realization of the relationship between the individual and society. In 1967, the university (then known as the Carnegie Institute of Technology) merged with the Mellon Institute, established in 1913 to conduct general research in the sciences and sponsored research for industry. Subsequently, Carnegie Mellon began a new phase in its history rapidly emerging as a research institution.

Carnegie Mellon University has built upon each of these historic advantages and is widely recognized for the excellence of its people and programs. As the list of Values and Traditions appended to Carnegie Mellon's current Mission Statement declares, "We build on our heritage of the Carnegie Plan to become a leading institution that combines first-rate research with outstanding undergraduate education through our focus on learning and problem-solving."

The university has seven teaching colleges or schools: the Carnegie Institute of Technology (engineering), the College of Fine Arts, the College of Humanities and Social Sciences, the Mellon College of Science, the Graduate School of Industrial Administration, the H. John Heinz III School of Public Policy and Management, and the School of Computer Science. All but the Heinz School offer undergraduate programs. In addition, Carnegie Mellon has thrived on interdisciplinary research and no less than 50 centers are chartered on campus as the institutional expression of this work. Carnegie Mellon is the only university with two National Science Foundation centers -- the Pittsburgh Supercomputing Center and the Data Storage Systems Center. The annual budget of the university is approximately $360,000,000 including funded research.

1.2. Organization of the University Libraries

The University Librarian is responsible for library operations at Carnegie Mellon and reports to the Provost. The staff includes 36 professionals and 50 staff. Like most academic libraries, it supports a significant workforce of students, around 45 FTE in all. The Libraries are a member of OCLC, the Center for Research Libraries, and cooperate closely with the University of Pittsburgh and the Carnegie Library of Pittsburgh in the Oakland Library Consortium. The Libraries' collections include more than 852,000 volumes; over 900,000 microforms and graphics; and 3,850 periodical subscriptions housed in three locations: Hunt Library (humanities, fine arts, social sciences and business), the Engineering & Science Library (engineering, mathematics, physics, computer science and robotics), and the Mellon Institute Library (chemistry and biology). Facilities include group study areas, reserve areas, music listening carrels, study carrels, and quiet study areas.

Several specialized collections distinguish the University Libraries. At Hunt, the Fine and Rare Book Rooms offer unique materials in literature, the arts, the history of science, and other subjects. The Engineering and Science Library maintains a notable collection of technical reports in computer science. The University Archives trace the history of the university from its beginning as Carnegie Tech to the present, and the Robotics and Artificial Intelligence Archives are of increasing importance in the study of computer science as a discipline. In addition the, University Archives includes political and policy collections like the Senator H. John Heinz III collection. The Architecture Archives document the history of architecture in Western Pennsylvania.

1.3. Organization of Information Technology Services

The Library Information Technology (LIT) department is responsible for day-to-day operations (e.g., installation and maintenance of system hardware and software) as well as research and development (e.g., system programming, cooperative work with partners, user testing). The libraries continually apply new technologies to improve services. LIT is divided into two departments: Operations, which is staffed by 8 FTE, and Research and Development (R&D), which is staffed by five FTE. The Head of R&D is responsible to the Head of LIT who reports to the University Librarian. In addition to TULIP, LIT is currently supporting several major technology R&D projects valued at around $2,000,000.

1.4. User Demographics

Carnegie Mellon is a highly selective small, private, coeducational university with approximately 4300 undergraduate students, 2400 graduate students, and over 550 regular faculty. The university population represents every region of the United States and over ninety foreign countries.

2. TULIP Promotion and Training

2.1. Description of Promotional Activities

The responsibility for administering the steering activities for the TULIP project changed hands several times during the four years of the project. The University Libraries began discussions with Elsevier to participate in the TULIP project in 1991. TULIP coordinating work moved to Computing Services in the Summer 1992 and returned to the libraries in the Fall 1993. This unsettled responsibility slowed the implementation of TULIP access on the Carnegie Mellon campus. By the end of 1993, the University Libraries had assembled the TULIP project team:

- Project Leader - Barbara G. Richards, Associate University Librarian (1993-1995).

- Project Manager - Denise A. Troll, Head of Research and Development, Library Information Technology (1993-1995).

- System Managers - Ryan Troll (1994), Joe Imbimbo, Stephen Hathorne and Brent Frye (1995), Library Information Technology.

- Documentation, Training, and Publicity - David Peck, Reference Librarian and liaison to the Materials Science and Engineering (MSE) Department, and Terry Wittig, Reference Librarian and liaison to the Physics, Mathematics, and Engineering and Public Policy (EPP) Departments (1993-1995).

- MSE Project Consultants - Prashant Kumta, Assistant Professor, and F. Haiskell Rogan, Research Associate (1993-1995).

- Bibliographic Consultant - Alice Bright, Serials Librarian (1993-1995).

- Technical Consultant - Art Wetzel, Research Programmer for Computing Services (1993-1994).

Promotional activities were scheduled to coincide with the release of the TULIP databases to the campus community. The TULIP bibliographic database was released to Carnegie Mellon students, faculty and staff in April 1994 and the image collection in June 1994. Access was provided through the Library Information System (LIS). In June 1995, TULIP was released on the World Wide Web (WWW), with access provided through WWW LIS. The releases were promoted on several electronic bulletin boards, including official.cmu-news, official.university-libraries and org.library. Announcements were also made to the Materials Science and Engineering Department bboard and in the Physics, Math and EPP departments. All engineering and science personnel were encourage to look at the TULIP databases as an example of electronic full text. A TULIP announcement also appeared in the Message of the Day (MOTD) service in LIS and in articles in campus newspapers and newsletters, including articles in the Computing Services' newsletter, *Cursor* (April, 1995), and in the *Oakland Library Consortium Newsletter*. The Libraries also announced the release of TULIP on their WWW page.

In addition, newsletters supplied by Elsevier were sent to members of the Materials Science and Engineering Department. When the Elsevier WWW site became available, it was publicized to the campus community. Elsevier also supplied large TULIP posters, which were displayed in various locations in the libraries on campus and in the Materials Science and Engineering Department, and small posters, which were sent to all Materials Science and Engineering Department faculty and students and to faculty in other relevant science and engineering departments -- with an invitation to see and hear about TULIP on Monday, March 6, 1995. About forty people attended this event, which included an introductory talk by Charles Lowry, a demo of the TULIP databases by Denise Troll, and a question/answer period in which several TULIP steering members participated. This was followed by an informal discussion and buffet lunch. This event was planned to be immediately prior to the release of TULIP to the campus community. Covers from the TULIP journals were displayed in the Engineering and Science Library (E&S) exhibit case during the month of March 1995. The large TULIP banner provided by Elsevier was used at the TULIP presentation in March and later at E&S to announce the release of the TULIP image collection.

Carnegie Mellon has talked and written about the TULIP project in a number of places for both on campus and off campus audiences. Since the TULIP database is the only image database currently available in the LIS, it is used extensively for demonstrations for campus students, faculty and staff as well as visitors. For a complete list of publications and presentations see the bibliography at the end of this report.

2.2. Description of Training Activities

At the outset TULIP was designed to use the same software and interfaces as the LIS system. LIS use has been taught in Computer Skills Workshop to all incoming freshmen for at least the last four years. Having been introduced in 1991, most campus users are familiar with its use. Users can get help from any reference librarian in a variety of ways: in the library at point of use, by email or on request in a classroom setting.

Special emphasis was given to TULIP by the liaison librarians at the E&S Library for relevant academic departments. The use of TULIP is taught in a library instruction session to a Materials Science department sophomore/junior class which has a required research paper. TULIP is talked about and demonstrated during orientation tours of the library, in particular to graduate students in MSE, Physics and Math at the beginning of the term. Much training is done at point of use when there is a specific need. If TULIP is appropriate, training is done at the E&S reference desk. TULIP materials were available at all the Fall 1995 orientation sessions for new faculty, graduate students and undergraduates.

Online and printed documentation were provided for TULIP. Online help was prepared for the Materials Science (TULIP) bibliographic database and for the Mercury prototype image user interface. In addition, several printed LIS handouts were revised to include TULIP information and instructions.

2.3. Effects of Promotion and Training

TULIP promotion and training seems to have stimulated use based on the logging statistics and feedback to librarians from users. As a result of the classroom instruction for undergraduates in the MSE research methods course, the database was used for their research papers. Requests for one-on-one help at the E&S reference desk are accompanied by TULIP information whenever appropriate. Also much positive response from researchers and graduate students was reported by E&S reference librarians. Graduate students especially were enthusiastic about this database and there were requests to the reference librarians for more material to be added to this database and for more full-text databases in general. An effect of promoting TULIP to departments other than Materials science has been to familiarize many campus user with the concept of full text. One frequently heard comment is the need to have more electronic journals available both from Elsevier and other publishers.

2.4. Conclusions and Recommendations

Promotion and training is a time consuming effort, but is a very important component in the attempt to modify users behavior in regard to journal use. However, the amount of promotion and training that can realistically be done needs to be balanced with the degree of stability and long term availability of the program being promoted. The TULIP project had many technological difficulties to overcome before the implementation was stable enough to begin PR activities. TULIP clearly demonstrated that student and faculty use of electronic journals for actual study and research requires a behavioral change. There is some evidence that this is beginning to happen, but it will not happen until such time as electronic texts are delivered in a way that fits the use that the individual has for the information. Promotion should be continued, but will only be useful if the product is one that meets users needs and the quality is such that they will continue to use the product. Training should be incorporated into the regular ongoing library instruction teaching that is already occurring.

Promotion and training for TULIP allowed the E&S Library staff to gather feedback on the TULIP project and electronic text. Based on conversations with Materials Science and Engineering faculty and students, electronic journal use is clearly acceptable, but our implementation needs improvements in functionality. The following have been mentioned as areas that need to be improved in order for users to change their use of the journal literature:

1. **Platform independence.** MSE users were very glad when TULIP journals appeared in a WWW format so that they could use the Macs and PCs on their desks instead of having to use a UNIX machine in the lab or in the library.

2. **Currency of data.** Users expect the electronic data to be at least as current as the printed journal; many expect that electronic texts will be MORE current than paper. This has implications for both the data provider and the libraries' processing.

3. **Printing.** There was general dissatisfaction with the process of submitting email requests to print TULIP images and to restrict printing to library printers. Most users did not bother to request prints because they knew that the journals were available in the library.

4. **Interface design and functionality.** Print is a very convenient, effective distribution method for journal literature and it is easy to use. Electronic texts need to be easy to use as well. Users would like to be able to highlight relevant passages, compare texts side by side on the screen, and have less labor involved with getting the texts. They requested better

indexing for chemical formulas, symbols, and non-roman alphabet characters, and to have improved screen resolution for better viewing of photographs.

The handling of electronic journals must be integrated into the work of the libraries so that is not just an experiment. Library staff will continue to promote and train on a stable, reliable product. The idea of a scholar's workstation is still very appealing to many faculty and students, but much work needs to be done to make electronic texts a viable alternative to print. User comments to reference librarians indicate that many users like the idea of working on a scholar's workstation, which they assumes delivers full-text to their desktop, where they can then print or download as they wish. At the same time, few people actually want to read articles on the screen. Many people still think that the easiest thing to do is to go to the library and read the journal. As long using an online journal is more difficult than going to the library, the library with the printed journal will remain the preferred option.

In spite of some current drawbacks, the consensus among users is that Carnegie Mellon should continue to work with electronic text in projects like TULIP. The general concept is worth pursuing even though the implementation is not yet optimal. As the use of computing for teaching increases on campus, the ability to find and use electronic texts will become more important. A survey of users regarding the current and future use of electronic journals should be undertaken to help determine the next steps in providing a wider range of electronic journals to campus.

3. User Behavior

The University Libraries conducted a survey in 1994 to assess the demographics, computer experience, and journal usage of potential TULIP users. The survey was designed by Elsevier in collaboration with the participating TULIP sites. The data was analyzed by Elsevier. The sections below describe human factors research designed and conducted by the University Libraries. The purpose of this research was to assess user needs and expectations regarding the design and functionality of electronic full-text journal information.

3.1. Research Studies

3.1.1. Printed Journals

To assess use of current periodicals, the University Libraries keep re-shelving and circulation statistics for unbound journals. The statistics indicate only that an issue of a journal title was reshelved, not what volume or issue was re-shelved. This statistics for reshelving current TULIP journals are shown in Part I, Section 3.2.1 of this report.

3.1.2. Electronic Journals

The University Libraries conducted three human factors studies related to TULIP:

- **April 1992 - User protocols of the first prototype image client.** Subjects in the protocols were graduate students in the School of Computer Science, and professional librarians. Images used in the study were Elsevier and IEEE computer science journals scanned by the University Libraries staff and linked to the INSPEC database.

- **March 1994 - User protocols of the third prototype image client.** Subjects in the protocols were graduate and undergraduate students in the School of Computer Science, and professional librarians. By design, this study closely resembled the April 1992 study so that the results of the two studies could be compared to determine whether significant improvements had been made. Because the TULIP data was still being loaded, this study was also conducted with Elsevier and IEEE computer science journal images linked to the INSPEC database.

- **July 1994 - Structured interviews about natural language retrieval.** The University Libraries conducted structured interviews to determine user needs and expectations regarding the design and functionality of a user interface for natural-language querying of full text ASCII (e.g., the TULIP raw data), and the retrieval and navigation of image documents. The subjects were faculty from different academic departments, librarians, and archivists. The interview questions focused on software developed by Claritech Corporation and demonstrated at the interview.

The results of these studies are summarized in Part I, Section 3.2.2 of this report.

3.2. Research Results

3.2.1. Printed Journal Usage Statistics

The Engineering and Science Library and Mellon Institute Library have kept re-shelving statistics on current (unbound) periodicals from January / February 1994 to the present. The data on reshelving current TULIP journals (to late November 1995) is shown in Table 1. These numbers reflect a conservative assessment of use because many people re-shelve the journals themselves and because the data do not reflect use of the boud journal backruns. According to the statistics, the most popular (print) TULIP journal is the Journal of Magnetism and Magnetic Materials; the least popular journal is Progress in Materials Science.

Table 1: Statistics on re-shelving unbound printed TULIP journals from January / February 1994 to late November 1995.

JOURNAL TITLE	NO.	JOURNAL TITLE	NO.
J. of Magnetism & Mag. Materials	119	Materials Science & Engineering A	10
Surface Science (MI)	86	Materials Science & Engineering R	10
Journal of Crystal Growth	55	Materials Letters	9
Thin Solid Films	41	Sensors and Actuators B	9
Solid State Communications	36	International Journal of Plasticity	7
Journal of Alloys & Compounds	35	Mechanics of Materials	7
Synthetic Metals	23	Composites Science and Technology	6
Materials Science & Engineering B	22	Chemical Engineering & Processing	4
Wear	22	J. of Electron Spect. & Related Phen.	3
Sensors & Actuators A	20	J. of Physics & Chemistry of Solids	3
Applied Catalysis A	19	Materials Characterization	3
Physica C	16	Chemical Eng. J. & Biochem. Eng. J.	2
Surface & Coatings Technology	16	Nuclear Instruments & Methods B	1
European Polymer Journal	13	Progress in Materials Science	0
Materials Research Bulletin	11		
SUBTOTAL	**534**	**SUBTOTAL**	**74**
		TOTAL	**608**

3.2.2. Electronic Journal Usability Studies

3.2.2.1. Design and Functionality of Image Retrieval

User protocols of the Mercury prototype image software conducted in April 1992 and March 1994 identified the following features and functionality as basic requirements for the desktop delivery and handling of full-text journals stored in image format. Their requirements indicate the print bias of the current academic library user:

- **Integrity of Documents.** Users expect the software's definition of a document and its model of a document collection to match their definition and model — which is based on print technology. For example, in a journal collection, the users' definition of a "document" is a journal issue. According to their model, a journal title is comprised of a collection of volumes, which are collections of published documents or issues, which are collections of articles and sundry other items. This print bias may or may not match the reality of electronic journals, but nonetheless has serious implications for interface design. Users expect the electronic environment to be at least as good as the print environment, and many need additional functionality as an incentive to change their environment and behavior.

- **Navigation of Documents.** Users expect to navigate pages, articles and issues for the same journal title in the same page display window, without having to resort to an hierarchical browser. Some users would like to navigate volumes (the entire holdings of a journal title) without resorting to a browser. It is acceptable to use a browser to select another journal title. Within the document display window, users expect to navigate Next Page, Previous Page, First Page, Last Page, Go to Page... (where they specify a printed page number), Next Article, Previous Article, Next Issue, Previous Issue. Users expect navigational features to be provided using standard menus, buttons, and scroll bars.

- **Tables of Contents.** Users expect to see the table of contents -- complete with author, title and page-range information -- when they select a journal issue in the hierarchical browser, not a list of page numbers or article titles. Users need an easy way to simultaneously display (or toggle between the display of) the table of contents for the selected issue and an article in that issue.

- **Images.** Users expect high quality images, no tilted pages, no distracting dots or jagged edges. They expect multiple, incremental levels of enlarging and reducing page size.

- **List Order.** Users expect dated information (e.g., lists of journal volumes and issues) to appear in the hierarchical browser in reverse chronological order, with the most recent information at the top of the list. They expect a list of article titles (a surrogate table of contents) to appear in the order in which the titles appear in the issue.

- **Context.** Users need a visual representation of their context displayed at all times or (at least) on demand because they frequently lose track of where they are on the page, in the document, or in the hierarchical document collection browser.

- **Vocabulary.** Users expect a standard or carefully designed and consistently used vocabulary.

- **Keyboard Use.** Users expect frequently used features to be provided with standard or carefully designed keyboard accelerators or mnemonics indicated in the user interface.

- **Online Help.** Users need easy-to-use online help with well-written help text, free of technical jargon, provided in an independent help window.

In addition to these basic requirements, the subjects in the user protocols suggested the following enhancements for journal (image) delivery and navigation:

- Provide an interactive table of contents, where they need only click on an entry to retrieve the first page of the article.[1]

- Enable users to navigate to the next and previous pages that contain figures or tables.

- Enable users to print entire documents, specified pages or page ranges.

- Enable users to view multiple pages of the same document at once.

- Enable users to view pages from multiple documents at once.

- Enable users to mark titles and insert bookmarks in databases, journal issues and articles. Enable the marks and bookmarks to persist across sessions.

- Enable users to annotate databases, journal issues and articles and link their annotations to specific pages or paragraphs in a document. Enable the annotations to persist across sessions. Enable users to set access control privileges on the annotations so that, for example, faculty could annotate articles and their students could read their annotations.

3.2.2.2. Design and Functionality of Natural Language Retrieval

In July 1994, the University Libraries conducted structured interviews to determine which features in the natural language retrieval software developed by Claritech Corporation should be integrated into LIS to facilitate retrieval of full text documents like the TULIP journals. The research was conducted using Claritech's prototype Motif client and natural language retrieval engine. One of the full-text databases, the Heinz Archives, was linked to document page images for display purposes. Research subjects met for an hour in groups of one or two with the Head of Research and Development for Library Automation, who demonstrated and described the software, and then asked the subjects a series of questions. The discussion was audio taped for later analysis.

Much of the discussion in the interviews focused on the design of the display users see immediately following a search. The demonstration compared the Claritech list of items retrieved with the LIS list of items retrieved. Both lists provide one line to describe each item. Since the volume of information that can be included on a line is limited, user input on the design of this display is critical. Table 2 shows how the research subjects prioritized the items in the Claritech and LIS lists. The Claritech and LIS lists are shown in Figures 1 and 2.

Table 2: The preferred design of the list of items retrieved.

DESIGN OF LIST OF ITEMS RETRIEVED	LIST	% USERS
Show whether the item has been seen or not	Claritech	88%
Show the relevance ranking of the items retrieved	Claritech	82%
Show the titles of the items retrieved	LIS, Claritech	82%
Show the date of publication of the items retrieved	LIS	82%
Show whether an item has been marked to keep [2]	Claritech	71%
Show whether an item has been marked to discard	Claritech	65%
Show the author's name for each publication (if available)	LIS	59%
Show the source of each publication	LIS	41%
Show the total number of items retrieved	LIS	41%
Show the database name [3]	Claritech	29%
Show the call number (if applicable)	LIS	24%
Show the change in ranking after refining a query	Claritech	6%
Show the score of the items retrieved	Claritech	0%

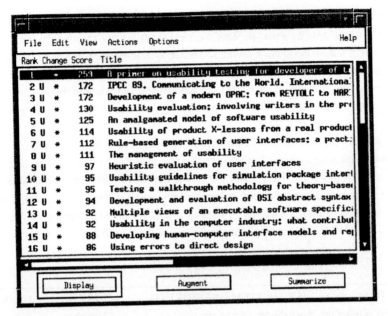

Figure 1: The display of the list of items retrieved in the Claritech prototype.

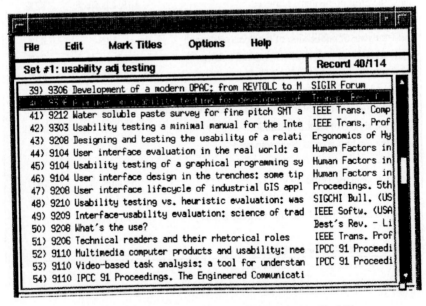

Figure 2: The display of the list of items retrieved in LIS.

Table 3 shows the percentage of subjects who responded positively to features provided by the Claritech prototype. Over 50% of the subjects stated that the the following features would be helpful: saving queries, positively weighting search terms, displaying a list of result sets, highlighting query terms in retrieved records, and generating hypertext links across databases "on the fly." Approximately 41% of the subjects thought that submitting all or part of a retrieved item as a new query would be helpful and that applying a negative weight to a term was an acceptable way to do a Boolean "not" operation. When asked what thy wanted to see when they retrieved a document, 47% of the subjects responded that they wanted to see the first page of the document.

Table 3: The design and functionality of a natural language retrieval interface.

QUERIES	% USERS
Save queries	65%
Submit all or part of retrieved item as a new query	41%
Delete queries	24%
TERMS	
Positively weight search terms	59%
Negatively weight search terms	41%
DISPLAYS	
Display a list of result sets and their accompanying queries	65%
Highlight noun phrases containing query terms in the retrieved records	65%
Display first page of document upon retrieval	47%
Highlight only query terms (not noun phrases) in retrieved records	24%
Display first occurrence of query term upon retrieval	12%
Display ranked list of terms in retrieved document	0%
PREFERENCES	
Specify maximum number of items to retrieve	29%
Specify maximum number of items to consider	6%
OTHER	
Generate hypertext links across databases	53%
Suggest query terms based on retrieved items	35%
Suggest query terms based on separate database	24%

Some of the Claritech prototype features may have received low scores because users are unfamiliar with natural language retrieval. In this case the user's bias is not print technology, but keyword-Boolean technology. Developers must carefully balance the trade-offs between matching the user's cognitive model of information seeking, and exploiting the possibilities that new technologies afford. Considerable research is required to achieve the appropriate balance.

3.3. Usage Research and Privacy Policies

3.3.1. Human Factors Research

The University Libraries' human factors research complies with the University's policy regarding the use of human subjects. The studies do not physically or psychologically put the subjects at risk, so no release forms are required. The subjects' identities are kept confidential in all reports.

3.3.2. Transaction Logging and Analysis

The University Libraries' usage monitoring complies, at least in spirit, with the University's policy regarding user privacy. It is unclear whether logging the identity of the user (e.g., the encrypted user ID) in the same transaction with the identity of the document (e.g., the TULIP document ID) protects the user's privacy, even though usage reports submitted to Elsevier do not contain the user's identity. Because of this lack of clarity, the University Libraries do not log document IDs for any project other than TULIP. Special code was developed so that usage monitoring can be project or database specific.

In addition to concerns about user privacy, the University Libraries are also concerned about the security of the transaction logs in the networked campus computing environment. The issue here is not what the libraries are logging, but what computer "hackers" can do if they breach the security devices surrounding the logs. Because of the concerns about user privacy, Charles Lowry (University Librarian) and Denise Troll (Head of Research and Development) met with the Faculty Senate in February 1995 to discuss LIS usage monitoring and seek their advice and consent. As a result of this meeting, a permanent statement was added to the LIS Message of the Day (MOTD) feature to alert users to the fact that LIS monitors what they do. Future plans include meeting with specialists in security, encryption, privacy and statistics to insure that LIS procedures are as stringent as possible, and exploring the provision of a "fire wall" between the transaction logs and the affiliation table used for post-processing the logs. Storing the transaction logs on a separate machine from the affiliation table would add an additional layer of security. A hacker would have to breach both machines to invade the user's privacy. Further details about usage monitoring are provided in Part II, Section 2.1.7.

3.4.   TULIP Usage

The TULIP bibliographic data was released in April 1994. The TULIP images were released in June 1994. Due to other projects and changes in personnel, the TULIP data was not updated again until April 1995. Another update is scheduled for the end of December 1995. Usage of the TULIP database and images has been light, in part because of the subject content (see Part I, Section 5.3) and in part because the data is old, e.g., no 1995 data has been released.

Figure 3 shows the number of TULIP searches submitted and the number of TULIP bibliographic records displayed from April 1994 through November 1995. Users submitted approximately twice as many TULIP searches and displayed twice as many TULIP bibliographic records in 1994 as they did in 1995. However, they retrieved ("hit") over twice as many bibliographic records in 1995 as they did in 1994; see Figure 4. Similarly, they displayed over twice as many page images in 1995 as they did in 1994; see Figure 5. To a large extent, the excess usage in 1994 is a result of the "novelty" effect of the release of this new service; peak usage in 1995 reflects testing prior to release of the updated database and image collecion.

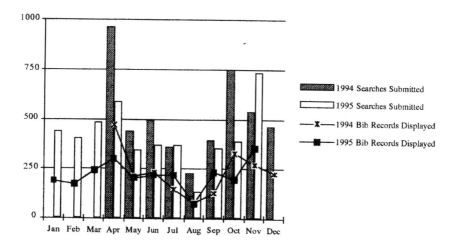

Figure 3: The number of TULIP searches submitted and bibliographic records displayed.

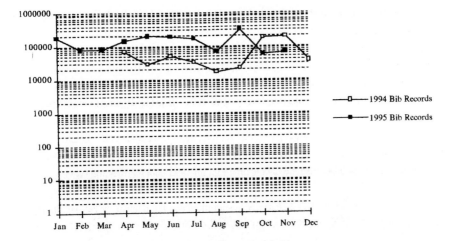

Figure 4: The number of TULIP bibliographic records retrieved.

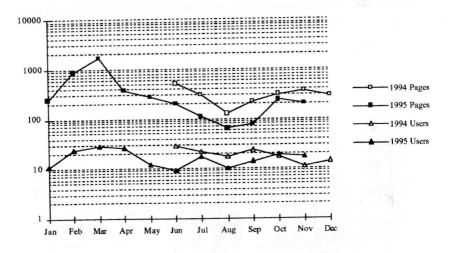

Figure 5: The number of TULIP page images displayed
and the number of unique users of those images.

LIS did not log save, mail and print transactions for bibliographic information until January 1995; see Figure 6. Of the total transactions, 14% were save, 11% were mail, and 75% were print transactions. LIS enables users to save, mail and print full bibliographic records, the titles or citations of marked records, titles or citations of all records retrieved, single citations and index terms. Figure 7 shows the distribution of the information that users saved, mailed, and printed. (See Part II, Sections 1.5.3.1 and 2.1.1.1 for details about the implementation of TULIP printing.)

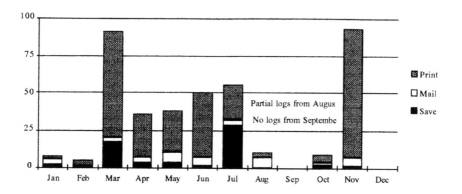

Figure 6: The number of TULIP save, mail and print transactions for bibliographic information in 1995.

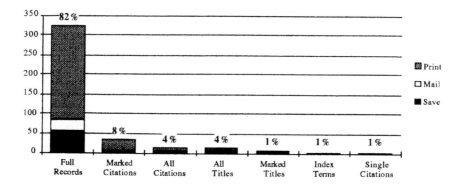

Figure 7: The distribution of TULIP save, mail and print transactions for bibliographic information in 1995.

3.5. Implications and Recommendations

The anecdotal evidence and usage data provided in Part I, Sections 2.4 and 3.4 of this report suggest that a better user interface is required for retrieving, navigating and printing full text journal articles -- an interface available on all hardware platforms, that the subject matter be expanded to include other academic disciplines, and that routine maintenance be provided for monthly updates of the bibliographic database and image collection.

4. Evaluation of Organizational and Economic Issues

Too often, work on digital libraries, not to mention much theoretical discussion, proceeds without a thorough grounding in the realities of cost. There are certain assumptions which precede this state of affairs, among them the notion that digital libraries somehow will be cheaper than print libraries, perhaps even free. One suspects that this arises from the misplaced hope that digital libraries will liberate us from the difficult cost dynamics of print libraries. There is also a presumption that electronic access will mean added value to library patrons, but it begs the question if the access is at a cost patrons are unwilling to pay. Recently, a neuroscientist stated in a library journal "I want all these [library] services to be affordable, and by 'affordable' I mean *free*".[4] So, exploring the underlying economics of the development of digital libraries is a critical feature of the work of TULIP.

In the first place, it seems clear that libraries will not have large amounts of new funding with which to purchase electronic materials, although it is not a zero-sum game. It follows that publishers may not expect to have large sources of new profits from the sales of electronic products that represent the scholarly information published today in books and journals. The economics of scholarly book and journal publishing, in short, how to make a profit from them, are well understood.[5] The profit largely arises from transactions with libraries in the form of subscriptions and book orders, not from sales to end users. The magnitude of the undertaking before publishers in the paradigm shift to digital libraries is no less daunting than that facing libraries. A few publishing statistics illustrate the point graphically.

Journals have been the format which has received most attention from publishers in attempts to begin providing refereed scholarly information in electronic form. A few publishers have begun converting existing print files into electronic formats using principally scanning or re-keying to ASCII, the former providing access to the images but no indexable text, and the latter providing indexable text but no access to the graphical materials. In addition to Elsevier's TULIP project, other projects have been undertaken by the few publishers or vendors who are working closely with publishers. These include University Microfilms Inc., IEEE's journal project, Institute for Scientific Information's recently announced biomedical journal project, and Information Access Corporation's ongoing ASCII project for full text. Among various full text efforts, there is a fair amount of duplication of conversion for key titles among "secondary publishers" like UMI and IAC, and a reasonable estimate is that the total number of titles available in electronic form is not more than 2,500. The 1994-95 edition of *Ulrich's International Periodical Directory* indicates that there are "more than 147,000 serials published throughout the world...."[6] Over 11,500 new titles were added during this period, and 9,532 ceased publication. The striking statistic is that less than 2% of the serials published world-wide are currently available in electronic format. These few are largely being digitized by the retrograde process of scanning or re-keying from the print.

Thus, serial publishers are faced with the large and complex task of moving to electronic publication, which means completely reorganizing their technology and workflow process to take advantage of electronic publishing. To make things more difficult, they will for some time have to produce both electronic and print formats, because they are publishing in an international market, which will require multiple formats. They will not be able to move away from print publication any faster than subscribers worldwide can build the infrastructure to receive electronic publication.

This does not even take into consideration the serious obstacles to converting books into electronic formats. It seems unlikely that books will be adapted to the needs of the digital library as quickly or easily as journals may be. The nature of monograph publication and use militates against this prospect. So do the numbers. "American book title output reached a peak in 1987, with a grand total of 52,027; three successive years of falling figures bottomed out in 1990, when the total output stood at only 46,743."[7] Data from the Bowker Annual indicates that 49,000 new titles were published for 1993. If one uses scholarly books as the primary target for digital publication, then the total for the same period (1993-1994) as reported by Blackwell North America is a smaller 33,630 titles.[8] With the exception of CD ROM formats for reference materials, almost nothing has been done to test electronic media for the purposes of publishing scholarly monographic materials. Thus far the work on the "electronic book" -- e.g., Bellcore's "Super Book", Sony's "DataDiscman", and Megaword's "Smart Book Text Pact" -- has not transformed book publishing. Even if a breakthrough technology appeared tomorrow, diffusion and general adoption would take ten years or more if the cycles for TVs and VCRs are any guide.

Three years into the TULIP project, it is possible to begin making estimates of the infrastructure costs to the library for managing print versus electronic text. In addition to TULIP, Carnegie

Mellon also has another online journal project -- "The CMU/UMI Virtual Library Project." This project exploits new technology implementation such as jukeboxes and a cache manager. Some comparison of both TULIP and UMI projects is helpful here to broaden understanding of the economic issues, but extrapolation is necessary in order to make legitimate comparisons of costs. Using the TULIP project as a basis, Carnegie Mellon subscribes to 29 of the 43 journals in materials science which are part of the project and, for these titles 85 volumes a year are bound.

Tables 4-6 illustrate the comparative costs for print, magnetic, and CD jukebox storage of journals. The key costs for print storage (see Table 4) are binding and the capital for library buildings and shelving. The cost for storing the print volumes from these 29 titles is $914 and the net cost for the 3.5 years is $3,199. The magnetic storage costs (see Table 5) includes a DEC Alpha 200 configured with five 9.1 GB Seagate disk drives, a 45.5 GB capacity. Only 30.1 GB is actually required to hold the 29 journal titles in compressed Group Fax IV TIFF images that conform to the 29 titles in the project for 3.5 years. The prorated cost for server and magnetic storage of TULIP journals is $16,891. Table 6 illustrates jukebox storage. The current cost for a 240-slot CD jukebox of the type used with UMI's PowerPages is $15,500. Each CD holds approximately 640 MB, and the entire jukebox full is 154 GB. At these capacities, the jukebox storage would cost $3,928 to store the equivalent information from the TULIP project. Thus, the CD format using jukeboxes presents a much more cost efficient medium for local storage than does the magnetic, but it is still 23% more expensive than print. It is striking that the annual maintenance for the floor space required for all three storage methods is relatively close–$19.37 for print, and $24 for either magnetic or jukebox storage (see Table 7).

Table 4: Print storage costs.

ELEMENT	EXPLANATION	TULIP COST
Library Binding	85 volumes per year @ $7.10 each	$604.00
Compact Shelving	69 volumes per sq. ft. @ $52/sq. ft.*	$64.00
Library Building	Construction $200 per sq. ft.*	$246.00
Annual Cost	**SUBTOTAL**	**$914.00**
Project Cost	**TOTAL (3.5 Years)**	**$3,199.00**

* Storage for 85 TULIP volumes will require 1.23 square feet.

Table 5: Magnetic storage costs.

ELEMENT	EXPLANATION	TULIP COST
Server	DEC Alpha 200 $7400	$4,895.00
Disk Space	Seagate 9.1 GB @ $3400 x 5 = $17,000	$11,246.00
Computer Room	Construction $250 per sq. ft.**	$500.00
Project Cost	**TOTAL (3.5 Years)**	**$16,641.00**

** Floor space for either magnetic or CD ROM storage requires approximately four square feet, but using racks to stack the data reduces the real requirements for space.

Table 6: Jukebox storage costs.

ELEMENT	EXPLANATION	TULIP COST
Juke Box	Kinotronics 240 CD Capacity	$15,500.00
Computer Room	Construction $250 per sq. ft.**	$1,000.00
Subtotal	**Cost for 154 GB Box**	**$16,500.00**
Project Cost	**TOTAL (36.4 GB Utilized 3.5 Years)**	**$3,928.00**

** Floor space for either magnetic or CD ROM storage requires approximately four square feet, but using racks to stack the data reduces the real requirements for space.

Table 7: Annual building maintenance.

ELEMENT	EXPLANATION	TULIP COST
Library	4.3 sq. ft. x $4.50 sq. ft.	$19.37
Computer Room	4 sq. ft. x $6.00 sq. ft.	$24.00

On the other hand, magnetic storage has dropped dramatically in price. For instance, in 1985 a mainframe 260 MB disk was $11,340 with a 40% educational discount. If prices had not dropped, the inflation-adjusted price of this disk would be $15,876 in 1994 dollars and 1 GB would have been over $60,000. But, today better storage may be purchased for a fraction of the cost -- 1 GB at about $374. In addition, storage costs for both TULIP and UMI are the result of the storage of inefficient TIFF images. There will be alternatives as publishers begin to exploit SGML and HTML, which are all "logical" descriptions of the page. These formats can be arbitrarily complex and refer to enormous images just like TIFF files. However, if you just want to record the text, with minimal markup, the space required is probably 5-10 KB per page. A

TIFF file for the UMI project will be somewhere between 60 KB and 125 KB. Thus, standards like SGML are about one-tenth the size, and that means one-tenth the storage cost. But no publishers are yet capable of supplying marked-up, formatted journals on a scale which would make this advantage useful. Moreover, the planning estimates used by Elsevier indicate that SGML may in the last analysis provide no real savings in storage capacity, only improved information retrieval.

As the tables clearly show, the current cost for magnetic storage is 5.3 times greater than print, and jukebox storage on CDs is 1.2 times greater. It is also worth considering that the typical book stack will last well over 30 years, but not the information technology. The $16,891 server and magnetic storage will have to be replaced at least every eight to ten years, and this is stretching the point. Based on a ten-year replacement cycle, digital storage and access will cost academic libraries 16 times as much as print to store locally. It seems unlikely that a persuasive case can be made for the added value of electronic access and retrieval without a dramatic change in the ownership concept. From firsthand experience, it is clear that jukeboxes are not nearly so robust and the replacement cycle on this technology will be every three to five years. It is also questionable that jukebox technology will continue to be available since it does not have a large number of applications, and is not widely used and manufactured. One final note on comparative capital expense–the cost of building will continue to increase at something like the CPI, and (if recent past is a guide) the cost of servers and storage will continue to fall at a more rapid rate. The problem is guessing correctly when these trend lines will cross and make digital storage cheaper than print.

5. Implications of TULIP for the Future

As much as any, Carnegie Mellon Libraries have participated vigorously in the work of digital libraries. It seems certain that within two decades electronic networked access to scholarly information will be the norm. That does not free us from critical analysis of the facts which may lead to better understanding of the problems and realistic decisions about what should be done to support libraries and scholarly information in the meantime. While there is cause for much optimism about the future of digital libraries, there is no cause for us to be "cockeyed optimists." The conclusions herein, based as they are on the facts of Carnegie Mellon's experience, are offered to temper optimism with reality. One thing should be stated emphatically, the whole publishing and library community owes Elsevier Scientific a large debt of gratitude for undertaking the TULIP Project. TULIP surfaced most of the fundamental issues which must be addressed in order to accelerate the pace of the the paradigm shift to digital libraries. While participants did not find all the answers, we now know the questions that must be asked, the experiments that must be conducted, and the problems that must be solved.

5.1. Infrastructure

Several observations should be made about the costing methods used here. These cost figures do not include any of the expense of stack maintenance by library staff, cost for computing staff, or cost for the necessary computing and telecommunications infrastructure to actually exploit electronic digital journals. Nor do they reflect the expense of the subscriptions to the journals. Perhaps it can be assumed that the maintenance of the print collection by the library staff or the electronic collection by computing staff is equivalent. It might also be assumed that the telecommunications infrastructure will ultimately be available on most campuses, and that students will routinely have small, inexpensive but powerful workstations at their disposal to access such information. Finally, it might be assumed that publishers will charge no more (perhaps less) for a subscription to the electronic version of a journal than to the print version. If these assumptions prove incorrect, then electronic text will be even more expensive to support than print.

However the rate of publication for serials and books is estimated, the plain fact is that electronic publication, which will be required to support the virtual library, is in its infancy. There are many inhibitors, both technical and human, to the process of converting to electronic publication. Thus, the answer to the question, "Should we build more library space in the next 15 years?" is "you bet." In addition, to fully understand the dynamics of cost, one must make comparisons between the various forms of storage, both print and electronic.

The current publishing environment and the cost analysis of the work at Carnegie Mellon does not support the notion that digital libraries are about to happen. The world of publishing is anything but monolithic. The comprehensive adoption of SGML-type editors in the next five to ten years is essential if the digital library is to emerge as the dominant paradigm, but it is not highly likely. SGML would provide full-text for indexing with advanced information retrieval technologies (e.g., natural language processing), and the intellectual markup that would facilitate familiar display and navigation (e.g., next table, figure, section).[9] In addition, the necessity to repeat capital expenditures on servers and storage will not encourage the development of digital libraries, even though hardware is becoming more of a commodity and storage costs may be trivial in the not-too-distant future.

Moreover, there are serious local information technology issues which must be resolved. The high-capacity telecommunications network at Carnegie Mellon enables the transmission of large image files, with little cost to the user in time waiting for a response. This is not the case on most campuses or, for that matter, on the Internet. In addition, the Library Information System supports efforts like the Virtual Library Project within the context of basic library access, rather than a stand-alone demonstration. These conditions must be prevalent on campuses everywhere for it to be an inducement to publishers to provide electronic information. These conditions are currently emerging as library vendors begin to incorporate state-of-the-art technologies into their systems; as colleges and universities improve their telecommunications networks (a necessary element in their educational effort); and as Internet capacity is improved. Ten years ago, Carnegie Mellon's telecommunications network was considered state-of-the-art and almost unique, but that is hardly the case today. Similarly, library automation vendors are moving vigorously to exploit the client-server distributed computing architecture. For instance, Carnegie Mellon Libraries work closely with Sirsi Corporation in order to ensure the likelihood that development efforts are not lost to the library community as a whole. These advanced infrastructure capabilities must be available "off-the-shelf" at affordable prices in supported product offerings.

5.2. Organization

One final telling conclusion may be drawn from the economic analysis. The traditional model of local ownership, which has dominated the vision of library organization and collection development for a century must change. The access model which is emerging will mean the libraries may subscribe or license access to information formerly packaged as a book or a journal, but it is not likely that they will store much of it on the local campus network. It only makes sense to share information technology resources among libraries and the cost of shared access to databases. Emerging networks like OhioLink are good examples of the opportunities which are presented. Smaller consortia like the Oakland Library Consortium may equally take opportunities for sharing such efforts. It also seems likely that the library vendor and publishing community will provide some forms of access. For instance, a large publisher such as Elsevier has opportunities to provide its own servers or even distributed servers to give good access to journal information. Similarly, University Microfilms has already begun experimenting with ProQuest Power Pages Direct, a server which will provide access to the same information now provided on CD. OCLC is also working on this problem. However, these are all new relationships. They mean that the nature of ownership must be carefully redefined and this will take time and it may not be very easy to accomplish. Publishers will want to know that their materials are being used appropriately. They will expect that access is for the campus community, that ILL and reserve reading conform to "fair use" and that authentication and authorization prevent the significant access to information for those who have not paid for it. Libraries will want to know that a subscription to a title gives them permanent access to the contents over time, that the server on which it is found will be consistently available, that the technology will be robust and stable, and that if the supplier (e.g., consortium, publisher, network) ever withdraws the service, then there is a plan for giving them the data they paid for. If such relationships are properly worked out, new types of subscribed access may be expected. For instance, a library may subscribe to a "block" of pages for electronic access to journals not in "core" collecting areas, but which faculty and students may need occasionally.

Whatever the model for shared access, the needs of the user for seamless, easy access must be given high priority. This means that the local library systems must be interoperable with remote servers. For instance, as previously noted, the cache manager being developed for the Virtual Library Project will be modular, so that with minimal work, images can be retrieved, not only from our local TULIP server and the UMI jukeboxes, but also from the Power Pages Direct server in Ann Arbor, Michigan. It is library users who will, in the end, play the key role in deciding how digital libraries are implemented. Systems which are not an improvement over current print organization, give inadequate information, or cost exorbitantly will not be used. Therefore, it is the user studies that will establish the best insights into the future and the clearest idea of the way to shape digital libraries. Carnegie Mellon Libraries are planning to undertake such studies using both the TULIP data and the UMI data in 1996.

5.3. Contents

There are two basic tasks which must be accomplished to build the virtual library infrastructure, and neither is trivial. First: build a foundation of information technologies (IT) that allows users to access electronic information easily, seamlessly -- and without becoming technology experts. This work is being done in tandem by libraries, computing centers and library IT vendors and publishers. Implementation of access to TULIP content on the Carnegie Mellon campus is indicative. TULIP here at CMU is well integrated into the Library Information System rather than existing as a stand-alone prototype system. Second, IT infrastructure of this type will be of little use unless a substantial amount of digitized scholarly information of immediate interest to students and faculty becomes available. Much, perhaps most, of this work will fall to publishers of scholarly information—including commercial and university presses, scholarly associations and secondary publishers. The networked environment will also stimulate much entrepreneurial experimentation with electronic publishing.

At this point, almost anything said about the subject content of electronic scholarly resources is speculative. There have been many "white papers" and published articles about digital libraries, but so far, not very much in the way of large scale presentation of scholarly information electronically. To some extent, TULIP participants learned less from TULIP than we had hoped, at least at Carnegie Mellon. Part of the reason is that the principle users in materials science were not well equipped to participate. They did not have Unix workstations on their desktops, and the original LIS/Mercury GUI and image browser was developed in MOTIF. Although the University Libraries loaned a Unix workstation to in the MSE Department, users still had to leave their lab or office to get access to TULIP images -- and since many of the TULIP journals were available in the Department Office, it was more convenient and less expensive to get the printed journal than to print the images in the library (printing TULIP images is discussed in Part II, Sections 1.5.3.1. and 2.1.1.1 of this report). In addition, they were not as sophisticated in their use of networked computing as other campus groups, and the availability of TULIP journals online required a change of basic behavior which was oriented towards print. Even though TULIP represents a technology area, it was not the best target of opportunity at Carnegie Mellon. Here it would have been better to select a field where there was already a strong propensity towards online information and no technology barriers -- people or machines. Computer science or business would be our choice. In the end, for digital libraries to succeed rapidly, they should be implemented where there are already conditions that encourage use. Early success will allow for other less susceptible disciplines to adopt digital libraries in an orderly and accelerating fashion.

From another perspective too, the University Libraries conclude that the choice of subject matter limited what was learned. The size of the TULIP data set (43 journal titles) is really very small, as is the period of time covered. Carnegie Mellon had only 29 journal titles available online. Materials scientists felt that they needed more titles available representing a larger corpus. In addition, the limited number of people who had interest in the TULIP titles exacerbated the issue of scale. If TULIP had delivered 29 journals in computer science or business, more use might have occurred simply because the user communities in these disciplines are much larger than the materials science community at Carnegie Mellon.

Another dimension of scale is the diversity of subjects and sheer volume of information. A much larger amount of scholarly information is needed to understand user behavior and really figure out the best methods of implementation. Observing just how users are going to behave with respect to digital libraries requires journal runs of five or more years covering a substantial part of a discipline or disciplines. These conditions do not now exist, but they must if digital libraries are to be viable in academe. To belabor the point somewhat, libraries are different from other electronic resources in that they are not as interactive. A "chat room" or a game on the Internet may attract a user repeatedly and for long periods of time because the data is the interaction created by the end user. In contrast, a digital library must substantially reward the end user with stored content, otherwise it will be viewed as a toy, or an incidental source of information. One final issue: when these more substantial digital libraries are available, they will require better retrieval tools than keyword-Boolean processing, e.g., natural language processing.

PART II

TECHNICAL IMPLEMENTATION

- DESCRIPTION OF THE CURRENT
  INFORMATION TECHNOLOGY ENVIRONMENT

- DESCRIPTION OF TULIP IMPLEMENTATION

1. Description of the Current Information Technology Environment

1.1. Hardware and Operating Systems

1.1.1. Server Types and Numbers

1.1.1.1. Library Information System (LIS)

LIS is a distributed system of UNIX clients and servers developed by the University Libraries. LIS provides public services access to the Library Catalog and other bibliographic and full text databases. The server hardware and software components in LIS are:

- **Retrieval Servers.** LIS currently has four retrieval servers that house thirteen ASCII databases (many of them replicated on multiple servers). The retrieval servers are DECstations (model 5000/200) running Ultrix 4.2. Each has 48 MB of memory. Total disk space on all four retrieval servers is approximately 50 GB.[10]

- **Image Servers.** LIS currently has one image server (for TIFF images), which houses the TULIP images. The TULIP image server is a Sun Sparcstation running SunOS 4.1.3 with 32 MB of memory and 34 GB of disk space. An additional image server, a Hewlett Packard (model 735) running HP UX with 64 MB of memory and 10 GB of disk space, will be added in 1996 for caching images provided by University Microfilms International (UMI) on CD ROM.

- **Reference Servers.** LIS currently runs four reference servers, which provide access control and database information for the system. The reference server software runs on three of the retrieval server machines (described above) and on the database testing machine (described below).

- **Database Building and Testing.** Databases are built on a DEC Alpha (model 3000/400) running OSF/1 1.3 with 64 MB of memory and 12 GB of disk space. Prior to being released to the production retrieval servers (Described above), databases are tested on a DECstation (model 5000/200) running Ultrix 4.2 with 48 MB of memory and 5 GB of disk space.

- **Intermediate (Client) Server.** An intermediate server, called library.cmu.edu, runs a captured login so that users can only invoke VT100 LIS (described below) on this machine. Library.cmu.edu is a DECstation (model 5000/125) running Ultrix 4.2 and AFS; it has 32 MB of memory and 500 MB of disk space.

With the exception of the image server currently in development (the Hewlitt Packard), all of the LIS servers reside in Computing Services' machine room on campus.

1.1.1.2. Unicorn

Unicorn is a distributed system of multi-platform clients and UNIX servers purchased from Sirsi Corporation. Unicorn provides integrated public services (e.g., access to the Library Catalog) and technical services (e.g., circulation, acquisitions, cataloging, and serials control). Currently, the production and test Unicorn retrieval server both reside on a DEC Alpha (model 3000/800) running OSF/1 2.0 with 128 MB of internal memory and 16.3 GB of peripheral disk space. Plans are to move the test server First Quarter 1996 to a DEC Alpha (model 5000/300) running OSF/1 1.3 with 64 MB of memory. The Unicorn servers are housed in Computing Services' machine room.

1.1.1.3. Other Projects and Servers

In addition to LIS and Unicorn, the University Libraries have several other research and development projects that entail server hardware and software. These include:

- **Heinz Electronic Library Interactive Online System (HELIOS).** The HELIOS project is developing a full-text and image legislative archive. The HELIOS server is a Sun Sparcstation 20 running Solaris 2.4 with 128 MB of memory and 18 GB of disk space. The HELIOS server is located in the Heinz Archives during the grant period while the system is being developed.

- **Pittsburgh Post Gazette (PPG).** This project is providing members of the Oakland Library Consortium (Carnegie Mellon University, University of Pittsburgh, and Carnegie Library of Pittsburgh) access to a full-text daily newspaper using natural language retrieval software developed by Claritech Corporation. When the prototype is available for testing it will contain ASCII full-text of the newspaper for the years 1991-present. The PPG server is a DEC Alpha (model 1000 4/233) running Digital UNIX 3.2 with 128 MB of memory and 5.6 GB of disk space. The PPG server is in Computing Services' machine room.

- **Usage Monitoring and Reporting.** Unicorn transaction logs are stored and analyzed on the Unicorn server. Transaction logs from LIS, PPG and HELIOS clients and servers are collected and analyzed on a dedicated machine. Currently the "logger" machine is a DEC Alpha (model 5000/300) running OSF/1 1.3 with 64 MB of memory and 4.15 GB of disk space; in 1996 the logging work will move to a DEC Alpha (model 200 4/233) running OSF/1 3.2 with 32 MB of memory.

The University Libraries also have several PC-based CD ROM products that deliver ASCII and image information. The Integrated CD ROM System (ICDS) is discussed in Part II of this report, Section 1.4.2.1.

1.1.1.4. World Wide Web (WWW)

The University Librarieshave implemented several WWW servers in conjunction with Unicorn, LIS, HELIOS and PPG. The WWW server for Unicorn WebCat runs on the Unicorn production server (described above). The WWW server for LIS TULIP images runs on the image server (described above). The WWW server for LIS database searching runs on the LIS database testing machine (described above).

Currently in development, the WWW servers for the HELIOS and PPG projects run on the project retrieval servers (described above).

1.1.2. Client Types and Numbers

1.1.2.1. Library Information System (LIS)

LIS has three UNIX clients:

- **Motif LIS** is a graphical user interface for users of UNIX workstations running X-windows (specifically Motif 1.2.4 and X11R5).

- **VT100 LIS** is a character-based client available to Internet guests and users of Macintosh and PC computers on the intermediate server called library.cmu.edu. It is also available on UNIX workstations. VT100 LIS emulates many terminal types.

- **LIS Look** is a command-line interface available on UNIX workstations. It also serves as the retrieval client running behind WWW clients like Mosaic or Netscape (invisible to the user) in the WWW implementation of LIS. The WWW client actually talks to LIS Look, which maintains state for the WWW client.

The three LIS clients are currently available for workstations running the Ultrix, SunOS, and HP UX operating systems. They may be ported to the Sun Solaris operating system in 1996.

Image handling in LIS is currently provided by prototype image software developed by Project Mercury in 1993. The image software is problematic for many reasons, but like all the LIS clients, its biggest drawback is that it runs only on UNIX workstations. Many users have Macintoshes or PCs running Microsoft Windows. Though these users can telnet to library.cmu.edu, run VT100 LIS and query the LIS (ASCII) databases, this character-based client cannot deliver images to the desktop. By the end of 1994, the University Libraries had two plans to provide desktop delivery of image documents on multiple platforms: Unicorn and the WWW. TULIP images were released in the WWW implementation of LIS in July 1995. Work continues with Sirsi to provide image delivery within Unicorn in 1996.

1.1.2.2. Unicorn

Sirsi Unicorn provides a multi-platform suite of graphical clients (for public and technical services) designed to run on the user's desktop machine -- on a Mac (System 7), PC (running MS Windows), or UNIX workstation (running Motif and X windows on a Solaris, AIX or OSF/1 machine). Unicorn also has a host-based, character-based client, comparable to VT100 LIS, that runs on the Unicorn server (described above). The character-based Unicorn client was released to campus in late June 1995; the graphical Unicorn clients will be released in 1996 following modifications to meet the needs of campus users and the campus computing environment.

1.1.2.3. Other Projects and Clients

The HELIOS digital legislative archives project is developing a graphical user interface for PCs running MS Windows. The various CD ROM database products run proprietary clients.

1.1.2.4. World Wide Web (WWW)

The WWW implementation of LIS was released in January 1995 . Because the WWW does not (yet) support authentication, which is required by commercial database licenses, with the exception of TULIP, only the Library Catalog and other campus information databases are provided.

Students and faculty in the Materials Science and Engineering Department at Carnegie Mellon use Macintosh computers, which means that they can not run the Mercury prototype client currently provided for image display and navigation in LIS. To gain desktop access to TULIP, they asked for TULIP to be made available over the WWW. On February 17, 1995, Jaco Zijlstra granted the University Libraries permission to use the WWW provided that access is restricted to clients running at IP addresses on the Carnegie Mellon campus, the Elsevier copyright statement is displayed, and the opening screen prompts users to identify their department and status, e.g., Materials Science graduate student.[11] TULIP was released on the WWW in July 1995. An additional TULIP/WWW release, specifically to support printing the images, is planned for December 1995. Details of this release are provided in Part II, Section 2.1.1.1.

WebCat, the WWW implementation of the Unicorn Library Catalog, was released in August 1995.

Claritech Corporation and the University Libraries are collaborating on the development of a WWW interface for HELIOS. Claritech and the Oakland Library Consortium are collaborating on a WWW interface for PPG. Both are scheduled for release First Quarter 1996.

1.2. Database Systems

The database-building and retrieval software used in LIS is OCLC's Newton, which has been optimized for keyword-Boolean retrieval over large databases. The retrieval software used in Unicorn is BRS; like Newton, BRS provides keyword-Boolean retrieval. Similarly, the CD ROM products support keyword-Boolean retrieval. In contrast, the search engine used in the full-text HELIOS and PPG projects is CLARIT, which provides natural language retrieval developed by Claritech Corporation. Long term plans are to integrate natural language retrieval into LIS and Unicorn for the retrieval of full text.

1.3. Central Storage Technology

Table 8 provides an overview of magnetic and CD ROM storage currently maintained by the University Libraries. The numbers in Table 8 include the storage required for the operating system, swap space, etc., not just the storage space available for data.

Table 8: Summary of current magnetic disk and CD ROM jukebox storage.

SYSTEMS & SERVERS	GIGABYTES
LIS - keyword-Boolean retrieval (all databases)	50
LIS - image retrieval (TULIP images)	34
LIS - intermediate server	00.5
LIS - logging & analysis	04.15
Unicorn - keyword-Boolean retrieval	16.3
MAGNETIC PRODUCTION SUBTOTAL	**104.95**
LIS - image retrieval (UMI images)	10
HELIOS - natural language & image retrieval	18
PPG - natural language retrieval	05.6
LIS - database building & software evaluation	12
LIS - database & software testing	05
Unicorn - database & software testing	00.87
MAGNETIC DEVELOPMENT SUBTOTAL	**51.47**
MAGNETIC TOTAL	**156.42**
CD ROM JUKEBOX TOTAL	**1,078**
GRAND TOTAL	**1,234.42**

1.4.   Network Typology

1.4.1.   Client-Server or Terminal Oriented

The University Libraries' primary information technologies, LIS and Unicorn, are client-server distributed systems. However, both provide host-based clients to support terminal emulation and access. The Claritech software currently used in the HELIOS and PPG projects is client-server, but it is not a distributed system, though work is underway to make it a distributed system.

1.4.2. Local Area Networks

1.4.2.1. The Integrated CD ROM System (ICDS)

The University Libraries operate an Integrated CD ROM System (ICDS) that provides access to thirteen databases. In comparison with LIS, the CD ROM products are less expensive than magnetic tape products, but they are not as accessible. With few exceptions, the CD ROM products are only available in the three University Libraries. The products are networked between the three libraries using the campus ethernet backbone. The networking software is Opti-Net, which integrates heterogeneous computing environments and supports up to 200 simultaneous users. At the present time there are only seven networked PC-based stations in the libraries. Remote access is supported for selected departments and affiliated libraries at Carnegie Mellon, e.g., the Software Engineering Institute (SEI) Library.

In addition to the thirteen networked CD ROM databases, there are five stand-alone CD ROM stations because the vendors prohibit networked access to these databases, forcing users to specific stations in specific libraries. Even vendors who permit networked access to a database restrict through licenses the number of simultaneous users of the database and the number of stations that the database is accessible from. From the library perspective, a more reasonable approach would be to not only restrict, but meter the number of simultaneous connections (based on performance criteria), so that the database could be accessible from any number of stations. This would allow, for example, five simultaneous connections from any of two hundred possible licensed clients. The inconsistent licensing practices of CD ROM database publishers translate into inconsistent library service, which puzzles and frustrates users.

1.4.2.2. The Electronic Journal Article Delivery Service (E-JADS)

The University Libraries also maintain a local area network in conjunction with the Electronic Journal Article Delivery Service (E-JADS) provided through LIS. Developed with University Microfilms International (UMI) to exploit their CD ROM-based journal image product called PowerPages, the LIS service enables users to search two bibliographic databases, specifically Periodical Abstracts and ABI/INFORM, and order laser prints of the articles indexed in the databases. Users complete an E-JADS online order form and submit it. LIS sends all of the relevant information in electronic mail to library staff. Staff read the mail and, using UMI's proprietary print (request) station, server, and printer, print the requested articles (images). The print station is connected to the print server by a Novelle network. The jukeboxes and printer are connected directly to the print server. Further details about E-JADS are provided in Part II, Section 1.5.3.1.

1.4.3. Wide Area Networks

All buildings on the Carnegie Mellon campus, including dormitories, are wired for Ethernet using the IBM cabling system. The buildings are connected to the campus backbone using 10 Mbits per second copper or fiber cable. The campus network is connected to the ANS backbone using 10 Mbits per second fibre link. Plans are to incrementally upgrade to 100 Mbits per second, starting with the backbone followed by the academic, administrative and residential buildings.

1.5. Printing Facilities

1.5.1. Printing ASCII Inside of the University Libraries

People who use the LIS and Unicorn workstations in the University Libraries print (ASCII information only) on dedicated dot matrix printers attached to the client workstation. Public LIS workstations support an alternate networked printer located in the library if the attached printer is not working. Public Unicorn workstations do not support an alternate printer.

Library staff print to either attached dot matrix printers or to (ethernet) networked laser writers.

1.5.2. Printing ASCII Outside of the University Libraries

People who use LIS outside of the University Libraries can print (ASCII information) on any accessible (ethernet) networked laser writer on campus configured to handle AFS ("Andrew") printing. Many printers on campus are configured to handle "Andrew" printing as well as Macintosh or PC printing.

Printing has not yet been implemented for people who use Unicorn outside of the University Libraries.

1.5.3. Printing Images

Users want to print images on networked laser writers across campus. However, in the absence of a networked billing server, required to track royalties and payments for publishers, the University

Libraries must track this information manually and restrict printing to printers located in the University Libraries -- so that users who do not have Carnegie Mellon charge accounts can pay for prints by copicard. This is an intermediate step to distributing journal images across the campus network. Plans are to have a networked billing server and to support networked printing of images by the end of 1996.

1.5.3.1. Library Information System (LIS)

Two of the University Libraries provide an Electronic Journal Article Delivery Service (E-JADS), specifically for printing images, in conjunction with two research and development projects. Fundamentally, the E-JADS services for the projects are the same, but for technical and historical reasons, their implementation and presentation to the user are different. Both services entail sending electronic mail to library staff, indicating what article is to be printed, and what payment and delivery method the user wants. The difference is in how this information is gathered and submitted:

- **UMI.** In this project (in production since 1992), two LIS bibliographic databases, Periodical Abstracts and ABI/INFORM, are logically -- but not electronically -- linked to two CD ROM-based databases: General Periodicals OnDisc and Business Periodicals OnDisc. When users search the bibliographic databases, they can submit requests to print many of the articles indexed in the database. In this implementation, submitting a print request entails selecting a payment and delivery method on the E-JADS online order form (i.e.., CMU charge account or copicard; pickup in the library or send through campus mail) and clicking a button (Motif LIS) or pressing return (VT100 LIS). The Motif LIS order form is shown in Figure 8. Users do not have to provide any information about what article is to be printed because the LIS client extracts the requisite information from the bibliographic record. They do not have to provide any information about who they are because they must be authenticated to access these databases -- therefore LIS "knows" their user ID. They do not have to know the email address to send the message to because LIS does. LIS sends the information about the article, the user, and the selected payment and delivery methods in electronic mail to Hunt Library staff. Staff read the mail every two hours and queue the prints using UMI's proprietary PowerPages hardware and software.

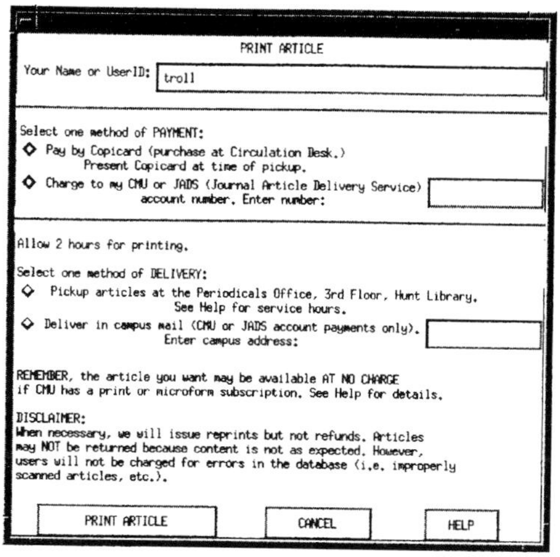

PRINT ARTICLE

Your Name or UserID: troll

Select one method of PAYMENT:
◇ Pay by Copicard (purchase at Circulation Desk.)
Present Copicard at time of pickup.
◇ Charge to my CMU or JADS (Journal Article Delivery Service) account number. Enter number:

Allow 2 hours for printing.

Select one method of DELIVERY:
◇ Pickup articles at the Periodicals Office, 3rd Floor, Hunt Library.
See Help for service hours.
◇ Deliver in campus mail (CMU or JADS account payments only).
Enter campus address:

REMEMBER, the article you want may be available AT NO CHARGE
if CMU has a print or microform subscription. See Help for details.

DISCLAIMER:
When necessary, we will issue reprints but not refunds. Articles may NOT be returned because content is not as expected. However, users will not be charged for errors in the database (i.e. improperly scanned articles, etc.).

PRINT ARTICLE | CANCEL | HELP

Figure 8: The Motif LIS E-JADS order form provided for UMI journal images.

- **TULIP.** In this project (in production since 1994), the Materials Science (TULIP) database is linked to journal images stored on magnetic disks accessible over the campus network. The TULIP images can be displayed as well as printed. The initial implementation of TULIP E-JADS (June 1994) was neither conspicuous nor user friendly. No E-JADS online order form was provided because by this time development of the production LIS clients had stopped; work had begun on an entirely new client. Instead, online help instructed users to copy and paste or type the citation and Print ID fields of the TULIP bibliographic record into an email window, to specify their payment and delivery method, and to address the email to E&S Library staff (the email address was provided). Staff read the email and queue the prints on a networked laser writer in the library using a script that logs the requisite information for Elsevier.

The lack of technical and interface support for submitting TULIP print requests no doubt contributed to the lack of TULIP printing. This situation is still the case in Motif and VT100 LIS because development of the new LIS client stopped in October 1994, when the University Libraries entered into an agreement with Sirsi Corporation that included the provision of a multi-platform suite of clients to replace the "home grown" LIS Unix clients. The TULIP E-JADS print service is different in the WWW implementation of LIS; details are provided in Part II, Section 2.1.1.1 of this report.

1.5.3.2. Unicorn

The University Libraries' current implementation of Unicorn does not support image printing. Future versions will.

2. Description of TULIP Implementation

2.1. Components

2.1.1. Functionalities

The following discussion describes TULIP features and functionalities implemented in Motif, VT100, and WWW LIS. Because previous TULIP reports have included pictures of the Motif user interface, which will be replaced in 1996, this report includes pictures of the WWW interface to TULIP.

2.1.1.1. Functionalities Implemented

User Access and Elsevier Copyright Display. Motif LIS users must authenticate themselves with a user ID and password before they can access TULIP. The WWW does not support authentication, so WWW access to TULIP is restricted by IP address. Nonetheless, WWW LIS prompts users to identify themselves; see Figure 9. Further details on LIS security are provided in Part II, Section 2.1.6 of this report.

In keeping with the agreement with Elsevier, both Motif LIS and WWW LIS display the Elsevier copyright statement before they display images for the user. Motif LIS displays the copyright statement before it displays the first image during the session. Because Web browsers are "stateless," WWW LIS has no approximation of a user "session," so the TULIP "home page" displays the Elsevier copyright statement along with the prompts for users to identify themselves; see Figure 9.

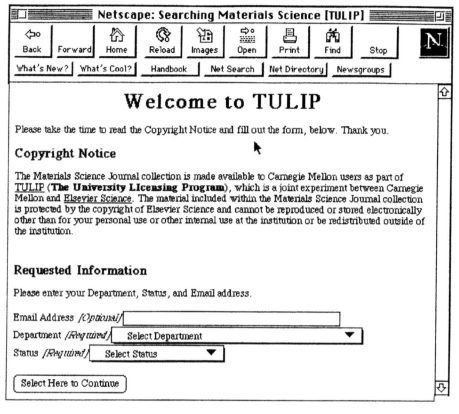

Figure 9: The TULIP "home page" in WWW LIS.

Bibliographic Information. From the user's perspective, the Materials Science (TULIP) bibliographic database offers the same functionality as all of the other LIS databases:

- Searching with keywords, Boolean and proximity operators, and field and index limits.
- Sorting the records retrieved, e.g., by date, author, title.
- Displaying the records retrieved.
- Marking the records retrieved (for navigating, saving, mailing and printing).
- Saving, mailing (electronic mail) and printing retrieved information, e.g., citations, bibliographic records, titles.
- Browsing database indexes and interactively constructing queries from index entries.
- Sending questions or comments to library staff.

The WWW implementation of LIS supports searching, displaying, and printing bibliographic database records, but not the other features listed above. Figure 10 shows the WWW LIS TULIP Search screen. All handling of bibliographic (ASCII) information is free.

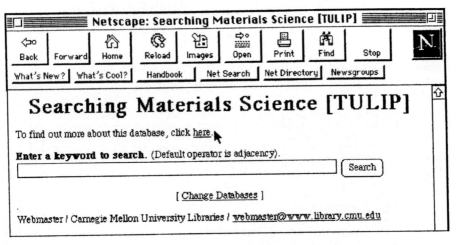

Figure 10: The WWW LIS TULIP Search screen.

Journal (Image) Collection. Motif and WWW LIS support viewing and browsing of the Materials Science Journals (TULIP) images. Users can search the Materials Science database, display a bibliographic record, and then click a button to retrieve the first page of the article indexed in the bibliographic record. They can also browse the Materials Science Journals collection by interactively selecting a journal title, issue, and article; see Figures 11 and 12. Motif LIS displays the Elsevier copyright statement before the first TULIP image is displayed; WWW LIS displays it on the TULIP "home page." Users can browse and view the TULIP images for free.

Using either the Motif or WW client, users can navigate to the next, previous, first and last pages of an article. Motif LIS users can also navigate to the next, previous, first and last pages of an issue, and they can specify any number of pages to move forward or backward in an article or issue. Motif LIS enables users to incrementally enlarge or reduce the size of the page. WWW LIS provides only two image sizes. Motif LIS displays TIFF images. WWW LIS converts the TIFF to GIF images "on the fly" for display in the WWW client.

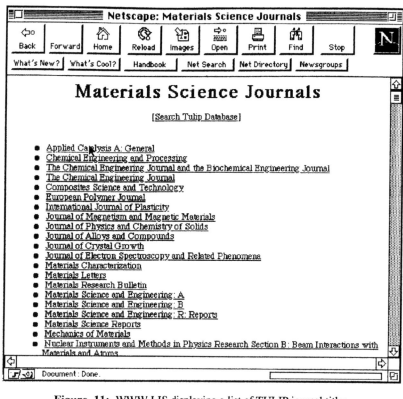

Figure 11: WWW LIS displaying a list of TULIP journal titles.

Printing Images. There is a charge for printing the TULIP images (to provide consistent service with other image collections, e.g., UMI, for which publishers require billing and royalty tracking). As described above, in the absence of a networked billing server, image printing is restricted to printers located in the University Libraries. Currently the TULIP images are the only images accessible using the WWW implementation of LIS. Compared to Motif and VT100 LIS (described in Part II of this report, Section 1.5.3.1), using WWW LIS to submit TULIP (image) print requests is conspicuous and user friendly. TULIP was released on the WWW in July 1995. In the initial release, users can print one page at a time using the Print option on the File menu in their WWW client. The quality of the printed image is not particularly good and the printed page includes the HTML buttons and text provided above and below the image. However, a WWW TULIP print service, complete with an E-JADS online order form, will be released by the end of December 1995 to facilitate printing TULIP images. From the user's perspective, the WWW

TULIP E-JADS print service is comparable to the UMI implementation in Motif and VT100 LIS --
with one exception. The exception is that users must enter their name and user ID in the TULIP E-
JADS online order form because WWW access to TULIP is restricted by IP address, not Kerberos
authentication, i.e., WWW LIS does not "know" the user's identity the way Motif and VT100 LIS
do. (Security is discussed in Part II of this report, Section 2.1.6.)

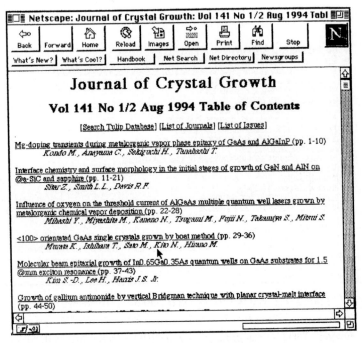

Figure 12: WWW LIS displaying a TULIP journal table of contents.

2.1.1.2. Rationale for Choice of Functionalities Implemented

The choice of functionalities was based on human factors research conducted by the University
Libraries from 1989-1994, e.g., focus groups and user protocols. The research relevant to the
design and functionality of a user interface for retrieving and navigating images is summarized in
Part I of this report, Section 3.1.

2.1.2. System Architecture

2.1.2.1. Implemented Browsing Technologies

TULIP users can browse bibliographic database keyword and phrase indexes using OCLC's Newton retrieval server software and clients developed by the University Libraries. They can browse the TULIP image collection using software developed by the University Libraries.

2.1.2.2. Implemented Searching Technologies

Similarly, users can search the TULIP bibliographic database keyword and phrase indexes using OCLC's Newton retrieval server software and clients developed by the University Libraries.

2.1.2.3. Implemented User Interfaces

The University Libraries implemented the Unix-based Motif and VT100 LIS retrieval clients for ASCII information. Carnegie Mellon's Computing Services implemented the Unix prototype image client available in Motif LIS. The University Libraries implemented the WWW LIS interface accessible on all platforms.

2.1.2.4. Image Viewing

The University Libraries take the position that quality control is the responsibility of the publisher or vendor, regardless of whether the journal is delivered in print or electronic format. There are no plans to enhance the images. TULIP users see what Elsevier delivers. Any modification of the viewable images is done on-the-fly as directed by the user via the client interface, e.g., zoom in.

2.1.2.5. Image Saving, Mailing, and Printing

LIS does not support faxing, emailing, saving or local printing of images. Image printing is discussed in Part II, Sections 1.5.3.1, 2.1.1.1, and 2.4.2.1 of this report. Features to support faxing, mailing and saving may be added over time in response to user demands.

2.1.3. Networking Issues

Use of the TULIP data has created no network traffic problems at Carnegie Mellon.

2.1.4. Data Preparation and Loading

2.1.4.1. Validation of Incoming Datasets

Incoming datasets are copied entirely to magnetic disks and validated using the checksum files.

2.1.4.2. Text Preparation

The bibliographic data from each DATASET.TOC is converted for use as an LIS / Newton database. Each EFFECT tag is assigned to a Newton field or subfield based on database specifications provided by the librarians. The structured nature of these tags corresponds well with Newton fields.

2.1.4.3. Image Preparation

No additional preparation is needed for storing the images. The DATASET.TOC files are used to index the images. (Managing the images is discussed further in Part II, Section 2.1.5 of this report.)

2.1.4.4. Indexing Bibliographic Data

After the EFFECT tags have been assigned to Newton fields or subfields, the TULIP bibliographic data is converted into ASN.1/BER format -- the input format for the Newton database-building software. The LIS / Newton database is then built, tested, and released to campus. William C. Dougherty and Edward A. Fox's article in the special TULIP issue of *Library Hi Tech* provides considerable detail about the steps required to build a Newton database.

2.1.4.5. Indexing Full Text Data

The University Libraries did not index the TULIP raw ASCII files for two reasons. First, because the quality of the files in the earlier datasets, available at the time the decision was made, was too poor to be of much use. Second, because the libraries' Newton retrieval engine does keyword-Boolean retrieval, which empirical research indicates is effective only in unrealistically small full-text databases. Plans are to index the raw ASCII files in 1996 using the Claritech natural language retrieval software.

2.1.5. Implemented Image Storage and Retrieval

The DATASET.TOC files are also used to index the images and determine the location of the data on disk. A pseudo-virtual device was created to manage multiple disks of varying types. One partition is used for keeping the structure of the images in the

```
ISSN/IssueID/Page
```

format defined by Elsevier. However, the IssueIDs are actually links to corresponding

```
Device/Dataset/ISSN/IssueID
```

directories that contain the actual data. This method is robust because, if one disk or partition fails, the entire image collection is not lost (as it would be using a true virtual device). The method is also easy to maintain and correct problems because the data retains the original dataset structure.

Each level of the `ISSN/IssueID/Page` structure has a corresponding catalog file that maps the natural language description of the data in the subdirectories to the subdirectory name. The parent of the ISSN directory contains the Titles of each viewable journal and a mapping to the ISSN of that journal. The ISSN directory contains the Volume/Number of each issue of the given journal mapped to the IssueID of that journal. The IssueID directory contains a listing of the articles with their corresponding TIFFs.

Each issue within the DATASET.TOC has a tag that defines which TIFF file belongs to a given physical page. In addition to the .TIF files that exists in each IssueID directory, a corresponding "p####" symbolic link is created. In the case of unnumbered or roman numeral pages, a "u###" or "IVXDLC" link is created.

Images are retrieved using different methods, depending on which client is used and how the image is located:

- **Motif LIS link in bibliographic record.** When users click the Display Article button in the Motif LIS Record window, the Motif client extracts the ISSN, IssueID, and beginning page number of the referenced article from the bibliographic record, and then requests the image based upon this information using the "p####" name for the image file.

- **Motif LIS browse image collection.** Using Motif LIS, users select a journal collection, title, and issue. When they select an issue, LIS displays the first page of the issue at the IssueID level.

- **WWW LIS link in bibliographic record.** When users click the Display Article button in the WWW LIS Record display, the LIS Look client (running behind the WWW client) extracts the ISSN, IssueID, and page range of the article from the bibliographic record and requests the article. The user can then look at the article as though it was found through the WWW browse mode.

- **WWW LIS browse image collection.** Like Motif LIS, using WWW LIS, users select a journal collection, title, and issue. Unlike Motif LIS, however, the issue level display in WWW LIS includes the GIF image of the journal cover, and, when users select an issue, WWW LIS displays an interactive Table of Contents at the IssueID level.

Image retrieval with the two interfaces is very different. Motif LIS uses a simple transfer mechanism with a two-command protocol: 'a <userid>' and 'g <path>'. The "a" (authenticate) command notifies the server that it should get a Kerberos ticket for the given user. The "g" (get) command gets the file specified in <path> for an authorized user. This command does not make any dependencies upon the data that is sent; in practice it is used to get both the CATALOG files and the .TIF image files. The Motif client decides how the data should be presented and enlarges or reduces the image at the user's request, freeing the server from this task.

WWW LIS runs directly on the machine that stores the TULIP images. The images themselves are not directly accessible to users. Instead, the interface determines which image is needed and converts it to GIF format "on the fly." This makes the image usable as an inline image in almost every available graphical Web browser. The user can specify the size of the displayed image, but in this case, the server enlarges or reduces the given image.

2.1.6. Implemented System Security

Motif and VT100 LIS use Kerberos authentication, developed at MIT, and authorization (access control) software developed by the University Libraries. Using Kerberos enables all Carnegie Mellon students, faculty, researchers and staff to login to the dedicated LIS workstations in the libraries with their University-supplied user IDs, freeing the University Libraries from having to maintain a separate set of passwords for user authentication. It also provides a user transparent

LIS authentication scheme for CMU users outside of the libraries; once they have logged into a UNIX machine, they do not have to login to LIS separately to use the system -- LIS uses the Kerberos authentication ticket they already have. In addition, TULIP is accessible to anyone who is physically in one of the University Libraries and who receives a guest user ID and password at the Reference or Circulation Desk. Guest user IDs and passwords work only on dedicated LIS workstations in the University Libraries. TULIP is not accessible to Carnegie Mellon alumni over the University-sponsored Alumni Network.[12]

WWW LIS limits TULIP access to machines with IP addresses affiliated with Carnegie Mellon University. Users of these machines must specify their status (e.g., Graduate student, Faculty, etc.), their department, and (optionally) their email address to search or browse TULIP. Once they identify themselves, they may use the system as much as they like. If, however, the machine is idle for ten consecutive minutes, their TULIP access is denied (times-out). They must specify their status and department again.

Using the WWW to access TULIP has certain advantages. For example, users can save URLs to images and, after "logging in" (specifying status and department) each session, easily return to those images and jump from point to point, as needed. Using the WWW does not require a specific client or system interface and therefore makes TULIP available to the widest possible University audience.

2.1.7. Implemented Usage Monitoring

In 1994, the University Libraries implemented a usage monitoring and reporting system for all LIS clients and servers, including a registry component to facilitate identifying user affiliations.

2.1.7.1. Collection of Usage Data

Elsevier requested very detailed usage monitoring of the TULIP data. When TULIP began, LIS monitored usage only on the server side of the distributed architecture. The LIS retrieval servers logged everything that was required by Elsevier for bibliographic information with the exception of document IDs and save, mail and print (SMP) requests, which required monitoring on the client side of the LIS architecture. Code was written and tested in 1994 to log document IDs and SMP requests at the client. Beginning in January 1995, SMP requests are logged for all LIS databases; document IDs are logged only for the TULIP database because of concerns about user privacy (see Part I, Section 3.3.2 of this report).

The Mercury prototype image server provided minimal usage monitoring, but did not log everything that Elsevier requested. Usage monitoring of the image server was revised in 1994 to provide more of what Elsevier wanted. No usage monitoring was added to the prototype image client because Computing Services ceased to support the client they developed and because library staff do not know raw X (details about the prototype image client are provided in Part II, Section 2.2.1 of this report). Requests to print images are logged by the print script that library staff execute when users send email print requests for TULIP articles (see Part II, Section 1.5.3.1).

Though LIS logged TULIP transactions from the time TULIP was released in 1994, the University Libraries began processing the TULIP transaction logs in the Summer 1995. Reports are now submitted monthly. In early December the 1995 reports were resubmitted to correct errors in the image display logs and to include additional retrieval client logs. With few exceptions, the TULIP reports provide all the information that Elsevier requested. What follows is an overview of the University Libraries TULIP usage reports:

- **Coverage:** The reports from April and May 1994 include usage of only the TULIP bibliographic data because the images were not released until June 1994. From June 1994 to the present, image data is also included in the reports. Reports on bibliographic usage from April 1994 to January 1995 cover only displayed bibliographic information because there was no client code to log save, mail and print transactions. Client-side bibliographic usage monitoring began in January 1995, so the reports from then on include the document IDs of displayed bibliographic records and save, mail, and print requests for bibliographic information.

  The reports are still missing information about the user because the University Libraries have not yet built the affiliation table required to convert encrypted user IDs to user department and status. This task is problematic because users change IDs, department and status over time. Plans are to design and implement an automatic way to keep the affiliation table up to date. The affiliation table will contain encrypted user IDs, user numbers and affiliation data. (A user's ID and affiliation may change over time, but the user's number will not.) When the affiliation table is built, all of the TULIP logs (from April 1994 to the present) will be post-processed to get the affiliation data for the TULIP reports. However, it is highly unlikely that the University Libraries will be able to reconstruct all of the affiliations that changed in 1994-1995. Post-processing will also replace encrypted user IDs in the logs with user numbers -- thus protecting user privacy in the stored logs.

- **Delivery date and time:**

  — Page images - Requests to display journal images include only the date and time when the request was logged at the image server, not the date and time when the image was delivered to the client, because the Mercury prototype image client does not log the date and time of image delivery. There are no plans to add usage monitoring to the prototype image client because it will be replaced by a new image client in 1996.

  — Bibliographic records - Requests to display bibliographic information are logged at the retrieval server, but the server does not time and date stamp the transaction. The retrieval server was revised in October 1995 to log the time and date of display requests. The new server is being tested now for release to campus. The retrieval client does log the time and date when the bibliographic record was delivered to the desktop and the SSDI of the record. Since delivery of bibliographic records is very fast, the TULIP usage reports use the same time and date for request and delivery of bibliographic records. The retrieval client also logs the date, time and SSDI of requests to save, mail or print bibliographic records. However, there is no log of when the item was actually saved, mailed or printed so this field is blank in the usage reports.

- **Image page numbers:** The Mercury prototype image server logs the printed page number of the image that was requested (e.g., p0541), not the electronic page number (e.g., 0053) that Elsevier requested. A preliminary investigation revealed that it will be difficult and time-consuming to change the server software to log the electronic page number. The University Libraries' TULIP usage reports therefore include the printed, rather than the electronic, page numbers requested by users.

- **Location:** Locating the user is problematic because it invades user privacy and because it is impossible to do accurately. LIS does log IP addresses, but machines are often moved from building to building without changing the address, so though the address may indicate an office location, the machine could really be in a dormitory or public computer cluster. Therefore the University Libraries decided to indicate only whether the user is in or out of the library. This too, however, turned out to be problematic.

The University Libraries' usage monitoring code strips the first two digits (e.g., 128.2) from the IP address of the client before encrypting and logging the information. This information was decrypted to determine whether it matches any of the dedicated LIS machines in the libraries. However, since the first two digits are stripped from the IP address, it is possible that an authenticated (CMU) user, for example, using a machine at MIT with the same final digits as one of the libraries' public LIS machines (e.g., 21.20) may show up in the usage reports as searching from inside of the University Library. The occurrence of this problem is probably so small as to be irrelevant.

Retrieval and image server transactions are logged on the server machine and automatically moved once a week to the logger machine (the hardware is discussed in Part II, Section 1.1). Retrieval client logs are sent to the logger machine in real time.

2.1.7.2. Assembly of Log File

Perl scripts are used to combine the data from LIS clients and servers and generate the TULIP usage reports in the format required by Elsevier. The TULIP report format is problematic in that it collapses multiple transactions into one, for example, the time and date when a request was received by the retrieval server and the time and date when the bibliographic record was displayed by the retrieval client.

2.2. History and Current Status

2.2.1. Successful and Abandoned Prototypes

The design and functionality of the Motif (UNIX) user interface for browsing image collections and displaying and navigating image pages was the University Libraries' biggest obstacle to releasing TULIP images to campus. Several image user interfaces were built and tested over a three year period (1991-1993):

- **1991-1992 - The first image client.** Developed by the Mercury Project, the first UNIX-based image client was implemented using raw X rather than Motif because the programmers believed that Motif would greatly reduce the speed of delivering images to the desktop. The initial prototype was comprised of two raw X windows: a Document Display window for displaying and navigating image pages and an hierarchical Document Browser for displaying and navigating image collections, e.g., the TULIP Materials Science Journals collection. The images available at the time were images of selected computer science journals scanned with the permission of Elsevier Science Publishers (ESP) and the Institute for Electrical and Electronics Engineers (IEEE). To increase the readability and usability of table of contents information, Optical Character Recognition (OCR) software was used to create (ASCII) interactive tables of contents of the Elsevier journals. The prototype client windows and an interactive table of contents are shown in Figures 1-3 of the "1993 Annual TULIP Report" from Carnegie Mellon University Libraries.

- **Spring 1993 - The second image client.** The Mercury Project ended in July 1992 and TULIP moved to Computing Services at Carnegie Mellon. At Computing Services' request, the University Libraries prepared detailed user interface design specifications for a new image display window and browser (based on the results of the April 1992 usability study), and submitted them to Computing Services in September 1992. The proposed design was rejected, and instead Computing Services implemented a Motif control panel for navigating images displayed in a raw X window, and a Motif browser. (The performance concerns that led Mercury to implement the Document Display window in raw X rather than Motif did not apply to the Browser, which displayed only ASCII lists of directory and file names.) The Motif browser resembled the initial raw X browser, not the browser detailed in the University Libraries' design specifications, i.e., it did not follow the principles established in the *Motif Style Guide*. The Motif control panel and browser are shown in Figures 4-5 of the "1993 Annual TULIP Report" from Carnegie Mellon University Libraries. Because many of the problems identified in the April 1992 usability study were not solved by the Motif control panel and browser, the University Libraries did not conduct a usability study or release the software to campus. Computing Services released the software to the School of Computer Science. It was not well received and was quickly abandoned.

- **Fall 1993 - The third image client.** By Fall 1993, Computing Services had developed another raw X Document Display window and another Motif Browser. The new display window was designed to look and feel like Motif without incurring the performance problems predicted with Motif. It somewhat resembled the design specifications submitted by the University Libraries in September 1992. The windows are shown in Figures 6-7 of the "1993 Annual TULIP Report" from Carnegie Mellon University Libraries.

The TULIP project returned to the University Libraries in January 1994. By then the University Libraries had decided to develop a new client for the Library Information System (LIS). The new client design included a new image Document Display window and Collection Browser, and an architecture that would facilitate natural-language as well as keyword-Boolean retrieval. While development proceeded on the underlying client software modules, two research studies were conducted in 1994 to develop user interface specifications for the new client. (See Part I, Sections 3.1.2. and 3.2.2.)

In the Fall 1994, the University Libraries signed an agreement with Sirsi Corporation to purchase their integrated library management system software called Unicorn, to conduct human factors research of the multi-platform graphical Unicorn clients, and to develop image system components and transfer them to Sirsi. The long-term plan now is to replace the LIS clients with the Unicorn clients. Consequently, work on the new image client stopped.

2.2.2. Migration to Production

The University Libraries released TULIP in April (bibliographic data) and June (image collection) 1994. Since then, there has been an unprecedented turn over in system management personnel responsible for updating TULIP. TULIP has had four different system managers. The learning curve is substantial with TULIP, given the problems in getting the data (in 1994), managing the data with the Newton and Depot software, and generating the usage reports required by Elsevier. Consequently, the TULIP data was (more often than not) out of date and usage reports were not generated until Summer 1995.

The turn over of system managers has aggravated an ambiguous distribution of system support between Operations and R&D tasks. In addition, the distinction between experimental and production systems was not clearly delineated. During TULIP, these organizational flaws were exposed and resolved. Basic practice now requires at least half of an FTE dedicated to system support tasks for R&D. In addition, projects will be fullymanaged within R&D for their duration. They will not be released to LIT Operations until they are fully supported services.

2.2.3. Problems and Solutions

The three most significant problems that the University Libraries encountered in TULIP are:

1. The provision of a suite of desktop clients for retrieving and navigating text and images that meets the needs and expectations of academic users. The proposed solution to this problem is described in Part II, Section 2.2.1 of this report.

2. The provision of an image print service that meets the needs and expectations of academic users and data providers. The proposed solution to this problem is described in Part II, Section 2.4.2.1.

3. The provision of sufficient maintenance and support, both in terms of personnel and hardware, to keep the database and image collection up to date. The proposed solution to this problem is described in Part II, Section 2.2.2.

2.3. Experiences

2.3.1. Quality of Data and Images

The quality of the TULIP data, particularly the images and the raw ASCII (full text), improved over time. For example, masking the images prior to scanning brought an end to the customer complaints about ugly black borders around the pages. The use of better OCR software provided less "dirty" text for indexing purposes, as well as x-y coordinates for mapping locations in the text to locations in the image.

2.3.2. Storage

The cost of magnetic storage for a seldom-used collection is not cost-effective given the cost of current electronic storage media and the cost of comparable storage for print. Part I, Section 4 of this report discusses the economics of TULIP.

2.3.3. Network Delivery to End Users

TULIP was not used heavily enough at Carnegie Mellon to "push the envelope" of the campus network. A larger, more comprehensive collection of broader interest is required to change the behavior patterns of students, researchers and faculty, such that their use of electronic full text stresses the network.

2.3.4. Viewing

Providing a powerful, yet user friendly client for multiple computer platforms was one of the most difficult problems encountered in TULIP. It is not cost effective for the University Libraries to develop a suite of clients. Though the popular WWW browsers provide a ready-made solution to the client problem, the WWW clients are not particularly well designed and have sufficient drawbacks (e.g., no authentication, no "state" or notion of a user "session") to make them less than an optimal solution. The University Libraries short term plans are to exploit the WWW clients while working with Sirsi Corporation to develop powerful, user friendly graphical clients for retrieving bibliographic information and full text (including images). The long term goal is to replace the Motif and VT100 LIS clients with a suite of clients (Motif, Mac and PC Windows) implemented by Sirsi.

2.3.5.   Printing

Users did not print the TULIP images because the print service provided was neither conspicuous nor user friendly. The new WWW TULIP print service (described in Part II, Section 2.1.1.1 of this report), scheduled for release by the end of December 1995, may change user behavior in this regard. Future plans for printing are provided in Part II, Section 2.4.2.1.

2.3.6.   Internet Delivery

The University Libraries were unsuccessful at FTPing TULIP datasets over the Internet. Since January 1995, TULIP data has been delivered on CD ROM.

No requests have been received to print TULIP images not in Carnegie Mellon's image collection, so no articles had to be FTP'd from Engineering Index or Article Express.

2.3.7.   Conclusions

There is still considerable technical work to be done to provide the optimal infrastructure to deliver electronic texts in the campus environment. The following issues remain unresolved:

- Purchasing or accessing the data cost-effectively.
- Determing whether to store the data locally or to access it remotely, based on the needs of campus users.
- Providing access to the data from all major client platforms in a distributed computing environment with a well designed user interface.

Solutions to these problems will drive future research and development efforts. Additional conclusions are provided throughout this report.

2.4. Future Developments

2.4.1. Additional Data Formats

The University Libraries plan to begin experimenting with additional data formats (e.g., SGML, PostScript, PDF, color images) in 1996.

2.4.2. Additional Functionality

2.4.2.1. Networked Image Printing Outside of the Libraries

The Mercury prototype image software used in Motif LIS does not enable users to print images. Adding print capability is a high priority. The University Libraries' goals are:

- To provide networked printing of documents in the image collections.

- To enable users to print image documents on their local printers.

- To enable users to print entire articles, selected pages or page ranges.

Technically, achieving these goals is not particularly difficult. A PostScript header can easily be added to the image files and the images printed on any networked PostScript level II printer on the Carnegie Mellon campus. To optimize security and performance, decompression software could be installed on the printers so that compressed images can be sent across the network and decompressed at the printer before printing. The obstacles to enabling this service are limited human and financial resources and stringent publisher requirements necessary to protect intellectual property.

Publishers expect to recover royalties for printing (if not desktop viewing) of image documents. With the exception of the Enhanced Journal Article Delivery Service (E-JADS) provided by LIS, printing is free at Carnegie Mellon. If the University Libraries enable the printing of images on networked printers across campus, there will be no way to recover royalties or printing costs. The University Libraries cannot afford to underwrite a free printing service for image documents.

In the absence of a networked billing server, the University Libraries must control billing and payment by more tedious means. (Refer to the discussion of E-JADS in Part II, Section 1.5.3.1. and the description of WWW LIS TULIP printing in Part II, Section 2.1.1.1 of this report.) To solve this problem, the short term goal (1996) is to integrate NetBill, a networked billing server developed by Carnegie Mellon's Information Networking Institute, into WWW LIS. NetBill provides billing and royalty tracking associated with NetBill debit accounts; use of NetBill will enable the networked printing of images outside of the libraries. Since all students, faculty and staff will not register and pay for NetBill accounts, the long term goal is to automatically log the print fee transaction in the Cashiers Office, i.e., to put it on the student's bill.

2.4.2.2. Natural Language Retrieval of Full Text

Plans are to index the TULIP raw ASCII files and other full text LIS databases with Claritech natural language retrieval software in 1996. In keeping with the TULIP license, users will search the full text ASCII, but display the images. The client will be WWW LIS.

2.4.3. Other

In cooperation with UMI, the University Libraries are developing UNIX Cache Manager software to create and maintain a magnetic disk cache of recent and popular articles stored (archived) on CD ROM. When the Cache Manager goes into production in 1996, images stored on CD ROM will be downloaded into the cache and delivered to the desktop at the user's request. System managers will also be able to download and lock images into the cache, creating a current awareness service for recent journal issues and (given copyright permission) an electronic reserve reading room for faculty and students. Once the cache manager is in production, plans are to use it to manage TULIP data delivered on CD ROM.

Notes

[1]   Though the ASCII interactive table of contents pages tested in April 1992 were very successful from the user's perspective, they were not successful from a maintenance perspective. It was not practical for the University Libraries to OCR and manually correct the table of contents for all of the TULIP journal issues. The University Libraries experimented with generating ASCII interactive tables of contents from the TULIP bibliographic data in 1994. Though the pages could be constructed quickly, problems in the Mercury prototype software made it impossible to use the interactive contents pages to retrieve one-page articles or pages numbered using Roman numerals or other alphabetic characters. In 1995, the University Libraries began providing interacive table of contents for the TULIP journals (to Carnegie Mellon students, faculty, and staff) using the World Wide Web (WWW) and the TULIP bibliographic data.

[2]   LIS enables users to graphically mark items in the list and to then act on the marked items as a group, specifically displaying (next and previous), saving, mailing and printing marked items on the list. The LIS mark is generic, i.e., an asterisk (*). In contrast, the Claritech software enables users to apply different graphical marks for a different set of functions, specifically keeping and discarding items on the list. Subjects in the structured interviews liked the different graphical markers and additional functionality provided by Claritech.

[3]   LIS enables users to query only one database at a time; the name of the database is recorded with the result set. The Claritech software enables users to query multiple databases at once, so all records in a result set are not necessarily from the same database.

[4]   Charles B. Lowry (ed.), "Managing Technology" Feature by Edward M. Stricker, "Managing the Information Revolution," *Journal of Academic Librarianship* 20, no. 5/6 (November 1994): 315-16.

[5]   Herbert White, "Scholarly Publication, Academic Libraries, and the Assumption That These Processes are Really under Management Control." *College and Research Libraries* 54, no. 4 (July 1993): 293–301.

[6]   Judith Salk (exec. ed.), *33rd Edition Ulrich's ™International Periodicals Directory, 1994-95,* The Bowker International Serials Database(New Providence, New Jersey: R.R. Bowker, A reed Reference Publishing Company, 1994): p. vii.

[7]   Catherine Barr (ed.), *The Bowker Annual, Library and Book Trade Almanac* ™, (New Providence, New Jersey: R.R. Bowker, A reed Reference Publishing Company, 1994): p. 532.

[8]   Blackwell North America, *Approval Program Coverage and Cost Study* , (Blackwood, N. J.: Blackwell North America, Inc., 1993): 10.

[9]   Charles B. Lowry, "Catching the Second Wave of Library Automation, Information Technology and Transformation," book chapter in Mel Collier and Kathryn Arnold (eds.), ASIS, *Proceedings of the First International ELVIRA Conference (1994)*, Milton-Keynes, UK, (May 3-5, 1995): 20-24.

[10]   The disk storage capacity noted in this report is the total space on the machine, including the space required for the operating system, applications, and swap space. It is not, strictly speaking, the space available for storing data.

[11]   It is understood that usage data gathered in this way is dubious because it is not authenticated, i.e., there is no way to be certain that the users are who they say they are.

[12]   The University plans to discontinue the Alumni Network in 1996 due to lack of interest.

Bibliography

PUBLICATIONS

Lowry, Charles B., and Barbara G. Richards. "Courting Discovery: Managing Transition to the Virtual Library". *Library Hi Tech.* Vol. 12, No.4 (1994).

Lowry, Charles B. "Catching the Second Wave of Library Automation, Information Technology and Transformation." ASIS,*Proceedings of the First International ELVIRA Conference (1994).* Edited by Mel Collier and Kathryn Arnol. Milton-Keynes, UK, 1995.

Lowry, Charles B., and Denise A. Troll. "Carnegie Mellon University and University Microfilms International, 'Virtual Library Project': If We Build It, Will They Come?" *The Serials Librarian.* Vol. 26, No. 3 / 4 (1996). Also to be published in *Serials to the Tenth Power: Tradition, Technology and Transformation.* Edited by Beth Holley and Mary Ann Sheble. North American Serials Interest Group, Inc. (NASIG). Forthcoming.

Richards, Barbara G. "Project Mercury: A Virtual Library Case Study." *Virtual Libraries.* Edited by Lavernna Saunders. Learned Information, 1995. Forthcoming.

Troll, Denise A., and Barbara G. Richards. *Carnegie Mellon University Libraries TULIP Annual Report* (1994). Carnegie Mellon University, 1995.

Troll, Denise A. *Carnegie Mellon University Libraries TULIP Annual Report* (1993). Carnegie Mellon University, 1994.

Troll, Denise A., Charles B. Lowry, and Barbara G. Richards. "TULIP at Carnegie Mellon." *Library Hi Tech.* Vol. 13, No. 4 (1995).

Troll, Denise A. "The Next Generation Digital Library at Carnegie Mellon." *Feliciter.* Vol. 40, No. 6 (June 1994).

Troll, Denise A. "Providing Bound Item and Document Delivery Services." *Interlending and Document Supply.* Forthcoming.

PRESENTATIONS

Lowry, Charles B. "Carnegie Mellon University and University Microfilms International, 'Virtual Li Project.'" *North American Serials Interest Group, Tenth Anniversary Conference.* Duke Unive Durham, N.C., June 1995.

Lowry, Charles B. "Courting Discovery at Carnegie Mellon Libraries." *Association for Information Dissemination Conference.* Clearwater, Florida, March 1993.

Lowry, Charles B. "If We Build It, Will They Come? Online Full-Text Journals at CMU." *Associ of College and Research Libraries New England Chapter Fall Conference.* Regis College, We Massachusetts, October 1995.

Lowry, Charles B. "LIS GUI View of Full Text Electronic Information." *First Electronic Library Visual Information Conference.* Milton-Keynes, UK, May 1994.

Richards, Barbara G. "Digital Images and the Transition to the Electronic Library." *Computers in Libraries '94*. Crystal City, VA, February 1994.

Richards, Barbara G. "Digital Images: Transition to the Virtual Library." *EDUCOM '93*. Cincinnati, OH, October 1993.

Richards, Barbara G. "Electronic Document Delivery." *American Library Association Annual Conference*. New Orleans, LA, June 1993.

Richards, Barbara G. "Managing Reference Services in the Electronic Library: Navigating Our Course or Adrift in the Sea of Change?" *SUNY/OCLC Network annual Reverence Services Conference*. New York, NY, April 1995.

Richards, Barbara G. "TULIP: Implementing at Carnegie Mellon University." *ASIS 1993 Midyear Meeting*. Knoxville, TN, May 1993.

Richards, Barbara G. "Virtual Libraries: An Introduction to Vision and Reality." *PreConference talk at Computers in Libraries '93 Preconference*. Washington, D.C., February 1993.

Troll, Denise A. "Document Delivery and Readability." *SURF '92*. Amsterdam, Netherlands, November 1992.

Troll, Denise A. "Providing Bound Item and Document Delivery Services." *International Interlending and Document Supply Conference*. Calgary, Canada, June 1995.

Troll, Denise A. "Toward the Electronic Library." *NORDINFO Conference*. Lund, Sweden, September 1993. Similar speech given in Copenhagen, Denmark.

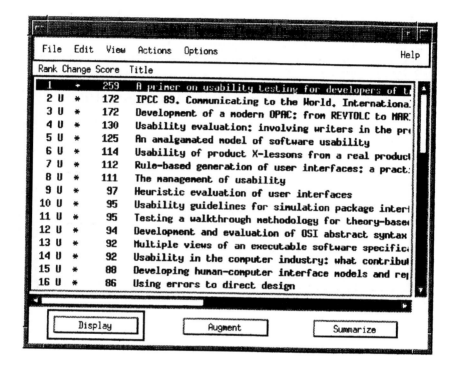

Rank	Change	Score	Title
1	◆	259	A primer on usability testing for developers of t...
2 U	*	172	IPCC 89. Communicating to the World. Internationa...
3 U	*	172	Development of a modern OPAC: from REVTOLC to MAR...
4 U	*	130	Usability evaluation: involving writers in the pr...
5 U	*	125	An amalgamated model of software usability
6 U	*	114	Usability of product X-lessons from a real produc...
7 U	*	112	Rule-based generation of user interfaces: a pract...
8 U	*	111	The management of usability
9 U	*	97	Heuristic evaluation of user interfaces
10 U	*	95	Usability guidelines for simulation package inter...
11 U	*	95	Testing a walkthrough methodology for theory-base...
12 U	*	94	Development and evaluation of OSI abstract syntax
13 U	*	92	Multiple views of an executable software specific...
14 U	*	92	Usability in the computer industry: what contribu...
15 U	*	88	Developing human-computer interface models and re...
16 U	*	86	Using errors to direct design

[Display]   [Augment]   [Summarize]

Figure 1: The display of the list of items retrieved in the Claritech prototype.

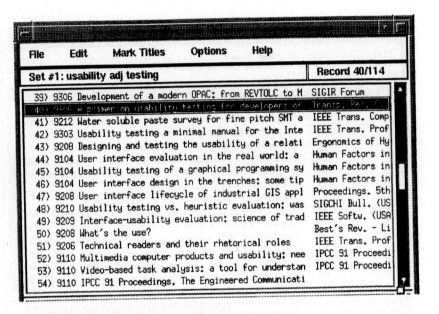

File	Edit	Mark Titles	Options	Help	
Set #1: usability adj testing				**Record 40/114**	

39) 9306 Development of a modern OPAC: from REVTOLC to M	SIGIR Forum
40) 9206 A primer on usability testing for developers of	Transc. Rev. T.
41) 9212 Water soluble paste survey for fine pitch SMT a	IEEE Trans. Comp
42) 9303 Usability testing a minimal manual for the Inte	IEEE Trans. Prof
43) 9208 Designing and testing the usability of a relati	Ergonomics of Hy
44) 9104 User interface evaluation in the real world: a	Human Factors in
45) 9104 Usability testing of a graphical programming sy	Human Factors in
46) 9104 User interface design in the trenches: some tip	Human Factors in
47) 9208 User interface lifecycle of industrial GIS appl	Proceedings. 5th
48) 9210 Usability testing vs. heuristic evaluation: was	SIGCHI Bull. (US
49) 9209 Interface-usability evaluation: science of trad	IEEE Softw. (USA
50) 9208 What's the use?	Best's Rev. - Li
51) 9206 Technical readers and their rhetorical roles	IEEE Trans. Prof
52) 9110 Multimedia computer products and usability: nee	IPCC 91 Proceedi
53) 9110 Video-based task analysis: a tool for understan	IPCC 91 Proceedi
54) 9110 IPCC 91 Proceedings. The Engineered Communicati	

Figure 2: The display of the list of items retrieved in LIS.

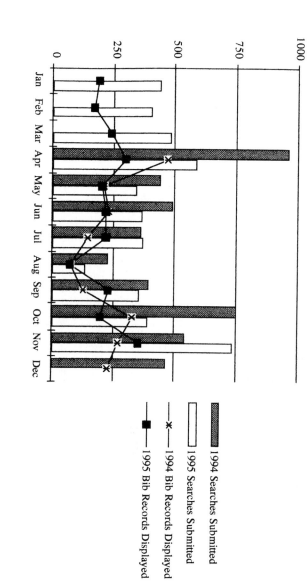

Figure 3: The number of TULIP searches submitted and bibliographic records displayed.

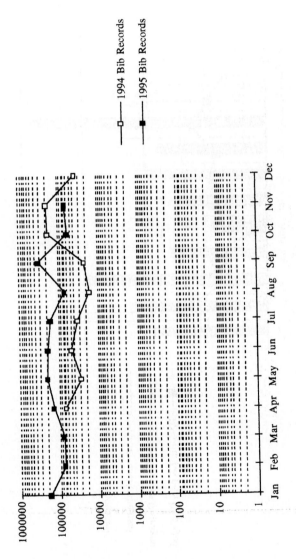

Figure 4: The number of TULIP bibliographic records retrieved.

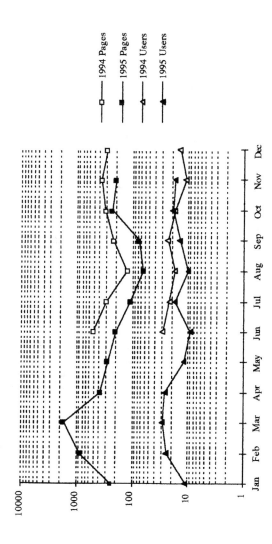

Figure 5: The number of TULIP page images displayed and the number of unique users of those images.

165

TULIP **Final Report**

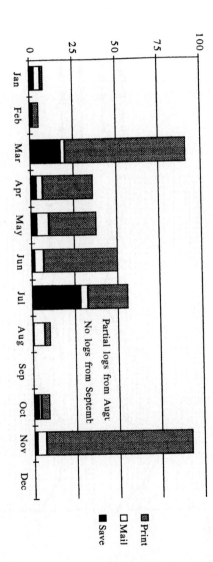

Figure 6: The number of TULIP save, mail and print transactions for bibliographic information in 1995.

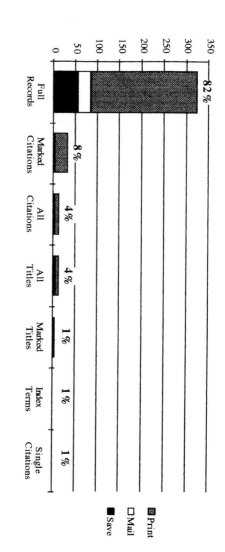

Figure 7: The distribution of TULIP save, mail and print transactions for bibliographic information in 1995.

```
┌──────────────────────────────────────────────────────────────┐
│  PRINT ARTICLE                                                 │
│                                                                │
│  Your Name or UserID:  ┌─────────────────────────────────┐    │
│                        │ troll                           │    │
│                        └─────────────────────────────────┘    │
│                                                                │
│  Select one method of PAYMENT:                                 │
│  ◇  Pay by Copicard (purchase at Circulation Desk.)            │
│          Present Copicard at time of pickup.                   │
│  ◇  Charge to my CMU or JADS (Journal Article Delivery Service)│
│          account number. Enter number:                         │
│                                                                │
│  Allow 2 hours for printing.                                   │
│                                                                │
│  Select one method of DELIVERY:                                │
│  ◇   Pickup articles at the Periodicals Office, 3rd Floor,     │
│          Hunt Library. See Help for service hours.             │
│  ◇  Deliver in campus mail (CMU or JADS account payments only).│
│          Enter campus address:                                 │
│                                                                │
│  REMEMBER, the article you want may be available AT NO CHARGE  │
│  if CMU has a print or microform subscription. See Help for    │
│  details.                                                      │
│                                                                │
│  DISCLAIMER:                                                   │
│  When necessary, we will issue reprints but not refunds.       │
│  Articles may NOT be returned because content is not as        │
│  expected. However, users will not be charged for errors in    │
│  the database (i.e. improperly scanned articles, etc.).        │
│                                                                │
│  ┌──────────────────┐   ┌──────────┐   ┌──────────┐           │
│  │  PRINT ARTICLE   │   │  CANCEL  │   │   HELP   │           │
│  └──────────────────┘   └──────────┘   └──────────┘           │
└──────────────────────────────────────────────────────────────┘
```

Figure 8: The Motif LIS E-JADS order form provided for UMI journal images.

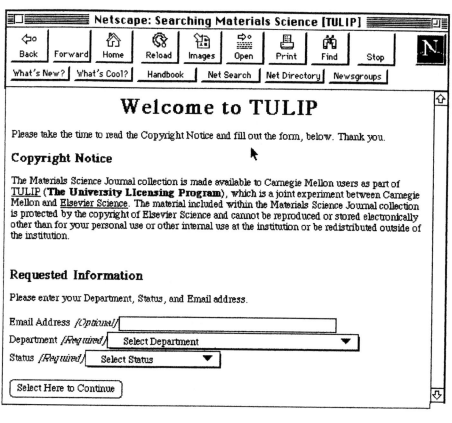

Figure 9: The TULIP "home page" in WWW LIS.

Figure 10: The WWW LIS TULIP Search screen.

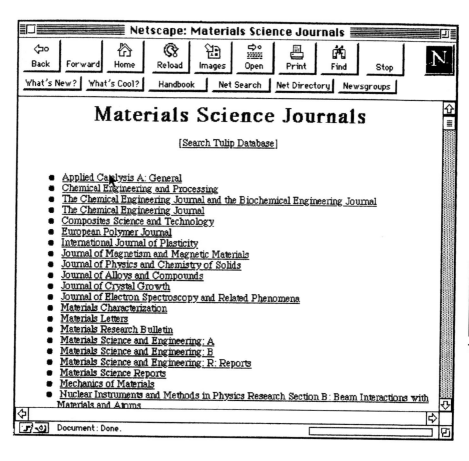

Materials Science Journals

[Search Tulip Database]

- Applied Catalysis A: General
- Chemical Engineering and Processing
- The Chemical Engineering Journal and the Biochemical Engineering Journal
- The Chemical Engineering Journal
- Composites Science and Technology
- European Polymer Journal
- International Journal of Plasticity
- Journal of Magnetism and Magnetic Materials
- Journal of Physics and Chemistry of Solids
- Journal of Alloys and Compounds
- Journal of Crystal Growth
- Journal of Electron Spectroscopy and Related Phenomena
- Materials Characterization
- Materials Letters
- Materials Research Bulletin
- Materials Science and Engineering: A
- Materials Science and Engineering: B
- Materials Science and Engineering: R: Reports
- Materials Science Reports
- Mechanics of Materials
- Nuclear Instruments and Methods in Physics Research Section B: Beam Interactions with Materials and Atoms

Figure 11: WWW LIS displaying a list of TULIP journal titles.

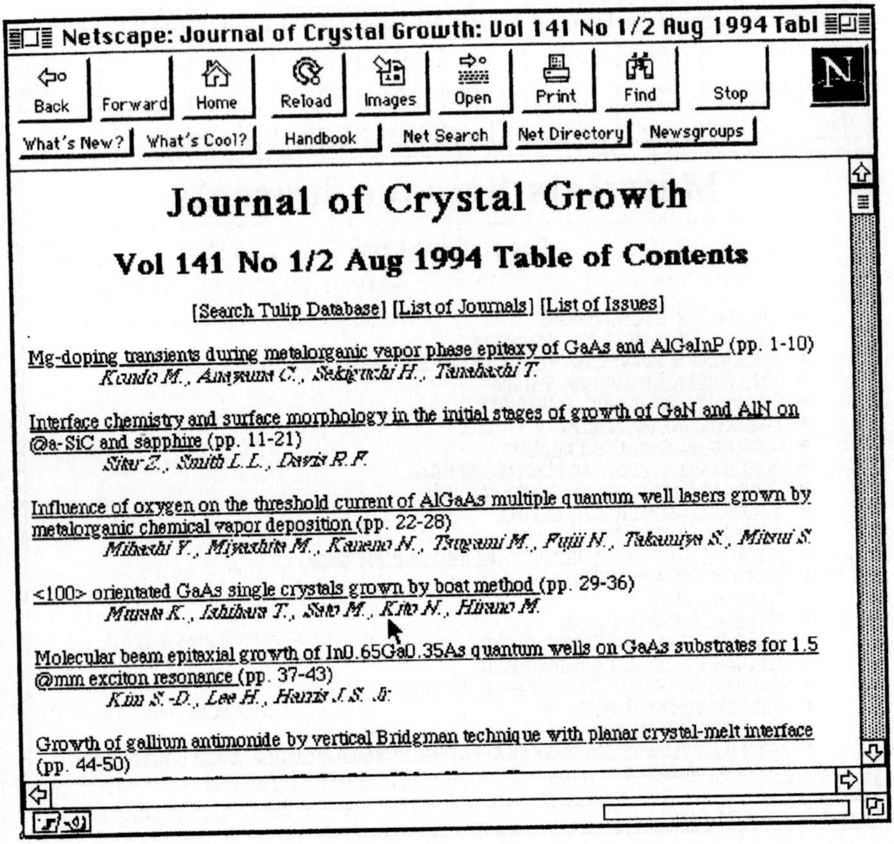

⇐o Back	Forward	⌂ Home	◎ Reload	🗎 Images	⇨o Open	🖶 Print	🔍 Find	Stop	N

| What's New? | What's Cool? | Handbook | Net Search | Net Directory | Newsgroups |

Journal of Crystal Growth

Vol 141 No 1/2 Aug 1994 Table of Contents

[Search Tulip Database] [List of Journals] [List of Issues]

Mg-doping transients during metalorganic vapor phase epitaxy of GaAs and AlGaInP (pp. 1-10)
  Kondo M., Anayama C., Sekiguchi H., Tanahashi T.

Interface chemistry and surface morphology in the initial stages of growth of GaN and AlN on @a- SiC and sapphire (pp. 11-21)
  Sitar Z., Smith L.L., Davis R.F.

Influence of oxygen on the threshold current of AlGaAs multiple quantum well lasers grown by metalorganic chemical vapor deposition (pp. 22-28)
  Mihashi Y., Miyashita M., Kaneno N., Tsugami M., Fujii N., Takamiya S., Mitsui S.

<100> orientated GaAs single crystals grown by boat method (pp. 29-36)
  Murao K., Ishihara T., Sato M., Kito N., Hirano M.

Molecular beam epitaxial growth of In0.65Ga0.35As quantum wells on GaAs substrates for 1.5 @mm exciton resonance (pp. 37-43)
  Kim S.-D., Lee H., Harris J.S. Jr.

Growth of gallium antimonide by vertical Bridgman technique with planar crystal-melt interface (pp. 44-50)

Figure 12: WWW LIS displaying a TULIP journal table of contents.

Table 1: Statistics on re-shelving unbound printed TULIP journals from January / February 1994 to late November 1995.

JOURNAL TITLE	NO.	JOURNAL TITLE	NO.
J. of Magnetism & Mag. Materials	119	Materials Science & Engineering A	10
Surface Science (MI)	86	Materials Science & Engineering R	10
Journal of Crystal Growth	55	Materials Letters	9
Thin Solid Films	41	Sensors and Actuators B	9
Solid State Communications	36	International Journal of Plasticity	7
Journal of Alloys & Compounds	35	Mechanics of Materials	7
Synthetic Metals	23	Composites Science and Technology	6
Materials Science & Engineering B	22	Chemical Engineering & Processing	4
Wear	22	J. of Electron Spect. & Related Phen.	3
Sensors & Actuators A	20	J. of Physics & Chemistry of Solids	3
Applied Catalysis A	19	Materials Characterization	3
Physica C	16	Chemical Eng. J. & Biochem. Eng. J.	2
Surface & Coatings Technology	16	Nuclear Instruments & Methods B	1
European Polymer Journal	13	Progress in Materials Science	0
Materials Research Bulletin	11		
SUBTOTAL	**534**	**SUBTOTAL**	**74**
		TOTAL	**608**

Table 2: The preferred design of the list of items retrieved.

DESIGN OF LIST OF ITEMS RETRIEVED	LIST	% USERS
Show whether the item has been seen or not	Claritech	88%
Show the relevance ranking of the items retrieved	Claritech	82%
Show the titles of the items retrieved	LIS, Claritech	82%
Show the date of publication of the items retrieved	LIS	82%
Show whether an item has been marked to keep [2]	Claritech	71%
Show whether an item has been marked to discard	Claritech	65%
Show the author's name for each publication (if available)	LIS	59%
Show the source of each publication	LIS	41%
Show the total number of items retrieved	LIS	41%
Show the database name [3]	Claritech	29%
Show the call number (if applicable)	LIS	24%
Show the change in ranking after refining a query	Claritech	6%
Show the score of the items retrieved	Claritech	0%

Table 3: The design and functionality of a natural language retrieval interface.

QUERIES	% USERS
Save queries	65%
Submit all or part of retrieved item as a new query	41%
Delete queries	24%
TERMS	
Positively weight search terms	59%
Negatively weight search terms	41%
DISPLAYS	
Display a list of result sets and their accompanying queries	65%
Highlight noun phrases containing query terms in the retrieved records	65%
Display first page of document upon retrieval	47%
Highlight only query terms (not noun phrases) in retrieved records	24%
Display first occurrence of query term upon retrieval	12%
Display ranked list of terms in retrieved document	0%
PREFERENCES	
Specify maximum number of items to retrieve	29%
Specify maximum number of items to consider	6%
OTHER	
Generate hypertext links across databases	53%
Suggest query terms based on retrieved items	35%
Suggest query terms based on separate database	24%

Table 4: Print storage costs.

ELEMENT	EXPLANATION	TULIP COST
Library Binding	85 volumes per year @ $7.10 each	$604.00
Compact Shelving	69 volumes per sq. ft. @ $52/sq. ft.*	$64.00
Library Building	Construction $200 per sq. ft.*	$246.00
Annual Cost	**SUBTOTAL**	**$914.00**
Project Cost	**TOTAL (3.5 Years)**	**$3,199.00**

* Storage for 85 TULIP volumes will require 1.23 square feet.

Table 5: Magnetic storage costs.

ELEMENT	EXPLANATION	TULIP COST
Server	DEC Alpha 200 $7400	$4,895.00
Disk Space	Seagate 9.1 GB @ $3400 x 5 = $17,000	$11,246.00
Computer Room	Construction $250 per sq. ft.**	$500.00
Project Cost	**TOTAL (3.5 Years)**	**$16,641.00**

** Floor space for either magnetic or CD ROM storage requires approximately four square feet, but using racks to stack the data reduces the real requirements for space.

Table 6: Jukebox storage costs.

ELEMENT	EXPLANATION	TULIP COST
Juke Box	Kinotronics 240 CD Capacity	$15,500.00
Computer Room	Construction $250 per sq. ft.**	$1,000.00
Subtotal	**Cost for 154 GB Box**	**$16,500.00**
Project Cost	**TOTAL (36.4 GB Utilized 3.5 Years)**	**$3,928.00**

** Floor space for either magnetic or CD ROM storage requires approximately four square feet, but using racks to stack the data reduces the real requirements for space.

Table 7: Annual building maintenance.

ELEMENT	EXPLANATION	TULIP COST
Library	4.3 sq. ft. x $4.50 sq. ft.	$19.37
Computer Room	4 sq. ft. x $6.00 sq. ft.	$24.00

Table 8: Summary of current magnetic disk and CD ROM jukebox storage.

SYSTEMS & SERVERS	GIGABYTES
LIS - keyword-Boolean retrieval (all databases)	50
LIS - image retrieval (TULIP images)	34
LIS - intermediate server	00.5
LIS - logging & analysis	04.15
Unicorn - keyword-Boolean retrieval	16.3
MAGNETIC PRODUCTION SUBTOTAL	**104.95**
LIS - image retrieval (UMI images)	10
HELIOS - natural language & image retrieval	18
PPG - natural language retrieval	05.6
LIS - database building & software evaluation	12
LIS - database & software testing	05
Unicorn - database & software testing	00.87
MAGNETIC DEVELOPMENT SUBTOTAL	**51.47**
MAGNETIC TOTAL	**156.42**
CD ROM JUKEBOX TOTAL	**1,078**
GRAND TOTAL	**1,234.42**

T U L I·P

Appendix II

Cornell University

Cornell University
TULIP Final Report

Ross Atkinson
ra13@cornell.edu

December 1995

I.   Description of the University

1.   Organization and Structure of the University.

Cornell University, founded in 1868, has a current enrollment of 19,000 students (13,000 undergraduates and 6,000 graduates), and a faculty of 1,600. The University is unusual in that it is partially public (it is the land grant university for the State of New York), and partially private. The University consists of thirteen colleges; eleven of these are in Ithaca, and two (the Medical College and the Graduate School of Medical Studies) are located in New York City.

2.   Organization and Structure of the Library

The Cornell University Library system contains 5.8 million volumes, 6.8 million microform items, as well as large collections of maps, video, sound recordings, and computer files. The Library system consists of nineteen libraries, two of which—the Engineering Library and the Physical Sciences Library—were the primary Cornell participants in the TULIP project. The Engineering and Physical Sciences librarians report to an Associate University Librarian, who reports to the University Librarian. The University Librarian reports to the Provost.

3.   Organization and Structure of IT Services

Cornell Information Technologies (CIT) consists of approximately 325 staff members, divided into three divisions: (a) Information Resources, (b) Support Services and Academic Computing, and (c) Network Resources.

4.   User Demographics

The science colleges of Cornell are the College of Agriculture and Life Sciences (411 faculty, 1,124 graduate students), the College of Engineering (218 faculty, 1,055 graduate students), the College of Veterinary Medicine (128 faculty, 334 students), the Medical College and Graduate School of Medical Sciences (661 faculty). There are additionally a large number of science faculty and students in the College of Arts and Sciences, especially in the fields of physics (45 faculty, 190 graduate students, 2 research associates), chemistry (31 faculty, 145 graduate students, 15 research associates), and astronomy (22 faculty, 43 graduate students, 25 research associates).

II.   TULIP Promotion and Training

1./2.   Description of Promotion and Training.

Throughout the three years of the TULIP project at Cornell, faculty and graduate students in materials science were informed through a variety of resources of the availability of online TULIP materials. Posters were mounted in the Engineering and Physical Sciences libraries. Form letters were sent to faculty through their departments, notifying them of training opportunities. Some faculty were also notified by e-mail of TULIP training sessions. When surveys of the use of the paper versions of the TULIP journals were undertaken, these included a note on each of the journals, explaining that the journal is also available in online form. An announcement of the availability of TULIP journals online was put on the Cornell Materials Science network, and a TULIP button was added to the Cornell Engineering Library web page. Despite all of this promotion, however, one of the most frequent comments by users on the paper survey forms was that they were unaware of the availability of the online versions. This is perhaps indicative of the endemic communication difficulties within the academy.

While TULIP availability was covered briefly in a variety of online training sessions presented by the Engineering and Physical Sciences libraries, the major TULIP training effort was concentrated in two special training sessions—one presented in November of 1994, and one in September of 1995. The first session presented information to graduate students and faculty on how to access the TULIP journals through the Cornell unix client. This was a somewhat complicated procedure, and access to the TULIP journals at that time was limited to users with unix machines—which did include many materials science faculty. Although that unix access is no longer available, a detailed outline of the procedure for gaining unix access to the TULIP journals has been retained on the Web at http://www.englib.cornell.edu/ccr/tulip/tuliphelp.html.

The second session, in September 1995, introduced some half dozen faculty members and two dozen graduate students to access to the TULIP journals by way of the Michigan Web server. This presentation was part of the Cornell Materials Science Colloquium Series, which ensured that it was broadly advertised ahead of time. The September 1995 presentation was somewhat more successful than the November 1994 presentation, not only because the access mechanism (the Michigan Web server) was much more user-friendly, but also because the presentation itself was more broadly conceived. Rather than talking exclusively about TULIP journals, the presenters began with a general discussion about the availability of scientific journals on the Internet. The increasing number of scientific publishers making full text available was noted, and the economic issues relating to online access were considered. TULIP access through the Michigan Web server was then demonstrated in some detail, with special emphasis on printing options for Cornell users. The TULIP journals were then contrasted with some other scientific electronic journals, such as Physical Review Letters.

3/4. Effects and Conclusions

As with so many other aspects of the TULIP project, our promotion and training effort seemed to require of us much more work than the final results appeared to justify. Despite frequent references to TULIP, we were unable to shift much use from the paper to the electronic versions, and we did not bring in nearly as many users (especially faculty) to our training sessions as we had hoped. Because we never managed to generate enough use of the TULIP journals to permit the creation of focus groups, the training sessions provided us with most of the direct user feedback we received. The main problem attracting users to training sessions was probably the sense on the part of the users that TULIP was a short-term, experiment—rather than a potentially fundamental adjustment to how users might gain access to the information they need for their research.

184

III. User Behavior

1. Description of User/Usage Research

We undertook two surveys of the TULIP paper journals, one between November 1992 and April 1993, and one between February and November of 1995. Our goal was to see how the use of the paper related to the use of the online versions. While only a small subset of the users of the paper materials took the time to complete the survey, it does perhaps provide us with information on the relative use of the TULIP journals in their paper form. When we have done an analysis of the—relatively light—use of the TULIP materials in online form, we can compare that information to what we learned from the paper surveys. The resulting of the paper surveys will be included in an Appendix I, and a selection of comments by users will be listed in an Appendix 2.

2. Findings

The paper survey resulted in few surprises, although it did provide us with a more exact understanding of the relative utility of the different TULIP journals. Some of the most useful information will be found in the reasons provided by users for not using the online versions. In most cases, the issue was one of convenience: the paper copies are still faster and easier to use—especially if one has a citation in hand—than the online version. And yet, it cannot be more convenient to come to the library, if one can access this information from home. The only conclusion we can draw is that the users are going to come to the library anyway, because they need access to all of the materials that are not remotely available; and since they must be in the library anyway, the paper copy is much more convenient. A possible goal for future experimentation may be, therefore, to determine what would be required to make the online version of an item preferable to the paper version for someone in the library. (That may in fact not be possibile in many cases.)

3.   Usage Research in View of Privacy Policies

The paper surveys were anonymous (or, if names were offered, we did not retain them). For the records of online access, random numbers were assigned to identify individuals, and even these will probably be deleted from the final report—leaving only the information on status (faculty, student) and possibly departmental affiliation. We feel we were able to gather use data, therefore, without compromising privacy.

4.   Evaluation of Usage of the TULIP System

We have data on the use of the Unix client, as well as the access from Cornell to the Michigan Web server. We are in the process of putting these data into the form you requested, and of drawing some conclusions. We will send this information to you shortly.

5.   Conclusions/Evaluation

In both training sessions, one of the clearest messages that we received from our users was the need for fast and effective printing. People do not want to use electronic materials, if they cannot print those materials easily. The system that we had set up that would permit users to order printed copies (at 600 dpi) was not acceptable to many users: they required the ability to print immediately—otherwise they would prefer to use the paper versions and photocopy.

The other message we received from users at the training sessions was that users were generally not willing to learn a new and special procedure for gaining access to a small number of journals for a limited time. If they knew that they would have access indefinitely to all of the core journals in their discipline (rather than the journals published by a single publisher), then it would be worth their time learning how to access those journals online and changing their research habits. Even for faculty users who regularly make use of (and have designed parts of) networked resources, the shift from paper to online access is taking place very slowly and even reluctantly. Most of the users who actually delved into the TULIP journals online probably did so more out of curiosity than with the expectation that this new format would replace the paper format upon which they have traditionally relied.

185

IV.   **Evaluation of Organization and Economic Issues**

Part way through the TULIP project, the Library made the decision to divide organizationally those projects considered to be experimental, such as TULIP, from regular and routine online services (e.g., online catalog maintenance) already in production. This was done mainly in order to protect the support for basic online services. While this decision had its liabilities, it did have the advantage of clarifying reporting relationships, which resulted in significant improvements in productivity: for the first time, we were able to guide the development of the TULIP effort, without constantly being compelled to interrupt our experimental work in order to support our production work. The main drawback of this decision has been that the experiments are no longer directly linked to the Library's overall online production effort; this increases the danger that experiment and production will proceed along different lines, potentially rendering the results of experimentation unacceptable to or impossible to integrate into the regular online service operation.

The TULIP project has provided us on the other hand, with excellent opportunities for the library and CIT staff to work closely together. The links established as a result of the TULIP project will remain in place for some time, and provide us with a head start on any future collaborative efforts.

While the Library provided administrative and public service support for TULIP, the main technical work on the project was accomplished by a combination of special support from CIT and grant funding received to further the creation of the Cornell digital library. CIT also assumed full responsibility for archiving the TULIP materials (on the Epoch server). If the Library is to assume responsibility for making electronic journals routinely accessible using similar methods to that of TULIP, the Library will need to identify significant storage space and appropriate technical staff.

Since we made the transition toward the end of the project from our own Unix client to the Michigan

TULIP database, the project also provided us with the opportunity to work with the University of Michigan. It is clear that we can rely on the server of another institution to provide us with full access to electronic journals, and we assume that such divisions of responsibilities will become an increasingly regular feature of online services.

Our views of the economics of the TULIP project changed over the years, due mainly to the departure of the Vice President for Information Technologies, Stuart Lynn. One of Stuart's goals for the TULIP project was to text the practicability of the "just fuzzy enough" thesis: publishers should allow all of their journals to move freely around the network, but those journals should be just fuzzy enough that the users will feel compelled to print them out—and the charge to the user should be for such printing (possibly as an alternative to subscription). The interest in establishing a procedure to charge users for printing was much greater early in the project, therefore, than later. At least after the first training session, we began to assume that the main purpose of printing was to provide users with copies—rather than to provide the publisher with revenue or to provide the library with a subsidy for the subscription. While it remains likely that users will need to pay for their printing in future, the charge for that printing may well be what is needed to cover those printing costs—but no more. We seem to be assuming generally, moreover, that the right for local users to print individual copies will be covered by the license, and will be assumed to fall under the same rubric of fair use that photocopy does in the paper environment.

The agreement to experiment with scanning and printing 600 dpi versions of all TULIP journals was also mainly a special experiment championed by Stuart Lynn—so that his departure reduced significantly the incentive to sustain that effort. While we continue to believe that there are some instances in which 600 dpi is necessary for effective graphics, 300 dpi appears adequate for most printing purposes. The cost of a special 600 dpi printing effort may not therefore necessarily be justified by the enhanced legibility. Again, what feedback we have received indicates that speed or immediacy of printing is much more important than the quality of the print: users would appear to prefer a print that is simultaneous but fuzzy to one that is pristine but delayed.

Because the online versions of the TULIP journals received only light use, it is doubtful that we would have been ready to pay additional charges for the online versions at this time. The pressures on our science materials budgets are too great to justify such expenditures. We can no longer provide access to paper journals now needed. We would therefore need to consider very carefully purchasing "added copies" online of items also held in paper at the expense of materials needed in paper form. If the costs of the online versions were less than the paper versions, then there would be some incentive to purchase online versions as an alternative to the paper—but the current Elsevier pricing policy (i.e., online versions on their own being more expensive than the paper versions) does not make that possible.

V.   Implications for the future

1.   Technical/infrastructure

Of all the technical conclusions we might draw from our participation in the TULIP project, two are perhaps most prominent. First, FTP does not work nearly as well as we thought it would for moving around such large quantities of information. Once Elsevier shifted from using FTP to sending CD-ROMs through the mail, a large portion of our production problems disappeared. Perhaps using text files rather than image files would reduce some of this problem, and perhaps future increases in network bandwidth will further improve the efficiency of FTP—but if the decision is to make such large quantities of information available in future, then at the very least Elsevier should ensure that the process is one whereby the institution "pulls" the information from the vendor, rather than relying on the vendor to "push" the information to the institution.

Second, the ubiquitous client, such as the Web, has many major advantages over the kind of proprietary clients we attempted to build at the outset of the project. In a way, many of our technical difficulties were a result of the fact that the project was started a few years too early. If we had begun the project after the broad acceptance of the Gopher and, especially, the World Wide Web, the project could have been much more effective, much earlier. That might, in fact, have changed dramatically the entire outcome of the project, at least at Cornell. We feel that in some ways we may have alienated our users from TULIP through the very slow and halting presentation of a difficult and tentative Unix client of our own making—so that it may be that we were never able to win them back to TULIP, even after we had access to the much more effective Web version from Michigan. If we had been able to provide Web access at the outset, we might have succeeded in moving some of our users from the paper versions to the online versions of the TULIP journals.

2.   Organizational

If online access to standard science journals is to become a reality, that material will probably need to be archived at one or more institutions of higher learning—rather than maintained by the publisher. There is too much distrust on the part of many institutions that—because the primary objective of the publisher is revenue—access could be denied or impaired as soon as it no longer generates revenue. Institutions therefore should own the archive, in the sense that they should have by license the right to make the archive available to its local users indefinitely. All institutions, which have paid for such licenses, should have that same right, even though they need not all hold the archive themselves: rather they should have the right to provide their local users with access indefinitely to an archive of the publication held either at their own or at another institution. In this way, different institutions can assume archival responsibility for large groups of subscribers, rather than expecting every institution to archive all publications. This arrangement also benefits the publisher, in the sense that the less money each institution needs to spend on archiving, the more it can spend on subscriptions. The cooperation between Cornell and Michigan in the TULIP project has demonstrated how effectively and easily such arrangements can be put in place. But while such arrangements are technically unproblematic, they do entail some political challenges. Institutions are not accustomed to working as closely together and relying upon each other to the extent that would be necessary for such cooperative access. Ensuring that institutions learn to cooperate more effectively will be therefore a primary prerequisite for moving scholarly publications online.

3.   Contents-Related

If the content of the TULIP journals was a problem, it was that there was either too little or too much of it. There was too little, in the sense that users would clearly have been much more inclined to make use of the TULIP journals, if all of the major materials science journals (rather than only those published by Elsevier) had been available in that way. As noted above, users appeared to be reluctant to change their research habits to gain access to only a subset of the items they need for a limited period. This would indicate that, while there are clear advantages for Elsevier to be in the forefront of electronic journal development, the real pay-offs may not be visible until the rest of the scientific publishing community feels compelled to follow suit.

If, on the other hand, there had been fewer TULIP journals—if we had concentrated on perhaps three or four journals, we could perhaps have identified the primary users of those journals—the scholars who make regular and heavy use of those journals for their work. We then could have worked individually with those particular users either to help them access the online versions or to determine with much more specificity why they find the online othing to stop us from using this approach in the course of the project, it never really occurred to us. If we can find the funding to continue our subscriptions to a few online versions of the TULIP journals, we may yet try this approach.

Technical Report

I.   Description of current information technology environment

1.   **Hardware and Operating Systems**
1.1.   *Server types and numbers*
1.2.   *Client types and numbers*

Cornell has operated a completely client/server-based infrastructure for several years. (The transition from timesharing occurred during the lifetime of the TULIP project.) Our network protocol is TCP/IP with pockets of AppleTalk and Novell. We have roughly 16,000 network connections on campus, including 6,000 in dorm rooms. Client workstations consist of Macintoshes, PC-compatibles, and Unix systems of all types. Cornell administrative and academic units operate hundreds of servers to support mail, network news, interactive chat, gopher, Web, and FTP. Additional hundreds of servers are run by individual students, faculty, and staff. Cornell is aggressively expanding the variety and importance of academic and administrative services offered primarily or exclusively by client/server-based computer systems, extending most recently to course registration. On November 30, Cornell was named the recipient of the 1995 CAUSE Award for Excellence in Campus Networking.

2.   **Database Systems and Development Tools**
2.1.   *Server*
2.2.   *Client*

Cornell's central administrative database systems are currently migrating from Adabas to a new vendor. The search for and evaluation of the new vendor are under way.

3.   **Central storage technology**
3.1.   *Types and current capacity of:*
- Magnetic disks
- Optical (WORM or Magnetic/Optical)
- Automated tape library

In a client/server environment with large numbers of distributed servers, this concept is meaningless. On any day, new servers could be introduced incorporating any of these storage systems, or existing systems could be decommissioned.

4.   **Network typology**
4.1.   *Client server or terminal oriented*
4.2.   *Local*
4.3.   *WAN*

This was covered in item 1.

5.   **Printing facilities**
5.1.   *Central (What types and how many)*
5.2.   *Decentral/Remote*
- What types and how many
- Types of connections

The central campus computing operation provides a network-connected Xerox Docutech 135 printing system. Hundreds of high- and low-capacity printers operate on LANs all over campus. Within a single LAN, AppleTalk or Novell might be used. The WAN technology is TCP/IP.

II.   Description of TULIP system

Note: Over the course of the project, Cornell has used three distinct digital-library systems to deliver TULIP material. The first was a locally developed client/server architecture with SUN-based servers and clients operating under X-Windows, DOS-Windows, and MacOS. The second was a connection to the Web-based TULIP system at the University of Michigan. The third was a Web-based environment created at Cornell utilizing techniques developed by our Computer Science Department as part of its Dienst system (see http://cs-tr.cs.cornell.edu). Except as noted otherwise, the descriptions below reflect the third system, that is, our local Web implementation.

1.   **Components**
1.1.   *Functionalities*
                 - Functionalities implemented
                 - Rationale for choice of functionalities

Text search of bibliographic fields. Full-text searching of abstracts and of complete content. Browsing within issues. Display of individual page bitmaps at multiple resolutions. Direct access to given journal page number. These functionalities were selected based on feedback from users of the two previous TULIP implementations as well as from users of the Dienst system.

1.2.   *System architecture*
1.2.1.   *Implemented browsing technologies*
1.2.2.   *Implemented searching technologies*
1.2.3.   *Implemented user interfaces*

                 - On which platforms

1.2.4.   *Image viewing (e.g. anti-aliasing, gray scaling, zooming)*
1.2.5.   *Image printing/exporting*
                 - Faxing
                 - E-mailing
                 - File transfer
                 - Local printing

Since this is a Web-based system, all platforms are supported. The user interface is server-driven. Because our digital library project is heavily influenced by preservation considerations, we are continuing to experiment with a variety of image-enhancing techniques. Depending on the collection, we will be storing several low-resolution versions of each bitmap. Which resolution(s) will be stored for the TULIP collection is still being determined. Printing is based on CUPID, the network-printing protocol developed by Cornell and a consortium of other organizations (named "Innovation of the Year" in 1994 by Xplor International).

1.3.   *Networking issues*
Covered elsewhere.

1.4.   *Data preparation and loading*
                 - Validation of incoming datasets
                 - Text preparation
                 - Preparing images
                 - Indexing bibliographic data from DATASET.TOC
                 - Indexing raw ASCII files
                 - Profiling

As implemented by Elsevier, FTP-based data distribution was completely unsatisfactory. Once delivery switched to CD-Rom, scripts could be written and executed without great difficulty.

1.5.   *Implemented storage & image retrieval*
Covered elsewhere.

1.6.   *Set up of security of the system*
Security for our Web servers is handled along with other centrally administered Unix servers.

1.7.   *Usage and logfiles issues*
1.7.1.   *Collection of usage data*
1.7.2.   *Assembly of logfile*

Nothing to report.

2.   History and current status of the project
2.1.   *Description of development process*
             - Successful prototypes and abandoned ones
             - Migration to production
             - Difficulties encountered, solutions found
Covered in preamble.

3.   Experiences
3.1.   *Quality of data/images*
3.2.   *Storage*
3.3.   *Network delivery to end users*
3.4.   *Viewing*
3.5.   *Printing*
3.6.   *Internet delivery*
3.7.   *Other*
3.8.   *Conclusions*

The 300-dpi images produced towards the end of the project seemed satisfactory for most journals. Earlier images had numerous problems, including black borders. Our current feeling is that users will demand very rapid page-turning capability, which will require clever implementation of pre-fetching and other techniques. (Cornell's current Web-based digital-library interface includes these features.) Network speed, even between campuses, is not seen as a serious problem, assuming on-campus connections. Delivery of bitmap images to community residences remains problematic, although events of the past 24 hours suggest that the commercial world may be working aggressively to provide solutions. With respect to printing, we have received the clear message from our users that immediate delivery of low-resolution images to a near-by printer is of more value than delayed delivery of high-resolution images. This has led us to expand CUPID to include linkages to LAN-based laser printers.

4.   Future developments
4.1.   *Additional data formats envisaged/ required, views on suitability*
4.2.   *Additional functionality planned*
4.3.   *Other*

The Cornell Digital Library is being designed to allow for newly emerging formats, since this seems to be an area still in rapid flux. The extent to which off-the-shelf Web browsers support these formats will be of great importance. The acceptance of Acrobat, for example, is severely hampered by its lack of easy access on many Unix systems.

T U L I·P

TULIP Final Report
Georgia Institute of Technology
Library and Information Center

December 13, 1995

I.   Current Information Technology Environment

1.1.   Hardware and operating systems

RS 6000/970
AIX
50 PCs available in Library
17,000 users have access via GTNET

2.1   Database systems

BRS search for UNIX
World Wide Web and Telnet

3.1   Storage

Magnetic disk with 8mm tape back up

4.1   Network

TCP/IP

5.1   Printing

Images are printed remotely at the computer center of faxed to the requestor

II.   Description of TULIP

6.1   Components

Users search the entire abstracts database or select journal title and issue.

TULIP is available as part of GTEL®, the Georgia Tech Electronic Library.

6.2.1   *Terminal interface—BRS/search scripts or WWW*

There is no image viewing software.

6.2.5   *Image Printing*

Fax or hardcopy printing used for images.

E-mail, file transfer and local printing are not used.

6.3   Networking Issues

None

6.6   Security

The system uses Ids and passwords and is restricted to GT students, faculty and staff.

6.7   **Usage and Logfiles**

(See attached report)

7.1   **Description of development process**

Project was developed bt the Library Systems Department and Reference staff. There were CPU problems in making the transition to WWW and insufficient disk space. New equipment will be purchased in early 1996.

8.   **Experience — covered in previous report**

9.   **Future Developments**

9.1   **SGML is desirable**

9.2   **No additional functionality is planned.**
GT is not planning large full text collections for in-house equipment. We prefer to obtain tull text from remote sources.

TULIP Technical Implementation

I. Public release date

09/01/94

II. Functionalities

1.   Our implementation of TULIP permits users to search the entire abstracts database, or to select a journal-orientated approach. If using the latter, the user selects a journal title, a specific issue, and an article from the table of contents. TULIP is available as part of GTEL, our OPAC. We are using a purely terminal/host approach at this time.

2.   **Browser-** no image browser in use.

3.   **Search engine-** BRS/Search for UNIX.

4.   **Interface-** terminal interface; BRS/Search scripts for searching and data presentation.

5.   **Image-viewing software-** none. Fax or hardcopy only for image delivery.

6.   **Export/print on desktop-** none.

III. Loading and distribution

1.   Loading of files

Last dataset loaded 68. Not using Article Express. When we have a partial dataset on our system, there's no way of knowing whether the kickoff system failed, or is merely paused during a transfer. We ended up waiting several days to see if anything new happens before assuming the transfer has been corrupted. An e-mail confirmation of a complete delivery (and even one for a delivery error) would be nice.

2.   Storage

Magnetic disk with 8mm tape backup. Although local storage offers us greater control over the files, the effort required to update the databases, and the cost of disk storage for this purpose argues for remote storage.

3.   Distribution on Campus

Journal images are printed at the computer center or are faxed to the end-user. Our OPAC may be accessed over local ethernet or dialup lines.

4.   Logfiles

Our dbms, BRS/Search, automatically logs searches and other transactions on our OPAC. For TULIP, we simply modified the native log format to fit project specifications. The user ids reflected in the logfiles are encrypted, so that privacy concerns are minimized, and searches cannot easily be tracked to the user who submitted them. At the same time, we have written software to categorize those users by department, faculty/staff/student status, etc.

II.   Promotion

When users first select the TULIP database (we call it MATS for easier recognition of the subject matter) a transaction is emailed to our system administrator containing user information. We then send out a packet to the user which includes a short description of the project, the TULIP survey, Elsevier-provided promotional material, and sample output of the page images as printed or faxed.

III.   Training

MATS training isincluded as part of the normal OPAC training conducted by the Library. To this point, no special MATS or onsite training has been conducted, although we anticipate offering such courses in the future.

IV.   User Behavior Research

None to date

V.   User community

All Georgia Tech faculty, staff and students may search the TULIP abstracting and indexing database. This population is about 17,000. Undergraduates (8,000) may not print or fax journal images, but graduates (4,000) and faculty/staff (5,000) may.

VI.   Subscription changes

None.

	January	February	March	April	May	June	July	August	September	October	November	December	TOTALS
Search Displays Requested	3225	3604	3227	2469	3289	1621	2337	1789	1376	2594			25531
Search Displays Provided	3225	3604	3227	2469	3289	1621	2337	1789	1376	2594			25531
Print Requests Requested	247	185	292	76	153	55	78	35	57	111			1289
Print Requests Provided	244	185	291	75	152	55	77	35	57	110			1281
FAX Output Requested	15	37	15	52	29	23	9	0	11	0			191
FAX Output Provided	15	37	15	52	29	23	9	0	11	0			191
LENDS Delivery Requested	0	2	2	1	0	0	0	0	1	0			6
LENDS Delivery Provided	0	2	1	1	0	0	0	0	1	0			5

TULIP **Final Report**

	January	February	March	April	May	June	July	August	September	October	November	December	TOTALS
Search Displays Requested	5	32	23	3	53	42	379	671	842	3783	3807	1626	11266
Search Displays Provided	5	32	23	3	53	42	379	671	842	3783	3807	1626	11266
Print Requests Requested									3	123	99	44	269
Print Requests Provided									3	123	99	44	269
FAX Output Requested									0	1	7	10	18
FAX Output Provided									0	1	7	10	18
LENDS Delivery Requested									0	1	1	1	3
LENDS Delivery Provided									1	0	1	1	3

TULIP

Appendix IV

Massachusetts Institute of Technology (MIT)

Massachusetts Institute of Technology
TULIP final report

December 1995

I. Description of profile of university

N.B. All quotes below are taken from: _MIT Bulletin: 1995/96_, vol. 130, number 1 (Cambridge: MIT), "Chapter 1: This is MIT", pp 11 - 16.

1. Organization of university structure/organization

"Education and related research - with relevance to the practical world as a guiding principle - continue to be MIT's primary purpose. The Institute is an independent, coeducational, privately endowed university, broadly organized into five academic Schools: Architecture and Planning, Engineering, Humanities and Social Science, Management, and Science. The five Schools house 21 academic departments, complemented by many interdepartmental laboratories, centers, and divisions, and the Whitaker College of Health Science and Technology." (p. 11)
. . .

"MIT's mission can be stated succinctly: to provide the highest quality programs of education and research in all areas of study and investigation where strength and competence have been developed, and to do so, with a strong commitment to public service and to a diversity of backgrounds, interests, and points of view among faculty, students, and staff." (p. 11)

2. Organization of libraries

"The MIT Libraries, with resources of more than 2.3 million volumes, are designed to support all of the Institute's programs of study and research. The library system is composed of five major (divisional) libraries as well as a number of smaller branch libraries. . . . More than 21,000 current journals and periodicals and extensive back files provide comprehensive resources in all major fields." (p. 15)

3. Organization of IT/information services

"Information Systems (IS) provides comprehensive computing, networking, and telecommunications services for all of MIT. IS services and facilities support the academic, research, and administrative use of a broad scope of information and computing technology, and include responsibility for the Athena Computing Environment and MITnet, the campus-wide computer network. The Athena Computing Environment offer computing resources designed for educational use by students and faculty. MITnet connects thousands of computers across the campus, and its connection to the Internet gives MIT access to computers around the world." (p.15).

At MIT, organization of the TULIP experiment took place within the context of the MIT Distributed Library Initiative (DLI), a collaborative effort led by the MIT Libraries and Information Systems. The TULIP implementation team was called BULB and was comprised of public services staff from the Libraries, programmer analyst expertise from Information Systems, a Research Associate from the Dept. of Materials Science, and a counselor from the MIT Intellectual Property Office.

4. User demographics

"MIT's total enrollment is approximately 9,800 students, with somewhat fewer undergraduates than graduates. In 1994-95, MIT students come from all 50 states, the District of Columbia, three territories and 101 foreign countries. . . . The MIT faculty numbers approximately 1,100, with a total teaching staff of over 2,000." (p. 12)

II. User behavior

1. Description of user/usage research (e.g. reshelving, statistics, surveys)

The user group for MIT was composed primarily of graduate students and faculty. They come from the following departments: Brain and Cognitive Sciences; Chemistry; Chemical Engineering; Electrical Engineering and Computer Science; Materials Science and Engineering; Physics; and Toxicology.

MIT made no analysis of reshelving.

MIT relied on Email and direct contact with lead users.

Aside from the Glickman Research Associates focus group, we engaged in no formal surveying. Using the logging requested by Elsevier, we did our own local analysis. Enclosed is the graph of usage by week up to the end of November 1995. Clearly the most usage took place during the spring term. Even in October and November of 1995 after announcement of our intention to discontinue, usage was on par with usage throughout the project.

2. Findings

From research:
MIT participated in the Focus Group run by Glickman Associates. The findings agreed with our other experiences, so all the conclusions are amalgamated in subsection 5 below.

User comments/ direct feedback:
"This is a fantastic system." - Graduate Student
"I finally got around to using TULIP and it is awesome!!" - Faculty
"It is great for the graduate students but I prefer the paper because the micrographs are clearer." - Faculty
"I do like the product and appreciate your efforts in developing it." - Graduate Student

Craig Counterman is a research associate in the MIT Department of Materials Science. He worked directly with the TULIP implementation team. He is both a user of some of the journals in the project, and a technically competent computer user. Thus he was able to give a perspective as a user, with the knowledge of the technical limitations involved in producing my ideal system.
Counterman was able to promote TULIP with his coworkers and in the department from within, supplementing the Library's efforts. He was also able to collect some comments, complaints, and problems which people weren't taking the time to report via formal channels. He gave technical aid to the developers from time to time.

3. Usage research in view of privacy policies

Reaching the balance between the gathering of use information and the protection of privacy was the key issue for the logging activity. MIT implemented the twelve metrics specified in Chapter 5 of TULIP: Specification of the Data Structure and of the Delivery Methods (Version 2.2, March 1994). MIT reached a balance between the capture of useful logging data and the MIT policy to preserve the privacy of members of the community. This balance is achieved by untraceable, anonymous user ID's and the informed consent of the user. At initial access to TULIP the user is presented with an information screen inviting them to contribute use information to the system. Assurances of privacy and an explanation of the type of information gathered and the use of that logged information is given. If the user accepts this offer a logfile is created and the user is normally not bothered again. This is discussed more fully in the Architecture Manual.

4. Evaluation of usage of the TULIP system

This system was used primarily by Graduate Students. They gave the system high praise in terms of ease of use and convenience.

5.   Implications and recommendations

Users found the system understandable and easy to use. The system was criticized for not fitting into people's existing processes of database search. Users would have preferred to have the option of accessing the images as a subset of the big databases they ordinarily use such as Inspec instead of the separate database covering only the TULIP journals.

The system was also criticized for having too small a subset of the desired publications online, and that the publications were limited to Elsevier publications rather than the ones they most frequently used.

From this we conclude that we need to focus our digital page image collection to sets that the customer perceives as complete. This means that if very large collections cannot be brought online as one corpus, smaller more focused collections must be dealt with.

III.   TULIP promotion and training

1.   Description of promotion activities undertaken

Time line:

March 1994	Letter sent to Researchers soliciting participants.
April 1994	Demo of prototype system.
May 1994	Meetings with Materials Science Chair and Graduate Council
June 1994	Site visit and demo to Materials Science Department
September 1994	TULIP Announced to Materials Science Community
October 1994	Formal announcement in letter to Mechanical Engineering, Chemical Engineering, Aeronautics & Astronautics, Chemistry, and Electrical Engineering Departments
October 1994	MIT Libraries Newsletter article on TULIP
November 1994	Two Open-House training Sessions on TULIP. TULIP Posters distributed
December 1994	Letter to Departments from Library and IS directors Jay Lucker and Jim Bruce announcing TULIP
January 1995	Letters sent out to faculty with printout of one of their articles from TULIP database (ongoing)
February 1995	TULIP article in MIT newspaper _TechTalk_
October 1995	Announcement on MIT TULIP WWW page of intention to discontinue TULIP service as of December 31, 1995.

2.   Description of training activities undertaken

The design of the Page Image Delivery System and the use of multi-purpose clients (Willow and Web browsers) minimized training requirements. Participants were encouraged to use Email for comments and training requests. Email turned up occasional opportunities for instruction, but for the most part, people trained themselves.

There was one site visit to the Materials Science department, and two open-house training sessions. The second session was poorly attended. One interpretation of the poor attendance is that users felt comfortable with the system. This view was corroborated by the focus group interview with students in summer 1995.

3.   Effects of promotion and training

Mapping dates from the promotions listed above onto the measured usage of the system shows no significant correlation between promotion and usage.

4.   Conclusions and recommendations

More than any effort on our part, the system spoke for itself. If the articles we had in the database were useful, people found them and used them. No amount of promotion could change the limited scope of the database.

No amount of promotion would change the processes our users habitually used to seek and utilize the information we made available.

IV.   Evaluation of organizational and economic issues

The foundation of the TULIP project at MIT was laid beginning in 1990 when MIT Information Systems and the Libraries began to meet and to discuss common interests and goals. TULIP was an early joint effort of the Distributed Library Initiative (DLI), the broad, umbrella program established to direct and coordinate electronic library efforts at MIT. Early discussions and activities about TULIP were led by the DLI Coordinating Committee, composed of IS staff (Marilyn McMillan, Tim McGovern, Bill Cattey, Connie Mitchell), Libraries staff (Greg Anderson, Tom Owens), and Library 2000 staff from the MIT Lab for Computer Science (Professor Jerry Saltzer, Mitchell Charity). As discussions moved beyond the initial planning and strategy phase, this committee created BULB, the TULIP implementation project team. The core BULB team was composed of a Senior Analyst Programmer (Cattey), the Reference Librarian for Materials Science (Suzanne Weiner), a Research Associate in Materials Science (Craig Counterman), and was convened by Anderson. Others participated in the BULB work as appropriate; for example, Connie Mitchell worked on the TULIP licensing agreement throughout the project. BULB met weekly and reported to the DLI Coordinating Committee.

Economic issues for TULIP at MIT revolved around the costs of content and the technical infrastructure. Because TULIP images were delivered during the experiment at no cost to MIT, the cost of content was not a factor in the experiment. The cost of building the Page Image Delivery System (PIDS) involved staff costs and technical costs. We estimate that the aggregate effort to build the delivery architecture has been 3 FTE for 2 years Because MIT's infrastructure is already in place, hardware costs for TULIP consisted primarily of the server and storage, in total, approximately $100,000. This seems like a relatively inexpensive effort with high return on investment.

With regards to continuing to purchase Elsevier electronic content, we have elected to discontinue loading content in the present mode primarily because the cost is too high and comes at a time of shrinking library budgets. We are excited about electronic content, and look forward to exploring other economic models that are a better fit with our economic realities. MIT is willing to pay for high value information but is under tremendous pressure to spend fewer dollars as time goes on. For example, electronic-only distributions are particularly attractive since they eliminate postal, paper, and packaging costs.

V.   Implications of the TULIP project for the future

1.   Technical/ infrastructure

Through development of PIDS to provide service to the TULIP images, MIT now has a robust, scalable architecture to deliver page image content to its community, regardless of discipline. We believe that page images will continue to be a critically important format for electronic library materials into the future. The TULIP project was the galvanizing effort that provided the focus and impetus to build this architecture.

For the future, MIT has a robust delivery architecture which it will populate with massive amounts of content, local, commercial, and scholarly.

2.   Organizational

TULIP demonstrated that an implementation team with representation by the key players - library, information technology, and target audience, is optimum. The BULB team maintained a balance of needs and perspectives, provided the necessary discussion and decision forum for the project to move forward, and it worked within the context of the DLI, building to and utilizing tools and services that provide a ubiquitous information access environment.

For the future, this implementation model will be replicated in other projects as appropriate. What has not yet been established is the best organizational model for moving development projects such as TULIP into an ongoing, operational mode.

3.   Contents related

At a format level, page image content will continue to be one key component of an electronic library. At a content level, academic communities prefer comprehensive electronic collections rather than a concentration of content from a single provider. Providing the critical mass of information that encourages scholars to use electronic resources will require coordination and collaboration among publishers, libraries, and the communities they serve.

For the future, MIT is interested in working with publishers to discuss and determine jointly viable models to provide content in electronic form to our community.

TECHNICAL REPORT

I. Description of current information technology environment

TULIP service was offered to the entire MIT campus community via Athena, the academic computing environment for MIT.

Athena has developed into a campus-wide networked computer system environment serving the needs of MIT's academic community. Athena has over 600 publicly-accessible workstations distributed around campus in both public and departmental clusters where students and faculty can go 24 hours a day, 365 days a year to do class work, write papers, do personal work, and even play games. . . . Athena is structured so that a student may sit down at any Athena workstation on campus, and have access to his or her own customized environment and personal files." In total there are over 1600 workstations in the Athena environment. These are UNIX workstations, running X/windows, and the network communications protocol is TCP/IP. The Athena system architecture is a client/server model; that is, "individual workstations (clients) access (or are supplied with) numerous services from other machines (servers) located elsewhere on the network. Most computations are still handled on the local workstation, but the storage of files and other services are actually delivered from elsewhere on the network — by machines devoted to delivering those services. The client/server model allows centrally-managed services to be concentrated so that a relatively small staff can support the system." (from _Welcome to Athena_)

1. Hardware and Operating Systems

1.1. Server types and numbers
RS/6000 520 running AIX 3.2

1.2. Client types and numbers
Sun Sparc with Solaris, Digital DECStation with Ultrix, SGI Indy with Irix, IBM RS/6000 with AIX. Also PC's and Macintosh via the World Wide Web interface.

2. Database Systems and Development Tools

2.1. Server
SiteSearch from OCLC, Dublin, Ohio

Code for on-the-fly conversion of Group IV FAX to gif for World Wide Web delivery comes from the University of Michigan.

NCSA World Wide Web server.

2.2. Client
Willow from the University of Washington.
MIT-written Image viewer: Tviewer.
Any Z39.50 search client.
Any World Wide Web client.

3. Central storage technology

All TULIP data at MIT resides on spinning magnetic storage. The pros include immediate access, standard, known management techniques, continuously decreasing costs, and known expansion/growth paths. Cons relate to any storage mechanism residing locally on the campus: management and ultimate scalability.

3.1. What types and current capacity of:
3.1.1. Magnetic disks
40 GB composed of 9 GB commodity SCSI drives.

3.1.2.   Optical (WORM or Magnetic/Optical)
None

3.1.3.   Automated tape library
None

4.   Network typology

4.1.   Client server or terminal oriented
Client/Server

4.2.   Local
100 Mb fiber ring to every building. 10 Mb UTP ethernet to every desk, and in every dorm room.

4.3.   WAN
Our Fiber ring is directly on the Internet.

5.   Printing facilities
5.1.   Central (What types and how many)
None

5.2.   Decentral/Remote
HP LaserJet 4simx are spread around campus in public computing clusters and department areas. They sit directly on the campus-wide network.

- Types of connections
10 Mb UTP ethernet.

II.   **Description of TULIP system**

6.   Components

6.1.   Functionalities

Functionalities implemented:
Bibliographic Search via Z39.50 Graphical Client. Record retrieved contains article abstract. From the Bibliographic record, the article page images can be obtained.
Browse search from World Wide Web pages that allow the user to traverse a hierarchy from Journal title, to list of issues, to issue table of contents naming the article titles and authors. Picking a particular title provides access to the article page image.
The MIT Page Image Delivery System (PIDS), the underlying system architecture supporting TULIP, provides both search and browsing capabilities. Search/discovery access is provided through the bibliographic search client, WILLOW (Washington Information Looker- upper Layered Over Windows), an X-based graphical, Z39.50 compliant access client. Journal title, issue table of contents browsing is provided via the World Wide Web. Both forms of access spawn the same page image fetch and browse system. For more complete information, see _MIT-PIDS — The MIT Page Image Delivery System: Architecture Manual_, by Bill Cattey, Senior Analyst Programmer, MIT Information Systems, February 1995. A user's eye view of the system would reveal three components: 1) a Z39.50 bibliographic search client (Willow) and the Tviewer image browser; 2) an article browse http client (Mosaic, etc.) and the Tviewer image browser; and 3) server hosts for Images, WWW Table of Contents (html), and Bib database server.

Rationale for choice of functionalities:
Students do research by bibliographic search, but professors keep up to date in the field by browsing the journals when they arrive.
TULIP at MIT is not integrated into the Libraries' OPAC (that system has recently changed, and the new system will provide those opportunities for integration in the future). The MIT PIDS system, however, is

also not a separate system. PIDS is an interoperable system composed of a consistent underlying architecture capable of supporting a variety of intellectual content data while serving that content via a variety of access/interface methodologies such as Willow or WWW. For example, TULIP is available along with a variety of other resources through Willow, and TULIP is one of many information resources available to the MIT community via the Web. TULIP is a linked resource possible from a variety of sources at MIT. As a point for future discussion, the distinctions between "separate" and "integrated" are becoming less significant in an interoperable, network-linked information environment.

6.2. System architecture

6.2.1. Implemented browsing technologies
A perl script converts TULIP Table of contents format into World Wide Web pages.

6.2.2. Implemented searching technologies
SiteSearch licensed from OCLC, Inc. is the bibliographic database server responsible for holding the bibliographic database consisting of a record for every article and its associated image identifiers. SiteSearch accepts and responds to queries from the Willow search client.

6.2.3. Implemented user interfaces
Collaborated with UW on integrating their GUI Search/Retrieve product, Willow.
On which platforms: Sun Sparc with Solaris, Digital DECStation with Ultrix, SGI Indy with Irix, IBM RS/6000 with AIX. The MIT Tviewer is supportable on Unix workstations but has not been ported to Macintosh or Windows platforms. The Table of Contents Browse program could be any WWW client. Willow, the bibliographic search client is being ported to Windows, but as yet there is no Macintosh port planned.

6.2.4. Image viewing (e.g. anti-aliasing, gray scaling, zooming)
MIT's Tviewer anti-aliases 300 dpi to 75 dpi or 150 dpi (in zoom mode) and tone scale transforms The anti-aliased image to enhance contrast. Tviewer provides several image enhancements; through efficient and robust caching techniques that can decode the Group 4 Fax TIFF images very fast. The viewer provides very fast page browsing forward and backward within an article and supports display of specific page numbers as requested. Tviewer provides Zoom capabilities (magnification) of images for highly readable displays for individual pages or for entire articles. Finally, Tviewer provides page or entire article printing capabilities that can be directed at any Athena networked printers. The TULIP 300 dpi monochrome images are anti-aliased to 75 dpi 17 gray levels. Handling of the 17 gray levels is to transform them via inverse-gausian to seven gray levels. For Zoom display, images are anti-aliased to 150 dpi, nine gray levels. The nine gray levels are inverse-gausian transformed to seven gray levels.

6.2.5. Image printing/exporting
- Faxing
  None
- E-mailing
  None
- File transfer
  None supported, but could have been feasable as a side-effect of the NFS delivery mechanism.
- Local printing
  The "Page Print" and "Article Print" buttons on Tviewer encode ASCII85, CCITT Fax Level II PostScript and send it to the printer. (The code is an ongoing collaboration among UW, Michigan, OCLC, and MIT.)

6.3. Networking issues

For delivery of the page images, we use NFS. NFS is high performance, but the file system mounting is integrated into the MIT-local name space. (We have our own interface "attach" which is called by a helper application from Willow or the WWW browser to fetch the image.) Using NFS and the MIT network, image transmission is essentially instantaneous compared to the time taken to decode the image. (You can turn a page in between one and three seconds. The viewer pre-fetches images, so page turning can seem instantaneous.)

We have experimented with on-the-fly conversion of the Group IV FAX image to gif and then deliver via the World Wide Web http protocol. Conversion takes on the order of two seconds. Delivery takes another couple seconds (depending on the performance of the WWW client and server). We keep the converted images in a local cache for increased performance. No pre-fetch seems possible at this time. This method forces the user to wait the maximum amount of time per page, but works on all computing platforms on our network, as well as allowing access from home (assuming a telephone link with PPP protocol, a typical image would be delivered in 30-60 seconds.)

6.4. Data preparation and loading

Validation of incoming datasets:
Our scripts always run the Sum checking. With the new MD5 based checksumming we no longer have to worry about customers reporting corrupt images that were not caught in the process, or additional work to confirm as valid images reported corrupt by the UNIX sum program.

Text preparation:
We do not use the RAW files. Their level of accuracy was deemed too low.

Preparing images:
All datasets prior to #EA000029 were cropped using code from the University of Michigan. Other than that, we copy the cd into the file server, rename the filenames to be upper case, and serve them up.

Indexing bibliographic data from DATASET.TOC:
Two parallel indicies are created:
SiteSearch for bibliographic search: A perl script converts DATASET.TOC format to SGML. SiteSearch utilities convert the SGML to BER and load it into an indexed database.
World Wide Web pages are created by a perl script which takes the DATASET.TOC file and generates a tree of html files.
Indexing raw ASCII files:
No indexing performed on the .RAW files.

Profiling:
No profiling other than the basic image viewing log was performed.

6.5. Implemented storage & image retrieval
Image storage is simple minded: Use the UNIX file system and export directly via NFS. Experimentally we can grab files, down-convert them to gif and export them via the World Wide Web http protocol.

6.6. Set up of security of the system
The SiteSearch database has no robust security challenge feature, so we keep the identity of the SiteSearch database a secret outside of MIT. We would prefer to make this bibliographic database widely available, but Elsevier insists on restricting access to the Abstract to only members of the MIT community.
The NFS export of the image files are restricted to the .mit.edu Internet domain through custom coding in the IBM NFS implementation which was eventually made a part of their standard release. (We are allowed to say "*.mit.edu" instead of naming explicitly all of the hosts at MIT that might use the images.)

The WWW browse access has no sensitive information so it is unrestricted. The experimental http delivery is unrestricted. We're just trying to get it to work at all at this point.

6.7. Usage and logfiles issues
6.7.1. Collection of usage data
Logging is done from inside the Tviewer program. A log entry is made via a message sent to a single central logging server. The data sent has been carefully designed to not reveal the individual identity of a user of the images.
No call out to the logger was added into Willow for bibliographic search.
No call out to the logger CAN be added to the WWW delivery system.

6.7.2. assembly of logfile

The central logger creates a file that is already in the format requested by Elsevier. Periodically a person moves the log file aside; restarts the logger, and sends the particular log file to Elsevier.

7. History and current status of the project

7.1. Description of development process

The TULIP implementation team at MIT, called BULB, involved reference staff from the Engineering and Science Libraries and a Research Fellow from the Materials Science Dept. to lead outreach, publicity, and training efforts. Throughout the project, the implementation team took a holistic approach, balancing technical development, building participation and interest in the user community, and relying upon interactions between librarians, researchers, students, and programmers to develop the system to meet user expectations and requirements. For example, in March 1994, a letter was sent to Materials Researchers soliciting interested participants for training. In April a demonstration was held for faculty and graduate students. BULB members were also added to key mailing lists for Materials Researchers and used that outlet to broadcast news about TULIP. Suzanne Weiner, Reference and Collections specialist in Materials Science met with the Materials Science and Engineering Dept. Head in May and with the Graduate Council of the Materials Science and Engineering Dept. In June another demo was given to graduate students and a core group was involved in TULIP testing through the summer. In September TULIP was announced to the MIT Materials Science and Engineering community and in October to the departments of Mechanical Engineering, Chemical Engineering, Aeronautics and Astronautics, Chemistry, and Electrical Engineering and Computer Science. The MIT Libraries Faculty Newsletter contained an article about TULIP in its fall issue. In November and December two more demonstrations of TULIP were held, and a letter encouraging participation was sent jointly by the Director of Libraries and the Vice President for Information Systems to Materials Researchers. TULIP posters were distributed to Libraries and to Materials Science departments. Suzanne Weiner began a specialized effort of searching TULIP for articles by MIT faculty, printing those articles and sending them to the faculty with a cover letter noting the TULIP service, the inclusion of the article(s) and encouraging further participation and support.

210

Successful prototypes and abandoned ones:
It is almost as if we had no time for failures. Depending on the success of the on-the-fly conversion and http delivery, we may phase out Tviewer. There will be a tremendous loss of performance, but the ubiquity of delivery platform and the escape from the software development/support business are very attractive prospects.

Migration to production:
When the customer said we had critical mass of functionality, we declared ourselves in production. But the system continues to be operated and maintained by its original developer. If the project had lasted longer we would have migrated to another person as operator.
The PIDS architecture is ready to migrate into production. Its design will accommodate page image information content, regardless of academic discipline. In August 1995, the MIT Libraries decided not to subscribe to the electronic version of the TULIP journals.

Difficulties encountered, solutions found:
Getting CCITT FAX PostScript to work was difficult and painful. It took meticulous work by far too many people at far too many sites to get it work. As mentioned above, data verification was a little problematic. Converting either FTP data or CD data to a form that is verified and tuned for delivery required the development of special scripts.

8. Experiences

8.1. Quality of data/images

The RAW files are not useful. Too many data errors. Elsevier is well aware of the number of improvements made as the scanning process became more refined. Proper alignment, cropping, and verification of the images was NOT there in the early datasets.

8.2. Storage
We managed to avoid many problems by keeping everything on magnetic storage.

8.3. Network delivery to end users
Getting the custom, NFS was interesting. Exploring http delivery of the images is an interesting, but not fully explored area.

8.4. Viewing
The chief architect of the Tviewer browse program is astounded that with so little image processing experience he could produce something so much better than what commercial companies were charging high prices for.

8.5. Printing
Getting CCITT FAX PostScript to work was difficult and painful. It took meticulous work by far too many people at far too many sites to get it work.

8.6. Internet delivery
From the first day MIT joined the project we said that the planned method of Internet delivery would not work. We were not surprised when it proved a horrendous failure. We proposed methods which, if tried, might well work. Too bad the project ended so quickly without any attempt to try more than the single failed method.

8.7. Other
We originally thought Group IV FAX was not the right image delivery format. We were wrong. It turned out to be compact, accurate, and quick to decode. Recent developments to down-convert to gif or other formats as they become ubiquitously supported with World Wide Web browsers will continue to keep this format viable for some time.
We never had any time to experiment with single-article delivery from Elsevier.

8.8. Conclusions
We should have tried other Internet delivery methods.
We should investigate various intermediate repositories for images and real-time request of articles, possibly billing through the copyright clearing house.

9. Future developments

9.1. Additional data formats envisaged/ required, views on suitability
Rendering the image in Adobe Acrobat and from SGML currently have the disadvantage that the rendering is slow, the viewed page is often ugly, and the deployment platform is a subset of what our customers actually have on their desks.

9.2. Additional functionality planned
Because of cost considerations we will discontinue delivery of the Elsevier journals. We will use all the infrastructure we developed to deliver images of materials we own.

9.3. Other
This has been an amazing project. MIT has been a big beneficiary:
TULIP has been a key success for MIT. Along with a few other projects in the MIT Distributed Library Initiative (DLI), TULIP provided the galvanizing reason and the actual content to move beyond the theoretical, discussion stage, to the actual construction of a page image delivery system that meets the requirements of TULIP but that is also flexible and open enough to meet the requirements of other types of scholarly content. MIT believes strongly in learning by doing, and Elsevier's risk-taking offer provided that forum to accomplish real work.
We have met and collaborated with others who are serving image content. We gained knowledge of how to do this developed an infrastructure for doing so where once we had none.
It is unfortunate that the high cost of Elsevier content coupled with the shrinking MIT library budget and the inability of MIT and Elsevier to come to agreement on inter-library loan have necessitated discontinuing the collaboration with Elsevier beyond the highly successful experimental phase.

Figure 1

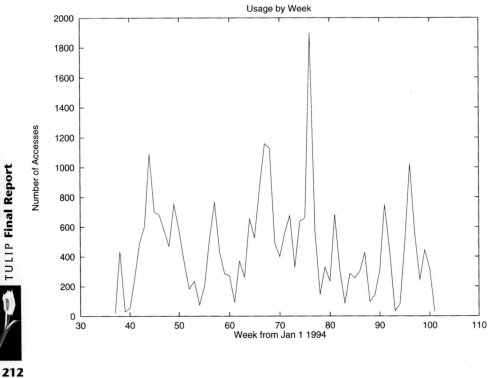

Figure 2

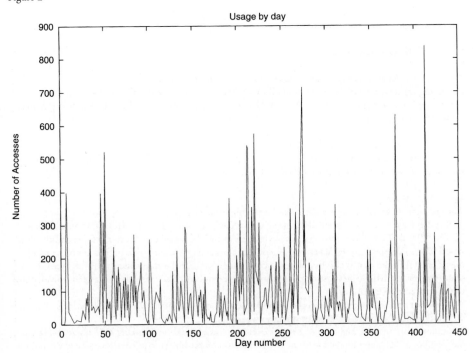

Figure 3

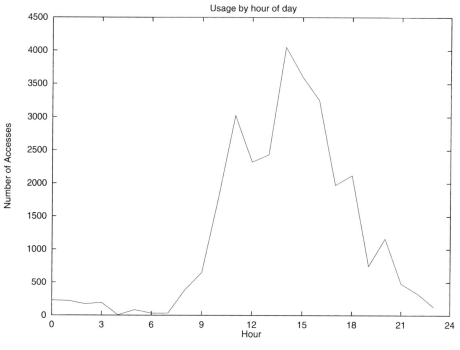

Figure 4

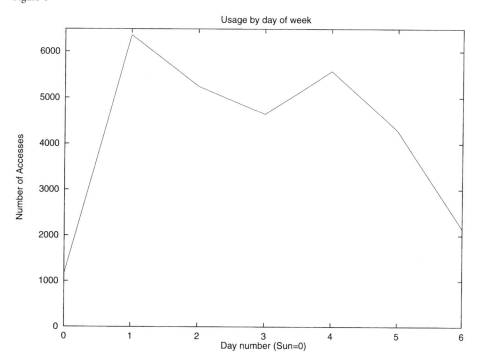

T U L I·P

Appendix V

The University
of California

University of California
1995 Final Tulip Report

University of California Profile

I. 1, 4 Organization, Structure of University/User Demographics

The University of California is one of the largest institutions of higher education in the world. It has 9 campuses, 167,000 students and 130,000 faculty and staff. They are composed of approximately 122,000 undergraduate and 40,000 graduate students, and 7,000 faculty and 32,000 other academic personnel. It has 5 medical schools, 3 law schools, extensive agricultural programs, and the largest university extension program of its kind. It has academic programs in over 150 disciplines, and 10 percent of all Ph.D's awarded in the United States come from UC. Its library system contains over 100 libraries on the 9 campuses, with collections totaling over 27 million volumes. The UC library system is surpassed in size on the American continent only by the Library of Congress in Washington.

The University also manages 3 government laboratories and 32,000 other with the Department of Energy: the Lawrence Berkeley Laboratory, the Lawrence Livermore National Laboratory, and the Los Almos National Laboratory. These laboratories conduct basic and applied research in nuclear science, energy production, national defense, and environmental and health areas. The 3 labs employ approximately 21,000 people.

The primary user community for TULIP was the material science, physics, and chemistry communities of the University. However, there were some users from other communities that used the system, not so much out of interest in the material but rather out of a desire to gain experience with the technologies that were used in the system.

Under the state of California Constitution, governance of the University is entrusted to a Board of Regents. They appoint the UC president and, with the president's advice, other officers of the university, including vice presidents, chancellors, and directors of the UC managed laboratories. Each campus is run by a chancellor. Authority in academic matters is delegated by the Regents to an Academic Senate which consists of faculty and certain administrative officers.

I. 3 DLA/MELVYL(1) Overview

The University of California MELVYL system is a computer based library system. created by the Division of Library Automation (DLA), in consultation with UC campuses, that allows users to search a variety of bibliographic databases, as well as connect to other databases at UC campuses and elsewhere. The MELVYL system provides access to three types of databases

- Databases of Library materials owned by UC and others
- Commercially produced databases for access to journal articles and other materials, available only to UC-affiliated users
- Databases produced by other libraries or organizations and available via the Internet

Currently, the following databases are mounted locally on the MELVYL system:

- The **MELVYL Catalog database** - a union catalog that contains records of UC's book holdings, as well as records of other materials such as maps and music. The Catalog includes the book holdings from UC, the California State Library in Sacramento, the California Academy of Science in San Francisco, the Center for Research Libraries, and the Graduate Theological Union In Berkeley. There are currently over 8.1 million unique titles representing 12.4 million holdings

- The **MELVYL Ten Year database** - a subset of the Catalog database consisting of records from the last ten years, currently consisting of approximately 1.8 million unique titles representing 3.8 million holdings

- The **Periodicals database** - includes over 790,000 unique titles of newspapers, journals, proceedings, etc., representing over 1.3 million serial holdings from UC, the California State Library, the California Academy of Sciences, the Center for Research Libraries, the Graduate Theological Union, Stanford University, the University of Southern California, the 19-campus California State University, and selected other libraries.

Several journal article abstracting and indexing databases acquired from commercial and public vendors. These currently include:

- **ABI/Inform** (2)- 1,000 business, management and finance journals indexed by UMI/Data Courier
- **Computer Articles**(3) - 200 computer related magazines and journals indexed by Information Access Company
- **Current Contents**(4) - tables of contents for 6,500 journals indexed by the Institute for Scientific Information
- **INSPEC** (5)- 4,000 physics, electronic and computing journals indexed by the Institute of Electrical Engineers
- **Magazine and Journal Articles** - the Expanded Academic Index(3) from Information Access Company indexing 1,500 magazines and journals
- **MELVYL MEDLINE**(6) **PLUS** - 4,000 medical and life sciences journals indexed by the US National Library of Medicine
- **Newspaper Articles**- the National Newspaper Index(3) from Information Access Company covering 5 major US newspapers
- **PsycINFO**(7) - 1,300 psychology journals and publications indexed by the American Psychological Association

In addition several databases from remote sources are available to UC affiliated users through the Z39.50 protocol. By this means, they can be accessed with the same command syntax as the locally mounted files listed above. Currently available databases are:

From the Research Libraries Group (RLG):

- **Anthropological Literature** - anthropology and archaeology materials indexed by Tozzer Library, Harvard University
- **Avery Index to Architectural Periodicals** - 1,000 journals indexed by the Getty Art History Program and the Avery Architecture and Fine Arts Library, Columbia University
- **Handbook of Latin American Studies** - journals, books, and conferences indexed by the Hispanic Division, Library of Congress
- **History of Science and Technology** - journal articles, conference proceedings, and books indexed by the History of Science Society and the Society for the History of Technology
- **Index to Foreign Legal Periodicals** - legal journals, essay collections, and congress reports indexed by the American Association of Law Libraries and the UC Berkeley Law Library
- **Inside Information** - 10,000 journals held by the British Library Document Supply Center
- **RLIN**(8) **Bibliographic Database** - holdings of 143 research and academic libraries
- **World Law Index - Hispanic Legislation** - laws, decrees, and regulations selected by the Hispanic Law Division, Library of Congress Law Library

From OCLC Inc.:

- **ArticleFirst**(9) - 11,000 magazines and journals, produced by OCLC Inc.
- **ContentsFirst**(9) - tables of contents for the magazines and journals indexed by ArticleFirst
- **ERIC** - article and report citations in the field of education indexed by the Office of Educational Research and Improvement of the US Department of Education and the ERIC Processing and Reference Facility
- **GPO Monthly Catalog of US Publications**
- **WorldCat** - holdings of 17,000 public, academic, and other libraries
- **Art Index** - 200 international arts publications indexed by H.W. Wilson

Several additional databases are available through a telnet pass-through mode to UC-affiliated users. These databases are accessed using their native system command modes. These currently include:

- **Congressional Quarterly's Washington Alert** - US Legislative and regulatory information
- **GeoRef** (at Stanford University) - geology and geophysics materials indexed by the American Geological Institute
- **ERIC** (at Stanford University) - same as the ERIC database at OCLC Inc.
- The **RLG** and **OCLC** databases listed above in Z39.50 mode

The telnet pass-through capability also has links to over 50 systems around the world that are available to anyone accessing the MELVYL system. These include major library catalogs, gopher systems, and other information retrieval resources.

In addition to developing, operating, and maintaining the MELVYL system, DLA is also responsible for operating the intercampus TCP/IP data communications network. In 1995 this network was upgraded from a network running at fractional T1 speeds to an SMDS network. One of the major justifications for this large increase in bandwidth was the need to adequately support applications like TULIP.

I. 2   Library Organization and Structure

The library system on each campus is headed by University Librarian. The University Librarians plus selected other individuals have a committee entitled Library Council which helps set university wide policy, advises DLA, and plans cooperative projects. Library Council also has several committees under its auspices which are comprised of library administrators, heads of departments and such in the areas of public services, technical services, system services, and collections development as well as some others. These committees help coordinate activities and policies on a university wide basis. For every major project such as mounting new databases DLA undertakes there is also assembled a liaison committee consisting of librarians with the appropriate expertise whose role is to help DLA on design implementation issues and be the contact point on their campus for that database or feature. The liaison committee for the TULIP project consisted of the material science or engineering librarian from each campus (a representative from the Lawrence Berkeley Labs was added in 1995). A list of the liaisons is given in Appendix A.

Tulip Technical Implementation Details

TII 1 Description of TULIP System- Functionalities
TIII.1 Functionalities
TIII.2 Architecture

At the University of California, the images have been linked to bibliographic citation records in the Inspec(1) and Current Contents(2) databases in the university's MELVYL(3) on-line public access system. Users perform normal MELVYL searches to retrieve records from those databases. If there is an image linked to a retrieved record, an informational message is displayed as part of the normal MELVYL system displays. There is also a facility to limit retrieved records to only those that have linked images.

Having retrieved records in the MELVYL system that have linked images, users can issue a DISPLAY IMAGE command to request that article images associated with a retrieved record be displayed on their output device. Currently, any output device capable of running the X windows protocol is supported for displaying the images. The images are stored on an optical jukebox controlled by a UNIX workstation, which also runs the software that projects the windows onto the end user's device.

When a user requests that article images be displayed, MELVYL gathers the necessary information and communicates it to the image server. The image server receives from the MELVYL system the requested citation and other information necessary to identify the end user, and using a database resident on the UNIX workstation, maps the article to the corresponding bit mapped image files which it fetches off of the optical jukebox. it then opens up windows on the user's workstation to display them. Facilities exist that allow the user to page back and forth in the article, adjust the size of the image, reverse the video, and print selected pages or the entire article. Currently, postscript printers attached to print servers that support the TCP/IP LPR printing protocol are supported.

Once an article has been displayed by using MELVYL display commands, facilities exist in the image viewing software that allow browsing around the issue in which that article was found, without the need to issue another request on the MELVYL system. There is an option to request the next or previous article, and to request browsing the table of contents for the issue. If that option is chosen, a table of contents window is shown to the user, who may then go directly to any article in the issue.

There is also a comprehensive statistical component built into the image viewing software. This facility allows us to gather both demographic data about the types of users who are using the system, and also extensive data about user behavior patterns that will help us gain more knowledge of how user's access and make use of electronic information of this kind. This knowledge and understanding will help us better design future systems of this type.

TI1
TI1.1, 2, 3, 4, 5
System Architecture- Browsing, Searching, Image Viewing & Printing

The UC MELVYL system runs on an IBM 9672/R61 computer. The user interface software was locally written and developed in PL/1. ADABAS from Software AG is the back end DBMS. The UNIX image viewing software was also locally developed and is written in C. It runs on a DECstation 5000 which is also used to control the optical jukebox on which the images are stored. This device is a DEC StorageServer 100. As mentioned above the X windows protocol is used to view the images. This allows the application to run on any device capable on running X (UNIX machines, X Terminals, PC's and Macintoshes) without the need to individually developed clients running locally on the user's machine. The TCP/IP LPR protocol is used for printing which occurs by print files being sent from the TULIP system at DLA to LPD daemons at the users' sites. There is currently no support for local printing to things like serially connected printers or local area network printing protocols such as Appletalk or Novell, except that some campuses do have gateways for such protocols to LPR. There had been plans for supporting output to fax machines by means of Internet fax gateways, but by the time the experiment ended in 1995 there had been no real development of such infrastructure on the 9 UC campuses.

TII2

TII2.1 Description of Development Process

The initial public release of the UC TULIP system occurred on January 16, 1994. However, there followed a several month period while campuses geared up to really make the system available to their users. The schedule of actual availability of TULIP varied on the individual 9 campuses. See below for details on overall usage of the system during 1994 and 1995.

Implementation Experience

Implementation of the system did not go as quickly or as smoothly as had been originally hoped. In retrospect, given that this was the first time we had attempted to deploy such a system, it might have been better not to have attempted to roll out the system on all 9 campuses simultaneously but to have done a staged deployment, rolling it out on each campus as they were prepared for it. For many of the campus librarians involved this was the first time they had used an X windows device and it took some time to get equipment installed and configured. Due to both technical and infrastructure issues printing has continued to be a problem in many places. The lack of sufficient bandwidth in the UC intercampus data network to support transmission of the amount of data required by TULIP images, as well as deficiencies in campus network infrastructures as well has made performance slower than desired to some locations. The UC intercampus network situation was addressed in 1995 by an upgrade to its bandwidth. In addition performance has been affected by the speed and available memory on some of the output devices employed by users. It should be stated, that even with the continued problems of printing, most of the initial problems that occurred were worked through and things have pretty much stabilized.

TII1.4 **File Loading and Distribution**

As of this writing the last dataset loaded is #82. Up until, dataset #60, UC used the "push" option where the data is ftp'ed directly to us from Article Express with no intervention on our part. AE sent mail notification when their verification process is complete. This was the signal for UC to process the new data and build the links to the mainframe MELVYL databases. An additional verification process is also undertaken on our end. That process had uncovered errors, corrupt images and missing files not found by the AE verification process which are then reported back to both AE and Elsevier. Without attempting to fix any blame, the ftp process had been one of the least successful portions of the entire project. There did not appear to be any determinable pattern or schedule to which the arrival of new data adheres and I do not believe any one dataset had arrived within the two week interval originally promised. For example, the time lag between receipt of dataset #60 and #59 was close to one month. It seems that the ftp process often broke down and had to be restarted, and that there had been some error we have uncovered in just about every dataset we have received this way. This lack of fixed predictable arrival of new data has been a barrier to acceptance and use of the system since there is no way to explain to users when they can expect to find new material by using it. Perhaps one of the most important lessons learned from the TULIP project is that internet delivery of this amount of material to end user sites is not yet practical given the current internet infrastructure.

Because of problems with ftp, starting with #61, UC (like all other sites) started receiving the data on CD-ROM's. Although there have still been some errors found by our internal validation routines, the quantity is much smaller than was the case with the ftp process, and as Elsevier has geared up for their new electronic product, the rate of receipt of the data has also improved to the point where in some cases the interval between receipt of the CD-ROMS has been less than the initially promised 2 weeks. It was initially hoped that the entire process of loading the data and running the links to Inspec and Current Contents would be taken over by our normal data production group rather than being handled by programming staff, because of the initial ftp problems and the switch to the CD-ROMS relatively late in the experiment, this did not happen, although the data does still get loaded and the links made within a couple of days of receipt of the CD-ROM.

One of the lessons that has been learned with TULIP is that timely receipt of new data is crucial to user acceptance of the system. While there were definite problems with using ftp and it is unclear how well it would scale to even larger amounts of data, it does represent a potentially faster method than CD-ROM for getting the material to the end user in a more timely manner. The method used in TULIP was to send all of the journals in one transmission when they were available. Methods such as smaller transmission as soon as possible after a journal has been scanned in potentially make electronic online transmission feasible in the future. In addition, many of the problems with ftp were caused by the extremely large filesizes and number of files involved in that single transmission. Newer electronic formats like SGML and PDF may also help in this area.

TII1.7 Storage/Distribution/Logfiles

As mentioned above, the TULIP data is loaded onto an optical juke box. Currently, all of the data is stored centrally at the central MELVYL computer site. Images are projected onto users' workstations by the image viewing software. At this time downloading of data to end user systems for manipulation by local software is not supported. One of the lessons learned is that access to data on optical jukeboxes is slow. The system does have a large amount of magnetic storage for caching purposes so recent or heavily used material will tend to be found on that caching storage. However, given the rapid decrease in the cost of magnetic storage that has occurred since the project was planned, future systems of this type will be much more heavily based on magnetic media.

Access to the images is provided across the university's TCP/IP intercampus network which connects to the individual campus backbone networks. Another of the lessons learned from the TULIP project was that the current bandwidth available on the intercampus network was not sufficient for real production transmission of this type of material, and the network is being upgraded because of that. Other factors that also affect performance to an individual user are the speed of that user's connection into their campus network and the speed of and memory available on their local workstation. Also many of these components have been found to vary greatly among the user community.

Most of the access to the TULIP material is coming from end user department workstations, although money was provided to each campus to ensure that there would be at least one in library device available to support public access.

The logfile data specified by Elsevier has been sent on a regular basis every month since the system went live. This file is generated and mailed automatically in the first full week of the month and contains the data for the previous month. The logfile data is extracted out from the much more extensive user behavior data the system collects. In addition, we currently produce from the more extensive data maintained by the system two monthly reports, one that gives a breakdown of usage of the material both in overall numbers and broken down by campus, department and user category, and a second report that tracks response time, user equipment type, and also breaks down usage by individual journal. Elsevier is sent copies of both reports. Again, this is handled by an automated process.

There was one problem that did occur based on the password system and the fact that expirations of passwords was not tied to the lifespan on the Tulip project (due unfortunately to the way the password system works). Many users' passwords expired at the end of July 1995. Some of them went and renewed their Tulip usage and were given new passwords with later expiration dates. Unfortunately, because of that, both UC and Elsevier lost the ability to track a single user's usage patterns after July 95 since the new password made them appear to be a different user. This has been corrected in some cases by requesting from the campuses, where they had the data, both the old and new password assigned to an individual. Elsevier (and UC) could then use that data to see where 2 different passwords represented the same user. In some cases, however, since demographic data such as department affiliation and user category is encoded into the password, the new password represents a change in the users' demographic data.

Details on usage of the system can be obtained from those reports. However gross usage numbers for 1994 and 1995 were:

1994 Pages Viewed:	7496
1994 Pages Printed:	4066
1994 Articles Viewed:	2447
1994 Articles Printed:	929
1994 Sessions:	2583
1995 Pages Viewed:	7093
1995 Pages Printed:	6291
1995 Articles Viewed:	1805
1995 Articles Printed:	1362
1995 Sessions:	2253

1995 Numbers are inclusive through 11/95. It should be noted that the Lawrence Berkeley Laboratory (LBL) was given access to the TULIP system in January 1995. Given that the numbers involved are relatively small, it is hard to make any definitive statements based on them, except to perhaps note that more printing occurred in 1995. This may reflect more of the way real users used the system as opposed to some of the initial demonstration and novelty effect patterns that occurred in the early months of 1994.

Overall usage of the Inspec and Current Contents databases in 1994 and 1995 was:

Inspec:

1994 Sessions:	259,773
1994 Find Commends:	752,611
1994 Records Displayed:	7,262,608
1995 Sessions:	316,088
1995 Find Commands:	894,097
1995 Records Displayed:	8,000,294

Current Contents:

1994 Sessions:	898,365
1994 Find Commands:	2,871,774
1994 Records Displayed:	28,733,569
1995 Sessions:	866,499
1995 Find Commands:	2,806,197
1995 Records Displayed:	27,340,677

The numbers for 1995 also reflect usage through November only.

II.1, 2, 3, 4 Promotion/Training/User Behavior

DLA, as part of the promotion and training aspect of the project, developed generic promotional and training materials that were distributed to the campuses and adapted by them. The campuses also developed their own specific training and promotional material and undertook specific activities like visits to relevant departments, notices in campus newsletters, user surveys and training sessions for users. This material has also been shared with Elsevier. More of this is detailed in the individual campus reports below. In addition, the viewing interface has both a built in help facility and a mechanism for users to send comments to DLA about the system. In spite of known problems with network bandwidth affecting performance of the system and problems with the university's printing infrastructure, response to the system has been very positive. A common comment that has been received from users has been a desire to see much more and more diverse material made available to them in this manner.

DLA staff along with Elsevier have visited many of the campuses during 1994 to talk to both librarians and end users in order to get feedback from them about the system, and have given presentations on

TULIP at several conferences. Both of these activities continued during 1995. Also in 1995 Elsevier conducted focus groups with graduate student users at Berkeley and Santa Barbara and individual interviews with faculty and graduate student users at Davis

As also mentioned above, the UC implementation of TULIP gathers much more extensive data on user behavior than the data required by Elsevier. Some of this more extensive user behavior data is reported out in a monthly report, and adhoc reports have been generated during 1994 and 1995 to answer specific questions. One of the intentions had been to do some extensive analysis of this data to better understand usage behavior patterns. Unfortunately, due to lack of resources at both UC and Elsevier, this was not able to be accomplished before the project terminated.

IV
IV1, 2, 3, 4
TII3   *Some Lessons Learned*

Several important lessons have been learned from the work done to develop the TULIP system and from the initial usage of it. These lessons, we believe, have important implications for future projects of this type.

Perhaps, the major general lesson that has come out of doing TULIP is that systems like TULIP are a lot harder to develop and deploy that might be apparent. And the reason for these difficulties has less to do with the technologies uses to build such systems than with the infrastructures needed to support them. TULIP was a limited prototype system with a relatively small number of journals and of interest to a small focused user community. Yet, with those constraints, the TULIP project highlighted several areas of deficiencies inside the University of California's infrastructure. Among the issues that the TULIP project has raised are the following:

TII3.2   Storage

1) **Storage** - The images for TULIP at UC are being stored on an optical jukebox. While more economical than magnetic disk storage, the costs are still significant for such a large amount of data. There are also performance implications for using optical technology. Optical technology is still much slower than magnetic disk technology. When combined with the fact that a jukebox is being employed, so that accessing material not actually resident in a drive requires a fetch and mount of an optical platter, access time for some material can still be quite slow. Caching techniques using magnetic disks try to keep the most requested material more immediately available, but variations in access patterns can effect the efficacy of those algorithms. However, given the recent introduction of high speed high capacity RAID magnetic storage devices, and what seems to be the rapid and constant advancement of magnetic disk technology, it is now becoming more practical to start using magnetic disks with their enhanced performance and response time capabilities for projects of this kind. It is likely that optical technology will still be used for less frequently accessed material where fetching it off of an optical jukebox once and then caching it to magnetic media will give acceptable performance.

TII3.3   Network Delivery to End Users

2) **Network Bandwidth** - Displaying bitmapped images requires a significant amount of network bandwidth. The recent increase of bandwidth in the UC intercampus network had a dramatic impact on performance, and use of compression techniques will also help in this area. There is also the possibility that other data formats such as PDF and SGML may be less intensive bandwidth consumers. The current widely deployed versions of the X Windows protocol do not contain support for moving compressed images. The newest version does add this support but it will be awhile until it is widely enough deployed so it will make sense to take advantage of that feature. And, as to network bandwidth, increasing it will certainly help but it may be hard to stay ahead of the ever increasing demand for it as new applications and data types become popular. The ever increasing popularity of the Web also has obvious implications for network bandwidth demands. In addition to the UC intercampus data network, there is also the issue of networking infrastructure on the campuses and in the buildings. While great advances have been made over the last several years, there still remains a lot of work to do in this area.

TII3.6 Internet Delivery

Another area in which available network bandwidth has an impact on the system is in the actual delivery of the data from the provider, in this case Elsevier Publishers. One of the goals for TULIP was to test the viability of delivering material to the participants using the Internet and the FTP file transfer protocol. For most of the TULIP participants who have chosen this method of receiving the material, this has resulted in the transfer of approximately 500 megabytes across the Internet every two weeks. Depending on network traffic, the process takes between 3-7 hours to transfer the material to each site. Given that the TULIP project only involved approximately 40 journals, and that the ftp transfer method had to be abandoned due to problems in transmitting that amount of data, and even with planned and projected enhancements to the Internet infrastructure, it is very unclear that this method could scale to any large scale delivery of electronic material.

TII3.1 Quality of Data/Images

3) **Equipment Infrastructure** - Systems like TULIP require a well networked user community. In preparing for TULIP, a survey was done of the installed equipment base among the material science and related departments on the university campuses. We found that there was a wide divergence among the campuses in the types and amount of computer equipment in those departments and in their connectivity to the campus networks. This problem only increases when considering providing electronic information to a more heterogeneous and widely diversified user community. As mentioned above, network bandwidth is a major factor in performance of systems like TULIP. However, the speed of the destination workstation CPU and the amount of memory available to it are also significant factors in performance as seen by the end user.

4) **Display Technology** - The TULIP images are scanned at 300 dpi. The average computer display monitor has a resolution of 75-100 dpi. The difference between the resolution at which the images are scanned and the one at which they can be displayed on-line has an effect on their readability. Higher resolution monitors are available but are still quite expensive. In addition, the size of the display device and whether it can support such things as greyscaling also have an impact on the usability of the images on-line. larger size monitors, that go beyond the type 14-16 inch range found on most PC's and Macintoshes, make the images much more readable, but come at a steep premium in cost that makes them still beyond the range of affordability for most users. The quality of the display device is an important factor in how receptive the user will be to actually using on-line images

TII3.5 Printing

5) **Printing** - One of the obvious things users want to do with the TULIP images is print them out. This is actually a much harder problem that it sounds due to the lack of a common unified printing infrastructure inside the university. Printing is currently supported on to any postscript printer attached to the campus TCP/IP networks that can be accessed via the LPR printing protocol. Unfortunately, there are a large number of printers in users' departments that do not meet those requirements, and thus can not be used to print from TULIP. These printers are attached to local area and departmental networks (or in many cases directly attached to a user's workstation) and can not be accessed by an application like TULIP that is running remotely. Until such infrastructure is put in place that provides better network connectivity for those locally connected printers, there will continue to be a population of user and departmental printers inaccessible to applications like TULIP. There is also the related issue of developing infrastructure and policies to determine what printers any user is allowed to access and doing the appropriate charging and accounting. Such infrastructure ideally should be developed on a university wide as opposed to a campus wide basis, to avoid there being separate and different solutions on each of the university campuses.

TII3.7 Other

6) **User Authentication** - Currently, TULIP uses a simple password scheme for user identification and verification. It has become clear that such a simple scheme will not scale well, and that much more sophisticated mechanisms are required for user authentication. This is especially true as more and more services come into being that require distinguishing among different classes of users for such things as accounting and charge back (like printing). However, while several of the UC campuses are experimenting with user

authentication systems (most notably with Kerbereous), there is not yet any generalized widespread user authentication infrastructure in place inside the university of the type that will be required for systems like TULIP to operate in a true production mode.

7) **Training and Support** - Systems like TULIP, because they utilize higher end technology like X Windows devices, may require more training and support than has been the case with more traditional on-line systems. In addition, because of the technology they use, they tend to require more complicated and customized configuration during their initial setup phases. They also may require new skills that will require reeducation of existing support and training staff in order for those personnel to become familiar and comfortable with the technology involved. This will put further pressure on already strained and decreasing library and computer center budgets. Mechanisms, such as good help systems, need to be designed into such systems to reduce their impact on support and training staff.

8) **User Interface Issues** - There has been a lot of discussion among the university community about whether the X windows based approach that was chosen for delivering the TULIP material was the proper method. Given the diversity of types of equipment within the university, a conscious decision was made to use X since implementations of it were available for just about all of the various platforms found within the university community such as PC's, Macintoshes, UNIX workstations and X terminals. There was a strong feeling that resources could not be made available to develop native implementations for all of those platforms. There was also the issue of the amount of resources that would be needed to support the distribution and management of a local client should one have been written for the TULIP project. The approach taken with X windows allowed the development of one client managed centrally, with the resulting interface projected onto the end user's device without the need for specialized software (except the X server code itself) to actually be resident. At the time TULIP was being designed the World Wide Web was just starting out, and there was no sense that it was going to be as popular or widely deployed as it has become. Given that WWW clients are now readily available for most platforms and are, in fact, widely being used by the university community, some of the issues surrounding the management of distributed software are no longer as great as they were in our initial design.

226 IV Future Developments

Final Observations

TULIP was UC's first foray into providing access to this type of material to its user community. As such, we feel it has been a landmark undertaking for the university in that it gave visibility to and forced us to confront the variety of issues surrounding how to provide access to this type of material. These issues include such things as providing adequate network bandwidth, user equipment infrastructure, printing infrastructure, user authentication and identification on a university wide scope, the proper storage medium for such material, managing distributed client-server access systems and the whole area of user support and training, and what models of access are appropriate for such material. Of course not all (if any) of these issues have been solved within the scope or lifetime of the TULIP experiment. But what has happened is that TULIP has provided a context for focusing on and discussing within the university community the issues it has helped raise. It has also become the model we plan on using for future systems we are planning on deploying for similar types of material.

From the point of view of a major technical and scientific publisher like Elsevier, TULIP has also raised some important issues for the future. These include economic models for delivery of the information to end users, access models, what models to use for delivery to sites like universities for further distribution to their users, and formats and types of data to make available. One of the limitations of the TULIP project which was somewhat of a barrier to acceptance was, that until 1995 with the additional 41 journals, there was a sense that the system did not have a critical mass of material to make it truly usable as more than just an interesting experiment. It is interesting to speculate how usage might have been different, and perhaps even different implementations models may have been chosen by the participating universities if those 41 additional journals had been available from the beginning of the project.

Finally, the question needs to be asked, was TULIP a success? There have been problems with deployments, performance, printing and the like, and this has caused frustrations for both the both the front line librarians who have to support end users and deal with user concerns and frustrations, and the end users themselves. Without attempting to diminish those frustrations in any way, it would seem that the answer would have to be yes. TULIP was an experiment to understand what the requirements were in both technology and infrastructure in order to deliver this type of primary content to end users. As such, it helped expose areas of infrastructure that were not quite up to the levels required to support this type of system, raise questions about appropriate technology to use, and in general, raise awareness among the university community about the requirements of such systems in a wide range of areas from network infrastructure and other technology areas through user support and training. If everything had worked smoothly from the beginning and there had been no problems, it would have been a less successful, and less interesting, experiment.

Campus Reports

1.   UC Berkeley

TULIP has continued to be used on this campus and this past year use seemed to mirror the cycles of the previous year: heavier usage in the periods March-June and September-December, falling off in the summer months. Since the originally issued passwords expired at the end of July, 20 individuals (primarily graduate students) obtained new passwords - 5 each in chemistry and expired at the end of July, 20 individuals (primarily graduate students) obtained new passwords - 5 each in chemistry and materials science, 2 physics, and 8 in other engineering departments. Likewise, a number of new users have come aboard since then; for example, at the Engineering Library, another 12 passwords were issued to first time users and activity at the Chemistry Library was similar. A number of these new TULIP passwords were issued after the IEEE journal page images became available in experimental mode on the MELVYL system - for users in some fields, it appears that the greater number of available images (with both IEEE & TULIP) heightened awareness of image delivery generally.

News of the end of the experiment has been received well by those users who have been told so far (basically all those who have recently acquired passwords). All have understood when apprised of the cost of continuing the project, knowing the state of the University's collection budgets. Reaction might have been stronger but for the fact of the small size and diffuse appeal of the set of TULIP titles; usually only a couple of titles out of the full set were generally of interest to any given user. Lack of critical mass has been one of the weaknesses of the project all along.

The experiment has been extremely useful in what we have learned regarding image delivery, support, promotion, instruction and - most importantly - user reaction. Even though the TULIP Project at UC will not be continued at this time, it has provided us with a solid base of knowledge which will inform and enhance future efforts in the electronic delivery of the scientific literature.

2.   UC Davis

Since last report, UC Davis has run a second article on TULIP in the IT Times, Information Technology's campus wide newspaper, described TULIP in the library's newsletter to faculty, Library Perspective, and posted Elsevier's posters. The poster seemed to generate additional interest in TULIP and lead to informal demonstrations and requests for passwords. Although we are not providing and centralized printing, we have not received any complaints about this feature. I believe UC Davis generated the highest use in the most recent TULIP monthly data.

We have distributed an additional 50 passwords for a total of about 100 TULIP passwords. About a third of these 100 passwords were given to faculty and graduate students in the core TULIP departments of Chemistry, Chemical Engineering, Physics and Material Science. Probably about a quarter are in the hands of library, computer, and telecommunications staff. The remainder have been distributed to a variety of users. Some users, the geophysicists in particular, have commented that they find the TULIP articles useful for their work; many others are probably curious about the new technology

In 1995 not much changed. There was no further publicity done and the number of passwords remained constant. Usage did drop off somewhat. Also TULIP at UCD remained slow due to the fact that intercampus network link to Davis has not yet been upgraded, as has been the case at most of the other campuses.

UCD was one of the UC sites that Elsevier conducted research at, conducting individual interviews with TULIP users instead of the focus group approach taken at UCB and UCSB. This occurred in November of 1995.

3.   UC Irvine

We continue to have ups and down with the printing configuration at the reference desk and in the reference room. The status of having TULIP function consistently has not been established at UCI. We constantly have to revise our instructions which I think is more of a function of our configuration than anything else. We have done very limited marketing this year - the new interest we have promoted has come from the Physics Dept. We at UCI welcome the ne journals that were added to the list of TULIP material should the university decide to include them. Toward the end of the project the greatest interest in TULIP came from Engineers and Physicists who came and used the system even without any promotion. They seemed to have learned about it through word of mouth. This interest may have been provoked by the fact that the system was about to go away and a desire to get maximum use of it before it was no longer available. Printing was still problematic as departmental and lab printers are not or can not be set for the needed postscript parameters.

4.   UC Los Angeles

The TULIP database on MELVYL was used primarily by four UCLA departments: Chemistry & Biochemistry, Chemical Engineering, Materials Science & Engineering, and Physics & Astronomy. Biomedical and Electrical Engineering users also showed interest in TULIP journals such as "Sensors and Actuators". According to the password categories, the heaviest usage came from Materials Science (as expected) and Chemistry/Chemical Engineering.

In the initial stages of the project, emphasis was placed on user equipment needs e.g. computers available with x-windows software, printing capabilities, etc. The Science & Engineering library provided two x-terminals in the public area and offered free printing in 1994-1995. As the project continued and usage of lab computers increased, emphasis was placed on providing concise, clear TULIP handouts along with passwords to enable the user to have a successful connection after leaving the library.

5.   UC Riverside

Based on the experience at UCR, I think the following points can be made:

1) we still have lots of technology lacks & limitations to overcome, in general.

2) user education can take lots of time: we've done steady advertising of TULIP, consistent with the peripheral subject area it covers for us, but, again, until someone needs it, or it connects somehow that "this is useful" all the advertising in the world won't help.

3) Most TULIP look-ups until very recently (maybe the last two months?) were primarily originated by reference librarians prostelytising or otherwise drawing it to people's attention, "Hey you need to see this!" whether for a specific need (such as knowing they needed an article from a journal we don't have) or to show off the technology.

Its also interesting to note that usage by real end users has picked up in the closing months of the experiment, reenforcing the sense that the TULIP experiment was not of a long enough duration, given the amount of time it takes to get infrastructure in place and users comfortable with these types of systems. More would have been learned if it ran for a longer amount of time.

6.   UC San Diego

The only thing to report for 1995 was that response time greatly improved due to the upgrade of the inter campus network link to UCSD. However, due to the use of the requirement of the LPR printing protocol and TCP/IP attached printers or print servers, printing problems still persisted.

Appendix A. Campus Project Liaisons

Karen Butter, Director Information Resources and Services, San Francisco (415) 476-8293
[kab@lib.ucsf.edu]

Beverlee French, Associate University Librarian for Science, Davis (916) 752-2110 [bafrench@ucdavis.edu]

Christy Hightower, Reference Librarian, San Diego (619) 534-1216 [chightow@ucsd.edu]

Julia Gelfand, Reference Librarian, Irvine (714) 856-4971 [jgelfand@Uuci.edu]

Kathryn Kjaer, General Science Librarian, Irvine (714) 856-8521 [kkjaer@uci.edu]

Carol Resco, Head, Physical Sciences Library, Riverside (909) 787-3511
[RESCO@UCRVMS.Bitnet]

Lizbeth Langston, Associate Librarian Rivera Library, Riverside (909) 787-2223 [lizbeth.langston@ucr.edu]

Camille Wanat Head, Physical Science Library, Berkeley (510) 642-0634
[cwanat@library.berkeley.edu]

Steve Watkins Reference Librarian, Santa Cruz (408) 459-2775 [watkins@scilibx.ucsc.edu]

Fred Yeungling, Physical Sciences and Mathematics Bibliographer, Santa Cruz,
(408) 459-3583 [yuengli@scilibx.ucsc.edu]

Charles Huber, Santa Barbara, (805) 893-2762 [huber@library.ucsb.edu]

Audrey Jackson, Librarian, Los Angeles (310) 825-3398 [ecz5ems@mvs.oac.ucla.edu]

Carol Backhus, Lawrence Berkeley Laboratory, (510) 486-6307 [cdbackhus@lbl.gov]

1) MELVYL is a registered trademark of the Regents of the University of California
2) ABI/Inform is a registered trademark of UMI/Data Courier
3) Computer Articles, Expanded Academic Index, and National Newspaper Index are trademarks of Information Access Company
4) Current Contents is a registered trademark of the Institute for Scientific Information
5) Inspec is a registered trademark of the Institute of Electrical Engineers
6) MEDLINE is a registered trademark of the US National Library of Medicine
7) PsycINFO is a registered trademark of the American Psychological Association
8) RLIN is a registered trademark of the Research Libraries Group
9) ArticleFirst and ContentsFirst are trademarks of OCLC, Inc.

TULIP

Appendix VI

The University
of Michigan

TULIP
University of Michigan Implementation and Research

Kenneth Alexander
Randall Frank
William Gosling
Wendy Lougee
James Ottaviani
Gregory Peters
Beth Warner
Katherine Willis

December   1995

TULIP **Final Report**

I Executive summary

I. Description of profile of university

1. Organization/structure of university

The University of Michigan, located in Ann Arbor, contains 18 schools and colleges and has an enrollment of 37,000 students. 30% are graduate students. During fiscal year 93-94, the University had a research volume of $386,000,000, the largest of any U.S. university. Its operating budget exceeds $2,000,000,000 of which approximately one half is committed to the Medical Center including the hospital. Governance of the institution is provided by the president, provost, chief financial officer and executive vice-president for research in consultation with the faculty senate and deans of each of the schools. Management follows a decentralized model with each administrative unit responsible for its operations and budget.

2. Organization of libraries

The University Library system includes Harlan Hatcher Graduate Library, Harold T. an Vivian B. Shapiro Undergraduate Library and 19 divisional libraries. The Law an Business School libraries are managed separately as are several special libraries. The University Libraries contain over 6, 600,000 volumes and 70,000 serial titles. All of these are accessible through MIRLYN, the libraries' on-line catalog and management system. Overall management of the library system is provided by the Dean of the Libraries.

3. Organization of IT/information services

The Vice-Provost for Information Technology provides campus-wide strategy and coordination of information technology. This is done in cooperation with the Schools, Colleges and major administrative units who maintain their own information systems. In 1994, the University implemented the University of Michigan Computing Environment, a distributed, client-server model, designed to meet the campus needs.

4. User demographics

The University of Michigan College of Engineering contains the largest number of materials scientists as well as computer scientists and others interested in the TULIP titles. However, users can also be found in the physics, and chemistry departments; and the Dental, Medical and Pharmacy Schools. Altogether, we estimate a potential user community of 500 faculty and students.

II. TULIP promotion and training

1. Description of promotion activities undertaken

Promotional activities were event-based in that our major efforts centered around significant changes in our TULIP offerings. An initial push occurred in the months preceding the introduction of the service. These included direct mailings, electronic announcements, and flyers describing the project. Upon introduction, significant changes in TULIP (introduction of the Web browser, addition of more titles) gave rise to similar publicity efforts. We also added color posters supplied by ES and special attachments to the unbound journals in the libraries to heighten awareness of the project at high traffic areas. UM library and ES marketing staff have worked together on promotional materials intended for wider distribution among TULIP users — ES is currently finishing up development on these.

2. Description of training activities undertaken

During the first months of TULIP's introduction, formal (classroom-based) training sessions were offered on both campuses at the University. Though the attendees stated that they found the training sessions useful, attendance was light. Because of this, and because of the care taken to make the three versions of the interface as straightforward as possible, after the initial effort further training occurred on an as-needed/as-requested basis. A dedicated station near the Engineering Library reference desk allowed librarians to observe and intervene in the use of Tulipview, the most complex of the three interfaces. Because the Engineering Library shared (and will continue to share) space with the CAEN, the Engineering College's information technology unit, staff were able to regularly offer point-of-need training. They also provided e-mail and phone training. The MASC database appeared to users in the familiar context (using the familiar search capabilities) of MIRLYN, UM's online catalog. As such, it presented fewer training issues. Similarly, the www browser offered simple access to the TULIP journals. Though the necessity of configuring the user's web browser to correctly handle printing caused some questions, for the most part training requirements for this interface were minimal.

3.   Effects of promotion and training

The use data on the TULIP journals shows that, for both the electronic and the paper versions, increases in use directly followed periods of strong promotion. Whether this is the result of promotion, or more closely tied to new developments (a new interface, a request for users to share their opinions on the project, addition of new titles) is unclear. But since most users accessed the TULIP journals on an irregular basis, the increased use near the times of heightened publicity and training efforts probably results at least in part from the increased promotion and training.

4.   Conclusions and recommendations

It is difficult to separate the influence promotion and training had from the influence of the availability of new features had on increased use. Highlighting new features, announcing new additions to the journals listings, and reporting bugs all require contact with our user community. It is clear, though that any new service that challenges a user's pattern of work requires a steady diet of promotion and training. Because faculty members (perhaps our most significant, and certainly our most stable, user group) have typically found a pattern of journal use that satisfies them, changes to this pattern have to be sold to them before they will use a new service such as TULIP. Promotion clearly fulfills this role. Training is also essential, but in a different way. If an information product requires a steep learning curve, users who have either already found a simple method for getting similar information or have invested time in learning an alternative way of getting similar information will hesitate to switch. The new system will be most readily accepted if it requires minimal training. So, it is essential to promote a new delivery mechanism as not only as good as the one it replaces (or, in the short term, supplements) but better. In terms of training, users will require, and often request a brief introduction. After this, though, the delivery mechanism will have to prove itself as not merely as easy to use as their previous methods, but easier.

III.   User behavior

1.   Description of user/usage research (e.g. reshelving, statistics, surveys)

User behavior was explored using a number of different measures, including : shelving statistics for both bound and unbound (current) issues, surveys of the user population both by Glickman Research and by library staff, and through statistics gathered electronically (reported elsewhere).

2.   Findings

- From research

We have estimated that our target group for TULIP here on campus is roughly 500 users. As of February, 1995, 360 different users had tried TULIP Of those, about 60 became "repeat" users, in that they have used TULIP in at least two different months in the past year. Our surveys demonstrate interest in TULIP, but the statistics we have gathered show only moderate use.

Statistics gathered in the library corroborate this. We have seen, and continue to see, moderate use of TULIP journals in paper form. We must be careful not to draw anything more than broad conclusions based on the reshelving data, though. Shelving statistics are not 100% accurate. Although we request that journal users don't replace the volumes/issues they use back on the shelves themselves, many do. The statistics collected are gathered by student workers with minimal training. High workloads (especially near the end of a term) result in erratic collection of the data. As a result of these and other factors [1], the sample sizes are small — and the differences noted are probably statistically insignificant in the strictest sense. Thus it is inappropriate to study individual titles, but instead have looked at the TULIP journals in aggregate to identify trends. For the titles we have information on:

41 unbound TULIP journals
    more use in 93 than 92: 23 journals
    more use in 94 than 93: 18
    more use in 95 than 94: 35 (projected)

Using the best information available (i.e., looking only at journals for which we have at least three years in a row of data), we see a similar pattern.

29 unbound TULIP journals
    more use in 93 than 92: 22 journals
    more use in 94 than 93: 15
    more use in 95 than 94: 26 (projected)

The overall pattern shows what may be a dip in unbound (current) journal use during 1994. Increases in current journal use occurred in 1993 and 1995. It is plausible that TULIP publicity efforts increased awareness (and therefore use?) of these journals in the first year of the experiment, and thus the journals were used more in 1993 than in 1992. After adding additional titles and in preparation for Glickman Research's focus group study, we made another publicity push in early 1995. Again, it's possible that the (projected) increase in use in 1995 over 1994 in part stems from this.

These data are also available for bound volumes. Unlike the current journals, we don't know which years of the bound volumes are getting used, so it's difficult to make even gross generalizations on the impact of TULIP. All we can say about 1994 use is that it was generally higher relative to the surrounding years than 1993 and 1995.
- User comments/ direct feedback

From January-March, 1995, Glickman Associates conducted focus group, individual and telephone surveys at the University. The resulting report provided a comprehensive review of TULIP users including an understanding of the information behavior of scientists and students, adoption of electronic products, and the role of promotion and training. Analysis of their feedback indicated that users hold higher expectations for digital resources than paper, particularly in speed of access and availability.

In addition to the Glickman survey, we conducted our own based on our need for feedback on what our next steps should be as the experimental phase of the TULIP project comes to an end in December, 1995 [2]. We targeted this mailing to faculty members with a known interest in the content of TULIP — in years prior to TULIP's inception, they received routed paper copies of the tables of contents information for one or more TULIP journals, and continued to receive TOC information in paper form during the project. After a brief background discussion of the project, we noted that our funding would not permit us to subscribe to both paper and electronic versions of the TULIP journals indefinitely. We asked them to choose how they would like us to obtain the information in the coming year, and requested their outlook on the long term as well.

From this we received a snapshot of use preferences for 21 titles of known interest:

    8 titles were recommended for electronic subscription,
    13 for both paper and electronic subscriptions, and
    16 for paper only.

Obviously, for some titles certain individuals requested that we retain paper exclusively while others preferred getting electronic subscriptions as well (or instead) for that same title. The mandate at this point is unclear. During follow-up correspondence, the thoughts on TULIP were similar to those reported by the Glickman study. The major concerns remained timeliness and image quality, both on screen and in hard copy. Cost was seen as a secondary factor, and those who acknowledged that we would have to choose someday either indicated a preference for paper or for taking a "wait and see" approach. A couple comments in particular stood out:

> "I could do 99% of my work with the electronic form. However, this is only true if we receive them as promptly as the paper journals. This is currently not the case... How well can photographs be reproduced from the electronic journals? If the quality is high, it seems to me that hard copies are not necessary...[but] after trying out the printing options I came to the conclusion that the electronic versions cannot replace the hard copies. My preference is to continue the hard-copy subscriptions."

> "In general, while it is inevitable that we will eventually go to the electronic form of publishing and we certainly should start setting up the hardware, software, and infrastructure now, I believe that we should hang on to the print form and not waste money buying duplicate electronic form for as long as financially feasible. This is because back issues of electronic form can always be ordered in the future, and probably at a fraction of the original issue costs since it has lost the time premium, whereas the opposite is true for the printed form. For most users, the latter will remain more convenient for a long time to come. The main drawback of the print form is on the side of library, not users, because of subscription and storage costs."

4. Evaluation of usage of the TULIP system

Though the data set is small, reflecting the moderate traffic we expected from our limited initial set of journal offerings, we have seen some patterns develop. Our agreements with ES and commitments to TULIP users regarding confidentiality prevent us from identifying specific researchers, but we have seen that apparently some groups prefer electronic access to journal literature over paper. When TULIP first became available, use of the paper copies declined as electronic use rose. On the other side, there appears to be a group of researchers who prefer paper — and perhaps because of the added publicity surrounding TULIP, have increased their use of these journals. Overall, TULIP use has risen slowly, but steadily. As we have increased both the number of titles we offer and the speed at which we make them available, we have been encouraged by the response.

5. Implications and recommendations

The "hard" data suggest that publicity and training make a difference in use of both the print and the electronic forms of journals. The subjective data we have collected while interviewing users about the steps they think we should take as the TULIP experiment comes to an end suggest that most are passively supportive of the program. We don't see an overwhelmingly positive response for three reasons:

Rightly or wrongly:

> People expect something to appear on their computer screen before it appears in their mailroom, or on the shelves in the library.

> People expect better quality printouts from laser printers than they get from photocopiers.

> People expect electronic resources to be cheaper then their print counterpart. (At best, they think they should cost the same.)

So, when promoting TULIP while pointing out that right now the electronic editions appears three weeks after their paper counterpart, that it gives them at best the same resolution as a photocopier, and costs more than the paper journals, few hear a "compelling" reason to switch. When pressed, they agree that

TULIP is how things will be done in the future. But they don't see a compelling reason to change "their way of doing business" right now. Searching and profiling are not as relevant as we might suspect to many of our researchers (especially faculty members). Few do searches themselves (most rely on their graduate assistants) and all have their own SDI network (predominantly their colleagues).

Jim Ottaviani
Head of Reference
Engineering Library

attached:
    TULIP Background
    Journals available via TULIP

Footnotes

[1] Other factors: We don't have data for all TULIP journals, for all years. (Science Library journals are not included at all.) Nor have we attempted to differentiate between data from TULIP journals added in 1995 vs. the initial set. And, use patterns can change for many reasons — changes on the journal side (editorial boards with new policies, competing journals, etc.) and on our side as well (funding changes, new/discarded research agendas).

[2]

July, 1995

Dear Prof. X

Since you currently receive, via our Messenger Service, table of contents information for
> journal x
> journal y
> journal z
> ...

I'm writing to alert you of upcoming changes in its delivery via the TULIP system.

The Library is nearing the transition point between receiving the above journals in paper or electronic form, and we need your reactions. We will soon have to choose in which format we provide these titles. We may be able to afford both print and electronic on a temporary basis, but this will not hold true in the long term. Currently, the situation looks like this:
* We have both paper and electronic subscriptions to 63 titles.
  (See the attached list).
* The cost of these journals for print alone is $116,000. For the past two and a half years of the TULIP experiment, the electronic versions have been given to us for free.
* Starting in January 1996, we will have to pay $11,600 - 40,600 (10-35%) more to get both print and electronic subscriptions.
* Though we may be able to buy both print and electronic subscriptions for a year, we cannot afford both in the long term.

So we need feedback from you:

1) Which of the above journals should we receive only on paper?
2) Which should we receive and store only electronically?
3) Which should we receive in both formats during the transition period?

Please place a 1, 2, or 3 next to each title listed above and return your response to me at the address below (or, if you are responding via e-mail, to jim.ottaviani@umich.edu). If you can spare the time, I would also appreciate you reviewing the full list and annotating it as well.

Thank you for your time and effort. In addition to the list of journals, I've attached a brief summary of our progress on the TULIP experiment. I would appreciate your thoughts on this issue in general, and would gladly to speak with you about any other ideas you have.

Sincerely,

IV.   Evaluation of organizational and economic issues

Development of a system that effectively manages and distributes electronic services requires a careful blending of human and technical resources. The knowledge and skill of librarians, system programmers, and marketing and communication professionals are all required. Michigan's culture of cooperation and multi-organizational activity enabled it to put together a small, functional team to implement TULIP. Supported by their bosses, they were allowed to develop the system without organizational interference and as a result, enabled scientists and students to begin using TULIP resources in 1993.

From the project's inception, the team anticipated gaining a base of knowledge about system building for electronic resources, user behavior with digital journals, and economic models applicable to the evolving hybrid print and digital environment They were successful in meeting the first two objectives but were unable to test economic models. The rapid evolution of the world wide web as an information environment presented the developers with a better approach to TULIP than possible during its initial implementation. However, the web does not yet support the kind of data collection that is necessary for testing economic models nor the level of security for financial transactions that we felt was necessary.

A review of faculty and student comments and patterns of use suggests how important a better understanding of economic models is if the TULIP concept is to be expanded. Clearly, we continue in a transitional phase with some users reporting their inability to sustain additional subscription costs for personal copies of favored journals and with the library, too, forced to make choices because of budget constraints. However, the scientists and students report a desire to retain a paper version as well as the electronic files as long as possible. Certainly, we need to know what are feasible pricing options that will enable us to continue to support our researchers' and students' information needs.

V.   Implications of the TULIP project for the future

1.   Technical/ infrastructure

TULIP will migrate from a research project to a production service, cooperatively managed by the University Libraries, the Information Technology Division and CAEN. It will become part of the University of Michigan Digital Library, an umbrella for campus-wide digital library products and services. Planning for this transition has been underway since June in order to assure no interruption for users. Technical support will be supported by the two technology organizations as well as the libraries' systems staff.

2.   Organizational

Through TULIP Michigan gained experience with an organizational model that took advantage of the special expertise of its library and technology organizations in providing digital resources to the campus. We expect to continue using multi organizational teams to support our digital library efforts.

3.   Content

For the last seven months, following the resolution of most of the technical problems related to delivery of the additional titles, the Engineering Library has made a monthly comparison of what was available via TULIP vs. what was available in paper form at UM libraries. Of the 62 journals available on the www version of our browser, roughly 15 journals/month don't get updated in TULIP, though the library receives new issues. Approximately 25 (nearly half) of the journals are two or more issues behind the paper copies in the library in any given month. In the last three months, performance has improved slightly: an average of roughly 12 journals not updated, 15 journals two or more issues behind.

Though the numbers are only approximations (as with other data discussed above, sample sizes and number of months checked are too small to call something a true average) the numbers are distressing. They indicate poor performance by Elsevier in delivering the electronic versions. Given scientists' and students' very high expectations, delays, like these, damage the credibility of the digital library and severely weaken the commitment of researchers to use its resources.

Electronic vs Paper Comparative Data
4/95-5/95
17 journals not updated in TULIP since the previous month (though new issues arrived in the libraries)
38 journals were 2 or more issues behind what was available in the libraries during this period.

5/95-
7 not updated
39 journals 2 or more issues behind

6/95-
25 not updated
37 journals 2 or more issues behind

7/95-
11 not updated
19 journals 2 or more issues behind

8/95-
8 not updated
14 journals 2 or more issues behind
9/95-
17 not updated
14 journals 2 or more issues behind

10/95-11/95
10 not updated
5 journals 2 or more issues behind

Technical aspects

I. **Description of TULIP system**
1. *Components*
1.1. *Functionalities*
- Functionalities implemented

The University of Michigan's world wide web implementation of the TULIP system supports browsing, searching, on screen image display, and local printing.

- Rationale for choice of functionalities

Use of the world wide web relieves Michigan of the need to develop client programs and enables us to leverage a very popular resource. Browsing, searching, viewing, and printing are the basic functionalities that someone would want.

MIRLYN was already a widely used system on campus. It allows access to the TULIP in a way that is familiar to many users on campus, including searching, citation/abstract display, and printing. It also supports users who have systems that cannot easily run a web browser.

1.2. *System architecture*
1.2.1. *Implemented browsing technologies*
In developing the www implementation, a hierarchical browser was built around the TULIP journals. At the top level is a list of journal titles, then a list of volumes and issues within each title, and finally a table of contents for a particular issue.

Browsing is also available through MIRLYN in a very rudimentary fashion. By searching on a journal's title and date of publication, a list of the articles in that issue is displayed. The user can then, in turn, select the citation for each item and scan it.

1.2.2. *Implemented searching technologies*
A search can be performed at any of the three levels of the web browser described above: all journals, within one journal, or within one issue. A user can do a simple fielded search by typing words into boxes for article title, journal title, author, abstract, or full text. Another page allows the entry of arbitrary Boolean or proximity queries.

Using the MIRLYN implementation, a user can perform author, title, and keyword searches. Keyword searches can be delimited to confine searches to specific fields such as article title, journal title, abstract, publication date, etc. Keyword searches can be either simple single-word queries or multi-term queries using the full range of Boolean and proximity operators (and, or, not, same, near, adj) and truncation. Online help is provided for formulating search queries.

1.2.3. *Implemented user interfaces*
Any forms-capable web browser can be used as an interface to the TULIP system. The MIRLYN interface is accessible with any VT100 or TN3270 terminal emulation package.

1.2.4. *Image viewing (e.g. anti-aliasing, gray scaling, zooming)*
Using the web browser, article images are viewed one page at a time. When a page is fetched, a program called tif2gif converts the 300dpi TIFF file into a 100-dpi grayscale GIF in a way that keeps it readable. The GIF is then used as an inline image by the client's web browser.

1.2.5. *Image printing/exporting*
- Faxing
- E-mailing

There is no faxing or emailing of images.

- File transfer

The images are sent to the client using the regular world wide web protocol.

- Local printing

Printing is accomplished through a helper application. The user can download this program and configure their browser to use it. We have set up a MIME type for a file containing a list of TULIP page images. The print button fetches this file, and a properly configured browser launches the print helper application. The print helper then fetches the individual full-resolution page images, converts them to postscript, and sends them to any printer that the client machine can access.

Printing from the MIRLYN interface is handled by passing the REQ DOC command and printer selection entered by the user from the mainframe via a print server to the TULIP image server. The image server retrieves the article images and passes them back to the print server where they are reformatted, prefaced with a banner page giving user and citation information, and sent to the user-selected printer.

1.3.   Networking issues
Most of the campus is wired with Ethernet, so network speed is not a problem when the system is used from campus locations. Modem access, especially at speeds below 14.4 baud, however, still presents challenges and in these situations, MIRLYN offers an alternative.

1.4.   Data preparation and loading
The TULIP server keeps the data in the same format as that on the CDs. Two additional types of data are created: a directory of reformatted citation/abstracts, and a fulltext index. Perl programs generate the browsable lists and pages, and the FTL search engine searches the fulltext. For the MIRLYN implementation, the citation and abstract data are reformatted into a psuedo-MARC record and loaded onto the mainframe. Author, title, and keyword indexes are generated and are searchable using the NOTIS search engine.

- Validation of incoming datasets

A perl program checks the incoming datasets to make sure that the TOC files are consistent with the data files and that the checksums are correct.

- Text preparation

The checker program also reformats the article abstracts and breaks them into separate files. In MIRLYN, the abstracts are loaded as a field in the citation record. Abstracts are fully indexed and are searchable using keyword.

- Preparing images

Images are kept in the same directory structure and format as on the CDs. They are not prepared except at viewing time, when they are scaled to grayscale GIF so they can be used as inlined images in a web browser.

Under the MIRLYN implementation, images are only prepared at time of printing. At that point, the print server reformats the TIFF images to Postscript Level II for faster printing.

- Indexing bibliographic data from DATASET.TOC
- Indexing raw ASCII files

The bibliographic data and raw ascii files are indexed together on the web server. An article is considered to consist of the reformatted abstract file and any number of raw text files. These are indexed with a locally-developed search engine called FTL.

Bibliographic and abstract data are indexed by author, title and keyword in MIRLYN. The raw ascii files are not used due to record size limitations.

- Profiling

A previous implementation supported the ability to store queries that would automatically be run against new datasets when they arrive, and the abstracts of matching articles were emailed to the user. The web implementation of TULIP does not yet support this, but will do so in the near future. MIRLYN also does not support profiling.

1.5.   Implemented storage & image retrieval
Images are stored in the same format in which they arrive. The images are by far the major component of the disk space. Currently TULIP is stored on five 9-gigabyte magnetic disks. As mentioned above, the images are converted to grayscale GIF at the time that they are viewed, and to Postscript Level II when printed through MIRLYN.

1.6.   Set up of security of the system
Security for the web implementation follows the world wide web model, which can restrict access by host-name range or IP address range. MIRLYN,users are asked to authenticate by social security number (SSN) and last name when searching and by uniqname and password for printing. The SSN and last name are verified against the Library's current patron file stored on the mainframe. Uniqnames are verified against a file of campus uniqnames matched against the patron file (to ensure the user is currently affiliated with the campus).

1.7.   Usage and logfiles issues
1.7.1.   Collection of usage data
The Web site usage data is collected from the http (world wide web) logfiles, which contain what was accessed and when. Usage under MIRLYN is logged by the standard or locally modified NOTIS log files. These logs capture terminal location, user type, search, display, and print request information.

1.7.2.   Assembly of logfile
A program converts the httpd log to the TULIP log format. Log information from MIRLYN is reformatted and added to the TULIP log format.

2.   History and current status of the project
2.1.   Description of development process
- Successful prototypes and abandoned ones
- Migration to production
- Difficulties encountered, solutions found

The Michigan TULIP project was originally designed to implement two different access systems in order to provide the widest availability possible and to take advantage of existing system development.

To begin, we adapted an existing system which contained information about campus events. Its Motif / X-windows, client program ran on any UNIX workstation, contacting a central server for searching. We modified it to work with TULIP by means of several additions including an image viewer. This system, called Tulipview, also allowed users to store queries and get notified automatically by email when new information matched.

Unfortunately, it had several limitations, including allowing searching but not browsing; an inadequate image viewer; and, a client program which only ran under UNIX, eliminating use from a Macintosh or PC. Nevertheless, it was released as a production system, and many people used it. Simultaneously with the Motif / X-windows system implementation, the citation/abstract data was made available through the MIRLYN. This system supports the Library's online catalog; 18 citation files including MASC [TULIP], Compendex, and Inspec; and provides links to 14 catalogs at remote institutions via the Z39.50 protocol. It uses the Ameritech Library Service's NOTIS LMS and MDAS software running on an IBM 9221 main-frame. Data loading and display formatting were very straight-forward using a locally written loader to convert the original TOC records to a psuedo-MARC format that could then be searched and displayed using the standard NOTIS MDAS software. The ability to request printouts of articles required local development since this was not a standard NOTIS feature at that time. We have since moved from the locally developed print request mechanism to the ALS NOTIS DocLink software (still with some local modifications). Close cooperation between Library and Engineering College programmers allowed us t o use a single image storage and delivery system for both the Motif / X-windows (and later the web) and MIRLYN implementations. One of the major limitations of the MIRLYN implementation is the inability to view an article before deciding to print. It also does not provide true browsing capability.

When the world wide web became popular we decided to use it for TULIP. This allowed people to access TULIP from any platform that had a forms-capable web browser. It also made it easy to implement browsing and a better way of viewing the images.

3. Experiences

3.1. Quality of data/images
The OCR'ed text, while it contains errors, is still useful for full text searching. However, a lot more could be done with correct fulltext. The images are of reasonable quality, after some initial difficulty at the beginning of the project with images that were skewed or had huge margins. A more faithful reproduction could be achieved with 600 dpi, but 300 dpi comes very close.

3.2. Storage
The images take up a lot of space. The system currently uses five 9-gigabyte drives to contain it. Keeping backups of this much data is difficult. We would like to switch to a RAID system in the near future, because RAID also provides protection against drive failure.

3.3. Network delivery to end users
Network delivery over campus Ethernet works well. Delivery to other sites can be slow if the remote site has a slow Internet connection, but we do not often have that problem. Dial-in access can also provide slow connections, depending on the speed of the user's modem.

3.4. Viewing
If done correctly, scaling to fit the screen can be fast and the resulting image can be quite readable.

3.5. Printing
An earlier prototype used centralized printing. We found that this was not a viable solution because of the difficulties involved in keeping an updated and reasonably complete printer list for an institution of Michigan's size. Local printing using the helper application works very well.

Centralized printing is still used in conjunction with the MIRLYN system since the mainframe cannot dynamically recognize the printers available on campus, nor can we offer local printing since the article images cannot be displayed at the user's workstation.

Initially, printing was a very time-consuming process. However, once a method was devised to convert the images from TIFF to Postscript Level II at the print server, printing greatly improved. In addition to reformatting the images, we also added a banner page that gave user and citation information, concatenated the images into a single file, and printed a line showing "Page 'x' of 'n' for [uniqname] [user name]" in the margin of each page to lessen the possibility of pages being separated and lost at the printer. This same procedure is still used when articles are printed via the MIRLYN system.

3.6. Internet delivery
Internet delivery of entire datasets from Elsevier to us turned out to be too slow and problematic.. Physical receipt of CDs of the files works well. Unfortunately, the time required to master and ship the disk delays arrival of the journals in their electronic format resulting in a substantial lag behind their paper counterparts.

Internet delivery of articles from our system to people using it at remote sites works well but is entirely dependent on the speed of the remote site's Internet connection. For major universities this isn't a problem, but some smaller institutions have fairly slow links and the delay in loading a page image is noticeable.

3.7.   Other

3.8.   Conclusions

Our www implementation provides our campus scientists with good browsing and searching capabilities, So too, our MIRLYN implementation, while not particularly 'glitzy', provides a very usable system for searching the citation / abstract information and requesting prints of articles regardless of the researcher's workstation or network connection.

As a project, TULIP provided valuable experience which is serving as the base for developing additional information services through both our web an MIRLYN implementations. Our TULIP URL is "http://tulipsrvr.engin.umich.edu/tulip/".

4.   Future developments

4.1.   Additional data formats envisaged/ required, views on suitability

Delivering TIFF plus OCR format has two limitations: the size of the TIFFs and the inaccuracy of the OCR text. A format such as SGML that takes less space and yet still includes accurate text and layout would be an improvement.

4.2.   Additional functionality planned

We have used the TULIP specification to evolve the content of the campus digital library, specifically implementing JSTOR which contains economics and history journals. In addition, we applied our experience to expanding MIRLYN's image delivery through a project called Core Journals. This matches citations from the Wilson Index files to images on CD in UMI's PowerPages system.

Future developments include implementing a web front-end to MIRLYN using an http-to-Z39.50 gateway during 1996. This should allow us to provide viewing capabilities for retrieved articles and to integrate the system more fully into the campus digital library. In addition, as TULIP moves from a research project into production, we will evaluate the feasibility of linking the Elsevier images / SGML files to citations in other databases which will provide fuller integration with existing information resources.

4.3.   Other

Throughout the development of TULIP, we found the interaction with the Elsevier technical team helpful and beneficial. We enjoyed the opportunity to work with them in achieving a service that provided our researchers with a new form of access to scientific information.

TULIP

Appendix VII

The University of Tennessee

TULIP FINAL REPORT
THE UNIVERSITY OF TENNESSEE, KNOXVILLE
December 1995

TULIP Team

Linda Phillips, Head, Networked Services, Project Leader
Gayle Baker, Electronic Services Coordinator (1992-93)
Margaret Casado, Electronic Services Librarian (1995)
Bob Conrad, ORNL Lockheed Martin Energy Systems (1995)
Lynn Davis, Electronic Services Librarian, Project Coordinator (1995)
Randy Hoffman, ORNL Martin Marietta Energy Systems (1993-94)
Tamara Miller, Head, Library Systems
Dianne Myers, Current Periodicals Supervisor
Richard Pollard, Associate Professor, School of Information Sciences
Earl Smith, Electronic Services Coordinator, Project Coordinator (1993-94)
Flossie Wise, Engineering Reference Librarian

249

Table of Contents

TULIP Final Report
The University of Tennessee, Knoxville
December, 1995

TULIP Technical Report

I. Description of Profile of University

1. Organization/structure of university

The University of Tennessee is the official land-grant institution for the State of Tennessee, with its main campus in Knoxville. UT Knoxville is a Research I University, the state's oldest, largest, and most comprehensive institution. The University offers more than 300 degree programs to its 25,000 students. More than 7,500 graduate and professional students are enrolled on and off campus in 85 master's and 52 doctoral programs. There are 1,600 faculty members. Developments in graduate education have been accompanied by expanded cooperation with Oak Ridge National Laboratory (ORNL) and the Tennessee Valley Authority and by growth of major research programs including those in the fields of energy, biotechnology, and robotics. The Science Alliance is the largest in Tennessee's Centers of Excellence for higher education. The Science Alliance's Distinguished Scientist Program, designed to strengthen cooperative instructional and research activities, attracts many eminent scientists to joint appointments at UTK and ORNL. Through public service activities, the University extends its resources throughout the state and nation. Continuing education programs, are offered in more than 40 locations across Tennessee.

2. Organization of libraries

The University of Tennessee, Knoxville Libraries own approximately 2 million volumes, more than 3.5 million manuscripts, 2 million microforms, 32,000 audio and video recordings, plus United States and United Nations documents. The UTK Libraries subscribe to more than 11,000 periodicals and other serial titles. The Libraries support the scholarship, teaching, and research of the University with a varied research collection, 185 full-time staff, and state-of-the-art information technology. A seven-story, 350,000-square-foot central library and five branch libraries serve the Knoxville campus. Library holdings are accessible via a sophisticated online library information system that can be searched in the central and branch libraries, from home and office computers, and is accessible worldwide through the Internet. Cataloging and interlibrary loan transactions are performed online through utilities that link UTK's library to thousands of libraries around the world.

3. Organization of IT/information services

UTK computing and telecommunications functions are divided among four units, Academic Technology, Computing and Administrative Systems, Network Services, and Telephone Services, with direct responsibility to the Vice Chancellor for Information Infrastructure. Academic Technology is concerned with research computing and the advancement of instructional technology. Computing and Administrative Systems supports various single- and multiple-user operating systems and applications, provides consolidated user services for computing and networking, provides consolidated business services and operations, performs database administration, and develops and maintains administrative systems. Network Services and Telephone Services connect mainframe computers, workstations, microcomputers and video terminals in a multivendor, heterogeneous environment. Emphasis is placed on the expansion of broadband communications facilities on campus and remote access for distance learning programs, based on published standards and with the capability of accommodating the rapid evolution of technology. Ethernet and fiber optics connect many buildings on the Knoxville campus to provide rapid access to data in remote locations and to support several protocols including TCP/IP, DECnet, LAT, Novell NetWare and Apple Appletalk. A terminal port selection and multiplexing system, which is connected to a similar system at the Oak Ridge National Laboratory (ORNL), provides access to the network through 200 dialup lines.

The university network is connected to the Internet which provides access to Internet sites via the Southeastern University Research Association Network (SURAnet). SURAnet connects to the National Science Foundation Network (NSFnet) which joins other state and The University of Tennessee Computing regional networks, and directly connects to the five NSF supercomputing centers. The Division of Information Infrastructure (DII) provides technical support for other departmental workstations on the UT Knoxville campus and maintains more than 150 microcomputers in remote user work areas and microcomputer laboratories on campus. Computing services are made available to the other UT campuses through remote links.

4. User demographics
The TULIP audience included faculty and graduate students in the UTK College of Engineering Department of Materials Science and Engineering, as well as ORNL researchers whose work involved materials science. There are fifteen UTK Materials Science faculty and approximately 100 graduate students. The Materials Science Department also has a small undergraduate program with 75-80 students enrolled. There are two materials science concentrations, metallurgical and polymer engineering. Metallurgical engineering areas of concentration include physical metallurgy, materials processing, welding metallurgy and materials joining, corrosion behavior, failure analysis, and mechanical and physical behavior of materials. Polymer engineering areas of concentration include rheology and polymer processing; polymer morphology; mechanical, physical, and chemical behavior of polymers; and composite materials. A secondary audience included faculty and students in departments of chemical engineering, chemistry, microbiology, physics, and engineering science and mechanics; the Center for Materials Processing; the Institute for Applied Microbiology; and the Institute for Resonance Ionization Spectroscopy.

The 38 faculty and graduate students who registered to receive full text of TULIP articles formed a target group for library communications about the project. Table 1 includes a summary of information collected on the registration profile form. A majority of this group were from Materials Science (22), although several related departments were represented: Chemistry (4), Chemical Engineering (3), Civil and Environmental Engineering (3), Mechanical and Aerospace Engineering (2), Engineering Science and Mechanics (1), Nuclear Engineering (1), Polymer

Engineering (1), and Structural Biology (1). Most of the registered TULIP participants were graduate students (20) or faculty (16); there was one ORNL researcher and one UTK post doctoral fellow. The participants reported variable lengths of experience with their research: 19 had less than five years, while 8 had five to ten years and 10 had over eleven years experience. A majority used the IBM platform (20), with 11 using Macintosh and 6 using UNIX. Regarding their familiarity with electronic access mechanisms, 30 of the participants used e-mail, 17 used the Gopher, and 13 used electronic bulletin boards. Since most of the demographic data was collected in early 1994 while the campus was primarily Gopher-based, it is not surprising that only 3 reported using the Web. Of the group 11 were familiar with FTP and 2 with WAIS.

Regarding user research habits, most reported using the UTK or ORNL online library information systems and about half used CD-ROMs and online database search services. On an open-ended question about most frequently used journals in their research, the following titles were given: *Macromolecules, Polymer, Polymer Engineering and Science, Journal of Polymer Science, Journal of Applied Polymer Science,* and *Journal of Physical Chemistry.* Using a list of preferred channels of information gathering provided by the TULIP Team on the registration form, the most popular were journals, books, conference proceedings, and personal contacts. Other sources were technical reports, preprints, reference works, and electronic bulletin boards.

A wider TULIP audience included any user of the UTK online library information system who wanted access to the journal tables of contents. Any UTK faculty, staff or student and any ORNL researcher was eligible to use abstracts and register for the use of TULIP full text of journal articles. Library staff were one segment of the TULIP audience that had no particular interest in the subject matter of the journals, but who were eager to understand the issues surrounding the development of electronic journals.

II. TULIP Promotion and Training
1. Description of promotion activities undertaken
Getting news of the service to the potential users was an important step in the TULIP project. A library news release (Illustration 1) invited the university community to take a look at TULIP, briefly explaining that the project provided online tables of contents and full article text for materials science journals published by Elsevier Science. The flier noted that the University Libraries and ORNL library were gathering data about user preferences, the mechanics required to deliver journals electronically, and the extent of use.

Flossie Wise, Engineering Reference Librarian, and other members of the TULIP Team met with faculty from Materials Science and Engineering, Physics, and Chemical Engineering departments as early as December 1991 to determine their

Table 1: Demographics of Registered TULIP Users

There are 38 registered users.		
By Department:	Materials and Science Engineering	22
	Chemistry	4
	Chemical Engineering	3
	Civil and Environmental Engineering	3
	Mechanical and Aerospace Engineering	2
	Engineering Science and Mechanics	1
	Nuclear Engineering	1
	Polymer Engineering	1
	Structural Biology	1
Status:	Graduate Students	20
	UTK Faculty (teaching and research)	15
	UTK Faculty (research only)	1
	ORNL Researcher	1
	Post Doctoral Fellow	1
Time in Research:	Less than 5 years	19
	5-10 years	8
	11+ years	10
Computers Available:	IBM or Compatible	20
	Macintosh	11
	Unix	6
Computer Services Used in Research:	E-mail	30
	Gopher	17
	Bulletin Boards	13
	FTP	11
	WWW	3
	WAIS	2
Information Services Used in Research:	UTK and/or ORNL Online Catalog	32
	CD-ROMS	15
	Online Database Search Services	14
Delivery Preference:	Departmental Mail	29
	Fax	6
Most Preferred Journal Titles:	Macromolecules	
	Polymer	
	Polymer Engineering and Science	
	Journal of Polymer Science	
	Journal of Applied Polymer Science	
	Journal of Physical Chemistry	
Most Preferred Channels of Information:	journals	
	books	
	conference proceedings	
	personal contacts	
	technical reports	
	preprints	
	reference works	
	electronic bulletinboards	

Illustration 1: Library News Release About TULIP

UTK Library News

THE PLACE OF KNOWLEDGE • THE PEOPLE WITH ACCESS • THE POWER OF INFORMATION

TULIP's Blooming

Read an electronic journal lately? Take a look at TULIP (The University Licensing Project), an experimental file of tables of contents and abstracts for 43 Elsevier journals in materials science. The University Libraries and Martin Marietta Energy Systems, Inc. (MMES) at ORNL are participating in a research project with Elsevier Science Publishers, Inc. and nine U.S. academic libraries to provide online tables of contents and full article text for materials science journals published by Elsevier. The libraries are gathering data about user preferences, the mechanics required to deliver journals electronically, and extent of use.

To use TULIP, begin with the Libraries' Online Library Information System menu. Select "Electronic Journals" and then "TULIP." From the TULIP menu, choose a desired journal title, and move to the tables of contents and abstracts.

UTK and MMES faculty, researchers, and students who would like to receive fax or laser printed copies of the article text without charge must register with the University Libraries. Send an e-mail query to **tulip@utklib.lib.utk.edu** or call Earl Smith (974-6797) or Flossie Wise (974-0016).

Internet Gopher Information Client v1.11

TULIP--Material Sciences Journals ❸

1. Welcome To TULIP !. ·
—> 2. How To Use TULIP.
3. Tulip Table of Contents/

Internet Gopher Information Client v1.11

Electronic Journals ❷

1. CICNet Electronic Journal Project/
2. EJournals Collection at Univ of Minn/
—> 3. TULIP - Elsevier Experiment at UTK/
4. Bryn Mawr Classical Review/

Internet Gopher Information Client v1.11

Online Library Information System ❶

1. Welcome to UTK Online Library Information System (OLIS)/
2. About UTK Libraries/
3. UTK Libraries Holdings/
4. Other Library Catalogs & Info Systems/
5. Electronic Books/
—> 6. Electronic Journals/
7. Electronic Reference/
8. Information by Subject/
9. Other Internet Resources/
10. Other UTK Information/
11. VERONICA: Search the World of Gopher for Information/
12. What's New in OLIS.
13. Search the OLIS menus <?>

Press ? for Help, q to Quit, u to go up a menu

Periodicals To Be Moved; Reserve To Offer Late Night Hours

Library users will soon find it easier to search for periodicals in the Hodges Library. And late night users of the Hodges Library will soon benefit from expanded services and additional study space.

On May 16th, the library will begin to move Periodicals (presently 235 Hodges Library) across the galleria to the (continued, over)

interest in the project. The Team kept the Engineering faculty apprised of developments as the project evolved. (Illustrations 2,3,4) All faculty in the UTK departments of materials science, chemical engineering, chemistry, and physics and ORNL researchers letters inviting participation and a registration form/profile sheet in December 1993. Colorful posters advertising TULIP were placed in the science buildings on campus and sent to researchers at ORNL: the TULIP Team created a poster (Illustration 5) that was distributed in Spring 1994; in Fall 1994 the Elsevier Science poster was distributed widely. In early Spring 1995 a TULIP poster and banner in the library's Current Periodicals section announced the availability of the project.

Librarians conducted several training sessions for groups of materials science faculty and researchers from both institutions to demonstrate and promote the service. Articles appeared in the campus newspaper, *The Daily Beacon*, and in the faculty newspaper, *Context*, describing TULIP and inviting inquiries. In April 1994 Linda Phillips made a presentation about TULIP at the Tennessee Library Association annual conference.[1] The *Tennessee Librarian* published an article by Earl Smith in Fall 1994, "TULIP Blooms in Tennessee."[2] Earl Smith and Lynn Davis collaborated on the "TULIP at The University of Tennessee, Knoxville," article published in the special *Library Hi Tech* issue devoted to TULIP.[3]

2. Description of training activities undertaken
Presentations to materials science faculty and students included both orientation and training for the use of TULIP. Printed materials (Illustration 6) and directions in the Gopher and Web files provided comprehensive instructions for getting access to the tables of contents, abstracts, and full text files. In library instruction sessions for the College of Engineering, Flossie Wise highlighted TULIP when student topics matched the subject matter of the journals available. Flossie presented TULIP as a research tool, as well as an example of electronic journals. Library staff in Current Periodicals, Reference, and Interlibrary Loan received training about TULIP so that they would be prepared to answer questions from users.

3. Effects of promotion and training
The immediate effect of promotion was user registration. Approximately 20 participants were registered at the conclusion of one presentation made to a group of faculty and students. Library staff incorporated TULIP access into their instruction to users who, at that time, were just becoming comfortable with the Gopher. When the Library implemented a Web-based system, TULIP was available in that format and used to demonstrate the improved graphics capabilities of the Web.

4. Conclusions and recommendations
Promotion and training activities gave the University Libraries and TULIP users an important learning experience and a beginning for studying issues of electronic journal delivery and access. Although the users clearly articulated their preference

Illustration 2: TULIP Progress Report for UTK/ORNL Participants

THE UNIVERSITY OF TENNESSEE
KNOXVILLE

MEMORANDUM

University
Libraries

TO: TULIP Participants

FROM: Linda Phillips *Linda*
         Head, Networked Services

DATE: November 30, 1992

SUBJECT: TULIP PROGRESS

Enclosed is a copy of the first TULIP Newsletter that has been issued
by Elsevier Science Publishers. It provides an up-to-date summary of
the current status of the TULIP project.

On the local scene, the University Libraries has received a CD-ROM test
file from Elsevier that includes three types of data from one issue of
each of the 42 materials science journals to be provided electronically:
1) Table of Contents in ASCII format; 2) Full text files in unedited
ASCII format; and 3) Bitmapped page images of the complete article in
TIFF format. Library Systems staff are experimenting with loading the
data into a menu format (Gopher) being developed for access to several
types of library information. We expect to install a NeXT computer in
the Hodges Library Database Training Room for demonstration of the TULIP
text and image files.

On November 19 I attended a meeting of national TULIP participants to
continue planning for the project. We will receive Table of Contents
files for all of the 1992 issues of the 42 journals. In 1993 UT and
Martin Marietta users will be able to see the journal tables of contents
through the library information system (Gopher-based) and get the full
text of the articles from Engineering Information. During the next few
months the University Libraries/MMES TULIP Team will be developing for
users an experimental process to view the Tables of Contents and acquire
the full text.

We want to involve you and our library colleagues in the design of the
access process. During December we will provide orientation sessions
for library staff, to be followed in January 1993 by orientation for
those on the TULIP mailing list. Once the first version of an access
process is completed, we will schedule orientation for potential users
of the journals.

The term **experimental** implies that there will be numerous changes and
improvements to the process before it reaches a point where is is
satisfactory for users! We appreciate your participation in this
pioneering effort to make electronic journals a viable option in the
research process. The current TULIP mailing list is enclosed. I
welcome your questions about the project.

Knoxville, Tennessee, U.S.A. 37996-1000

THE UNIVERSITY OF TENNESSEE
KNOXVILLE

University Libraries
John C. Hodges Library
Knoxville, Tennessee, U.S.A. 37996-1000

MEMORANDUM

TO: UTK Materials Science & Engineering Faculty
MMES Researchers
TULIP Project Mail List

FROM: Linda Phillips
Head, Networked Services

DATE: December 10, 1993

SUBJECT: TULIP UPDATE

TULIP Open for Business at UTK and MMES

The University Libraries and Martin Marietta Energy Systems have moved from the planning to the implemention phase of TULIP, a cooperative research project between Elsevier Science Publishers, Inc. and over a dozen research libraries across the country. Tables of contents and abstracts from Elsevier materials science journals may be viewed through UTK's Online Library Information System (OLIS). During the remainder of the FY 93/94 academic year UTK and MMES users who register may also receive, without charge, copies of these articles. During 1994, the second year of this three-year project, we will be experimenting with delivery of bit-mapped journal page images.

How TULIP Works

Every two weeks UTK Electronic Services receives journal table of contents files via Internet from Engineering Information (Ei), a document supply company working for Elsevier Science Publishers. The ASCII data is run through a parsing program which converts it to the table of contents format displayed in OLIS. Users who register with Electronic Services may send us requests for articles they wish to receive by providing the "item identifier" given in the article citation. Each day a student assistant collects incoming requests and places orders for article text via electronic mail to Ei. Ei sends the text to us electronically; we print the articles on a laser printer and deliver them to the user.

Options for Receiving TULIP Articles

In the TULIP REGISTRATION/USER PROFILE you may elect to have articles delivered in printed format or sent via fax. If you have appropriate equipment and software, you may receive articles in electronic format. Contact Earl Smith at smithec@utklib.lib.utk.edu for details about hardware and software requirements.

Illustration 3: TULIP Update for UTK/ORNL Participants (page 2)

Evaluating TULIP

The registration form provides baseline information about TULIP users. Occasionally during the next two years we will ask about your satisfaction with the project through short surveys. We will appreciate your comments immediately, however, both positive and negative--please contact Earl Smith or any of the TULIP Team members named below.

TULIP's Future

During Spring 1994 we will begin experimenting with TULIP image files. In TIFF format, they are quite large, and require special hardware and software to be viewed at a computer workstation. Further, the image files must be compressed for speedy transmission via Internet, and then decompressed for viewing. We have assembled the necessary components for viewing in the library, and will be exploring options, including hypermedia, for making the images more conveniently available electronically. Please contact one of the TULIP Team members for a demonstration of the existing files; we'll let you know when we have something more advanced to show.

TULIP Team

The following people meet on a regular basis to implement TULIP and evaluate progress. Complete addresses are given on the enclosed mail list.

Earl Smith, Electronic Services, University Libraries (TULIP Team Coordinator)
Randy Hoffman, Collection Development, MMES
Tamara Miller, Systems, University Libraries
Dianne Myers, Current Periodicals, University Libraries
Linda Phillips, Networked Services, University Libraries
Richard Pollard, Graduate School of Library & Information Science (Research Coordinator)
Flossie Wise, Reference Services,

Enclosures:
TULIP Newsletter
TULIP Mail List
User Profile/Registration (included for those who have not yet registered)
Instructions for Accessing TULIP

TULIP **Final Report**

259

Illustration 4: TULIP Memorandum to UTK Engineering and Science Faculty

THE UNIVERSITY OF TENNESSEE
KNOXVILLE

University Libraries
John C. Hodges Library
Knoxville, Tennessee, U.S.A. 37996-1000

MEMORANDUM

Date:	March 15, 1994
From:	Flossie Wise, Engineering Librarian The John C. Hodges Library, Reference Services (WISE@UTKLIB.LIB.UTK.EDU or 974-0016)
To:	Engineering and Science Faculty
Subject:	TULIP Project (The University Licensing Program)

Many of you are already familiar with the TULIP project, but for those who aren't, an explanation is in order. TULIP is a cooperative research project between Elsevier Science Publishers and several research libraries across the U.S., including the UTK Libraries and the Martin Marietta Energy Systems Libraries. The project objective is to look at the technical and economic feasibility of using campus networks and the Internet for electronic distribution of scientific information, ideally to the researcher's desktop.

Forty-three materials science journals published by Elsevier make up the test group. Even though this may not be your field, we ask that you take a look at the listing in order to have an idea of what may be in store for the future.

Currently the 1993-present table of contents and abstracts from the 43 journals can be accessed through the Library's Online Library Information System (OLIS). To view the list:

- Connect to OLIS
- Select Electronic Journals
- Select TULIP (the journals are listed here)
- Select journal/volume/issue
- View abstract

Please note that each citation/abstract has an item identifier which also serves as an order number. If you are interested in obtaining copies of articles from the 43 journals, you will need to register with UTK Libraries' Electronic Services. A registration form and user profile is enclosed for those who have not previously registered.

Registered users will receive copies of articles from the test group free of charge during the experimental period. The copies are delivered to your mail box or can be faxed to you. In the future it may be possible to receive articles in electronic format, as the next phase of the project will look at delivery of bit-mapped journal page images.

For further information or assistance, please contact Earl Smith at SMITHEC@UTKLIB.LIB.UTK.EDU.

TULIP...
Electronic Journals in Materials Science

What is TULIP?
- access to 43 journals from Elsevier Science Publishers
- online tables of contents and abstracts
- articles faxed or laser printed without charge

To use TULIP:
- from the Libraries' OLIS menu, select Electronic Journals
- from the Electronic Journals menu, select TULIP
- from the TULIP menu, select journal, volume and issue
- read the abstracts and record item identifier

To order articles:
- request a user profile and instructions via e-mail from:
    TULIP@UTKLIB.LIB.UTK.EDU
- order articles via e-mail
- articles will be delivered to departmental mailboxes or faxed

For more information, contact:
- Earl Smith, Electronic Services Coordinator
  SMITHEC@UTKLIB.LIB.UTK.EDU
  974-6797
- Flossie Wise, Engineering Reference Librarian
  WISE@UTKLIB.LIB.UTK.EDU
  974-0016

THE UNIVERSITY OF TENNESSEE, KNOXVILLE LIBRARIES   3/94

TULIP **Final Report**

261

Illustration 6: Instructions for Accessing TULIP

Accessing Tulip At UTK/MMES

ACCESSING TULIP AT THE UNIVERSITY OF TENNESEE, KNOXVILE & MARTIN MARIETTA ENERGY SYSTEMS

TULIP, The University Licensing Program cooperative research project between Elsevier Science Publishers, Inc. and several research libraries, is now available for access at UTK. The University Libraries and Martin Marietta Energy Systems are collaborating with Elsevier to provide on-line table of contents and full article text for materials science and engineering journals published by Elsevier. The first phase of the experiment at UTK/MMES is now available to faculty and researchers who register with the University Libraries.

To Register

Contact Earl C. Smith (smithec@utklib.lib.utk.edu) or Flossie Wise (wise@utklib.lib.utk.edu) at 974-6797 to complete a preliminary information form and profile. The profile will have a section in which you can indicate your preferred method for delivery of full-text articles.

To Browse TULIP Tables of Contents

❶ Connect to the Library OLIS menu (see attached OLIS guide).

❷ From the OLIS menu, select Electronic Journals.

❸ From the Electronic Journals menu select TULIP.

A list of available journal titles is shown. Eventually, the list will include a total of 43 titles in Material Sciences.

❹ Select a journal title, volume and issue from the menus.

❺ The Table of Contents for each issue contains brief bibliographic information plus an item identifier (needed to order individual items) and an abstract number (used to link citation to a corresponding abstract file). Note the abstract number(s) of interest.

❻ Return to the previous menu and select the desired abstract by its abstract number (see step 5).

To Receive Articles

Eventually, we will experiment with the delivery of full text to your workstation. At present, however, we will request article text from Engineering Information. Library staff will request documents from Ei via e-mail and receive them over the Internet. Text and graphics will be printed on a laser printer at 300 dpi (dots per inch).

To Order an Article

❶ Send the item identifier and your name via e-mail to tulip@utklib.lib.utk.edu or by paper (if you do not have an e-mail account) to TULIP, Networked Services, University Libraries, 149 Hodges Library.

❷ Articles will be delivered to departmental mailboxes or fax machines according to the specifications in your profile (see registration).

for desktop access to full text of journal articles, the actual promotion and training concentrated on what was possible at the time the project began. Promotion focused on the steps to use TULIP in its current stage of development, rather than on what future electronic journals might offer. The experiment with Elsevier Science was an excellent opportunity to observe researchers' initial reactions to electronic journal files.

III. User Behavior

1. Description of user/usage research

Users provided survey and profile data as they completed the registration forms (Appendix I). The registration/profile form, collected information such as name, address, ID number, delivery preference (fax,courier), status (professor, graduate student, researcher, etc.), number of years active in materials science research, and research subject areas. The form requested information about computing capabilities and use of technology such as e-mail, news groups, FTP, Gopher, online catalogs, database searching, and WWW. Users also provided information about which journals were priority reading, which Elsevier Science journals they used, how they stay current in their field, how they obtained articles in previous months, and how many articles they usually obtained in a month.

A Gopher program collected data electronically and recorded access to TULIP files. A student programmer wrote two PERL-based extraction programs to automate the analysis of TULIP Gopher logs. One program converted data to the format requested by Elsevier Science. The other generated a report showing frequency of access to the files, addresses of computers from which the files were used, and the number of uses by journal title. On the first day of each month, a student library assistant downloaded data from the Gopher logs, forwarded a copy to Elsevier, and produced a hard copy for the use of the TULIP Team members.

Throughout the project, librarians from the TULIP Team, particularly the Engineering librarian, communicated with faculty about the development of the user interface. Faculty reactions to the presentation style and steps in the document ordering process were incorporated into revisions.

In early 1995 the TULIP Team held focus group meetings with registered TULIP users to obtain feedback concerning the usefulness of the project. The participants were contacted personally and encouraged to attend. In these meetings the TULIP Team asked a series of questions to collect information on users' perceptions of strengths and weaknesses of TULIP.

2. Findings from research and user comments

Comments from participants in the focus groups indicated that low use of the TULIP files is due primarily to the limited number of journal titles available and their narrow scope; the journals available were of marginal interest. This observation is confirmed by participant lists on the registration form of their most frequently used journal titles, in which few Elsevier Science titles are included. A wide assortment of titles in other areas of study would have contributed to increased use. Those who did scan the tables of contents tended to browse the titles not held by UTK.

Suggestions for improvement from the focus groups included making the process easier to order full text of articles, providing the ability to do keyword searches on subsets of the files, the ability to limit searches by years, and quick delivery of articles. Users would have liked full text at their workstations, more titles available, more variety in tables of contents services, and electronic access to the journals of professional societies. A report on the focus group discussions appears in Appendix II.

Randy Hoffman and Earl Smith met with ORNL researchers about TULIP in February 1994. The sharp contrast between the computing resources available at UTK and ORNL was reflected in the researchers' suggestions for improvement. Many of the ORNL researchers had high-end UNIX workstations. They wanted gray-scale image quality in the printed copy and on the screen display. In contrast, most equipment available to UTK Materials Science faculty had inadequate page displays for viewing the images from the TULIP journal titles. Also, many ORNL researchers were participating in a current awareness service and were receiving citations according to their interests. TULIP would have been of more value to them if an automatic profile service had been available.

3. Usage research in view of privacy policies
Logfiles recorded the name of the computer which accessed TULIP, not the name of the person. For example, the logfile recorded that UTKLIB.LIB.UTK.EDU retrieved the TULIP Welcome file on Sunday, January 23 and that UTKVX1.UTK.EDU consulted a TOC file that day, but it was not possible to link this data to names. The registered participants were only identified by name for distribution of promotional information, invitations to focus group discussions, and for full text delivery preference in the event a request was placed. Reports to Elsevier Science were made in the aggregate.

4. Evaluation of usage of the TULIP system
Data gathered show that the use of tables of contents and abstracts was moderate and varied from month to month, totaling a low of 4 in December 1994 to a high of 812 uses per month in January 1994 (Table 2). However, the number of requests for full text of articles was very low, no more than ten from registered users throughout 1994 and 1995. Although some members of the TULIP Team speculated that the requirement for registration and library intermediation was in part responsible for the virtual non-use of full text in any format, participants in the focus groups indicated that the TULIP journals were not those seminal for their research. The use of TULIP journals in the Current Periodicals room was also low (Table 3), as was the circulation of bound copies of TULIP journals (Table 4). Interlibrary Services statistics

also revealed minimal requests for articles from TULIP journals. A summary of the total uses of table of contents and abstract data for individual TULIP titles is shown in Table 5.

Data from all sources confirms the information provided on the participant registration forms: key journals for the primary audience were not TULIP titles. The Elsevier Science citation analysis revealed a comparatively lower publication rate for UTK faculty in TULIP titles than for faculty at other TULIP institutions. However, the online browsing of TULIP tables of contents and abstracts indicates a level of interest in the titles, and suggests that the brief information available through contents and abstracts was useful. Use of the available electronic files also suggests that if the full text were conveniently available, particularly with full-text search mechanisms, use might increase. In fact, electronic access could be the only format that would generate use of the TULIP titles at UTK.

TULIP Team members speculated that polymer science journals would have been a better match for UTK and ORNL research interests, as would have journals in another field, such as biomedicine. Elsevier Science expressed a willingness to explore these alternatives, but such an expansion of the project would have required additional time and resources.

5. Implications and recommendations

Early in the TULIP development we gleaned useful information about implementing access to electronic journals. The TIFF data format made information delivery problematic at best, prohibitive at worst, because of the complexities of delivery to various computer platforms. Another helpful finding was that users preferred keyword access to cumulative TULIP data, rather than browsing for information on a volume and issue basis. TULIP confirmed our sense of the widely divergent campus equipment capabilities and researcher familiarity with the network.

With the numerous hardware platforms on campus, developing an interface for each one would have been prohibitive. Interface development required a combination of programming skills and an understanding of the scholarly research process. Finally, the successful implementation of TULIP required a team approach; library staff who comprised the Team contributed a needed mix of faculty liaison, systems, current periodicals, management, and research skills.

IV. Evaluation of Organizational and Economic Issues

A key organizational issue concerns the availability of equipment at the UTK faculty desktop. Although the University Libraries provides equipment in the library that is adequate for viewing page images, TULIP has shown us that Materials Science and Engineering faculty are more likely to use electronic resources in their offices.

Table 2: Uses of TULIP Via UTK Gopher for 1994 and 1995

	Total Accesses	Unauthorized Searches	TOC Retrieved	Abstracts Retrieved
January-94	812	150	89	137
February-94	301	14	30	31
Mar 1994-May 1994	2032	179	221	208
June-94	540	17	98	42
July-94	637	6	136	52
August-94	252	2	47	52
September-94	216	4	43	26
October-94	351	6	38	113
November-94	251	2	43	26
December-94	4	0	0	1
January-95	433	2	93	51
February-95	114	2	18	25
March-95	135	4	11	22
April-95	421	3	21	61
May-95	102	3	8	7
June-95	227	11	41	16
July-95	179	7	13	33
August-95	128	8	22	6
September-95	97	4	12	10
October-95	89	10	6	6
November-95	301	22	57	34

Table 3: Current Periodicals Reshelving Statistics for TULIP Titles: UTK, p.1/5

Journal Titles	Oct-92	Nov-92	Jan-93	Feb-93	Mar-93
Applied Catalysis A: General	3	4	3	0	0
Applied Catalysis B: Environmental	1	0	0	0	0
Applied Surface Science					
Chemical Engr. Journal and athe Biochemical Engr. Journal	0	0	1	0	0
Chemical Engineering and Processing	0	0	0	0	0
Composite Structures					
Composite and Science Technology	0	0	0	0	0
Diamond and Related Materials					
European Polymer Journal	2	1	1	1	0
International Journal of Applied Electromagnetics in Materials					
International Journal of Plasticity					
Journal of Alloys and Compounds	0	0	0	0	0
Journal of Crystal Growth	1	0	0	0	0
Journal of Electron Spectroscopy and Related Phenomena	0	1	0	0	0
Journal of Magnetism and Magnetic Materials					
Journal of Molecular Catalysis	0	2	0	0	1
Journal of Non-crystalline Solids	1	0	0	0	0
Journal of Nuclear Materials	0	0	2	0	0
Journal of Physics and Chemistry of Solids	0	0	0	0	0
Materials Characterization	1	0	0	0	0
Materials Chemistry and Physics					
Materials Letters					
Materials Research Bulletin	0	0	0	0	0
Materials Science & Engineering A. Structural Materials: Properties, Microstructure and Processing	0	0	0	0	0
Materials Science & Engineering B. Solid-State Materials for Advanced Technology	0	0	0	0	0
Materials Science & Engineering C. Biomimetic Sensors and Systems					
Materials Science & Engineering, Section R					
Materials Science Reports					
Mechanics of Materials					
Nuclear Instruments & Methods in Physics Research, Section B	0	2	0	0	0
Optical Materials					
Physica C, Superconductivity	0	0	0	0	0
Progress in Materials Science	0	0	0	0	0
Sensors & Actuators A: Physical					
Sensors & Actuators B: Chemical					
Solar Energy Materials and Solar Cells					
Solid State Communications	1	0	0	0	1
Surface and Coatings Technology					
Surface Science	1	0	0	0	0
Surface Science Reports					
Synthetic Metals	0	0	0	0	0
Thin Solid Films					
Vacuum					
Wear					

Journal Titles	Sep-93	Oct-93	Nov-93	Dec-93	Totals
Applied Catalysis A: General	3	1	0	1	15
Applied Catalysis B: Environmental	1	7	0	0	9
Applied Surface Science					
Chemical Engr. Journal and athe Biochemical Engr. Journal	1	0	0	0	2
Chemical Engineering and Processing	0	0	0	0	0
Composite Structures					
Composite and Science Technology	0	0	0	0	0
Diamond and Related Materials					
European Polymer Journal	1	0	1	0	7
International Journal of Applied Electromagnetics in Materials					
International Journal of Plasticity					
Journal of Alloys and Compounds	0	0	0	0	0
Journal of Crystal Growth	0	0	0	0	1
Journal of Electron Spectroscopy and Related Phenomena	0	0	0	0	1
Journal of Magnetism and Magnetic Materials					
Journal of Molecular Catalysis	0	0	0	0	3
Journal of Non-crystalline Solids	0	0	0	0	1
Journal of Nuclear Materials	1	0	0	0	3
Journal of Physics and Chemistry of Solids	1	0	0	0	1
Materials Characterization	0	0	0	0	1
Materials Chemistry and Physics					
Materials Letters					
Materials Research Bulletin	1	0	0	0	1
Materials Science & Engineering A. Structural Materials: Properties, Microstructure and Processing	0	0	0	0	0
Materials Science & Engineering B. Solid-State Materials for Advanced Technology	0	1	0	0	1
Materials Science & Engineering C. Biomimetic Sensors and Systems					
Materials Science & Engineering, Section R					
Materials Science Reports					
Mechanics of Materials					
Nuclear Instruments & Methods in Physics Research, Section B	0	0	0	0	2
Optical Materials					
Physica C, Superconductivity	0	0	0	0	0
Progress in Materials Science	0	0	0	0	0
Sensors & Actuators A: Physical					
Sensors & Actuators B: Chemical					
Solar Energy Materials and Solar Cells					
Solid State Communications	0	0	0	0	2
Surface and Coatings Technology					
Surface Science	0	1	16	0	18
Surface Science Reports					
Synthetic Metals	0	0	0	0	0
Thin Solid Films					
Vacuum					
Wear					

Journal Titles	Jan-94	Mar-94	Dec-94	Jan-95	Feb-95
Applied Catalysis A: General	0	0	0	3	0
Applied Catalysis B: Environmental	0	0	0	6	0
Applied Surface Science					
Chemical Engr. Journal and athe Biochemical Engr. Journal	1	0	0	1	0
Chemical Engineering and Processing	3	0	0	0	0
Composite Structures					
Composite and Science Technology	0	0	5	0	0
Diamond and Related Materials					
European Polymer Journal	0	0	0	0	0
International Journal of Applied Electromagnetics in Materials					
International Journal of Plasticity					
Journal of Alloys and Compounds	0	0	1	0	0
Journal of Crystal Growth	0	0	1	0	0
Journal of Electron Spectroscopy and Related Phenomena	0	0	0	0	0
Journal of Magnetism and Magnetic Materials					
Journal of Molecular Catalysis	1	1	2	3	1
Journal of Non-crystalline Solids	0	0	0	0	0
Journal of Nuclear Materials	0	0	0	0	0
Journal of Physics and Chemistry of Solids	2	0	0	0	1
Materials Characterization	0	0	0	1	0
Materials Chemistry and Physics					
Materials Letters					
Materials Research Bulletin	1	0	0	0	0
Materials Science & Engineering A. Structural Materials: Properties, Microstructure and Processing	0	0	3	0	0
Materials Science & Engineering B. Solid-State Materials for Advanced Technology	0	0	0	0	0
Materials Science & Engineering C. Biomimetic Sensors and Systems					
Materials Science & Engineering, Section R					
Materials Science Reports					
Mechanics of Materials					
Nuclear Instruments & Methods in Physics Research, Section B	0	0	0	0	0
Optical Materials					
Physica C, Superconductivity	0	0	0	0	0
Progress in Materials Science	0	0	0	0	0
Sensors & Actuators A: Physical					
Sensors & Actuators B: Chemical					
Solar Energy Materials and Solar Cells					
Solid State Communications	0	0	3	0	0
Surface and Coatings Technology					
Surface Science	0	0	0	0	0
Surface Science Reports					
Synthetic Metals	0	0	0	0	0
Thin Solid Films					
Vacuum					
Wear					

Table 3: Current Periodicals Reshelving Statistics for TULIP Titles: UTK, p.4/5

Journal Titles	Mar-95	Apr-95	May-95	Jun & July 95	Total
Applied Catalysis A: General	0	0	4	3	10
Applied Catalysis B: Environmental	0	0	4	1	11
Applied Surface Science					
Chemical Engr. Journal and athe Biochemical Engr. Journal	1	0	0	0	3
Chemical Engineering and Processing	0	0	0	0	3
Composite Structures					
Composite and Science Technology	0	0	0	0	5
Diamond and Related Materials					
European Polymer Journal	0	0	0	0	0
International Journal of Applied Electromagnetics in Materials					
International Journal of Plasticity					
Journal of Alloys and Compounds	0	0	0	0	1
Journal of Crystal Growth	0	0	0	0	1
Journal of Electron Spectroscopy and Related Phenomena	0	0	0	0	0
Journal of Magnetism and Magnetic Materials					
Journal of Molecular Catalysis	0	0	4	1	13
Journal of Non-crystalline Solids	0	0	0	0	0
Journal of Nuclear Materials	0	0	0	0	0
Journal of Physics and Chemistry of Solids	0	0	0	0	3
Materials Characterization	0	0	0	0	1
Materials Chemistry and Physics					
Materials Letters					
Materials Research Bulletin	0	0	0	0	1
Materials Science & Engineering A. Structural Materials:	0	0	0	0	0
Properties, Microstructure and Processing	1	0	6	0	10
Materials Science & Engineering B. Solid-State					
Materials for Advanced Technology	1	0	0	0	1
Materials Science & Engineering C. Biomimetic Sensors and Systems					
Materials Science & Engineering, Section R					
Materials Science Reports					
Mechanics of Materials					
Nuclear Instruments & Methods in Physics Research, Section B	0	0	0	0	0
Optical Materials					
Physica C, Superconductivity	0	0	0	0	0
Progress in Materials Science	1	0	0	0	1
Sensors & Actuators A: Physical					
Sensors & Actuators B: Chemical					
Solar Energy Materials and Solar Cells					
Solid State Communications	0	0	0	0	3
Surface and Coatings Technology					
Surface Science	0	1	0	1	2
Surface Science Reports					
Synthetic Metals	0	0	0	0	0
Thin Solid Films					
Vacuum					
Wear					

Table 3: Current Periodicals Reshelving Statistics for TULIP Titles: ORNL, p.5/5

Journal Titles	*Mar-94	*May-94	Total
Applied Catalysis A: General			
Applied Catalysis B: Environmental			
Applied Surface Science	0	1	1
Chemical Engr. Journal and athe Biochemical Engr. Journal	0	0	0
Chemical Engineering and Processing			
Composite Structures			
Composite and Science Technology			
Diamond and Related Materials			
European Polymer Journal			
International Journal of Applied Electromagnetics in Materials			
International Journal of Plasticity			
Journal of Alloys and Compounds	5	4	9
Journal of Crystal Growth	3	4	7
Journal of Electron Spectroscopy and Related Phenomena	2	4	6
Journal of Magnetism and Magnetic Materials	1	2	3
Journal of Molecular Catalysis			
Journal of Non-crystalline Solids	2	8	10
Journal of Nuclear Materials	11	15	26
Journal of Physics and Chemistry of Solids	3	3	6
Materials Characterization	0	0	0
Materials Chemistry and Physics			
Materials Letters			
Materials Research Bulletin	6	3	9
Materials Science & Engineering A. Structural Materials: Properties, Microstructure and Processing	7	13	20
Materials Science & Engineering B. Solid-State Materials for Advanced Technology	2	1	3
Materials Science & Engineering C. Biomimetic Sensors and Systems	0	1	1
Materials Science & Engineering, Section R			
Materials Science Reports			
Mechanics of Materials			
Nuclear Instruments & Methods in Physics Research, Section B	5	12	17
Optical Materials			
Physica C, Superconductivity	7	6	13
Progress in Materials Science	2	0	2
Sensors & Actuators A: Physical	4	0	4
Sensors & Actuators B: Chemical	5	0	5
Solar Energy Materials and Solar Cells			
Solid State Communications	2	1	3
Surface and Coatings Technology			
Surface Science	10	20	30
Surface Science Reports	6	6	12
Synthetic Metals			
Thin Solid Films	5	1	6
Vacuum	1	0	1
Wear	6	6	12

* Data for one week in March and one week in May

TULIP **Final Report**

271

Table 4: Circulation of Bound TULIP Titles from UTK for 1993 and 1994

Journal Titles	1993 Circulations	1994 Circulations
Applied Catalysis A: General	2	8
*Applied Catalysis B: Environmental	-	-
*Applied Surface Science	-	-
Chemical Engineering Journal and the Biochemical Engineering Journal	1	-
Chemical Engineering & Processing	1	0
*Composite Structures	-	-
Composites Science & Technology	5	9
*Diamond and Related Materials	-	-
European Polymer Journal	7	2
*International Journal of Appled Electromagnetics in Materials	-	-
*International Journal of Plasticity	-	-
Journal of Crystal Growth	15	18
Journal of Electron Spectroscopy and Related Phenomena	2	3
Journal of Alloys and Compounds	8	10
*Journal of Magnetism and Magnetic Materials	-	-
Journal of Molecular Catalysis	3	8
Journal of Non-crystalline Solids	3	9
Journal of Nuclear Materials	27	7
Journal of Physics and Chemistry of Solids	3	
Materials Characterization	2	1
*Materials Chemistry and Physics	-	-
*Materials Letters	-	-
Materials Research Bulletins	2	4
Materials Science & Engineering A. Structural Materials: Properties, Microstructure, and Processing	3	11
Materials Science & Engineering B. Solid-State Materials for Advanced Technology	4	5
*Materials Science & Engineering C. Biomimetic Sensors and Systems	-	-
*Materials Science & Engineering, Section R	-	-
Mechanics of Materials	1	1
Nuclear Instruments & Methods in Physics Research Section B	12	0
*Optical Materials	-	-
Physica C, Superconductivity	22	13
Progress in Materials Science	3	2
*Sensors & Actuators A: Physical	-	-
*Sensors & Actuators B: Chemical	-	-
*Solar Energy Materials	-	-
Solid State Communications	12	9
*Surface and Coatings Technology	-	-
Surface Science	15	30
*Surface Science Reports	-	-
*Synthetic Materials	-	-
*Thin Solid Films	-	-
Vacuum	1	0
Wear	1	0

* Titles are not held by University Libraries

Table 5: TULIP Use By Journal Title at UTK for 1994 and 1995

Journal Titles	1994 Abstracts	1994 TOC	1995 Abstracts	1995 TOC
Applied Catalysis A: General	75	69	18	9
Applied Catalysis B: Environmental	10	15	24	1
Applied Surface Science	28	31	16	18
Chemical Engr. Journal and athe Biochemical Engr. Journal	5	14	7	4
Chemical Engineering and Processing	10	14	4	7
Composite Structures	22	26	8	7
Composite and Science Technology	17	20	22	2
Diamond and Related Materials	32	28	8	8
European Polymer Journal	97	66	48	89
International Journal of Applied Electromagnetics in Materials	11	11	2	2
International Journal of Plasticity	9	17	0	2
Journal of Alloys and Compounds	19	11	5	8
Journal of Crystal Growth	49	33	0	2
Journal of Electron Spectroscopy and Related Phenomena	5	4	0	2
Journal of Magnetism and Magnetic Materials	4	4	4	2
Journal of Molecular Catalysis	7	12	0	1
Journal of Non-crystalline Solids	14	6	2	5
Journal of Nuclear Materials	8	11	8	12
Journal of Physics and Chemistry of Solids	7	7	1	1
Materials Characterization	8	12	0	1
Materials Chemistry and Physics	3	10	1	3
Materials Letters	8	9	2	3
Materials Research Bulletin	5	7	4	1
Materials Science & Engineering A: Structural Materials: Properties, Microstructure and Processing	2	11	9	10
Materials Science & Engineering B: Solid-State Materials for Advanced Technology	2	5	0	2
Materials Science & Engineering C. Biomimetic Sensors and System	0	2	0	1
Materials Science & Engineering, Section R	3	13	3	1
Materials Science Reports	2	6	7	11
Mechanics of Materials	19	8	5	3
Nuclear Instruments & Methods in Physics Research, Section B	12	19	4	8
Optical Materials	6	10	0	3
Physica C, Superconductivity	30	25	5	3
Progress in Materials Science	9	16	18	9
Sensors & Actuators A: Physical	11	11	1	2
Sensors & Actuators B: Chemical	3	5	1	2
Solar Energy Materials and Solar Cells	23	8	8	4
Solid State Communications	6	11	3	6
Surface and Coatings Technology	7	8	0	4
Surface Science	14	44	1	8
Surface Science Reports	2	4	8	8
Synthetic Metals	42	33	4	4
Thin Solid Films	13	18	7	4
Vacuum	13	19	3	2
Wear	15	28	2	7

Wide variation exists in the computer expertise of researchers. Some individuals need considerable coaching to be proficient computer operators; others need minimal training and would like more features and capabilities. Differences among operators are matched by disparities in the equipment they use.

Some researchers have viewing and full text capabilities at their workstations; others are using outdated equipment that is unable to present images and print full text. Needs for equipment and training are being addressed in UTK academic departments, and the campus network is rapidly expanding. The University Libraries offers an Information Technology Forum series for UTK faculty, staff and students to learn and use specific information access tools, such as current awareness sources, Web sites relevant for various disciplines, and downloading, with time for hands-on practice.

From the library computing perspective, Web-based access to electronic journals presents a more attractive option than local interface development and management, storage, and delivery of bit-mapped image files. The university has recently acquired a subscription to *Current Contents* which will provide tables of contents and abstracts for a large number of scholarly journals, including most of the TULIP journals. TULIP set a precedent for internal interface development, and some programming is being done for *Current Contents* presentation via the Web, while we monitor the commercial market for options such as SilverPlatter's software that could provide an appealing interface. The Elsevier Science Web pages are attractive, and if searchable abstracts could be included in that format, the service would be a compelling option for consideration. One by-product of the local *Current Contents* development is that programmer attention will be directed to improving authorization. While authorization by IP address will continue in the near future, the ability for an individual to bypass IP authorization would be disabled.

The non-use of TULIP full text meant that we could not measure willingness of the researcher or the library to pay for articles. UTK's Interlibrary Services conducted a study during 1994-95 where several commercial document suppliers were used to fill requests. (An article about the study by Alice Mancini will be published in a 1996 issue of *College and Research Libraries*.) The generally speedy turnaround and good quality copies have resulted in continued use of these suppliers to fill rush requests. In this model the library continues to serve as intermediary in order to control unknown costs. However, several libraries have begun to experiment with direct user access to commercial suppliers with the library paying the bills.

The model being used by the Johns Hopkins University Press, a flat subscription rate for electronic journals, is appealing. With this model the library pays one amount for use of articles from a journal title. Like the subscription model for printed journals, one payment covers access for a year, and whether articles are used once or many times, the price is fixed for that year. Only through sustained use of refereed, scholarly journals will enough data be generated to inspire other options for appropriate pricing.

V. Implications of the TULIP Project for the Future

Elsevier Science sponsored TULIP at a timely juncture for the future of scholarly research and publishing. TULIP represented a unique collaboration among publishers, librarians, academic faculty and researchers for exploring delivery of full text to the desktop. The project gave the libraries considerable experience with using outside programming service to assist with interface creation. At the time TULIP started, librarians and their clientele had had little exposure to scholarly electronic journals, and Gopher was an innovative development. With the advent of Web capabilities, we discovered a much more viable medium for image delivery. The fact that Elsevier Science journal tables of contents are now available via the Web suggests that this direction holds promise for the future.

Sustained communication among libraries and Elsevier Science as we probe electronic frontiers together has surely resulted in higher levels of understanding about the differing concerns that we bring to the arena of electronic journals. TULIP libraries have gained first-hand experience with a publisher's perspective on the costs of changing from a traditionally accepted format to an experimental, rapidly changing electronic medium. Perhaps Elsevier Science has benefitted from working closely with libraries in the developmental process to discover values and constraints that inform library acquisitions decision-making. UTK and ORNL greatly appreciated the opportunity to work with Elsevier Science and the other TULIP participants.

Notes

1. Phillips, Linda L., "TULIP at UTK: an Electronic Journals Experiment." Tennessee Library Association Annual Conference. Nashville, TN. April 28, 1994.

2. Smith, Earl C., "TULIP Blooms in Tennessee," *Tennessee Librarian* 46(4):26-31 (Fall 1994).

3. Smith, Earl C. and Lynn J. Davis, "TULIP at The University of Tennessee," *Library Hi Tech* 13(4):44-46,60 (1995).

TULIP TECHNICAL REPORT

I. Description of Current Information Technology Environment

The UTK/ORNL implementation was to mount and store tables of contents and abstracts locally. Page images would be provided by Engineering Information (Ei) on demand via Internet. This decision made implementation of TULIP a fairly standard process and allowed the implementors at UTK to use tools, such as Gopher, WAIS and WWW that were freely available on the Internet to provide access to the TULIP datafiles. Considering the availability of equipment, networking and technical support on the UTK campus, and the amount of storage required, this approach proved to be practical.

TULIP files were delivered to UTK approximately every two weeks via the Internet, and later on CD-ROM as a diverse set of electronic files. The first file included a tagged table of contents file (journal title, volume, issue, author, abstract, etc.) and a plain text file containing bibliographic information with links to the remaining TULIP files. Also included were electronic text (ASCII) files that contained the full-text for each article indicated in the table of contents. The raw ASCII files were not used for display purposes, since they were uncorrected and unformatted, and were only delivered with the group of files because they contained special coordinate information that could be used by each site to help navigate the image files. The final batch of files were the image files which are laser printer quality (300 dots per inch) black and white images about 90 kb each compressed and about 1 mg each uncompressed.

1. Hardware and Operating Systems

1.1 Server types and numbers

Hardware included an Intel 486DX 66 with 24 megabytes of RAM, a one gigabyte hard drive, and a CD-ROM drive. The operating system was LINUX, a freely available version of Unix for Intel platforms. Other software included The University of Minnesota's Gopher server software, NCSA HTTP server software, and Free-WAIS server software for searchable Index.

1.2 Client types and numbers

Users, primarily Materials Science faculty at UTK and their counterparts at ORNL, accessed TULIP from their offices by browsing the table of contents via the UTK library's Gopher server. Of 10 Materials Science faculty, 5 had Macintosh computers and 4 used IBM machines. One had no desktop workstation. Of 14 Chemical Engineering faculty who may have had occasion to use TULIP, 11 had Macintosh and 3 had IBM. Several Materials Science graduate students used Unix. The University Libraries provided IBM workstations for use in the library.

2. Database Systems and Development Tools

2.1 Server

UTK hired student programmers for 20 hours per week to write a program to parse the raw TULIP table of contents files into standard bibliographic citation format. In addition to the table of contents file, a separate file was created for the abstracts, so that they could be indexed for searching by users. The abstract files included bibliographic information as well as the unique item-identifier for each article.

WAIS server software was used to index the abstract files, which enabled researchers to perform keyword searching on the abstract files. This feature was integrated with the Gopher server, so that keyword searching was available from the TULIP Gopher menu.

Finally, the World Wide Web server was used to provide a graphical page for TULIP in anticipation of adding bitmapped images to the server. The resulting Web page hooked into the existing Gopher server so that all the initial development could be leveraged.

These phases of the project proceeded quite smoothly overall. A barrier to the implementation in this phase was the deciphering of the sometimes cryptic documentation for the server softwares and the steep learning curve for UNIX. Once the pieces were in place, the first phase of TULIP implementation was complete.

2.2 Client

Researchers accessed TULIP by browsing the table of contents of the menu for each journal categorized by volume and issue. Once the researcher had identified the journal of choice, the table of contents for the issue could be viewed. If abstracts for the articles existed, they would be indicated by an abstract number. The researcher could then go back and pull up the abstract of interest by its number. The approach was straightforward and primitive because it forced the researcher to drill down menus to find articles. Feedback from users indicated that they desired the ability to perform keyword searches, so the TULIP implementors acquired the WAIS server software FreeWAIS for this purpose.

3. Central Storage Technology

3.1 Types and current capacity of magnetic disks, optical disks

As noted above, data for tables of contents and abstracts was stored on magnetic disks on a library server. Because the implementation acquired full text on demand from Ei, no other central storage was needed.

4. Network Typology

4.1 Client server or terminal oriented

The university computing network primarily terminal oriented, but has the capability to support client/server technology.

4.2 Local

Ethernet and fiber optics connect many buildings on the Knoxville campus to provide rapid access to data in remote locations. The network supports several protocols including TCP/IP, DECnet, LAT, Novell NetWare and Apple Appletalk. A terminal port selection and multiplexing system, which is connected to a similar system at the Oak Ridge National Laboratory, provides access to the network through 200 dialup lines.

4.3 WAN

The DII network provides access to Internet sites via the Southeastern University Research Association Network (SURAnet). SURAnet connects to the National Science Foundation Network (NSFnet) which joins other state and The University of Tennessee Computing regional networks as well as directly connecting to the five NSF supercomputing centers. DII provides technical support for other departmental workstations on the UT Knoxville campus and maintains more than 150 microcomputers in remote user work areas and microcomputer laboratories on campus. Computing services are made available to the other UT campuses through remote links.

5. Printing Facilities

5.1 Central (types and number)

The university uses a Digital LPS-32 Postcript Iser printer to produce high quality printed output. The Imagen printer can also produce graphics at 300 dots per inch. A Xerox DocuTech Production Publishing System, located at UT Graphic Arts Services includes a 600 dpi laser printer connected to a scanner nd network media server. It permits electronic transmission of documents for processing from computers on the campus computing network.

5.2 Decentral/Remote (types, number, types of connections)

Laser printers are used with Ethernet and Appletalk connections in various academic departments.

II. Description of TULIP System

1. Components

1.1 Functionalities (implemented and rationale for choice)

The Gopher server was used to provide access to the bibliographic data for the 43 TULIP journals. It presented researchers with a menu for each journal categorized by volume and issue. Once the researcher had identified the journal of choice, the table of contents for the issue could be viewed. If abstracts for the articles existed, they would be indicated by an abstract number. The researcher could then go back and pull up the abstract of interest by its number. The approach was straightforward and primitive because it forced the researcher to drill down menus to find articles of interest. The Gopher file included instructions for registered users who wished to receive full text of an article. When the researcher identified an article of interest, he or she sent a delivery request via electronic mail to the library, including the unique item-identifier, so that Ei could locate the article on its server. A student library assistant checked the TULIP e-mail account daily and sent the request electronically to Ei. When the page images were received, they were printed and sent to the requestor by fax or courier, according to instructions provided on the initial registration form.

1.2 System architecture
1.2.1 Implemented browsing technologies
Implementors at UTK used tools, such as Gopher, WAIS and WWW that were freely available on the Internet to provide access to the TULIP datafiles. Student programmers were hired at 20 hours per week to reformat the raw DATASET.TOC files. The TULIP Team decided on a format that looks similar to a traditional table of contents. The abstracts include bibliographic information as well as the unique item-identifier for each article. The programmer followed the design of the committee and implemented the screens that are now available through the TULIP Gopher server. (Appendix III) New DATASET.TOC files were parsed as they were received over the Internet, and later via CD-ROM, and then moved into the server for browsing by TULIP users.

1.2.2 Implemented searching technologies
The WAIS server software was used to index the abstract files, which enabled researchers to perform keyword searching on the abstract files. This feature was integrated with the Gopher server, so that keyword searching was available from the TULIP Gopher menu.

1.2.3 Implemented user interfaces (on which platforms)
Initially the NEXTSTEP operating system for Intel (IBM) computers was chosen as the system to use for TULIP implementation because the UTK Libraries were already providing access to the Internet with a Gopher server running on a NeXT workstation, and the NEXTSTEP operating system was extremely well suited for handling images. But, because the first release of NEXTSTEP for Intel was not quite ready for prime-time and we experienced many problems in configuring our IBM ValuePoint to work with NEXTSTEP, we ultimately chose an alternative Intel-based operating system called LINUX. LINUX was a cost-free publicly available version of UNIX for Intel 386/486 platforms. LINUX provided the power of UNIX to the TULIP project and allowed the project to take advantage of the many publicly available information access programs that run under the UNIX operating system including Gopher, WAIS, and WWW.

1.2.4 Image viewing (e.g. anti-aliasing, gray scaling, zooming)
Not applicable

1.2.5 Image printing/exporting (fax, e-mail, file transfer, local printing)
          When page files were received from Ei via Internet, the files were
checked to see that they were complete. Image files were visually inspected on the
Unix workstation to make sure that the article was the correct one requested; and that
all pages had been received and were not corrupted due to Internet transmission.
Once this step was completed, a program was run to prepare the files for printing.

          From the beginning of the TULIP project, printing was problematic.
Because each page image was at least a megabyte in size when decompressed,
printing would take 15 to 30 minutes a page. Since the average TULIP article was
eight pages, it could take up to four hours to print one article on the average laser
printer. When this problem was brought up at a TULIP technical meeting, it was
ultimately solved by a small amount of programming and use of Adobe Postscript
Level 2 printers. Adobe Postscript Level 2 is able to interpret fax group four
compressed images by sending the pages directly to the printer without first
decompressing them. With the new printing software, printing times per page
averaged 30 seconds to one minute per page. Still there were some problems with
particular pages that refused to print. A new version of the Elsevier Science code for
printing solved this problem and made it possible to process efficiently the image files
for printing.

1.3 Networking issues
          Some Materials Science faculty had only dial-in access. Lack of high
speed access in the academic departments prohibited the delivery of image files to the
desktop. Further, UTK did not have computing storage space available that would
enable the project to store or deliver images.

1.4 Data preparation and loading (validation of incoming datasets, text preparation, preparing images, indexing bibliographic data from DATASET.TOC, indexing raw ASCII files, profiling)
          See II.1.2.1 above.

1.5 Implemented storage and image retrieval
          Not applicable

1.6 Set up of security of the system
          The TULIP server was secured through IP authorization. A public client
residing on the university's VAX fooled the TULIP server into authorizing an external
client as a local user. TULIP Team members worked with computing center staff to
resolve this problem, but it had not been fixed by the conclusion of the TULIP project.
UTK needs an authorization and authentication system.

1.7 Usage and logfiles issues

1.7.1 Collection of usage data

Data on TULIP use was collected at several points. The Engineering Librarian and other members of the TULIP Team met with Materials Science faculty to demonstrate the service. During the demonstration several of the participants completed registration profile sheets that provided demographic data about them, as well as instructions for article delivery. Filling out a profile sheet was stated as being a requirement for the delivery of documents. Section III.4 of this final report contains more detail about usage data.

Current Periodicals staff monitored usage of Materials Science journals during the six-month period prior to the inauguration of the TULIP project at UTK and during the project. ORNL conducted a current periodicals use studies for one week in March, 1994 and another in May, 1994. Users marked the TULIP issues as they were reshelved. Logfile statistics were collected electronically by the Gopher program and reported monthly to Elsevier. Tables 2-5 contain aggregate data collected during 1994 and 1995.

1.7.2 Assembly of logfile

The logfile process ran in the background and provided up-to-date information on which table of contents files and abstracts were being accessed and at what frequencies. Additional programs were developed and run every month by the TULIP Coordinator to reformat the Gopher logfile data according to the format requested by Elsevier Science. The logs were sent to Elsevier Science via FTP on a monthly basis.

2. History and Current Status of the Project

2.1 Description of development process (successful prototypes and abandoned ones, migration to production, difficulties encountered, solutions found)

Covered in above sections.

3. Experiences

3.1 Quality of data/images

Generally, the data received from Elsevier Science was of good quality. From time to time there were problems during the dataload from the Internet or CD-ROM files, and Elsevier Science technical staff were most helpful.

3.2 Storage

The one gigabyte of storage on the TULIP server was inadequate after one year due to the space needed for storing data and indexes.

3.3 Network delivery to end users

See network discussion in II 1.3 above.

3.4 Viewing

When page files were received from Ei via the Internet, the files were checked to see that they were complete. The image files were visually inspected on the Unix workstation to make sure that the article was the correct one requested, and that all pages had been received and not corrupted due to transmission over the Internet. Once this step was completed, a program was run to prepare the files for printing.

3.5 Printing

See printing discussion in II 1.2.5 above

3.6 Internet delivery

Delivery of datasets over the Internet was not optimal because of slow transmission speed. CD-ROM was the preferred medium for dataset delivery.

3.7 Other

3.8 Conclusions

In terms of developing an awareness of and direct experience with several issues pertinent to electronic scholarly information, the TULIP project was of immense value to UTK. The project was somewhat premature for UTK network development; we are now in a better position to experiment with image delivery, and look forward to future opportunities.

4. Future Developments

4.1 Additional data formats envisaged/required, views on suitability (SGML, Acrobat PDF, other)

Ideas for expanding the use of TULIP focused on three areas. The first was to add 40 more materials science titles that included polymer science. The low number of article requests from TULIP journals, and Current Periodicals usage statistics showing infrequent use of the same, supported users' comments that the initial TULIP titles did not match their interests. A second possibility was to explore the means to access tables of contents, abstracts, and full text in Standard Generalized Markup Language (SGML). SGML would address some of the problems with the file transfer and manipulation associated with TIFF images, and would provide access to the full text of articles. Acrobat PDF is a promising format with commercially available viewers. Finally, access to Elsevier Science titles via the Web seems to be a vehicle that will appeal to many users. Web access could remove the library from the intermediation process, and provide an aesthetically pleasing interface for the user.

4.2 Additional functionality planned (for instance combining journal collections from other publishers or other sources, links with other sources of information)

The use of commercial suppliers by interlibrary loan will expedite document delivery for users who may identify citations through the Elsevier Science Web pages. An internal prototype multidisciplinary journals database, Mockingbird, is being developed at UTK to combine information found in other databases, online resources, and reference sources into a unified decision support system. Mockingbird promises to provide a quick guide to the best way to gain access to a document.

TULIP REGISTRATION/ USER PROFILE

To participate in the TULIP research project that provides electronic access to Elsevier materials science and engineering journals, please provide the following information. Filling out this profile is required if you plan to request articles. There will be no charge to users for articles requested through TULIP.

Name_____

UTK/MMES ID Number_____

Telephone_____

E-mail Address _____

Department_____

Departmental Building & Room Number_____

Please deliver articles that I request by the following route: (Check one)

    ❏ Deliver to me at the departmental address given above
    ❏ Deliver to me via fax at this number:_____

Status: (Check one)

    ❏ UTK Faculty (Teaching & Research)
    ❏ UTK Faculty (Research Only)
    ❏ MMES Researcher
    ❏ Post Doctoral Fellow
    ❏ Research Staff
    ❏ Graduate Student
    ❏ Undergraduate Student

How long have you been active in Materials research: (Check one)
    ❏ Less than 5 years
    ❏ 5-10 years
    ❏ 11 years or more

Research subject areas:_____

COMPUTING CAPABILITIES:

Do you have a personal computer or terminal available at work?

    ❏ Yes
    ❏ No

If Yes:

    ❏ IBM (or Compatible) PC; with Windows
    ❏ Macintosh (specify model):_____
    ❏ UNIX workstation (specify model):_____
    ❏ X Terminal (specify model): _____
    ❏ Other (specify model): _____

What type of printer do you use?

    ❏ Laser printer (specify model)_____
    ❏ Other   (specify model)_____

Is this a PostScript printer?

    ❏ Yes
    ❏ No
    ❏ Don't Know

Where is the printer located?

    ❏ Your office
    ❏ Lab
    ❏ Departmental office
    ❏ Other location (please specify):_____

To which of the following networks do you have access?

    ❏ Local Area Network (LAN)/Campus Network
    ❏ National and International Networks (e.g. Internet)

Do you have a computer or terminal at home?

    ❏ Yes
    ❏ No

What computing services have you used recently for your research or teaching?
(Check all that apply)

    ❏ Electronic Mail
    ❏ Bulletin Boards/Listservs/Electronic Newsgroups
    ❏ FTP (File Transfer Protocol)/Archie
    ❏ Gopher
    ❏ WAIS
    ❏ World Wide Web (WWW)

What information services have you used recently for your research or teaching?

    ❏ UTK Online Catalog
    ❏ MMES Online Catalog
    ❏ CD-ROMS (Applied Science & Technology, COMPENDEX, etc.)
    ❏ Online database searches

Please rank the following computer services (1-10) in importance to you with 1 being most important.

_____Electronic Mail
_____Bulletin Boards/Listservs/Electronic Newsgroups
_____FTP (File Transfer Protocol)/Archie
_____Gopher
_____WAIS
_____World Wide Web (www)
_____UTK Online Catalog
_____MMES Online Catalog
_____CD-ROMS (Applied Science & Technology, COMPENDEX, etc.)
_____Online database searches

USAGE OF SCIENTIFIC INFORMATION AND OBTAINING JOURNAL ARTICLES:

Which five journals are priority reading for you?

1._____
2._____
3._____
4._____
5._____

Which journals have you cited most frequently in your recent publications?

1._____
2._____
3._____
4._____
5._____

Which journals **on the attached list** did you read in the last year (Please check)

Which information sources specified below do you use for your work; please rank with 1 being most important and 8 least important.

_____Journals
_____Personal Contacts (e.g. colleagues, students)
_____Conference Proceedings
_____Books
_____Pre-prints
_____Technical Reports
_____Electronic Bulletin Boards
_____Reference Works

Browsing and Searching

What methods did you use last month to keep up-to-date with relevant literature ? (Check all that apply)

- ❏ Browsing journals in the library
- ❏ Browsing journals using your personal/department/colleague's subscription
- ❏ Looking through a table of contents service such as:
    - ❏ Current Contents (ISI)
    - ❏ Library Current Awareness Service
    - ❏ Other (please specify)
- ❏ Using an on-line bibliographic Database (INSPEC, Chemical Abstracts, Compendex, etc)
- ❏ Looking through and electronic table of contents service such as:
    - ❏ Current Contents on Diskette
    - ❏ Current Contents On-line
    - ❏ CARL's Uncover
    - ❏ Contents Alert
    - ❏ Other (please specify):_____
- ❏ Other methods (please specify):_____

If you have used electronic table of contents services (such as Current Contents On-Line/Uncover) before how often do you use these services?

- ❏ Every week
- ❏ Once a month
- ❏ Occasionally

Ordering

How many articles did you obtain last month and from what source? (Please check)

❏ Available in UTK or MMES library and photocopied/printed by you (or personal assistant):

#articles: ❏ 1-5 ❏ 6-10 ❏ 10+

❏ Ordered and/or obtained by UTK or MMES library staff through interlibrary loan.

#articles: ❏ 1-5 ❏ 6-10 ❏ 10+

❏ Ordered and/or obtained through UTK library Express:

#articles: ❏ 1-5 ❏ 6-10 ❏ 10+

❏ Ordered yourself not using the library:

#articles: ❏ 1-5 ❏ 6-10 ❏ 10+

Please specify commercial Document Delivery Service used (e.g. ISI, UMI, Uncover):

_____

❏ Received from colleagues (originals or copies):

#articles: ❏ 1-5 ❏ 6-10 ❏ 10+

Thank you for your time. We appreciate your help in providing this new service. ——The Tulip Team.

Please fold and staple so that the return address is showing. Return via campus mail.

ELSEVIER TULIP MATERIALS SCIENCE JOURNALS

____ 1.   Applied Catalysis A: General
____ 2.   Applied Catalysis B: Environmental
____ 3.   Applied Surface Science
____ 4.   Chemical Engineering Journal and the Biochemical
           Engineering Journal
____ 5.   Chemical Engineering & Processing
____ 6.   Composite Structures
____ 7.   Composites Science & Technology
____ 8.   Diamond and Related Materials
____ 9.   European Polymer Journal
____ 10.   International Journal of Applied Electromagnetics in
           Materials
____ 11.   International Journal of Plasticity
____ 12.   Journal of Crystal Growth
____ 13.   Journal of Electron Spectroscopy and Related Phenomena
____ 14.   Journal of Alloys and Compounds
____ 15.   Journal of Magnetism and Magnetic Materials
____ 16.   Journal of Molecular Catalysis
____ 17.   Journal of Non-crystalline Solids
____ 18.   Journal of Nuclear Materials
____ 19.   Journal of Physics and Chemistry of Solids
____ 20.   Materials Characterization
____ 21.   Materials Chemistry and Physics
____ 22.   Materials Letters
____ 23.   Materials Research Bulletin
____ 24.   Materials Science & Engineering A. Structural Materials:
           Properties, Microstructure and Processing
____ 25.   Materials Science & Engineering B. Solid-State Materials for
           Advanced Technology
____ 26.   Materials Science & Engineering C: Biomimetic Sensors and
           Systems
____ 27.   Materials Science & Engineering, Section R
____ 28.   Mechanics of Materials
____ 29.   Nuclear Instruments & Methods in Physics Research Section B
____ 30.   Optical Materials
____ 31.   Physica C, Superconductivity
____ 32.   Progress in Materials Science
____ 33.   Sensors & Actuators A: Physical
____ 34.   Sensors & Actuators B: Chemical
____ 35.   Solar Energy Materials
____ 36.   Solid State Communications
____ 37.   Surface and Coatings Technology
____ 38.   Surface Science
____ 39.   Surface Science Reports
____ 40.   Synthetic Materials
____ 41.   Thin Solid Films
____ 42.   Vacuum
____ 43.   Wear

TULIP Focus Meetings Report

Friday, January 27, 1995
Tuesday, January 31, 1995

University Libraries
The University of Tennessee, Knoxville

February 1995

TULIP **Final Report**

291

TULIP Team

Lynn Davis
Linda Phillips
Richard Pollard
Flossie Wise

Preparations

In early to mid January 1995 the UTK TULIP Team began preparing for two TULIP Focus Meetings. The goal was to learn about the user's perception of TULIP's availability and usefulness.

Flossie Wise reserved Room 405, Dougherty on UTK's campus for Friday, January 27, 10:00-11:00 a.m. and Tuesday, January 31, 3:30-4:30 p.m.

Linda Phillips prepared the agenda. First, a brief laptop demonstration by Flossie Wise would allow users to both view TULIP on the gopher and the Web and ask any questions they had about electronic access, the full-text ordering process or other related issues. Next, Linda would ask the users a series of questions:

1. If you have been using TULIP, have you accessed the files regularly? Do you use TULIP for current awareness? For what other purposes do you use TULIP? How useful has it been?

2. If you have not been using TULIP, do you have a need for the files? If you have a need for the files, but have not been using TULIP, are there factors that prohibit its use?

3. How can we improve TULIP?

4. What would the ideal journal current awareness service be?

5. How do you keep current with new developments in your field?

Richard Pollard was scheduled to take notes at the Friday meeting and Lynn Davis on Tuesday.

We invited the TULIP users whose names are registered. The users were contacted by telephone and were invited to attend one of two meetings. The telephone calls were followed by one of two e-mail notices. If the user indicated he would attend one of the two dates, his acceptance was followed by an e-mail reminder containing the corresponding date, time, location and purpose of the focus meeting. If the user was not available by telephone or had not decided which meeting he would attend, an e-mail was sent notifying him about both dates, times, location and purpose of the focus meetings, and was asked to indicate (either by telephone or e-mail) which of the meetings he would attend (see II. Correspondence below). After the telephone calls were made and e-mail was sent, the responses indicated we would have eight users at the Friday, January 27 meeting (six attended), and four users at the Tuesday, January 31, meeting (one attended).

Correspondence

(Distributed to users who were not available by telephone or who had not decided which meeting they would attend.)

INTEROFFICE MEMORANDUM

Date: 25-Jan-1995 01:15 pm EST
From: Lynn Davis
     LDAVIS
Dept: Networked Services
Tel No: 974-3652

Subject: TULIP User Focus Meeting

Dear TULIP Registrant:

This is the beginning of the third and final year in the TULIP (The University Licensing Program) project. TULIP is a cooperative research project between Elsevier Science Publishers and, locally, the research libraries at The University of Tennessee, Knoxville and Martin Marietta Energy Systems to provide on-line table of contents and full article text for materials science and engineering journals published by Elsevier.

As a registered TULIP user we are inviting you and the other registrants to attend a focus meeting to help us determine TULIP's strengths, weaknesses, and future direction.

A brief presentation will demonstrate access to TULIP through the gopher and Web, including keyword searching. Even if you do not use the TULIP service your comments about why you do not use the service will be helpful to us.

WHERE: Dougherty Hall
          Room 405
WHEN: Friday, January 27, 10-11:00 a.m.
          or
          Tuesday, January 31, 3:30-4:30 p.m.
Please telephone or e-mail:
     Flossie Wise, 974-0016, wise@utklib.lib.utk.edu
     Lynn Davis, 974-3652, ldavis@utklib.lib.utk.edu
to let us know which date you plan to attend.

We look forward to seeing you there.

Lynn Davis
(For user response data see III. TULIP User table below.)

Focus Meeting Notes

Friday, Jan. 27, 1995

Present: TULIP Team: Linda Phillips, Flossie Wise, Richard Pollard
(recorder), Lynn Davis
TULIP User: Dr. Jim Chambers, Dr. Charles Feigerle, Dr. Joe
Spruiell, Darnell Worley, Dr. Z. Ben Xue, Scott Liter (sent as a
substitute, new registrant)

Absent: TULIP User: Colin Huang, Man-Ho Kim, Ping Li, Gang Zhou

Notes:

Q1.   If you have been using TULIP, have you accessed the files regularly?

A.   Looked at it before Christmas
Haven't used it for 9 or 10 months
Used it a couple of weeks ago
Haven't used it much because I don't use those journals

Q2.   Do you use TULIP for current awareness? For what other purposes do
you use TULIP?

A.   Look at table of contents for TULIP journals not held by UTK
Libraries (2 respondents)
Used keyword search (3 respondents)
I printed abstracts from the screen

Q3.   How useful has TULIP been?

A.   You only get the abstract. I really need the whole article.
Took three weeks to get articles (participant last used TULIP 9 to
10 months ago)
Tried to order hard copy of an article but didn't get any response.
Thought there was a cost for using TULIP so I ordered the articles
through ILL

Q4.   If you have not been using TULIP, do you have a need for the files?

A.   Most respondents reported having used TULIP but the journals
seemed to be of marginal interest.

Q5. If you have a need for the files, but have not been using TULIP, are there factors that prohibit its use?

A. Presentation and layout of information on the screen seemed not to be a problem.
Registration process not a barrier to use

Q6. How can we improve TULIP?

A. Get more polymer journals
Ability to do keyword searching on a subset of the TULIP journals or on certain years
Ability to perform keyword searching on full text of articles
Deliver full articles within 2-3 days

Q7. What would the ideal journal current awareness service be?

A. Table of Contents service provided by the Library
Library would provide access to society journals (e.g. JACS or Macromolecules) on CD-ROM
Full text of journals available at workstation

Q8. How do you keep current with new developments in your field?

A. It's a struggle (don't like to have to go to library)
Go to current periodicals weekly/daily to browse
Send grad students to current periodicals once or twice a week
Respondents didn't seem to be aware of Uncover or the ability to examine table of contents at no cost.
Material Science respondents didn't seem to be aware of Current Contents (Chem subscribes to this service)

Tuesday, Jan. 31, 1995

Present: TULIP Team: Linda Phillips, Flossie Wise, Lynn Davis (recorder)
TULIP User: Dr. Edward S. Clark, Materials Science Engineering

Absent: TULIP Team: Richard Pollard
TULIP User: Dr. Roberto S. Benson, Dr. Edward S. Clark, Dr. Marion G. Hansen, Khaled Mezghani

Notes:

Dr. Clark described the deterioration of the field of Materials Science. He said research efforts have greatly decreased and production is currently the primary focus. He indicated that the decline of the field also has had a negative effect on the quality of Materials Science journals.

In regards to electronic journal access, Dr. Clark says he has used UNCOVER to search for subjects not journal titles. He says he is aware that some of the [registered] graduate students are using TULIP.

Other User Comments

Some of the registrants did not attend the meeting but made comments on the telephone or by e-mail. Four users made a comment similar to the following:

> "The journals available in TULIP are not titles which interest me."

Additional comments included:

> "... [I] hope this would soon change." (Related to first comment, above.)

> "If TULIP contained Civil Engineering or Geology journals, as opposed to Materials Science, it would be more useful to me."

> "TULIP is a great idea, however, I deal with other journals in a conventional way so TULIP is not helpful to me."

> "I'm not a good person to ask [for comment] since I haven't used TULIP. I jumped on it because it was something new."

> "If available, I would appreciate receiving some documentation for accessing TULIP through the Web." (Lynn Davis provided this information to the registrant via e-mail.)

> "I once made a request but received no information."

> "Thanks for the notice, but I will not be attending. I have not pursued the use of the [TULIP] system."

> "I have not used TULIP but would like to attend the focus meeting if my schedule allowed it."

Synthesis

Question #5 points out that there are few requests for files in addition to checking for TULIP-related problems restricting user access to files. The frequent users' comments that there are few titles of interest indicate this may be more the reason for few file requests than a problem stemming from the users' interaction with TULIP. Perhaps it also accounts for the low use - four users either have not browsed at all or only once since spring of 1994. However, it is evident that some users do not seem to fully understand the ordering process and the slow delivery of full text may discourage further requests.

The users' widespread comments that the TULIP Materials Science titles are limited, and users would like to see more titles added seems to at least imply continuing interest in a service such as TULIP. The user's response that "it's a struggle to get to the library" also suggests there is likely support for electronic browsing and delivery. In addition, users seem to perceive electronic availability as a useful supplement to print journals for current awareness. The electronic format is useful to users when searching for a particular topic, and TULIP's print capability and abstract availability are also used/useful.

User "wants" include added searching capabilities, faster delivery service, and the users' have been asking for full-text delivery to the workstation since the time the TULIP project originated. Both they and we were not fully aware of the requirements necessary to reach that goal. As technology progressesand the hardware and software are better understood and met the opportunity for delivering full-text is getting closer.

Gopher Menu

Welcome To TULIP!

How To Perform Keyword Searches On TULIP

How To Use TULIP

Tulip Table of Contents

Welcome to TULIP! Please read How To Use TULIP for instructions
on browsing and ordering.

This service is brought to you by:
Elsevier Science
The University of Tennessee, Knoxville
Martin Marietta Energy Systems at ORNL
The TULIP Team

Thanks for your interest in TULIP. Let us know what you think of the service.

Lynn Davis
Electronic Services Librarian
University of Tennessee, Knoxville
ldavis@utklib.lib.utk.edu
974-3652

.

********** TULIP UPDATE ****************

Keyword searching is now available under the Tulip Table of Contents menu:

    Choose "Search TULIP by keyword"
    Type in keyword(s) (and, or and not Boolean operators are supported)
    EXAMPLE: A search for polymer and smith will retrieve files
    that contain *both* polymer and smith in their body.

Truncation is also supported:

EXAMPLE: A search for super* and film* will retrieve documents that contain:

superconductors and film or superconduct and films, etc.

Please let us know what you think of the searching capabilities.

Thanks,

    The TULIP team

ACCESSING TULIP AT THE UNIVERSITY OF TENNESEE,
KNOXVILLE & MARTIN MARIETTA ENERGY SYSTEMS

TULIP (The University Licensing Program) a cooperative research
project between Elsevier Science Publishers and several research libraries, is
now available for access at UTK and MMES. The University Libraries and
Martin Marietta Energy Systems are collaborating with Elsevier to provide
on-line table of contents and full article text for materials science and
engineering journals published by Elsevier. The first phase of the experiment
at UTK/MMES is now available to faculty and researchers who register with
the University Libraries.

NOTE: YOU MUST REGISTER IN ORDER TO RECEIVE FULL TEXT ARTICLES!

TO REGISTER:

Contact Lynn Davis (ldavis@utklib.lib.utk.edu) or Flossie Wise
(wise@utklib.lib.utk.edu) at 974-6797 to complete a preliminary information
form and profile. The profile will have a section in which you can indicate
your preferred method for delivery of full-text articles.

TO BROWSE OR SEARCH (BY KEYWORD) TULIP TABLE OF CONTENTS:

1. From the OLIS menu, select Electronic Journals.

2. From the Electronic Journals menu select TULIP-Elsevier Experiment at
   UTK

3. Choose TULIP-Material Sciences Journals. Then choose TULIP Table of
   Contents.

The list of journals is displayed in alphabetical order (43 items total).
At the top of this list is the option to Search TULIP by Keyword (See step 5).

4. You can select a specific journal title, volume and issue from the menus or
you can perform a keyword search for articles using the Search TULIP by
keyword option.

Keyword Searching allows you to search the entire on-line TULIP
database by any keyword of interest and also supports the boolean
operators and, or and not.

EXAMPLE: Searching for polymer and smith will retrieve files that
contain *both* terms and will exclude those files that do not contain
both terms.

Truncation is also supported.
EXAMPLE: Searching for polymer* will retrieve files that contain
polymer, polymers, polymerization, etc.

5. The Table of Contents for each issue contains brief bibliographic
information plus an item identifier (needed to order individual items) and
an abstract number (used to link citation to a corresponding abstract file).
Note the abstract number(s) of interest.

6. Return to the previous menu and select the desired abstract by its abstract
number (see step 6). IF YOU WISH TO ORDER THIS ARTICLE NOTE ITS ITEM IDENTIFIER

--Write it down and read how to order articles.

TO RECEIVE ARTICLES:

Eventually, we will experiment with the delivery of full text to your workstation. At present, however, we will request article text from Engineering Information. Library staff will request documents from Ei via e-mail and receive them over the Internet. Text and graphics will be printed on a laser printer at 300 dpi (dots per inch).

TO ORDER AN ARTICLE:

1. Send the Item Identifier and your name via e-mail to tulip@utklib.lib.utk.edu or by paper (if you do not have an e-mail account) to TULIP, Networked Services, University Libraries, 149 Hodges Library.

2. Articles will be delivered to departmental mailboxes or fax machines according to the specifications in your profile (see registration).

Gopher Menu

Search TULIP by Keyword

Applied Catalysis A--General

Applied Catalysis B--Environmental

Applied Surface Science

Chemical Engineering Journal&Biochemical Engineering Journal

Chemical Engineering and Processing

Composite Structures

Composites Science and Technology

Diamond and Related Materials

European Polymer Journal

International Journal of Applied Electromagnetics in Materials

International Journal of Plasticity

Journal of Alloys and Compounds

Journal of Crystal Growth

Journal of Electron Spectroscopy and Related Phenomena

Journal of Magnetism and Magnetic Materials

Journal of Molecular Catalysis

Journal of Non-Crystalline Solids

Journal of Nuclear Materials

Journal of Physics and Chemistry of Solids

Material Science Reports

Materials Characterization

Materials Chemistry and Physics

Materials Letters

Materials Research Bulletin

Materials Science and Engineering A

📁 Materials Science and Engineering B

📁 Materials Science and Engineering C

📁 Materials Science and Engineering: R: Reports

📁 Mechanics of Materials

📁 Nuclear Instruments and Methods B

📁 Optical Materials

📁 Physica C

📁 Progress in Materials Science

📁 Sensors and Actuators A--physical

📁 Sensors and Actuators B--Chemical

📁 Solar Energy Materials and Solar Cells

📁 Solid State Communications

📁 Surface Science (including Surface Science Letters)

📁 Surface Science Reports

📁 Surface and Coatings Technology

📁 Synthetic Metals

📁 Thin Solid Films

📁 Vacuum

📁 Wear

Gopher Menu

📁 Volume 31 1995

📁 Volume 30 1994

📁 Volume 29 1993

📁 Volume 28 1992

Gopher Menu

📄 Table of Contents for Volume 31 No.6

📄 Abstract 1

📄 Abstract 2

📄 Abstract 3

📄 Abstract 4

📄 Abstract 5

📄 Abstract 6

📄 Abstract 7

📄 Abstract 8

📄 Abstract 9

📄 Abstract 10

📄 Abstract 11

📄 Abstract 12

📄 Abstract 13

📄 Abstract 14

📄 Abstract 15

EUROPEAN POLYMER JOURNAL

Elsevier Science
Oxford, United Kingdom

Volume 31 No.6   Table of Contents   June 1995

Author(s): Troitskii, B.B.   Troitskaya, L.S.

Abstract: 5
Page(s): 533-539
Item Identifier: 0014-3057(94)00198-7

Title: Poly(dialkoxyethyl itaconate)s - I: Some properties of dimethoxyethyl itaconate and its polymer

Author(s): Popovic, I.G.   Stanojevic, N.G.   Katsikas, L.
Petrovic-Djakov, D.M.   Filipovic, J.M.   Velickovic, J.S.
Diesner, K.

Abstract: 6
Page(s): 541-545
Item Identifier: 0014-3057(94)00213-4

Title: Spontaneous copolymerization of phthalic anhydride with aziridine or 2-methylaziridine

Author(s): Pooley, S.A.   Canessa, G.S.   Rivas, B.L.

Abstract: 7
Page(s): 547-553
Item Identifier: 0014-3057(94)00204-5

Title: Addition of radicals to quinones: ESR study of some radical reactions of 3,3',5,5'-tetra-tert-butylstilbene-4,4'-quinone

Author(s): Simandi, T.L.   Rockenbauer, A.   Simandi, L.I.

Abstract: 8
Page(s): 555-558
Item Identifier: 0014-3057(94)00207-X

Title: Cation binding properties of polyanions bearing fluorescent crown ether units

Author(s): Shirai, M.   Matoba, Y.   Tsunooka, M.

Abstract: 9
Page(s): 559-563
Item Identifier: 0014-3057(94)00209-6

Title: Synthesis and characterization of fluoridated azo primers: Application t study of the the chain termination reaction during styrene polymerization

Author(s): Boutevin, B.   Bessiere, J.M.   Loubet, O.

Poly(dialkoxyethyl itaconate)s - I: Some properties of dimethoxyethyl itaconate and its polymer

Author(s): Popovic, I.G.   Stanojevic, N.G.   Katsikas, L.
Petrovic-Djakov, D.M.   Filipovic, J.M.   Velickovic, J.S.
Diesner, K.

Item Identifier: 0014-3057(94)00213-4

Abstract: The preparation of dimethoxyethyl itaconate and its polymerisation are described. Some of the properties of the monomer and polymer were determined with special emphasis on the experimental determination of the solubility parameter of the polymer, $@d"p$. Possible reasons for the relatively high experimentally determined value of $@d"p$ 21.6 $(J/cm^3)^{@2}$ are discussed with comparison to calculated and experimentally determined values for poly(di-butyl itaconate).

Citation: EUROPEAN POLYMER JOURNAL   , Volume 31 No.6, June   1995, 541-545 .

Article Type: Full Length Article

Correspondence for Item: I.G.Popovic, Faculty of Technology and Metallurgy, Belgrade University,   Karnegijeva 4, PO Box 494, YU-11001 Belgrade, Yugoslavia

TULIP

The University LIcensing Program

 About Tulip

 Using Tulip...

 Registration (*Need Form Capability*)

 Search TULIP by Keyword

 Order an Article (*Need Form Capability*)

View journals by:

- Cover Icon (*Warning: Possibly long download time!*)
- Title

Comments / Questions / Information

ELSEVIER
SCIENCE **About TULIP**

The University LIcensing Project is a cooperative research project between Elsevier Science Publishe
research libraries. The University Libraries and Martin Marietta Energy Systems are collaborating with
on-line table of contents and full article text for materials science and engineering journals published b
of the experiment at UTK/MMES is now available to faculty and researchers who register with the Un

Return to TULIP Home Page

ELSEVIER SCIENCE
ACCESSING TULIP AT THE UNIVERSITY OF TENNESEE, KNOXVII MARTIN MARIETTA ENERGY SYSTEM

TULIP, The University Licensing Program cooperative research project between Elsevier Science Pu research libraries, is now available for access at UTK. The University Libraries and Martin Marietta E collaborating with Elsevier to provide on-line table of contents and full article text for materials scienc published by Elsevier. The first phase of the experiment at UTK/MMES is now available to faculty an with the University Libraries.

Registration

Contact Linda Phillips (phillips@utklib.lib.utk.edu) or Flossie Wise (wise@utklib.lib.utk.edu) at 974 preliminary information form and profile. The profile will have a section in which you can indicate yo delivery of full-text articles.

To Browse TULIP Tables of Contents

1. Connect to the Library OLIS menu (see OLIS guide).
2. From the OLIS menu, select Electronic Journals.
3. From the Electronic Journals menu select TULIP. A list of available journal titles is shown. E include a total of 43 titles in Material Sciences.
4. Select a journal title, volume and issue from the menus.
5. The Table of Contents for each issue contains brief bibliographic information plus an item ide individual items) and an abstract number (used to link citation to a corresponding abstract file number(s) of interest.
6. Return to the previous menu and select the desired abstract by its abstract number.

Ordering Articles

Send the item identifier, citation, and your name via e-mail to Tulip@utklib.lib.utk.edu or by paper (if

account) to:
TULIP
Networked Services
University Libraries
149 Hodges Library.

Articles will be delivered to departmental mailboxes or fax machines according to the specifications in registration).

Eventually, we will experiment with the delivery of full text to your workstation. At present, however text from Engineering Information. Library staff will request documents from Ei via e-mail and receiv Text and graphics will be printed on a laser printer at 300 dpi (dots per inch).

Return to TULIP Home Page

ELSEVIER
SCIENCE **Registration for Services**

Purpose

This document is a TULIP registration for services form. This is to collect basic information on you so th.
send you the material you need to use TULIP. Please fill out this form completely if it is to be submitted.
send you another more detailed profile after submital, so that we can know how to serve you best.

What is your:

: Full Name
: E-Mail Address
: Department Name
: Office/Campus Address
: Phone Number
: FAX Number (optional)

What type of computer will you be using for access?

What is your prefered method of article/form delivery?
Mail
FAX

Click One :

Return to Instructions
Return to TULIP Home Page

gopher://libpc50.lib.utk.edu/77/TULIP/T

Gopher Search

This is a searchable Gopher index. Use the search function of your browser to enter search terms.

This is a searchable index. Enter search keywords: [   ]

ELSEVIER SCIENCE   Ordering Articles

Instructions

To order articles you must be a registered TULIP user. Completely fill out the form below and we wil process your request. As soon as we recieve the article from Engineering Information via Internet, we will send it to you by fax or courier delivery. All we need from you is the citation and item identifier from the article abstract and, of course, your name.

Ordering the Article

	: Your Name

	: Citation

	: Item Identifier

or

Return to TULIP Home Page

ELSEVIER
SCIENCE **Journal Covers**

   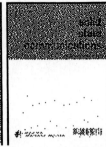

Return to Tulip Home Page

ELSEVIER SCIENCE Journal Titles

- Applied Catalysis A - General
- Applied Catalysis B - Environment
- Applied Surface Science
- Chemical Engineering & Processing
- Chemical Engineering J., The and The Biochemical Engineering Journal
- Composite Structures
- Composite Science and Technology
- Diamond and Related Materials
- European Polymer Journal
- International Journal of Plasticity
- International Journal of Applied Electromagnetics in Materials
- Journal of Alloys and Compounds
- Journal of Crystal Growth
- Journal of Electron Spectroscopy and Related Phenomena
- Journal of Magnetism and Magnetic Materials
- Journal of Molecular Catalysis
- Journal of Non-Crystalline Solids
- Journal of Nuclear Materials
- Journal of Physics and Chemistry of Solids
- Materials Characterization
- Materials Chemistry and Physics
- Materials Letters
- Materials Research Bulletin
- Materials Science and Engineering A
- Materials Science and Engineering B
- Materials Science and Engineering C

- Materials Science and Engineering R
- Mechanics of Materials
- Nuclear Instruments and Methods B
- Optical Materials
- Physica C
- Progress In Materials Science
- Sensors and Actuators A - Physical
- Sensors and Actuators B - Chemical
- Solar Energy Materials and Solar Cells
- Solid State Communications
- Surface and Coatings Technology
- Surface Science (including Surface Science Letters)
- Surface Science Reports
- Synthetic Metals
- Thin Solid Films
- Vacuum
- Wear

Return to Tulip Home Page

T U L I·P

Appendix VIII

The University
of Washington

The University of Washington

The University of Washington ceased participating in the TULIP project in 1994. They have not submitted a final report.

TULI·P

Appendix IX

Virginia Polytechnic Institute and State University

(Virginia Tech)

TULIP PROJECT - FINAL REPORT
VIRGINIA POLYTECHNIC INSTUTE AND STATE UNIVERSITY

Submitted — December 16, 1995
Charles A. Litchfield
Virginia Tech Libraries

I. Description of profile of university

1.   Organization/structure of university

Virginia Polytechnic Institute and State University (Virginia Tech) is the largest state supported institution of higher education in the Commonwealth of Virginia and a Land-Grant institution. Over 23,000 students are enrolled in graduate and undergraduate education in nine different colleges. The College of Engineering has over 5000 students enrolled in courses taught at both the main campus in Blacksburg and around the state through televised or regional campus courses.

2.   Organization of libraries

The Virginia Tech Libraries consist of a main library (Newman Library) and three branch libraries (Architecture, Geology, and Veterinary Medicine) at the main campus in Blacksburg, and another branch library in Fairfax, Va., at the Northern Virginia Graduate Center. There are six administrative units that comprise the University Libraries — Administrative Services, Collection Development, Library Automation, Special Collections, Technical Services, and User Services. Library personnel consists of 40 professional librarians, 110 support staff, and approximately 63 FTE of student assistants, reporting to the Dean of University Libraries, who in turn reports to the Vice President for Information Systems.

3.   Organization of IT/information services

Within the University Libraries all IT services, equipment installation and repairs, software and network maintenance, etc., are provided by the Library Automation Department. Campus-wide IT services are provided mainly by other Information Systems groups, such as the Computing Center, Communications Network Services, and Media Services, but Library personnel do participate in various IT outreach projects that affect a broad spectrum of the University community. Internally to each college, most hardware, software, and networking issues are addressed by personnel reporting to that college's administration.

4.   User demographics

The focus group for this project was to consist primarily of the faculty, graduate and undergraduate students in the area of materials science. These efforts span three colleges and and approximately ten departments. The Materials Science and Engineering Department, with 20 faculty, approximately 50 graduate students and 50 undergraduate students, complemented by approxoimately 50 additional faculty and 50 graduate students from related fields such as Chemical Engineering, Chemistry, Engineering Science and Mechanics, Electrical Engineering, Mechanical Engineering, and Physics form the basis for our focus group. The initial user group will be the MSE department.

II. TULIP promotion and training

1.   Description of promotion and training activities undertaken

Because of difficulties at the start of this project, and long delays before enough data was available to make user training feasible, very little was done in the way of promotion or training. The system has been demonstrated to about 20 MSE faculty members, and instuctions have been distributed as to how to download the client from a WWW site and use it to access the database. (See URL http://www.eng.vt.edu/eng/materials/seminars/tulip.html) A double-sided handout was prepared, giving basic searching instuctions and information about the titles that can be found in the database. At this point, only a small number of students have been trained to use the system.

2.   Effects of promotion and training

Use of what data are available (about 1 and 1/2 years of the most current information) has been very light. Promotional and training activities are planned for the Spring 1996 semester, if our proposal for an extension of the project is approved by Elsevier.

3.   Conclusions and recommendations

At this point, it is hard to draw conclusions or make recommendations about promotion and training since we have done very little. In general, I would suggest that promotional activity should be targeted specifically at the user group most likely to benefit from the available data. Also, the training materials should be concise and clearly written. In our case specifically, I would think that the problem of client distribution has added to our difficulties of promotion and training, and that if possible the client should be changed to a WWW interface. We have been informed that OCLC is moving in this direction, and may have a WWW interface available in the first half of 1996. It might be useful if the OCLC Guidon client could be made an integral part of a WWW browser like Netscape.

III.   **User behavior**

1.   Description of user/usage research (e.g. reshelving, statistics, surveys)

Because of the low use of the system, no impact has been noticed in the reshelving of paper copies of the TULIP journals. There was also a problem with the statistical gathering portion of the system software, so that only a few weeks of usage statistics have been captured to date.

2.   Findings - From research

no research performed todate.

- User comments/ direct feedback

Comments from Faculty and students that have seen or tested the system have been favorable. They generally like the idea of access to full text data in their subject area, and the added search features of the client software. They are dissatisfied with the method for distributing the client, and would prefer a WWW interface, which did not exist at the start of the project. There are concerns about the amount of data that has been loaded to date, and the need for a "critical mass" of other journals in the same format. Concerns have been voiced that the faculty would not like to see the hardcopy journals cancelled until the electronic access is more stable, and the system has "matured" as a method for online retrieval of the same information.

3.   Usage research in view of privacy policies

N/A

4.   Evaluation of usage of the TULIP system

Usage has been too small to make a large scale evaluation.

5.   Implications and recommendations

At this point, it appears that there is great interest on the part of faculty and students for access to this type of online information. Our University has a high enough level of available hardware and networking expertise in our user population to make the switch to online access of journal literature feasible. Our problems in this project have been the result of difficulties with hardware, software, and loading of data, on the systems management side of the project, not the user side.

IV.　　Evaluation of organizational and economic issues

For a project such as ours, using "off the shelf" hardware, and software provided by a third party vendor, care needs to be taken regarding unrealistic expectations as to what can be accomplished using part-time and volunteer labor. The project should have full time staff totally devoted to meeting stated goals and objectives, and committed support from the highest level of the University administration. There needs to be a broad spectrum of journal literature available from a full array of vendors, with a "critical mass" of titles that are useful to a majority of our university community. Most likely, the method of access should be a WWW browser interface to a remote storage location through an ATM connection, with the availability of document delivery through network printing facilities, as well as local printing.

V.　　Implications of the TULIP project for the future

1.　　　Technical/infrastructure

Access must be to remote storage of data, as local storage on the scale that would be necessary given the current form of the TULIP data would be prohibitive to most academic institutions. Printing could be at the individual workstations, or could be networked to campus printing centers if higher quality printing is desired, or costs for access need to be recouped from the user population.

2.　　　Organizational

The successful distribution of fulltext journal literature such as that in the TULIP Project, could have a tremendous impact on the organizational structures of all academic and research libraries. There are many fundamental problems that will need to be addressed, such as bandwidth restrictions, copyright, enduser printing, archival responsibilities, etc., but there is no doubt that the easy access of online, fulltext literature of this type will drastically, and irrevocably change the way libraries function. If article level information can be accessed and printed on demand at every workstation in an academic community, then many activities performed in libraries for the last four thousand years will be altered forever. A good portion of the mundane tasks now occuring in libraries will no longer be necessary. Hardcopy issues of magazines will not have to be checked in, cataloged, bound, placed on shelves, and reshelved after they are used. Many people will have to move to more "service" oriented positions, and less "behind the scenes" activities will have to be done. Libraries will have to adopt a larger educational role, instead of the more "keeper of information", archival position they now occupy. The change can be gradual, with shifts in most positions being done through attrition, but in some institutions the change may be swift, with abrupt alterations in workflow and job responsibilities.

3.　　　Contents related

The succssful move to online storage, access, and distribution of fulltext article literature will be dependent on several factors. 1) The information will have to be available from a common access mechanism. It can be devided by subject, but not by publisher, or point of origin. 2) Storage will have to be at remote sites, as most users will not be able to afford the costs of local storage. 3) The user interface will have to be easy to acquire, easy to use, and function across all equipment platforms. 4) Local printing options will have to be flexible, providing varying degrees of "quality" printing, allowing for networked and individual printing needs, as well as "free" and cost recovery situations. 5) There will need to be a "critical mass" of journal titles available that provide comparable coverage to the titles currently available in hardcopy. 6) And most important, the issue of archival copies for the literature has to be addressed to everyone's satisfaction, or there will be less willingness to give up the hardcopy issues in favor of the online versions. Without the ability to switch from one form to the other, most libraries will not be able to afford to move agressively toward the online titles.

TECHNICAL REPORT - TULIP PROJECT
VIRGINIA POLYTECHNIC INSTITUE AND STATE UNIVERSITY

Submitted — December 16, 1996
Charles A. Litchfield
Virginia Tech Libraries

I. IT Environment

1. Hardware and Operating Systems
1.1. Server Types and numbers

IBM RS/6000, Model 560, with 128Mb of RAM under version 3.2.5 of AIX Operating System. Indexing, loading, and database storage is handled by this single CPU. (Server software is provided by OCLC, Inc. of Dublin, Ohio, and uses Newton database technology.)

1.2. Client types and numbers
GUIDON client (also provided by OCLC, Inc.) is currently the only access tool to reach indexed data. GUIDON runs on WINDOWS-PCs only, but produces full text images on the desktop.

2. Database Systems and Development Tools

2.1. Server
See above. All database manipulation is handled by code developed by OCLC, Inc.

2.2. Client
See above. All client access is handled by code developed by OCLC, Inc.

332

3. Central Storage Technology

3.1. Types and current capacity of
Magnetic disks are used exclusively for storage of indexed TULIP data. Currently we are maintaining 15Gb of indexed data, with anticipation of eventually holding 50Gb. OPTICAL storage solutions were abandoned earlier in the project's history due partly to increased seek times, and partly to incompatible hardware. Tape backups of indexed data are created by the systems administrator using the TAR utility. No automated solution has been pursued to date.

4. Network Topology

4.1. Client Server or terminal oriented
Access to TULIP databases is through a client-server model.

4.2. Local/4.3. WAN
Network structure on-campus is ethernet to FDDI backbone. Off-campus users employee SLIP connections through high-speed modems. GUIDON will work with either configuration.

5. Printing Facilities

5.1. Central
No centralized printing services have yet been established, but this is currently under investigation. The University owns two Zerox Docutech machines that may eventually be able to act as campus-wide printers for a document delivery service.

5.2. Decentralized/Remote
The GUIDON client currently allows local printing through WINDOWS set-up screens to slave printers attached to the PC. Laser printing gives highly readable output.

II.   Description of TULIP system

1.   Components

1.1.   Functionalities

Full text of scanned articles is currently implemented. This decision was based on discussions with the developer, OCLC, Inc.

1.2.   System Architecture
1.2.1.   Browsing/1.2.2. Searching

Searching really dictates the browsing capabilities as a return list must be generated before any browsing can be performed. Full keyword searching of article text is supported, along with searching on author(s), article title and subject, and journal title. Once a result list is available, the user can browse brief entries (title, author, journal issue) before viewing the full text article.

1.2.3.   User Interfaces

Currently only available through WINDOWS based PCs, but a WWW client is due in early 1996, which should allow MACs and X-Stations to interface with the data as well.

1.2.4.   Image viewing

Zooming is currently possible with the client, as are all WINDOWS viewing functions.

1.2.5.   Image printing/exporting

Local printing is possible, as is capturing images for FTP or e-mail purposes. Clarity will be dictated by viewing monitor.

1.3.   Networking Issues

No significant problems were encountered using TCP/IP and ethernet network internet connections. The Guidon client was designed by OCLC for this environment. Some minor problems with SLIP connections occured because of the SLIP drivers being used, but OCLC was able to develop a "fix" that solved the problem.

1.4.   Data preparation and loading

Each dataset is passed through an 18 step procedure which performs the following functions:

If this is a new database, directories are created. Then the Elsevier supplied data is checked and verified against the DATASET.TOC file. SGML tagged files are then created from the raw text, as are page versions, and thumbnail images. Records are then copied into the Newton database, then sorted, and then inverted index files are created. Each Newton database (made up of one or more Elsevier data- sets) is comprised of 5 separate files.

1.5.   Implemented storage and image retrieval

The five files which make up an individual Newton database are stored in two different file systems, and spread across more than one physical volume. This allows performance of the GUIDON client to be optimized as the index file, which contains pointers for the actual image data, never resides in the same file system or on the same phycsial device as the images.

1.6.   Setup of security of the system

Access to the system is in no way restricted for users who possess the client. All databases are protected with routine UNIX permission security, and write access is restricted to a single user id.

1.7.   Usage and logfile issues

The OCLC software provides for usage and logfile data collection. Because there have not been many users per se, there has not been much chance to collect usage data.

2.   History and current status of the Project

See article in Library Hi Tech, v. 13, no.4, 1995, pp.54-60.

3.   *Experiences*

3.1.   Quality of data/images
Generally the data recieved has been of high quality. Only 2 out of now 84 datasets caused problems at this site.

3.2.   Storage
A major (if not the major) cost factor in the project. Once the data is indexed, backup of the file systems poses logistical headaches as the tar utility is quite slow.

3.3.   Network delivery to end users
Those that have experimented with the system find it easy to use and considerably faster than anticipated. On campus ethernet users tend to have better results than off campus SLIP users.

3.4.   Viewing
On-screen viewing of images has been excellent on a 1024x768 screen driver. The speed at which images could be viewed has varied on campus, depending on the internet traffic on local subnets during peak use hours of the day.

3.5.   Printing
Users find local print quality superior to photocopies of the original journal articles, except for TEM (Transmission electron microscope) images and other micrograph-optical reproductions, such as from scanning electron microscopes. Here, the image quality is lost and the figures are of reduced value. It may become necessary for images of this type to be scan at a higher resolution than 300 dpi so that higher quality reproductions can be printed by those that have the capability to do so. Experiments have begun with downloading articles to a central printing facility, using Xerox Docutech machines, but the process is not ready for use at this time by patrons searching the database.

3.6.   INTERNET delivery
A complete disaster; perhaps partially due to the fact that the vendor providing the FTP access was running SCO/UNIX on a 486 PC. The CD-ROM delivery has been much easier to deal with.

3.7.   Other
Because no two of the institutions dealt with the data in the same way, problems experienced here were not always experienced elsewhere, and vice versa. In this way Elsevier was able to learn a good deal more about the data they were producing, but changes made during the course of the project were not met with equal enthusiasm.

3.8.   Conclusions
From a purely technical standpoint, such activity as has been required to load, index, and present the data for user access was time consuming, I/O intensive, and required almost constant oversight. Unless the data can be delivered in a manner that requires less manipulation by institutions before users can view it, this model cannot be considered cost effective.
From an end user standpoint, it appears that the University has a significantly high population of users with the equipment and understanding to take advantage of full text online information, distibuted in a manner similar to this project. Preliminary results from a limited set of users in the MSE department are very favorable regarding the ease of use of this technology. The major limitations at this time would be the need and method for distribution of the client software, the current lack of software compatability across hardward platforms, and relatively small size of the data sets, both in number of titles and years of coverage, available for research use.

4.   **Future Developments**

The University Libraries of Virginia Tech, in cooperation with the Computing Center and the Department of Materials Science and Engineering, has requested an extension of the TULIP Project. Because the project took so long to mature at this institution, successful use of the system did not come about until the final months of the four year project. Due to the interest on campus among our materials science user community for access to this data, a proposal has been made to Elsevier requesting that the full text data for the materials science journals continue to be sent to Virginia Tech for an extended period of time. This extension would allow the participants in the project to refine the application software, test client distribution methods, better guage user satisfaction, and study collection development issues affecting the transition from hardcopy to electronic dissemination of journal literature.

If the extension request is approved, OCLC has agreed to continue to allow the use of their software, and to provide updates and new versions as they become available. The development of a WWW browser interface may also be possible in the first half of 1996. Elsevier will also be using a new method for distributing the data, that will potentially streamline and shorten the data loading process.

T U L I·P

Appendix X

Checklist of aspects to be considered for the implementation of a 'digital library'

Checklist of aspects to be considered for the implementation of a 'digital library'

It is hard to specify exactly which aspects need to be considered for the implementation of a 'digital library' at an institution, as this is very much dependent on the installed base, as well as on the desired functionalities. That is why we have chosen to discuss solutions which require a lot of investments in time and/or money to implement, as well as solutions which require (relatively!) less investments, in order to get a sense of the impact of these alternatives. A 'low cost' solution could have a menu-driven, character-based interface, which can run on any terminal emulation, with typically remote printing. Although not very sophisticated, the TULIP project has proven that this approach can work. Alternatively, as Web browsers have become commonplace, and implementing Web based systems has become less problematic, choosing this route has emerged as a good solution at relatively low cost, providing a lot of the more sophisticated functionality usually associated with the higher investment solutions. A 'high investment' solution could be characterized as having a (proprietary) graphical user interface, allowing for flexible page image viewing, a lot of sophistication in terms of browsing and searching, and printing to a local printer.

The basic infrastructure needed will differ for each solution, and is described first, as it is the foundation for what follows. The rest of the paper lists the additional resources (hardware, software, infrastructure, organization) needed to implement a digital library system. Wherever appropriate and possible, some explanation is given of the requirements listed.

1.   Lower cost solution

1.1   Basic infrastructure needed
It is assumed that a basic infrastructure is in place as described in the following points.

1.1.1   *Existing systems*
- A **local area network** for locally attached PCs, Apple Macintoshes and other decentrally located workstations. Most common is a network based on Ethernet and TCP/IP. With such a network it is possible to give external users access via Dial-in SLIP or PPP protocols. Similar possibilities exist for Token Ring based networks with Novell Netware, Lan Manager or other network protocols.
- Central **computer center** facilities with mainframe or minicomputers.
- Locally placed **desktop computers** with network possibilities. In the case of a TCP/IP based network this requires Ethernet boards, network drivers and terminal emulation software and/or World Wide Web client software, such as NCSA Mosaic or Netscape Navigator.
- Some form of high level **printing** will have to be possible. Printing facilities could range from centrally located high volume laserprinters, such as Xerox Docutech type machines, to decentral office laser printers, directly connected to the LAN.

1.1.2   *Organization*
- **IT production environment**
  As the description of systems infrastructure above indicates, the implementation of a digital library system requires a certain systems infrastructure. Similarly, it presupposes a certain capacity in the organization to maintain systems once these have been installed.
- **Development staff:**
  If there is no development staff in house, a 'turn key' solution, such as the OCLC system, which consists of a search engine plus a user interface could be considered.
- **Library staff/relations with IT**
  A digital library system has to be developed in close cooperation between the library and the IT department. The library will have to involve end users to get feedback and will also have to train/promote.

1.2 Functionalities needed

To be developed by institution.

1.2.1 User interface

There are basically two options for the development of the EJS on a restricted scale:

- Based on an **existing library system interface**, most probably the OPAC, which is available to at least Telnet-VT100 based clients.
- If there is already a library system in place, this probably needs adaptation. Most 'older' systems are based on terminal emulation ('Telnet' or similar) to let users type in queries and browse the results. The bibliographic data format as, for instance, provided by Elsevier Science, is based on common practice in secondary databases and provides typical information units such as titles, authors, keywords, abstracts, etc. Systems already aimed at providing this type of information will probably need minimal change. Users are already accustomed to the interface and need no special training for it.

Main concerns are:

- The development for converting and loading the EES data format to the internal format.
- The development/implementation of a file or database system to hold the large amount of page images. A possible solution is to purchase a standard hierarchical storage manager system, composed of an image server (a dedicated processor) and a `staged' storage area of magnetic disk, jukeboxed optical disk storage, and a tape library.
- Adequate linking mechanisms to connect bibliographic records in the library system to the associated pages in the page image collection.
- The printing infrastructure needs to be defined since the volume of page images is different from traditional office applications, for instance:
  - local print of bibliographic data on `ordinary' office laser printers;
  - central printing facility or;
  - dedicated decentral office laser printers especially set up for image printing (e.g. PostScript level 2 with CCITT Fax Group IV support), controlled by central server.
- **WWW interface**

If there is no library system available or if it is decided to develop an entirely new system, the best option at this moment seems to be to use the very popular World Wide Web as user interface. This brings the following additional points into play:

- The look-and-feel of a WWW based user interface should be developed and proper HTML files and HTML-generating procedures need to be developed
- A choice needs to be made, to develop full text search software, or to purchase this software and adapt this to the preferred other components. A multitude of choices is commercially available such as Information Dynamics Basis+, BRS Search, Verity Topic, Oracle SQL*Text and others. This choice is dependent on the desired functionality. For instance, sophistication in Boolean search, truncation/wildcard operators and presentation, needs consideration. Also, the integration aspects need attention, e.g., is a complete turn-key full text database preferred, or are a number of different toolkits from several suppliers favored
- Online viewing of page images on computer displays should be avoided if no sufficient performance can be guaranteed.

1.2.2 Searching

- Information searched:
  - Bibliographic data only.
- Searching methods:
  - Boolean search;
  - Truncation/wildcard operators;
  - Presentation of hits in reversed chronological order.

1.2.3 Browsing

- Selection by choosing journal title -> issue -> article.

1.2.4 Viewing

- Bibliographic data only in the case of a character based solution, viewing of (downgraded) page images is possible in the Web solution, performance is a consideration.

1.2.5 *Printing*
- Local print of bibliographic data
- Central printing facility for page images
- Decentral (identified) office laser printers for page images controlled by server.

1.3 Additional infrastructure needed
To be acquired.

1.3.1 *Text management database*

1.3.2 *Standard Hierarchical Storage Management system (HSM) for page images*
- Image server
- Magnetic disk storage, optical disk storage, tape library.

1.3.3 *Printing*
- High volume central printing facility
- Dedicated office laser printers, especially set up for image printing.

1.3.4 *Network*
No upgrades assumed.

1.4 Organization
Attention points:
- Project management;
- Introduction;
- Promotion;
- Training;
- Support.

2. Higher investment solution

2.1 *Basic infrastructure needed*

2.1.1 *Existing systems*
Additional to the lower cost solution described above, the following points need to be considered for development/implementation of this solution; the main difference lies in the more sophisticated display of page images on computer displays.
- **High capacity network**
  The network needs to have sufficient bandwidth for fast delivery of (large) page images from the central server to the desktop machines. Dial-in connections should use the highest capabilities available, e.g. minimally 14.400 bits/sec, but preferably 28.800 bits/sec or higher (e.g. 64Kbits/sec ISDN connections).

- **Desktop computers** need to be high end PCs (486 or Pentium), PowerMacintoshes and/or workstations, able to provide realtime viewing, browsing and zooming (anti-aliased) page images in World Wide Web software (Mosaic, Netscape, etc.), or dedicated page viewing helper applications.
- **Printing** facilities
  - Fast office laserprinters, running PostScript level 2 with CCITT Fax Group IV support.

2.1.2 *Organization*
- IT production environment
- Development staff
- Library staff/relations with IT.

2.2   Functionalities needed

2.2.1   User interface
- Graphical User Interface, WorldWide Web based (Netscape, Mosaic, etc.).
- Integration with other collections in same user interface. Formats to be supported:
  - Page images;
  - PDF files;
  - Word processors;
  - Spreadsheets;
  - SGML files;
  - HTML files;
  - Graphics formats (JPEG, TIFF, GIF, EPS).

2.2.2   Searching
- Information searched:
  - Bibliographic data;
  - Full text search by using raw ASCII files;
  - Searching through different collections in one go (requires deduplication).
- Searching methods:
  - Boolean search;
  - Truncation/wildcard operators;
  - Phonetic search;
  - Presentation of hits in reversed chronological order;
  - Relevance of ranking of hits;
  - E-mail notification by means of user profile.

2.2.3   Browsing
- Selection by choosing journal title -> issue -> article.

2.2.4   Viewing
- Bibliographic data
- Anti-aliased 100 dpi or 75dpi page images.

2.2.5   Printing
- Local print of bibliographic data
- Central printing facility for page images
- User-designated, decentralized laser printers for page images controlled by server.

2.3   Additional infrastructure needed
To be acquired.

2.3.1   Server + software

2.3.2   Sophisticated text management database

2.3.3   Hierarchical Storage Manager (HSM) with large magnetic cache for page images
- Image server
- Magnetic disk storage, optical disk storage, tape library.

2.3.4   Printing
- High volume central printing facility
- Dedicated office laserprinters, especially set up for image printing.

2.3.5   High capacity network
No upgrades assumed.

2.4   Organization

Attention points:

- Project management;
- Introduction;
- Promotion;
- Training;
- Support.

TULI·P

Appendix XI

Internet delivery problems

Internet delivery problems

The different problems concerning Internet delivery ranged from operational problems at the sending or the receiving side, to more generic problems with the Internet and the FTP protocol:

- For one, problems occurred at the receiving end of the Internet delivery process, such as magnetic disk space limitations, account quotas, invalid passwords, account restrictions, invalid permissions and university hosts off-line. All of these situations occurred on a frequent basis with most of the participating sites. When one of these situations occurred, the delivery of the Dataset could not proceed. Since these responses were not anticipated, they were not 'programmed' into the original system and investigative work was needed each time to determine the reason why the Dataset delivery aborted or did not take place. This in turn would lead to the delayed delivery of a Dataset.

- There have been unanticipated bottlenecks, not only on the receiving side, but also on the delivery side. The setup at Article Express was developed and implemented in 1992, based on certain assumptions regarding automated procedures, human resource capacity, stability of Internet transfer and the universities receiving each Dataset consequently, that is all in one batch. For instance, the idea was to have only a fairly small number of Datasets online to fulfil deliveries.

  At the point in the project where the needs to keep more Datasets online became apparent, in order to deal with the different speeds of Dataset loading at the Universities, Article Express started adding more disks. However, the SCO UNIX-based 386/486 systems at Article Express had unforeseen restrictions in dealing with multi-gigabyte hard disks.

- Even though the Internet service providers claim that they provide continuous connection to the Internet, difficulties were frequent. The TULIP delivery mechanism was set up to transfer material in a continuous stream between two UNIX hosts. Any interruption into this process resulted in incomplete deliveries and deadlock situations.

  A manifestation of intermittent FTP connections is a condition known as 'text file busy'. This is the error message which FTP reports, when an FTP process attempts to overwrite or replace a file which has been previously locked by an FTP transfer, which was in turn aborted due to communication difficulties on the Internet. When this condition was reported by the host universities, a deadlock situation occurred, which could only be resolved through manual intervention at either end.
  Since this was an unanticipated condition when the delivery system was implemented, there was no automated facility for alerting the university. Therefore, the approach taken was to wait for the university to clear up or delete any pending FTP processes that had 'aged' more than 24 hours or so. This, of course, prevented a successful validation step in the delivery system procedures, which in turn resulted in delayed delivery of the Dataset.

- The implementation of the FTP program operates in batch mode. A series of FTP commands is written to a local file and the file is submitted to the FTP program for execution. The results of the FTP program, i.e. the output status, are then written to a local disk file. After all of the commands are executed, the status file is parsed and searched for success and error codes. For most error conditions, this mechanism works well. It also works quite well when there are no error conditions. It does not work well when Internet communications are interrupted and no status is returned from the FTP program, particularly in deadlock situations.

T U L I · P

Appendix XII

Gray scaling and anti-aliasing

Gray scaling and anti-aliasing

300 dpi page images are too large to fit on most common computer displays. Consider that an average 300 dpi page image is 7" wide and 10" high, which is 2,100 pixels wide and 3,000 pixels high. A typical 14" computer display running in SVGA is 600 pixels high and 800 wide. At least the full width of the page should be entirely visible for good readability. This means that the 2,100 pixels should be down-scaled by two thirds to 700 pixels, to allow for space for window borders and scroll bars, giving a total width of 800 pixels.

The following 300 dpi input (enlarged 10 times) is taken as an example:

When simple down scaling to one third (i.e. 300 dpi to 100 dpi) is applied, every rectangular area of 3 x 3 pixels is considered for each pixel in the result. If only 0-4 pixels are black, the resulting pixel is white. If 5-9 pixels are black, the resulting pixel is black. The end result (enlarged 30 times) is as follows:

However, applying the anti-aliasing technique yields better images. For every rectangle a gray-value percentage is calculated, based on the number of white and black pixels. For instance, zero one black pixel yields 0%, one black pixel means 11%, two pixels equals 22%, etc. and nine black pixels signifies 100%. Because computer displays are able to show different grades of gray, the anti-aliased result of the down scaled example (enlarged 30 times) looks like this:

T U L I·P

Appendix XIII

Interview Guide

Materials Science Data Delivery Study

I   Introduction (5 minutes)

Introduce subject: review of current data delivery, evaluation of your needs and how well these needs are met, changes, trends, role of electronic publishing in the future.

Brief profile of respondent: name, areas of responsibility and interest.

II   Current Information Needs Patterns (10 minutes)

Before we get into specifics regarding your data needs, I would like to ask some general questions ... (Build 'grid' on flip chart) ... (Brief, 5 minutes, max on first three questions.)

1. Role
   As a scholar, you may wear many hats ...what are some of the roles you play during the year which may lead you to seek information?

   Probe: Professor, researcher, reviewer, author, review research grants, prepare presentations, pleasure reading/study ... etc.?

2. Need
   In each role, what are primary information needs?

   Probe: ...   Author versus reader?
            ...   Proposal writing? Any different needs?

3. Source
   For each need, what are your primary information sources? How often do you typically access each source?

Background information (10 minutes)

4. When you use journals, what is your typical pattern?

   Probe   (only if necessary):
           ...   Review abstracts
           ...   Review TOC
           ...   Scan/browse (what % read?)
           ...   Usually read actual articles or copies
           ...   Do you read/use special issues (e.g. conference proceedings) differently than regular issues?
           ...   How important is serendipity?
           ...   How important is stimulation of new ideas?
           ...   How important is validating ideas?

Probe: How often do you

    ... cut out articles/info to save

    ... copy/Xerox materials

    ... order copies or reprints from library or publisher

III   Electronic Information (10 minutes)

5.   What do you use your computer for?

    ... On-line databases

    ... Reviewing abstracts (source?)

    ... Internet

    ... E-mail

    ... On-line journals

    ... On-line catalogues

    ... Other

Probe: If Internet ... what do you do with the Internet?

    ... How much time do you spend using WWW browsers (like Mosaic)? What do you use them for?

6.   Which electronic information sources do you use most and why?

Probe (likes/dislikes)

    ... INSPEC

    ... Science Citation Index

    ... Current Contents (ISI)

    ... Compendex+ (Engineering Index)

    ... Contents Alert (ES-APD)

    ... Campus sponsored sources versus independent sources?

IV   TULIP Evaluation (60 - 80 minutes)

Initial reactions to TULIP

7. How did you first hear about it? (Trace usage pattern from initial awareness through trial - to present) Do you use TULIP? ... Were you trained in the use of the system? Did the training help?

    ... If stopped using: why? (then continue - ask appropriate questions)

8. When you first heard about TULIP, what did you expect from the service?

    Probe

        Has it provided up to your expectations? Why/why not?

        ... Probe for positive characteristics:
- ○ ease of use?
- ○ helps me identify useful articles?
- ○ timeliness of materials (no 3 mon lag?)
- ○ convenience?

        ... Negatives?

9. How do you usually access TULIP?

    Options
1. Browser using WWW - access via Netscape or Mosaic. Order ... browse journal list, volume/issue list, article list, jump to page images ...
2. Search interface under X-Windows (WILLOW) - search bibliographic info (not full text), receive 'hits' including abstracts, then retrieve page images.

10. How often do you use TULIP?

    ... Under what circumstances do you use TULIP, i.e. do you have a set time of the day/week? Ad hoc when you need information? At random when you think of it?

    ... Has your frequency of use been influenced by the 'profiling' feature?

    ... For what purpose do you use it? (Browsing, searching, printing, etc.?)
Which searching mode of TULIP is most useful? (Title, author, keyword.)
    ... What other mode(s) would be useful if available? (Free text? Reference?)

    ... How does TULIP use relate to your specific roles as (as appropriate)
- ○ professor/teacher
- ○ dept head
- ○ administrator
- ○ researcher
- ○ etc.

    ... What do you usually do just before/after using TULIP i.e.
- ○ prepare key word lists
- ○ 'accumulate' needs/questions?
- ○ save trips to the library/make extra trips?

11a. What sources of information might TULIP replace?

11b. How do you view the relationship between TULIP and a service such as INSPEC? Do they compliment one another or are they redundant ... In what ways, i.e. find it in INSPEC/verify you want it with TULIP.

11c. Which best describes TULIP ... it is really a set of journals or it is a source of articles? Why?

12. Do you still read the paper journal? Why?

13. Thinking of some of the journals which you typically use which are included in TULIP, has availability of TULIP influenced your use of these journals in any way?

        ... Probe: Especially in your role as "author".

General factors which can influence usage

        [Unaided - initial question]

14. What, if any, are some of the problems you encounter in your day-to-day search for information or data?

    Probe: With paper journals? Going to the library, library staff, current awareness services, secondary databases, etc.

        [Follow with probed questions, as appropriate]

15. Journal selection

        ... Do the journals included in the system provide enough critical mass? If not, what other kind of journals should be included? (More depth or breadth, other journals?)

        ... Has your reading of the 43 journals increased/decreased/remained the same during this electronic experiment? Why?

16. Physical access

        ... Where are journals located on campus? (Core/non-core/TULIP.)
- ○ Departmental subscriptions
- ○ Central versus specialized libraries
- ○ Rotating between sites
- ○ Just too far away.

        ... Does TULIP make it easier for you to access these important journals?

        ... Would your usage of TULIP change if it was only available at the library and **not** at your desktop?

17. Timeliness

        ... How current are shelf copies in the library?

        ... Are issues available when you want them?

        ... Do you feel access to TULIP can or might speed up your actual speed of access to journal articles?

... When you access an article or issue, do you spend more or less time (i.e. number of minutes) when you use TULIP versus hard copy? More or less times accessed?

18. Sharing information

... How important is it to read (or have access to) the same set of papers as your colleagues or supervisor?

... How important to know what they think is excellent or poor?

... Can TULIP help? Ever forwarded articles? Annotated?

TULIP features

19. Comments on the following features of TULIP:

... the versions available;
... up to date/timeliness of materials
... search features (for key words, authors, etc.;
... complex searches);
... browse features;
... printing facilities (quality of print);
... bitmapped pages/quality of image;
... reading from screen;
... speed of access - of the program;
... profiling feature;
... 'help' feature.

20. What is missing from TULIP?

... What other types of information would you like to be able to access or link through the system? (Raw data, simulations?)

... How should different types of information be linked?

21. In what way(s) could the service be improved?

22. How often do you actually print materials?

... Do you order from library or have your own printer access?

... How do you typically decide to print, i.e. do you usually just review an abstract; read articles on screen; review TOC; other?

... Do you obtain prints more/less often using TULIP? Why?

23. How do you pay for information you need? Library pays all - do you share any cost?

   ... Grants

   ... Personal budget

   ... Do you expect to pay more yourself in the next five years? How much more? What would be acceptable or reasonable?

   ... What could be done to help control the cost of your professional journals in the future? Any ideas?

   ... Do you associate electronics with potentially higher or lower costs for obtaining needed data in the future?

   ... How would you feel if advertising appeared on screen in electronic journals of the future?

   ... How do you think information in electronic format should be billed; that is, would it be better to pay for 'availability' (such as you now have by subscribing to a journal) or would it be better to pay for 'use'?

   ... Do you think it would be appropriate to price individual articles by some formula which relates the cost to the level of usage of the piece?

24. Would you miss TULIP if the program was discontinued? Discuss

25. In your opinion, what would be the best way to introduce a service like TULIP? What media would be best?

   ... How could users be kept up to date about the service?

26. What else would you like to tell me about TULIP to help us better understand your feelings about it and to help us improve the next generation of the service?

Professional journal usage

Please list the professional or scientific journals which you use most often. This may include any materials science journals which are available in TULIP **or** from any other source or publisher.

Priority reading: Please list a maximum of five journals

1. _____

2. _____

3. _____

4. _____

5. _____

Read now and then: Please list a maximum of five journals

1. _____

2. _____

3. _____

4. _____

5. _____

T U L I·P

Appendix XIV

Detailed findings of the
qualitative research

Detailed findings of the qualitative research

The interview guides used for the focus groups and the one-on-one interviews have been adapted for each site in order to fit the particular implementations of TULIP and/or the specific situations on each campus (see Appendix XIII for the interview guide used at MIT). Nevertheless, all interview guides covered the same issues, so we were able to compare the results.

The major findings are reported according to the sequence of the interview guides, which first addressed a few generic topics regarding information behavior (problems encountered, expectations for the future, electronic information sources, etc.), before discussing the specific TULIP topics. In short:

1. Current information and search behavior
2. Electronic information sources
3. Evaluation of TULIP.

When reading these findings it should be kept in mind that only three TULIP sites have been involved in the qualitative research. Most of the findings of the research activities conducted by other universities (to the extent that they are comparable) concur with these results.

Ad 1. Current information and search behavior

Patterns used to review journals
- Looking through the table of contents a first selection of relevant articles is made. The following step is reading the abstract and skipping through the article to see if any pictures or figures catch the eye.
- Although abstracts (in this discipline, Material Science) are considered to be a helpful scanning device, their quality could be improved: better than half of the abstracts are considered to adequately describe the full article (60-75%).
- In general, respondents do not read most articles in-depth: an estimated 5-30% is read thoroughly.
- Since scientific papers require considerable time to read in-depth, photocopies are made to bring back to the office/lab or home. Faculty members seem to make less photocopies than students.
- Most students read journal articles in their office, while faculty members also read journals at home.
- Graduate students almost always have a particular subject in mind when looking for information. Therefore, most visits to the library begin with a database search (INSPEC, Current Contents).
- Faculty also make use of on-line searches, but are more likely to know better what they are looking for, for instance, because their network of personal contacts indicated relevant sources. On the other hand, they are more likely to browse or pleasure-read a journal.
- A high percentage of both faculty and students indicated that they subscribe to one or more core journals from which they read a high percentage of the articles.

Physical access to the libraries is frequently mentioned as a problem, especially when more than one library has to be visited (sometimes scattered around campus), this is considered a cumbersome task. Distance to the library, things like traffic and finding a parking space, appear to be of direct influence on the likelihood/frequency of library visits.

The lack of availability of information sources is another problem mentioned frequently. Canceled subscriptions, journals not subscribed to, journals out to be bound or placed in storage (archival material) and many other barriers occur when looking for information.

Cost
In particular, the costs related to the use of electronic databases have been mentioned as prohibitive (e.g. Inspec, Current Contents). Meanwhile, cost for both primary and secondary information is rarely 'out of pocket', and therefore plays a minor role on a day-to-day basis, either lost in the overall university structure or covered by grants.

Recent changes and expectations for the future
According to many respondents, their current search capabilities have improved compared to the recent past as a result of access to such services as Inspec and the Internet.
Respondents not only expect more and faster online information to become available in the future, but also strongly desire this.

Ad 2. Electronic information sources

The time spent on a computer varies considerably: from 1 hour per day to 'all day'. The computer is used for a wide variety of activities: word processing, communication (e-mail), simulations and other scientific 'number-crunching' applications, electronic searching, 'surfing' the Internet, etc. Electronic information sources are used 'when needed', which can range from several times per week to a few times per year.

Use of sources
The most frequently used electronic information sources are:
- INSPEC;
- Science Citation Index;
- Current Contents: considered to be less useful (because abstracts are not included) and very expensive;
- Within UC, INSPEC and Current Contents are used far more frequently than other electronic sources. Appreciated elements of INSPEC are the online abstracts, back issues as far as 1968, and the available information on conference proceedings. The greater scope of materials and the automatic background searches (mailed every couple of weeks), are considered as positive points of Current Contents.

The Internet is not widely used for gathering information: it is considered to be time consuming and therefore not very productive.

Ad 3. Evaluation of TULIP

Launching TULIP
The general feeling at the sites involved in the qualitative user research is that getting started on TULIP did not require a great deal of training, because it is quite simple to use.
Users had different expectations of TULIP, ranging from a feeling that it would be a 'toy', to being intrigued about its ability to provide full text. Some were pleasantly surprised to find out what TULIP did offer, others were disappointed by its slow speed or technical problems.

Frequency of use
The use of TULIP by the individual researchers is rather infrequent. Most access is randomly, as needed. Users believe that TULIP would be used more often if it were expanded to include more journals. TULIP usage is, of course, very much influenced by the user friendliness of the implementation: at UC several students tried TULIP only once or twice, because they never succeeded in installing the necessary X-Windows software to run TULIP on their PCs.

Advantages/benefits
Overall, there is enthusiasm about the concept of TULIP: desktop access to full text articles. The possible time-savings and convenience offered by desktop access to articles is considered very favorably. It replaces going to the library and it can be used any time of the day.

Disadvantages/limitations
The following disadvantages and/or limitations were mentioned. These were sometimes reasons for stopping or reducing the use of TULIP.
- Insufficient journal coverage: this is generally considered to be the greatest limitation; several core journals are not Elsevier publications and the time coverage is limited; it does not go back far enough in time.
- Difficulties in accessing TULIP: no X-Windows available on the desktop, no connection to printers in the lab or office, no knowledge of how to access TULIP with a MAC, are a few of the difficulties men-

tioned. At UC, virtually all respondents had difficulties installing the system due to equipment and software problems.

- Printing problems: at all sites printing is considered to be too slow ('every page is like agony'). At UC, most respondents could not figure out how to print from TULIP. After spending (too) much time, nearly all abandoned their attempts.
- The print quality of text is considered as acceptable, but opinions about the quality of the photographs and graphs are much less favorable.
- The quality of the image on screen is strongly dependent on the implementation. Users at MIT felt that the TULIP image quality was quite good, while those at UM complained about poor image quality of the Web implementation. However, many respondents do not like to read information on a computer screen.
- Speed: mostly at UC, complaints have been heard about TULIP's response times.
- A particular problem at UC is switching between TULIP and MELVYL: respondents consider loading X-Windows time consuming and a task that should not have to be done by the user. The fact that each time the user re-enters MELVYL from the TULIP image viewer he must begin a new search and reset the defaults, is also considered to be a serious drawback.

The effect of TULIP on readership of paper journals

The general feeling is that TULIP represents an addition to, rather than replacement of, the paper journals. The serendipity of paper journals is missed when doing an electronic search. People still like to spend some time with the printed version, which is easier to browse and where there is a greater likelihood of 'finding without looking'. Many respondents simply enjoy browsing through a journal or book: there is an 'emotional' relation with paper products. The 'fun' aspect of reading a book or a journal should not be underestimated: 'Seeing material on the computer is work, holding a book is fun'.

According to the users, usage of TULIP does not appear to have a significant impact on readership of the journals involved. (However, there is some evidence that the publicity and communication efforts around TULIP has increased the awareness of the TULIP titles and, by consequence, their usage.)

Evaluation of specific features

- Searching: This appears to be one of the most valuable features of TULIP. Providing full text makes TULIP superior to a service like INSPEC. Despite these positive perceptions, many users have difficulty in using the search feature. This is sometimes related to more general difficulties with keyword searching.
- Profiling: Most users were unfamiliar with this feature, but were quite enthusiastic about the concept. Those who tried the profiling feature (at UM), however, had minimal success.
- The help feature: Most respondents did not use this feature.
- Browsing: Most respondents did not (like to) use the browsing feature. Browsing through a hard copy is preferred (emotional touch, quicker, easier).
- Timeliness of materials: Most respondents felt that the information on TULIP is timely, but many of them did not appear to be aware of the actual updating of the TULIP database. When asked specifically, a few respondents commented that there seems to be a delay in adding new issues.
- Response time: There were numerous complaints at UC, and to a lesser extent at UM, about TULIP's processing speed, in particular printing documents was felt to be much too slow. At MIT, TULIP's response time for articles and printed output was considered to be acceptable.

Missing items/suggestions for improvement

As noted above, the major shortcoming of TULIP is its limited coverage.
- TULIP could be improved by expanding it to:
  - all the core journals;
  - conference proceedings, books, etc.;
  - back issues;
  - secondary journals and trade journals (i.e. not scientific journals);
  - visual images (video, sound, 3D).

However, respondents envisage some other improvements as well:
- The linking of TULIP information to other information sources is frequently suggested by the respondents. Mentioned are links to:

- references;
- other publications of an author;
- company profiles;
- Science Citation Index.

• There have been a few suggestions regarding alternative search methods. Allowing for keyword searching in the body of the text has been mentioned, as well as backward and forward 'chaining': linkages to references mentioned in an article (backward) and linkages to other articles in which the article has been referenced (forward).

• Simplifying and making the access to TULIP faster and easier has already been mentioned. One of the suggestions in this context was to put TULIP on the Web.

• Adding a bibliographic formatting feature that would allow users to 'grab' certain bibliographic citations and put these directly into a paper, would also be appreciated by several users.

Cost/payment
Cost is of moderate importance to students, because they do not personally subscribe to journals. Faculty members are more concerned: they fear that the cost of using the final product may be prohibitive. Respondents indicated avoidance of various databases currently available to them because of expense.

At UC respondents were asked how electronic information should be billed. All concurred that it should be charged for availability only, not on a 'per use' base.